BELOVED ENEMY

"I don't want to see war between our countries," Arielle said, "but if it comes, I won't spy for either side. You have my promise on that, Byron. I won't betray you, or my people."

"I'd not suspect you of it," he assured her. He rose and drew her to him, rested his forehead against hers for a moment.

Arielle tilted her head to kiss him and pulled him into her embrace. "The first time you kissed me," she whispered, "I knew there was something very, very special about you."

"But you ran away."

"You were the enemy then."

Byron wrapped his arms more tightly around her and pulled her even closer. "Are you afraid of me still?"

"I love you so dearly I would set fire to a dozen ships rather than leave you," she said, and smiled.

Arielle found his lips and, with a teasing sense of wonder, showed him all he need ever know of love.

PHOEBE CONN

BELOVED LEGACY

ZEBRA BOOKS
KENSINGTON PUBLISHING CORP.

ZEBRA BOOKS are published by

Kensington Publishing Corp.
850 Third Avenue
New York, NY 10022

First Printing: August, 1996
10 9 8 7 6 5 4 3 2 1

Printed in the United States of America

One

Grand Pré, Nova Scotia, September 1755

"Oh, please, Madame Douville, isn't there something more you can do for Mother?"

Arielle drew the distraught young man away from the dying woman's bedside. She was a midwife, but with Acadian physicians few in number, she was frequently called upon to expand her services to include the treatment of illness. Most patients responded to her herbal remedies, liberally laced with prayers, and made a full recovery. Sadly, there were others, like this dear lady, who suffered only from the infirmities of advanced age and whose natural course of life could neither be altered nor delayed.

Arielle had been awake all night, but the conscientious young woman took care to speak in a sympathetic whisper. "Your mother's been blessed with a long and happy life. She's been loved by two devoted husbands, eight attentive children, and how many adorable grandchildren are there now, forty-four?"

André nodded, and Arielle continued. "My herb potions have eased her pain, but they can't prolong her life. Be grateful for the many years you've shared. Have everyone come in to kiss your mother good-bye, and send her into the next world radiant with the love that surrounds her here."

André succeeded in choking back his tears, but, heartbroken, he gave in to his rage. "It's the accursed British who have killed her. Had they only left us alone, as their Queen Anne promised, Mother would never have fallen ill."

Arielle had to agree, for his mother was only one of many of Grand Pré's elderly residents who had become terrified by the recent British occupation. To have to share their town with an armed camp of rustic colonial lads who showed them not the least amount of respect had unnerved them all, but it had taken a serious toll on their older citizens. Minor complaints they had endured for years were swiftly becoming serious ailments, and in Marie Mouflet's case, the unrelieved tension had brought a rapid decline.

Arielle glanced toward the bed. Withered by the years, Marie was so tiny her bony figure made only a small lump beneath the quilt. She had been a proud woman, and, respecting her, Arielle had dressed her that morning in a freshly laundered nightgown and brushed her hair so that even in death, she would look her best. Arielle stood by the aged woman's bedside to pray a moment with André, and then, leaving her patient in her family's care, she gathered up her basket of herbs, and left for home.

The road inclined gradually as it led away from the bay, and, walking with her head down, Arielle would have run right into a well-dressed Englishman at the corner, had he not seen her coming and stepped out of the way.

"*Bonjour, mademoiselle,*" he offered warmly.

Not fooled by the young man's pleasant greeting, Arielle replied in English. "It is *madame,* but because I will not bother to speak to the likes of you again, you will have no need to remember."

A well-bred Virginian, Byron Barclay had merely extended the usual courtesy one stranger showed another back home, and he was taken aback by the fierce hostility of the young woman's response. However, he was not so badly insulted that he failed to notice she was exceedingly comely, and he studied her with an openly curious glance. She was tall, and very blonde. Her blue eyes were framed with long dark lashes, and while filled with a furious disgust, held an unusual hint of aqua that lent a unique beauty to her delicate features.

Byron had learned many of the Acadians could trace their roots to Normandy, and back centuries, even further to Viking invaders. Clearly, this lovely fair creature had a Norman heritage. Then he realized she had spoken fluent, if slightly accented, English. He was relieved, for he had already exhausted what French he knew.

"We have scarcely met," he argued. "Are you always so hasty in your judgments?"

"When it comes to British swine, yes!" Arielle would have struck him with her basket had he not already moved aside. She dismissed him with a curt nod and continued on her way.

Byron had arrived on a supply ship that very morning, and wanting to see something of Grand Pré he had been out for a stroll before offering his services to John Winslow, the man overseeing the British occupation. While having no wish to confront a jealous husband, he was sufficiently intrigued by the irate young woman to follow at a discreet distance.

Unaware that she had inspired his admiration, Arielle did not once glance over her shoulder as she walked home. She lived on the edge of town, in a small frame house that was indistinguishable from its neighbors. There was a sprinkling of flowers in the yard, but the path leading to the front door was overgrown with weeds.

Taking care not to be seen from a window, Byron moved past the house before turning back to study it at length. He put his hands on his hips and pursed his lips thoughtfully. A fresh coat of paint would have made the unassuming dwelling utterly charming, but clearly the owners lacked either the pride, or the funds, to maintain it properly.

Unlike the neglected front yard, the lush kitchen garden in the rear promised an abundance of produce. He had heard the Canadian winters were severe and that its residents had to cultivate and harvest great amounts of food to survive in good health.

Turning back to the road, Byron walked on toward the farms where the meadows were filled with ripening wheat. Cows were grazing contentedly, and the peacefulness of the countryside belied the area's uncertain future. In the distance, wooded hills framed the idyllic scene. Restless, he turned back and gazed out toward the Bay of Fundy. The view had a pristine clarity in the fresh morning air, but if all of Grand Pré's residents shared the blonde's view, Byron doubted he would enjoy his stay.

He laughed to himself then, for, embittered after battling the French in the Ohio Valley, he hadn't come to Acadia to vacation, but to do whatever damage he could.

Gaetan Le Blanc rapped lightly at Arielle's back door, and when there was no response, he stepped into the room that served as a combination kitchen and parlor without waiting to be welcomed. He was disappointed not to find a fire burning in the fireplace. Usually Arielle's kitchen was invitingly warm and filled with the delicious aroma of freshly baked bread, or a simmering stew whose delicate spices always made sharing a meal with her a veritable treat. Not that he was interested in her for her culinary skills; it was the joy of the delightful young woman's company that drew him back time and again.

Her basket sat on the table, so he knew she was at home, and, growing even more bold, he inched open the door to her bedroom. It wasn't like her to be in bed at noon, but he assumed she had been up late to deliver a baby and deserved her rest. What he thought *he* deserved was to share her bed, but she had made him wait a full year after her husband's death before she would even receive his calls. He had no hope he would ever sample her favors before marriage and unfortunately, thus far, she had been maddeningly disinclined to accept his proposal.

An agile man despite his muscular build, he tiptoed over to the canopy bed, and was grateful the warmth of the day had made closing the draperies unnecessary. In sleep, Arielle had an angelic sweetness he was content to appreciate in adoring silence for almost a quarter hour before he thought of a way to curry her favor. He returned to the kitchen then, built a fire, and made some hot cocoa for her. When he carried it into the bedroom, she was already starting to stir.

Arielle opened her eyes when she heard Gaetan set the cup of cocoa on the nightstand. Torn between equally strong impulses to thank him and to accuse him of trespassing, she sat up very slowly. She hadn't bothered to braid her hair before getting into bed, and it fell across her eyes in a silken curtain she quickly swept aside. Her lace-trimmed nightgown provided a modest covering, but she pulled the blue-and-white quilt up over her breasts to add another layer of fabric between them.

She tried to show the proper indignation and give Gaetan the scolding he deserved, but the width of his good-natured grin made it extremely difficult to be harsh. He was rakishly handsome, with curly black hair and green eyes; but she had learned as a child that in both men and women good character was of far more importance than the superficial asset of attractive appearance. She liked Gaetan enormously, but she did not admire him as she had her late husband, and that kept her from deepening their friendship as he continually urged her to do.

"I don't recall giving you permission to come and go here as you please."

Gaetan picked up the cup of cocoa and handed it to her as a peace offering. "When you didn't answer the door, I feared you might have fallen ill. What kind of a friend would I be if I allowed you to languish in your bed all day unattended?"

Arielle regarded him with a skeptical glance. "You know I am never ill."

"While that may have been true in the past, the possibility still exists." Pleased with himself for having invented such a considerate excuse for roaming her home at will, Gaetan pulled up a chair and sat down so close to the bed that his knees were pressed against the feather mattress.

"You shouldn't be living here all alone, chérie, not with Englishmen prowling our streets in search of whatever booty they might steal. None of our womenfolk are safe, and I don't want you to come to any harm."

"Neither do I," Arielle assured him. She took a sip of the cocoa, burned the roof of her mouth, and set it aside to cool. For a brief instant she was tempted to describe the Englishman who had spoken to her that morning. His clothes and manners had been far more sophisticated than the others of his kind who had arrived uninvited, and, like an evil blight, had refused to go away.

Had he been a Frenchman, she would have found his appearance pleasing, but now as she recalled him, there had been a troubling weariness to his gaze. His eyes had been very blue, but filled with the deadened sadness of one who has lost someone precious. She had seen the same terrible grief reflected in her neighbors' eyes all too often of late. While she could not help but wonder who it was the Englishman had lost, she feared mentioning him would only provide fuel for Gaetan's argument, and thought better of it.

"I sat up all night with Marie Mouflet," she explained instead. She's very old, and unlikely to get any older. She may already be dead."

"That is a shame. She was a good woman."

"Yes, but death is easiest to accept in the elderly. It is only when a babe dies that I cry with the parents."

Knowing her fondness for children, Gaetan leaned forward. "You and I would make such beautiful babies together. Why won't you marry me?"

Finding her feelings impossible to put in words when they weren't what he longed to hear, Arielle used an oft repeated excuse. "Not every widow reweds after a year of mourning, Gaetan. Some of us require much longer to fall in love again."

Gaetan sat back slightly. "It's been nearly two years since Bernard was killed by the Iroquois. Do you plan to mourn him forever?"

Stalling for time, Arielle took a second sip of cocoa, and finding it sufficiently cooled, drank another, but its delicious taste didn't ease her growing discomfort. "I'd like you to leave, please. You ought not to have come in on your own in the first place, and while I appreciate your concern and thoughtfulness, I'd really like to go back to sleep."

Gaetan saw something entirely different in her averted glance. When they talked about other people, she always looked him in the eye, but when he wanted to discuss their future, she would turn away, as if the mere sight of him were distasteful. The other young women of Grand Pré considered him a fine catch; why didn't she? She never compared him aloud to Bernard Douville, but each time she dropped her gaze, he felt she was dwelling on memories.

Hurt by her constant rebuffs, he rose so quickly he

nearly overturned his chair. "You don't think I'm good enough for you, do you? Well, there's a meeting this afternoon at the church and none of us expects good news. In the days ahead, you may have need of a strong husband to protect you, and I'm warning you, I won't be kept waiting much longer!"

He came toward her, and, fearing he was about to slap her, Arielle flinched, but rather than raise his hand, he leaned down and placed a hasty kiss on her cheek and then strode from the room. She heard him stomp through the kitchen, and then the scrape of a chair against the plank floor when he careened into it. In a loud accent of his displeasure, he slammed the door on his way out.

She had slept only a few hours and was still tired, but sat slowly sipping the cocoa until she had finished it all. She was sadly afraid that she had handled Gaetan's infatuation with her very badly, and she could not fault him for his anger when she had been less than honest all along.

After setting the empty cup aside, she slid back down under the covers and closed her eyes. As always, Bernard's dear face appeared in her mind's eye. He had not been tall like Gaetan, nor impressively built, and she was the only woman who had ever considered him handsome, but he had been honest, and kind, and so bright and charming that the three years of their marriage had been the best ones of her life. She would always miss him. Perhaps the pain of his death would never leave her, but she still believed she had been one of the luckiest women on earth for, like Marie Mouflet, she had been truly loved, and whenever death overtook her, she would die content.

* * *

It had been Massachusetts' governor, William Shirley, who had first proposed an invasion of Acadia, and he had chosen John Winslow to raise two thousand volunteers to carry out the plan. A farmer with considerable military experience, Winslow was a popular leader and had easily assembled a force made up of farmers, fishermen, tradesmen, and shopkeepers. There had been no French opposition to the invasion, and, lacking support, the Acadian soldiers and private citizens who had joined their ranks had surrendered in June.

The troops from New England had agreed to serve for only one year, however, preventing a lengthy occupation. Believing the French would attempt to regain the province, with the full support of the Acadians, Charles Lawrence, the governor of Nova Scotia, and Shirley had decided to deport them all. Sending them to Canada would only aid the French cause, so they were to be transported instead to the English colonies. Now encamped at Grand Pré, Winslow was faced with the onerous task of carrying out the expulsion of the local populace. Heavily burdened by that responsibility, he welcomed Bryon Barclay to his camp.

While Byron was proud to have been part of two campaigns, both had been so widely reported as devastating defeats that he knew he need not recount the details. "I've been serving as a captain in the Virginia militia," he began. "Last year, I fought the French with Lieutenant Colonel Washington at Fort Necessity, and I served with General Braddock this past summer. I intend to fight again when war with France is finally declared, but until then, I thought I might be of service to you here."

Winslow nodded sympathetically when, like Arielle, he noted the young man's eyes held the glaze great suffering can impart. He judged Byron as in his twenties, but his light-brown hair was noticeably graying at the temples and there was no trace of boyishness in his demeanor. Despite his soft-spoken manner, Byron Barclay impressed Winslow as being both tough and resourceful.

"Yes, I can use a man of your talents. My soldiers are good men," Winslow exclaimed, "but most are simple folk who lack the skills to handle administrative duties. Although you commanded troops while serving in the militia, what I really need is someone who can keep track of the citizens of Grand Pré so that adequate preparations can be made for their removal. Would you be willing to serve with us in that capacity?"

Byron had already known there would be scant opportunity to fight and he wasn't disappointed. "Yes, sir, I would."

"Good. Governor Lawrence wants families separated and dispersed to widely distant colonies, but after these poor souls have lost their homes and farms, I can't add to their suffering by making them lose each other. I want you to take special care, therefore, to make absolutely certain that families remain intact. It will make your work more difficult, but if we expect to absorb these people into our society, we must treat them kindly."

"They could have signed the oath required of loyal British citizens," Byron reminded him.

"That is unlikely. We excused them from ever having to bear arms, but that wasn't enough, and even had all their terms been met, I doubt they would have been satisfied. This has been British soil for forty years, but the people have stubbornly remained French. Their loyalty will now cost them dearly."

Winslow shrugged slightly. "Perhaps we should take some of the responsibility for not vigorously colonizing Nova Scotia. Had there been some English residents here, their influence might have created an entirely different attitude among the Acadians."

A man in his fifties, Winslow's face was round and smooth, his wig a stark white frame for a ruddy complexion. The strain of his assignment showed in his expression, and Byron, noticing and appreciating that fact, adopted a more moderate tone. "I doubt the loyalties of generations could be changed in such a short span," he argued. "Would you have forgotten you're English if Massachusetts had fallen to the French when you were a child?"

"No, of course not." Winslow frowned slightly, and then leaned forward. "I've called a meeting of all the men in the area for three o'clock this afternoon at the church. You'll want to be there. There have been rumors, of course, and speculation, but a formal announcement of the expulsion hasn't been made. When it is, I expect confusion of the worst sort. I plan to arrest every last man and march them back here to the stockade. They'll be unarmed, so there shouldn't be any violence. Do you speak French, by any chance?"

"No, but I'm certain I can quickly master whatever phrases I'll need to make an accurate tally of the families."

"Yes, you'll need a few words at least to make yourself understood. Now as to your quarters, I'm afraid I haven't much to offer. I'm staying at the priest's house, and we're crowded as it is.

"I've already taken a room at the inn."

John Winslow had recognized Byron as a man of substance the moment he had introduced himself. "May I assume money is no problem for you?"

"Absolutely none," Byron responded with a slight smile. "In fact, keep whatever funds you might have given me for your men."

"That's very generous of you. Until three o'clock then."

The steeple was visible from the bay, and Byron knew he would have no trouble finding the church. As he left Winslow's camp, he decided to make a list of every possible question he might have to ask. He would then have them translated, and be ready to start work in the morning. He returned to his inn for paper and ink, but as he began to make notes, a provocative possibility occurred to him.

He doubted that Grand Pré had more than a handful of residents who spoke English, and he considered it a good omen that he had already met one. He would not be able to return to the comely blonde's home until the announcement of the expulsion order had been made and her husband arrested, but then he would definitely seek her out. The sorry state of her home was convincing proof she was in need of money, and he could afford to pay her well for translating for him.

Inspired by his clever plan, he wrote down not only the most obvious questions, but some that were decidedly obscure so that he would have enough material to keep his prospective translator busy long enough to seduce her.

Byron arrived fifteen minutes early for Winslow's meeting, but the church was already crowded. He couldn't help but wonder which of the Acadians streaming into the church was the pretty blonde's husband. He doubted she was more than twenty, but because women frequently wed much older men, he could not really dismiss any but the most elderly gentlemen as unlikely mates.

Most of Grand Pré's male citizens were farmers and fishermen dressed in homespun garments, their deeply tanned faces etched from years of toil in the sun. There were a few pale and pudgy merchants clad in fine clothes, but none struck him as a proper spouse for the aqua-eyed beauty. Then a tall man, with unruly black curls and bright green eyes, came through the door. As the Acadian glanced his way, Byron felt a sudden shock of recognition although he was certain they had never met. The man's posture and expression were not downcast or sullen as so many of his companions but openly defiant. Undaunted, Byron took up the challenge, returned his stare with the coldest glance he could affect, and felt triumphant when the Acadian was the first to look away.

Byron despised the French, and with good reason after the terrible losses his troops had sustained in the Ohio Valley. He wasn't surprised to be regarded with equal loathing, but there was something more than mere hatred in this man's contemptuous gaze. A soldier brushed by him then, and, distracted, Byron moved aside and lost sight of the green-eyed man in the crowd. Feeling overly warm, he stepped outside for a moment to draw a deep breath. If that menacing individual was his prospective translator's husband, then seducing her carried far more risk than he had imagined. Fortunately, the battles he had survived in the last couple of years had taught him to thrive on danger and he wasn't in the least bit intimidated.

A small crowd of women and children were gathered across the street. Fearful as to the subject of the meeting, they had been unable to wait patiently at home to learn of its outcome. Byron scanned the anxious faces of the women, and was disappointed not to see the one he sought. He hoped her absence meant that she had little regard for her husband's welfare, but he doubted the opposite were true.

At three o'clock, Byron followed the last of Grand Pré's adult males into the church and resumed his place against the back wall. Lieutenant Colonel Winslow, backed by several of his officers, then appeared. Byron had seen the uniformed men earlier, and recognized them as the same hearty folk with whom he had served in Virginia. Strong men, toughened by New England winters, he knew them fully capable of controlling the four hundred unarmed Acadians attending the meeting.

With a translation provided by a merchant named

Beauchamp, John Winslow announced the king's orders: The Acadians had been declared rebels, their lands and goods were therefore forfeited to the Crown. They were to be immediately taken prisoner, and when ships arrived to transport them to the English colonies, they, along with their families, would be deported.

The words were met with a stunned silence. Then, fearing they had misunderstood Winslow's announcement, the Acadians began leaning forward to question their friends, and the whispered replies soon swelled to a rumbling groan as full comprehension of the dire nature of their predicament took hold. Seated near the rear, Gaetan Le Blanc leapt to his feet and denounced King George II in such colorful terms it was a shame only those fluent in French understood him, but he was quickly subdued by the officers Winslow had brought along for just such a purpose.

As he was dragged out the door, Gaetan again caught Byron's eye, and the green-eyed Acadian included him in the vile string of insults. He spit at his feet and damned him to hell with every other Englishman on the face of the earth, but Byron didn't even blink. Instead, he tipped his hat in mock salute and laughed at Gaetan's fury. In that instant, Gaetan memorized his face, and swore if he could kill only one Englishmen in Grand Pré, he would send this blue-eyed devil to hell.

Two

Escaping her ruffled cap, Michelle Mouflet's dark-brown ringlets bounced to a hysterical beat as she raced from her grandmother's house to Arielle's. Out of breath, she pounded on the door with a shaking fist. When Arielle answered her summons, she collapsed in her arms.

"Madame, oh, madame," the young girl sobbed.

Accustomed to distraught callers demanding her attention at all hours, Arielle gently guided Michelle into a seat at her table and poured her a soothing cup of herbal tea. "Marie is gone," she assumed aloud, "but you need the priest, and the undertaker now, chérie not me."

Flustered, Michelle grabbed up the teacup, and, shaking badly, spilled more of its contents than she swallowed. Arielle picked up a towel to wipe away the puddle on the table, but she had to repeat the gesture several times when the overwrought girl continued to sob. Arielle set the damp towel aside, and began to rub her back in easy comforting circles.

Michelle managed to speak after coming forth with a loud hiccup. "Oh, Madame Douville, Grandmother died not long after you left this morning, but that's not why I'm here. The most dreadful thing has happened!"

With that ominous announcement, Michelle began to weep again. Fearing she was in for a long wait before she learned what dire circumstance had prompted Michelle's visit, Arielle poured herself a cup of tea, and sat down across from her. Michelle was fifteen, and a budding beauty who would surely have been courted by several eager suitors next spring had the British not chosen this summer to disrupt their lives.

"I hope no one has fallen ill," Arielle offered in hopes of inspiring Michelle to continue.

Michelle shook her head, again sending her ringlets dancing. "No," she wailed. "It's what's happened to the men!"

"The men? Gaetan told me there was to be a meeting for them all this afternoon. Is that why you're crying?"

Having finally heard the subject of her fears stated aloud, Michelle pulled a handkerchief from her sleeve and blew her nose. "It was a horrid trick," she managed to explain between hiccups, "a dreadful ruse to gather the men in order to arrest them. They've all been locked up in the stockade and I fear we'll never see any of them ever again!"

This time it was Arielle who placed her teacup on the table with trembling hands. "It's only a few minutes past four," she pointed out. "Perhaps you misunderstood why the men were taken to the stockade. Maybe they'll all be released before nightfall."

Michelle drew in a breath, then spoke in a hoarse rush. "No, you're wrong. I waited outside the meeting with the other women. The men truly were arrested, and the order came from King George himself."

Stunned, Arielle leaned back in her chair, unable to do more than watch as Michelle continued to dab ineffectually at her tears. There had been rumors all summer, but, busy tending the increasing numbers of people falling ill, she had not paid much attention.

She reached out to Michelle, but as her fingertips brushed the girl's sleeve, another loud knock at the door demanded her attention. She found one of her favorite neighbors hopping from foot to foot outside. "If you've come to tell me the men have been arrested, Sophie, I've already heard, but come in and have a cup of tea with us."

Sophie's bodice strained at the seams as she heaved a great sigh. "No, I've left my babies alone and I can't stay, but what are we going to do? They may have arrested only the men today, but there's talk we're all to be deported soon."

Alarmed, Arielle stepped outside and drew her door closed to assure their privacy rather than risk upsetting Michelle any further. "Deported where?"

Sophie's usual rosy complexion was drained of all color. "To the English colonies, I was told."

Gaetan had presented such a stirring example of defiance in the face of the British occupation that Arielle's first thought was of him. He had offered to protect her, for certain never dreaming his arrest would make such an effort impossible.

While horrified by the prospect of deportation, Arielle feared there was a more immediate danger to the women of Grand Pré. She could easily imagine some of the rude English lads demanding favors from women who no longer had men to defend them from unwanted attentions. Outraged at such a ghastly possibility, she gave Sophie's pudgy shoulder an encouraging squeeze.

"I'll go to see Winslow immediately. I might not be able to convince him to release the men, but I can at least demand that he tell us his plans. Go home and make supper for your family. I'll stop by to tell you what I've learned when I get back."

"Thank you, Arielle, I knew you would know what to do."

While she was pleased by that show of confidence, Arielle wasn't at all certain what ought to be done.

After bidding Sophie farewell, Arielle went back inside and returned to the table where Michelle was just finishing the last of her tea. She told the young woman Sophie had come to confirm the grim news. "Come with me," she urged. "I'll walk you home and then I'm going to speak with John Winslow. He may think the women of this town will be too lost without our men to object to what he's done, but he'll soon find out just how wrong he is."

Inspired by Arielle's courage, Michelle matched her brisk stride as they walked into town. "I knew you would help us, madame. You are the very best of *femmes sages.*"

Arielle nodded half-heartedly to acknowledge her young friend's compliment. She was being asked to cure the whole town of the English malady and she knew of no herb powerful enough to banish them all.

As they neared the center of town, Arielle and

Michelle stopped to listen as an elderly fisherman told a gathering of anguished women and children that Winslow had agreed to allow twenty men per day to leave the stockade and visit their families. Holding the rest of the men as hostages, the Englishman was assured he would not lose any of his prisoners.

"You see," Michelle wailed. "What I told you is true."

"Yes, it obviously is," Arielle agreed. Michelle's home was just around the corner, and she urged her to go on alone. "I'll stop by later to tell your family what I've learned," she promised.

Arielle hurried on, and while the fisherman hadn't mentioned anything about anyone being sent to the English colonies, he had left before anyone had had the chance to question him. Determined to learn the details of the British plan for her city, her expression grew as determined as her stride. As she approached the stockade, the guards, if they could be called that, were standing in careless poses beside the gate.

"I wish to see Colonel Winslow," Arielle announced bravely.

"Do you now?" The taller of the two young men winked at his fellow guard. "If you'll just wait an hour, I can take care of you myself."

Arielle ignored the man's sappy grin and his companion's raucous laughter. "I wish to see Winslow now," she repeated through clenched teeth. "Whatever business I have is with him rather than the likes of you."

Still not impressed, the guard straightened his shoulders and gestured for her to move along.

"Winslow isn't seeing anyone today. Come back tomorrow."

Knowing the colonel had taken up residence at the priest's house, Arielle debated going there to wait for him, but, deciding he would have to come out the gate to make his way there, it made more sense for her to remain right where she was. She folded her arms under her bosom and looked the sarcastic soldier in the eye. "If you lack the manners to tell Winslow I've come to see him, then I shall have to report you when he appears."

That threat brought peals of deep laughter from both guards, but Arielle gave no sign of being offended. She just observed them with a smoldering glance, and waited. It was growing dark, and she was now sorry she had failed to wear her cape, but she was not going to leave her vigil just because the evening breeze held a hint of autumn's chill. When the Englishman she had met earlier in the day came through the gate, she cast an eager glance behind him, hoping John Winslow would soon follow, but when she realized he was alone, she sighed unhappily.

"Madame?" She was clearly livid, and while Byron could readily understand why, he couldn't ignore her distress. "This must have been a very difficult day for you," he offered sympathetically. "May I be of some service?"

Arielle opened her mouth to tell him to be on his way, then caught herself in case he might be of some service to her. She tried to smile, but wasn't certain she had succeeded. "I need to speak with John

Winslow, but these impertinent oafs have refused to allow me to do so. Can you get me inside to see him?"

"It would be my pleasure." Byron turned, and at a wave from him, the surly guards opened the gate. "I'm Byron Barclay," he revealed. "Ask for me if anyone else proves to be less than cooperative and I'll see that he's punished."

Surprised by that vow, Arielle turned to face him. Even in the gathering dusk she could make out the brightness of his smile, but the sadness she had noted earlier had not left his gaze.

He offered his arm, but she refused to take it and remained several steps to his side as they walked to Winslow's headquarters. She had seen Winslow a time or two, and recognized him immediately. He was seated at his desk, apparently tallying figures, but she didn't care about interrupting his work.

Not waiting for Byron to speak, she stepped forward. "I am Madame Douville," she stated proudly, her English superb, having been raised as a smuggler's daughter. "You have apparently announced your plans to the men you have enslaved, but because we were excluded from your meeting, the women have no idea what is happening. We need to be told at once."

Struck first by his belligerent visitor's stunning beauty, and then by the fact she had addressed him in English, John Winslow rose, and gestured for Byron to pull up a chair for the young woman. "I am so pleased to meet you, madame, but you misunderstand; I've not taken any slaves."

"The men are free to go then?"

"Well, no, they will have to remain here for the

time being." He picked up his pen and searched through the papers littered across his desk for a blank sheet. "Give me your husband's name, and I'll see he is among the next group of prisoners released for a day."

"I am a widow," Arielle informed him. Having to describe herself as such brought back memories of Bernard's tragic death so intense they made her wince. "If you have established such a policy for the men you've kidnapped, then I would like to request that you allow the ones related to Marie Mouflet, whose death your occupation undoubtedly hastened, to attend her funeral."

"Madame, really, I've kidnapped no one."

"What do you call it when you compel men to attend a meeting and then forbid them to leave?"

Exasperated, Winslow turned to Byron. "Since Madame Douville is your friend, could you possibly help me here?"

"We are not friends," Arielle denied with a venomous disdain that made an insult of the word.

Byron knew he had only himself to blame for the embarrassment Winslow was suffering. He had already been stung by the Frenchwoman's temper and should have known she would treat the colonel no more kindly. Focusing on her complaint rather than her mood, he prompted the answer she had sought.

"Despite her lack of tact, Madame Douville has a valid point," he began. "The women of Grand Pré have *not* been adequately informed of your plans. It is assumed that the twenty men who were released this afternoon will begin spreading the word, but there are undoubtedly some, like Madame Douville, who might miss being informed. Perhaps a bulletin can be printed and distributed tomorrow to end the confusion."

Winslow's frown lightened. "Excellent suggestion," he admitted. "Until then, let me say that I have brought the men of Grand Pré into the stockade to facilitate their prompt deportation to the English colonies. I fully intend to send families together on the same ship, and just as soon as those ships arrive, the deportations will begin."

"You have no right!" she cried.

Winslow nodded to Byron, who rose and moved behind Arielle's chair. "This is British soil, and as your menfolk learned this afternoon, the Acadians have been declared rebels and their goods forfeited to the Crown. I would have made that announcement to the entire city but for fear of violence. Not wanting to risk injury to women and children, I excluded them, but you needn't fear you'll be separated from your men."

"I have already been separated from my man!" Arielle reminded him. She sprang from her chair, and would have leaned across his desk to slap him had Byron not moved quickly to prevent it. He caught her wrist, and, holding it tightly, attempted to pull her toward the door. Arielle relaxed as though she meant to follow meekly, but when he slackened his grip, she immediately yanked her hand free and turned back to Winslow.

"Your ill-bred soldiers at the gate were rude to me, and now that we have no men to protect us, I fear that disrespect will take even more blatant forms.

Have you a dire penalty for rape, or will you simply expect it?"

Out of his seat now, Winslow raised his hands. "Madame Douville, please. We wish the people of Grand Pré no harm."

"No harm! You have imprisoned the men and threaten to deport us all! You intend to destroy our city and yet you say you wish us no harm? Liar!"

Byron had seldom been witness to a more shameful spectacle, and yet he thought Madame Douville's defense of her town absolutely splendid. Fearing John Winslow might think otherwise, he wrapped both arms around her narrow waist, lifted her off her feet, and carried her outside. Still holding her tightly, he whispered in her ear. "That was wonderful, but hush now, or you might also end up a prisoner."

Had Byron not sounded so sincere, Arielle would have continued kicking and clawing, but, amazed to find him sympathetic, she ceased to struggle. When he put her down on her feet, she quickly adjusted her clothes and straightened her cap before turning toward him. "You're British; if you were even capable of understanding our anguish, you'd not have caused it."

Byron had been elated to learn she was a widow. Noting she was wearing pale blue rather than black, he assumed her loss had not been recent, and that fact cheered him all the more. He clasped his hands behind his back, and continued to address her in a conspiratorial whisper.

"I admire your spirit, madame, if not your cause, and I assure you that the women of Grand Pré are in no danger from our troops. You have my promise that bulletins detailing Winslow's plans will be distributed as soon as they can be written, translated, and printed."

Arielle thought him a handsome liar. "What did you say your name was?" she asked.

"Byron Barclay," he repeated with a mock bow, pleased that she would inquire.

"Well, Mr. Barclay, I don't think the English have the faintest concept of honor, or they would not have broken the promises given to us by their own Queen Anne, and I don't believe a word you say." She turned her back on him and started for the gate with the same long, fluid stride that had brought her into town.

Byron had already had ample evidence that the fiery Madame Douville would not be easy to seduce, but even after abandoning his original plan, he wanted to see her again. "It's gotten dark," he warned as he caught up with her. "I'll walk you home."

"Why should you bother? According to you, I'm in no danger."

"A gentleman never permits a lady to walk alone after dark," Byron explained.

"Really? Then it is a great pity all the gentlemen in this town have been taken prisoner."

Having tried his best to befriend her, Byron could not resist hurling an insult of his own. "To what did your late husband succumb? If he survived that wicked tongue of yours without injury, I can't imagine that could have sent him to his grave."

Just inside the gate, Arielle could have bolted through it to avoid him, but she could not abide his making fun of Bernard. "My husband," she told him in a burst of cold fury, "was the finest gentleman to ever walk this earth. If you ever mention him again, I shall take great pleasure in sending you into the next world to meet him!"

Byron nodded to acknowledge her colorful threat, then let her walk out the gate alone. He laughed to himself as he started back toward John Winslow's headquarters because he knew if she were to meet any amorous soldiers, her blazing wit would instantly cool their ardor.

Arielle went to the Mouflet home first, where, already mourning Marie, the women were in a pitiful state. All six of her daughters had survived her, and along with their two brothers' wives and all their children, the house was alarmingly overcrowded. Spreading with the speed of a deadly epidemic, the news of the coming deportations had already reached them, but they were too numbed by grief to fully appreciate the fact they would soon lose their homes.

Arielle moved among them. After patting tear-wracked shoulders and cuddling cranky babies, she began to give practical advice. "You must take care not to go out alone," she warned them. "Travel in pairs, or in threes, but do not let the English soldiers find you out walking alone. They know there are no men in our homes, so bar your doors even during the day, and especially at night. Let's not give them even the slightest opportunity to torment us."

Gradually, the look of fear in the women's eyes was replaced by one of calm determination. "We Acadians are a hardy people," she reminded them. "We have learned to survive here, and wherever we are tossed, we'll survive there, too. Our unity is our strength. That's why the British are afraid to leave us here, but they can never take that from us."

She left then, but as she passed by the next house, and the next, she heard the anguished sounds of weeping. She didn't stop now, but she would tomorrow. She might have no blood relatives in Grand Pré, but all of its citizens were like family to her.

Sophie had already tucked her children into their cribs. "I can see by the sadness in your face that all I heard was true," she greeted her, still anxious for news.

Joining her friend by the fire, Arielle shook her head sadly. "Winslow promises to keep us together, but how can he? We'll be lucky to keep families intact, but all of Grand Pré will never be able to stay together."

"Come with us," Sophie urged.

Arielle thanked her, but made no promises. "Some people will surely return," she hoped aloud. "If not to Acadia, then to Canada. I'm sure that's why Winslow arrested the men, to prevent them from going now, and fighting for the French."

Sophie filled a bowl from the pot of rabbit stew simmering over the coals. "You must have something to eat," she insisted.

"I'm not one of your babies," Arielle chided.

"Perhaps not, but I can still see that you're well fed. Besides, this is very good and I want you to share it."

After the first spoonful, Arielle was grateful for the offering. "You are a wonderful cook," she enthused.

Sophie stirred the pot. "Do you suppose the English will allow us to take a few things, like this old iron kettle, to prepare our meals?"

It took Arielle a moment to respond, but she spoke from the heart. "Had you lost your reason for living, you'd know how little possessions matter. If you have Jean and your children, you'll have all you'll need."

Sophie nodded, but tears welled up in her eyes. She glanced around the room, taking in the furnishings Jean had made with his own hands and the slew of things they had accumulated over the years. Many had been gifts from friends and family no longer alive, and were doubly precious. "I will burn everything myself rather than give it to the British," she vowed.

Arielle finished the stew, and bid her friend good night. As she started home, she heard a twig snap, and felt rather than saw someone lurking nearby. She stopped, strained to listen and, hearing nothing, moved on, but as soon as she had taken a few steps, she heard a rustling in the tall grass at the edge of the road. She had left home before needing a lantern, and had not expected to be away so long. Even so, there was enough moonlight for her to see the way.

Certain it could not be one of her neighbors, she chose to speak in English. "Who's there?" she called, but there was no answer. "With all the noise you're making, you might as well come out and walk with me. Well, come on. I'm not afraid, no matter who you are."

Feeling rather foolish, Byron came forward. "After you left the stockade, I began to worry about you," he explained. "I walked out to your house, and when you weren't there, I feared you might not arrive safely. I waited until I began to feel very foolish, and I had just started back into town when you came along."

"So you stepped into the shadows so I'd not know you've discovered where I live?"

Byron knew he could lie and say that he had asked for directions to her house in town, but because he had never been one to resort to a convenient fabrication, he didn't consider it now. "It wasn't what I'd call a discovery," he admitted freely. "I was just out exploring this morning, and having no real destination in mind, followed you."

"Why?"

Byron laughed softly to himself. "Because you're a very beautiful woman."

"One who clearly despises you, so why did you bother?"

Byron found it difficult, if not impossible, to explain. "I was out for a stroll; you caught my eye, and I followed. There's nothing more to it than that."

"You've turned up with a maddening frequency today," Arielle mused thoughtfully. "But you ought not to prowl the town alone at night, Mr. Barclay. Not all of our citizens are as friendly as I am."

"You're not friendly at all," he complained.

"Good. Now you understand what danger you're in."

"I had another reason for coming out here," he suddenly confessed. "I wanted to apologize for my tasteless remark about your late husband. He must have been very dear to you and I shouldn't have mocked him. I hope that however he met his fate, he did not suffer."

"He was slain by the Iroquois," Arielle replied, and, impressed by Byron's politely worded apology, she continued. "He was on a trip to Quebec when his party was overtaken by savages. It has always been a comfort to me to know that he was killed by a single arrow to the heart and spared the days of hideous torture the beasts often inflict on their captives."

Apparently believing their conversation over, she turned away, but Byron reached out to stop her. "Wait, as long as I'm here, I might as well walk you home."

"I live just up ahead."

"Yes, I know." Byron fell in beside her. "I truly am sorry about your husband. My only brother was killed by the Abenaki last spring, and it was a tragic loss. He was a fine man." Byron then spoke more to himself than her. "It should have been me."

"I beg your pardon?"

"Oh, it's nothing, I was just deploring the fact that Elliott died rather than me."

"That explains the sadness in your eyes."

"It shows?"

"Yes, I imagine it's apparent to anyone who bothers to look."

"I'm amazed that you did."

They had reached her door, and this time, Arielle realized perhaps she had been the one to admit too much. "Good night, Mr. Barclay. I trust if we put our minds to it, we can avoid ever having to see each other again."

Byron stared at her a long moment. He was hungry, and the night had grown cold, but he had not really minded waiting for her. He had known she would not invite him inside, but the finality of her dismissal was still disappointing. Pretending an agreement he did not feel, he bowed slightly and turned away to hide his smile. He did not care how much it cost him to hire her to translate for him, he would willingly pay it.

Three

Arielle had worn black for a year following Bernard's death, and as she took out mourning attire in preparation for Marie's funeral, she decided it was the only appropriate way to dress again. As she saw it, the whole town had been placed under a death sentence, and anything more colorful would simply be an insensitive denial of the British scourge.

Bernard had always wanted her to dress fashionably, and her mourning clothes, despite their dark hue, had been as pretty as her other things. She brushed off the velvet bodice and smoothed the creases from the taffeta skirt. She had even worn black lace at the neckline rather than a white fichu. Once dressed, she slowly drew the delicate strip through her fingers before tucking it inside her bodice.

When she had last been clothed in black, she had been too sick at heart to pay any attention to its effect on her appearance, but now, when she turned to judge the effect in the mirror, she was almost ashamed of how attractive she looked. Embarrassed to even be thinking such selfish thoughts on the day of a funeral, she chastised herself severely, and left for the church.

The day was cool, and after the funeral mass, as

Marie's coffin was lowered into the ground, dark clouds blew across the sun in what the mourners took as an omen of the sadness still to come. They crossed themselves hurriedly, and stood in huddled groups exchanging their fears in hushed whispers. The Mouflet men were all there, and several approached her to thank her for interceding for them with John Winslow.

As Arielle assured one such grateful male relative that it had been a pleasure, she caught a glimpse of Byron Barclay at the cemetery gate. Shocked that he would intrude at such a time, she sent him an angry glance and turned her back, concentrating on listening to a particularly heartwarming memory one of Marie's daughters wished to share. When it came time to leave the gravesite, she was relieved to find Byron had gone.

Byron, she scolded herself silently, for she did not want to even think of the man by his first name. That he was attractive, and behaved in a gentlemanly fashion, was completely irrelevant. He was British, and she detested him as much as she did John Winslow and all the others. She tried to join him in her mind with the obnoxious soldiers who had refused to take her seriously at the stockade gate, but his image failed to merge with the scurrilous pair.

She joined the other mourners at the Mouflet home, but too disturbed by the plight of the town to share their loss in a sufficiently potent manner, she excused herself as soon as was politely possible. On the way home, she thought of Gaetan, and knowing he would not be deported without a valiant struggle, actually found herself admiring him. Then she noticed Byron Barclay waiting by her door.

She shook her head sadly. "Mr. Barclay, really, I thought I had made my objection to your following me about very clear last night. I've absolutely nothing more to say to you, nor will I ever."

"This is not a personal visit," Byron informed her, "not that I wouldn't enjoy the pleasure of calling on you." Arielle greeted that comment with such an astonished gaze that he hurried on before she interrupted with what he feared would be another of her strident insults.

"Colonel Winslow has given me the responsibility of taking a census, to assure him that family members aren't separated during the deportations." As proof of his intentions, he removed the list of questions from his coat pocket. "Because you speak English as well as French, I was hoping that you'd translate my questions for me so that I can begin my work this afternoon. You'll be well paid for your help."

Byron had been wearing dark gray the previous day, but was now dressed in a coat and breeches of beige wool. His waistcoat was a paler shade, and his shirt and stockings snowy white. She was certain the buttons on his coat were real silver, as were the buckles on his black leather shoes. Even his tricorne hat looked brand new. It was obvious he could afford to pay her well, but she was not impressed by his offer.

"With what?" she asked. "Thirty pieces of silver?"

Having anticipated her reluctance to assist him, Byron easily countered her objection. "Please, Madame Douville, I'm offering you the opportunity to be of service to your people during a difficult time. Won't you please help me make the relocation of your friends easier to bear?"

The left corner of his mouth rose slightly in the beginnings of a smile and, determined not to allow his handsome appearance to distract her, Arielle glanced away. "Where is your home, Mr. Barclay?" she asked.

"I'm from Virginia."

"What is it you do there?"

"My family raises tobacco."

Surprised, Arielle again regarded him with a skeptical stare. "Farmers don't dress as well as you, Mr. Barclay."

Amused that she had noticed his apparel when he had left far finer clothes at home, Byron's smile grew wide. "I'm not a farmer. We own a plantation with considerable acreage. I don't have to tend the plants with my own hands."

Arielle lifted her chin slightly. "Farming is honest work."

"Yes, indeed it is. I didn't mean to imply otherwise."

After a moment's pause, Arielle continued. "What would your reaction be should our positions be reversed? Would you translate for me had I arrived to deport your family?"

Byron took a deep breath and released it slowly. He had known winning her cooperation wouldn't be easy, but he had not anticipated that question. Somehow he knew instinctively that she would accept nothing but the truth. "Should Virginia ever be invaded, I would fight to the death rather than surrender as the Acadians did. I realize there were powerful influences in Canada who incited your people to resist and then provided no assistance in that endeavor, so I can't fault the Acadians for lacking the will to fight on alone. In my view, your people have already been betrayed, and any help you give me can be regarded only as an act of kindness toward your neighbors."

There was no trace of a smile gracing his well-shaped lips now, and, convinced by his spirited defense of his own principles, Arielle nodded slightly. She extended her hand. "Give me your questions. I'll put them into French and have them ready for you in an hour."

That was another demand Byron had not foreseen, but he immediately shook his head. "No, I'd much rather work with you on them so you can help me with the pronunciation of the French words."

Arielle straightened up to her full height. "It may interest you to know that I've already warned every woman I've seen to bar her doors both day and night to prohibit our being overrun by your soldiers. Do you honestly expect me to willingly invite you into my home?"

Byron tried to appear insulted, but he actually found her challenging nature very appealing. He had also noted how beautifully her black gown complemented her fair coloring, but knew better than to say so. "Madame Douville, before coming here, I served as a captain in the Virginia militia. While I'm not clad in a military uniform, I will give you my promise as an officer that I would never attempt to take advantage of you. Indeed, were I quartered in your house, you would find me a perfect guest."

"I would burn my home to the ground before I would invite you into my bed!"

"Madame Douville!" Byron replied in an equally shocked tone. "You must have completely misunderstood me, for I said nothing about sharing your bed. I merely made a passing reference to being quartered in your home, which is something entirely different. This is a perfect illustration of why we must work together while you translate my questions. Otherwise, I fear I will merely confuse everyone I meet, as apparently I have confused you."

Embarrassed she had misinterpreted his remark, Arielle reluctantly opened her door and invited him inside. "I hope you will not compare my home unfavorably to yours," she admonished.

"I wish you would give me the opportunity to prove myself rather than thinking so badly of me," Byron protested. He surveyed the combined kitchen and parlor of the simple two-room dwelling and found no reason to complain. The air held a comforting fragrance of freshly baked bread mixed with the heady perfume of the herbs she had drying along one wall. He walked over to admire her collection.

"Do you use all these in cooking?" he asked.

"Are you planning to ask to stay for dinner?" When Byron again looked pained by her response, Arielle answered his question. "No, I use them to treat the ailments common here. In addition to being a midwife, that's how I support myself."

"Really, I had no idea." Byron took care to stand well away from the table as Arielle brought out a pen and ink. He had extra paper, and when she sat down, he handed her the blank sheets as well as his questions. Now that he knew her better, he feared she might immediately recognize how superfluous many of them were. He held his breath as she read through them, and when she offered no complaints, he sighed aloud.

"You sound exhausted," she advised. "You better sit down while I do this as it may take me awhile."

Byron pulled out the chair opposite hers, considered asking if he would be too close, then not wanting to provide an opportunity for her to object, sat down. He placed his hat on the chair beside his. "Even upside down I can appreciate the clarity of your writing. That's unusual in a left-handed person."

"Is it? Most of the *femmes sages* are left-handed," she remarked absently.

"Femmes sages?"

"Those of us who provide herbal cures."

"Ah, yes, now I understand." Byron tried not to watch her so closely that he would make her nervous, but he found it difficult to look away when she was so wonderfully attractive. He could see only a hint of her blond hair at the front of her cap, and wondered how long it might be. He could easily imagine the silken strands slipping through his fingers.

Arielle looked up to find Byron staring at her with a glance so full of desire that she had to hurriedly return to her task. Then, flustered, she couldn't recall precisely what she had been writing and had to reread his question. While Gaetan had taken supper with her several times, having him seated across from her had never been so disconcerting, and she feared inviting Byron inside had been a grave mistake.

"I'm almost finished," she assured him.

"Please, take all the time you need." As he continued to watch her, Byron began to imagine the tasks that usually kept her occupied, then was interrupted in his musings hearing Arielle clear her throat as she laid her pen aside. "There you are," she declared, and handed him the translation.

Byron stared down at the neatly penned words and winced. "Let me try and read the questions now, and tell me if I come close to being understood."

"Of course."

Taking a deep breath, Byron read the first, which was a simple query intended to elicit the names of the residents of each household. When he looked up, Arielle's pained expression gave clear evidence of his shoddy performance. "Did I do that poorly?" he asked. "After all, you have an accent in English, but I have no trouble understanding you."

"I fear this is going to take far longer than we anticipated," she confided as she rose to put the tea kettle over the smoldering remains of the fire. "Try reading that again," she urged.

Making every effort to enunciate clearly, Byron struggled to improve his delivery, but again, Arielle looked perplexed. "You read it for me then," he exclaimed as he handed the sheet back to her.

Arielle read the words slowly and distinctly, then gave the paper back to Byron for another try. After several such exchanges, she moved her chair to the end of the table to sit beside him so they could both read without having to pass the paper back and forth. She could tell Byron was making a sincere effort to read the French questions exactly as she had written them, but no matter how hard he tried, they sounded so peculiar, she feared he would inspire ridicule rather than cooperation.

She got up to make the tea. "I don't have any of the tea the English drink," she apologized, "but several varieties of my own making. Would you care to try one? The peppermint is very good."

What Byron wanted to drink was something far stronger, but he doubted she kept spirits. "Thank you. We use it at home for upset stomachs, so I'm sure it won't hurt me."

"Do you actually believe that I'd try to poison you, Mr. Barclay?"

Byron turned to watch the lovely young widow as she placed the peppermint leaves into a china teapot to steep. "No, not at all, I only meant that even if it's usually used as a medicine, I'd like some."

She brought the pot and two cups to the table, and sat down again beside him. "Just who are you?" he asked.

"I'm Arielle Douville, no more, no less. What is it you expect me to say?"

"You're a very bright woman," he complimented softly.

"Why does that surprise you? Were you led to believe all Acadians were such stupid dolts we could scarcely remember our own names?"

"No, of course not, it's just that—"

A knock at the door interrupted him, and Arielle rose to answer. It was Sophie, and Arielle tried without success to step outside and pull her door closed before her friend saw her caller.

"Who is that!" Sophie cried.

"He's an Englishman who needs some translation done. Now what can I do for *you?*" she asked with as pleasant a smile as she could affect.

Shocked to the marrow to find an Englishman in Arielle's home, Sophie frowned, opened her mouth to make a comment, and then, with a wave of her hand, turned away and hurried back toward her home.

Arielle went back inside, and, certain the tea was now ready, poured two cups and sat down to take a fortifying sip.

Byron sampled the tea, found it surprisingly good, and then gave his first question another try. "How did it sound that time?" he asked.

"Better, truly it was," Arielle assured him, but without convincing enthusiasm.

Disappointed by her response, Byron sat back in his chair. "At this rate, everyone will already have been deported before I master these questions." Thoroughly frustrated, he then caught a blinding glimpse of the obvious. "There's also the problem of understanding the answers. If people reply with a list of names, Jacques, André, Marie, whatever, I can transcribe them competently enough. But what if they wish to request special consideration for an invalid niece or aged grandmother? I won't understand them and that might lead to a disastrous mistake in their travel arrangements."

Arielle nodded. "There are merchants who speak enough English to translate for you. Monsieur Beauchamp is one. Perhaps you ought to take him with you."

Byron was rapidly beginning to believe conversing

with Arielle Douville was like playing chess, for he not only had to be careful in his own remarks, but anticipate hers as well. Fortunately, he came up with a plausible objection to her suggestion. "That would be unfair to the other men if he were permitted to leave the stockade every day to traverse the town freely while they aren't."

He then regarded her with a knowing smile. "But I think your idea that I have a translator accompany me is a very good one."

Who he had in mind was so readily apparent, Arielle instantly rebelled. "What is it you really want from me, Mr. Barclay?"

Byron would have liked to have brought her hand to his lips to kiss her palm and suck her fingertips, but thinking such a romantic confession would only infuriate her, he made no such provocative declaration. "Help in taking the census," he admitted sincerely.

"I had honestly believed it would be a simple matter of having these questions translated and then tallying the answers. Now I realize how badly I overestimated my ability to master the French language quickly. Please come with me," he urged gently. "We can start this very afternoon, and I doubt that we'll need to spend more than a few minutes at each house, so we should finish up in a week or so. I will pay you for your time, and if ever you're needed to attend a birth, or treat someone who's ill, I won't object."

"How very kind of you." Arielle picked up the list of questions. "It will take far longer than you expect if you ask all these questions at every house. Forgive me if I'm insulting you, but some are rather silly."

Arielle looked away for a long moment. She didn't want to spend another minute with Byron Barclay, but she was far more concerned about the fate of the populace of Grand Pré than she was about whatever passing distress having to work with him might cause. Her decision made in an instant, she sat up straight and faced him.

"We need ask only two questions: the names of the people who occupy each house, and with whom they wish to travel. That will simplify your task considerably."

While inordinately pleased to have won her consent for the project, Byron dared not gloat. "Thank you so much. I promise you'll not regret this."

"I'm heartbroken there's even a need for such a thankless task, so I already regret it. Now, you said you wanted to begin today. Shall we go?"

"I'll need to gather paper and writing supplies." Byron feared that made him sound totally unprepared. "I had expected to return to my inn before starting out."

"We can use my supplies today, and you can replace them with your own later."

"Excellent idea. Would you like to change your clothes before we go?"

Nonplussed by his comment, Arielle nonetheless gave an immediate reply. "Whatever would possess you to make such a presumptuous suggestion? Does my present attire offend you?"

"Oh, no, not at all," Byron hastened to explain.

"In fact, it's extremely becoming, but I thought you had dressed especially for Marie Mouflet's funeral."

"No, I have decided to don mourning indefinitely, Mr. Barclay. Now the sooner we begin, the sooner we can complete this odious task." She got up to fetch more paper and a small basket to hold it and her pen and ink.

Odious task, Byron murmured under his breath. He also rose and tugged on his cuffs to adjust the fit of his coat. He tried to remember when he had last been so intrigued by a woman. He had left home without even telling Sarah Frederick goodbye. While she might have once considered herself his sweetheart, after his lack of attention in the last year she could not possibly still harbor that illusion. She was Arielle Douville's exact opposite, petite and dark, so eager to please she was flirtatious in the extreme, but her considerable charms no longer moved him. That Arielle had so little, or rather, *no* interest in him was maddening, but he had always relished a challenge.

"I'd planned to canvas the town in a systematic fashion, but we might as well begin with you," he called to her. "Just for practice if you will. Now who lives here?"

Not wanting to remain indoors with him, Arielle carried the basket to the door, and paused there. Thinking such practice totally unnecessary, she rolled her eyes, but answered, "I do."

"And with whom do you wish to travel?"

Arielle reflected on the possibilities a long moment. There were friends of whom she was very fond, and Gaetan. She knew she ought to consider his feelings. Finally, she shrugged slightly. "I'd rather not make my choice now. After all, I shan't have to sail with the evening tide."

Byron picked up his hat and came forward. "You have no family you wish me to list?"

"No. Now let's be on our way." They had taken only a few steps along the path from her door to the road before she stopped and turned back to face him. He might have thought his questions were innocuous, but they had forced her to accept the painful fact she was a widow with no family who faced the loss of her home and deportation. Now horribly uncomfortable, she couldn't ignore her feelings.

"I must warn you this survey of yours is only going to upset the women we question even more than they already are. Why don't we just use the church records to list everyone?"

"The priest keeps track of marriages, baptisms, confirmations, deaths; that sort of thing?" When Arielle nodded, Byron gave her suggestion brief consideration but then rejected it. "His records may be inaccurate or out of date, madame. They could also be altered to exclude whole groups of families, and in the case of the unmarried women, we might have to search back many years for any mention of them. No, I'm afraid that just won't do. We must conduct the census personally. Now, can we finally be on our way?"

"You needn't use such a scolding tone," Arielle responded, but she hurried on without waiting for him to apologize. The first house they went to belonged to Sophie and Jean, but when Sophie appeared and saw Arielle had brought an Englishman with her, she promptly shut the door in her face.

"Is this woman always so hostile?" Byron asked.

"No, she's the one who came to my door earlier. She's one of my best friends." Although uncertain how to proceed, Arielle again rapped lightly at Sophie's door. After a long delay, Sophie finally opened it just wide enough to peer out at them.

After assuring her friend she need not be afraid, Arielle attempted to begin their survey. "Mr. Barclay has asked me to help him conduct a census, so that adequate travel arrangements can be made for everyone in Grand Pré."

"Travel arrangements?" Sophie repeated in an astonished gasp. "We're being robbed of everything we own and deported! How can you refer to it as anything other that what it is?" To emphasize her displeasure, she again slammed her door soundly.

Taking a firm hold on her basket, Arielle led the way back out to the road. "I know Sophie's family, so I'll list them for you, along with a reference to their relatives. It's plain she's not going to ever be cooperative."

"What did she say?"

"There's no reason to translate when I'm positive you understood her meaning. I warned you that we'd upset everyone."

"I see what you mean. Well, let's give it another try. Perhaps the woman at the next house will be more cooperative."

"She's a widow, and unlikely to appreciate being sent away any more than Sophie. Rather than bother her, I'll just list her and her relatives, too."

Byron removed his hat and bounced it against his thigh as he spoke. "I realize that you mean to be helpful, but we ought to speak with everyone, or they'll complain of being neglected. They may not want to hear our questions or answer them, but if we don't ask, they'll run straight to John Winslow and accuse us of plotting against them."

"Not 'us,' Mr. Barclay, but *you* and the rest of the British scourge." Confident she had made her point, she led the way to the widow's home where they were threatened in such abusive language she was very glad Byron didn't understand French.

Badly embarrassed, Byron was still convinced they needed to stop at every residence, and refused to alter his plans. He did feel sorry for Arielle, though. "While it certainly isn't my responsibility to apologize for the rudeness of your neighbors, I do want you to know I had no idea you'd be subjected to such sorry displays of anger."

"How can you expect us to react otherwise, Mr. Barclay? You've already admitted you'd fight to the death rather than surrender your plantation. I hope you'll respect the dignity in our anger."

"Believe me, Madame Douville, I have the utmost respect for you."

As he replaced his hat, at what Arielle considered far too jaunty an angle considering the grimness of their task, she was struck by the laughter lurking in his gaze. Yesterday, she had seen only sorrow, and she could not imagine what could have caused the change in his mood. Fearing that he took a perverse delight in torturing the citizens of Grand Pré, she started off down the road, but with every step she felt as though she were trodding on her own anguished regrets.

Four

Arielle encountered curious glances when she appeared in church the next morning still clothed in black, but after she explained the reason for the somber choice, several other young women also volunteered to adopt mourning attire. Then hushed innuendoes began to circulate about her association with a certain handsome young Englishman. Rather than issue denials of the gossip, she left church holding her head high and ignored the talk.

Sophie was carrying her youngest daughter, while two more girls and her son skipped along by her side. They walked along in companionable silence for a few minutes, and then Arielle shared her thoughts aloud. "I agreed to work with Mr. Barclay for the good of the town. I thought there might be some unkind remarks about my helping the British until the purpose of the survey was understood, but it had to have been the very women who know what it's about who were giving such free, and unfortunately vocal, rein to their imaginations."

"Well, Arielle, you brought it on yourself by inviting him into your home. What were you thinking? You're an attractive widow, and he's, well, for an Englishman, he's pleasant enough to look at."

"I didn't think you'd had time to notice. Besides, you're the only one who knows he's seen the inside of my house. No one else does, or will, unless you tell them, and I really thought you were a better friend than that."

Flustered only a moment, Sophie continued to argue her point. "Granted, all anyone else knows is that you're helping the British, but there are men who can count heads as easily as you. Because they've all been arrested and have no say in the matter, no one can call them traitors for helping with a census."

"Is that what people were saying? I thought it was Byron's looks that had started all the gossip."

"Byron!" Sophie shrieked. "You're calling him by his first name?" They were nearing her house, and, eager to get home, she picked up her pace.

Exasperated with herself for making such a slip, Arielle quickly denied the accusation. "No, of course not, not to his face certainly. I address him as Mr. Barclay and he calls me Madame Douville. There's nothing scandalous about this, Sophie. It's just a business proposition."

Now at the front of her home, Sophie waited until her older children had rushed inside to reply. Then she lowered her voice to a malevolent whisper. "You must be more careful, or people are going to start questioning what business you're in!"

Arielle was too shocked by that outrageous warning to respond with more than an astonished gasp. Her cheeks growing hot with a deep blush of shame, she hurried on to her own home, and, horribly embarrassed, flopped across her bed, and lay there for nearly an hour. She hadn't wanted to work with Byron, *Mr. Barclay*, and now rather than being recognized for her efforts to help her neighbors, one of her closest friends had stopped just short of calling her a whore!

She had a miniature of Bernard in a gold frame beside her bed. She reached over to pick it up, and pressed it to her heart. Grateful her dear Bernard would never hear such scandalous tales, she wondered how anyone could think of her as being anything other than the virtuous young woman and faithful wife she had always been. Although they had been wed three years, and Bernard had continually assured her they would have children someday, her dreams of motherhood had not come true. Tragically, she had gone from being a loving bride to a heartbroken widow all too soon, but she had no intention of now running the risk of being called a strumpet!

Propping her head on her elbow, she gazed at the small painting of her beloved. Like hers, his dark hair had lacked even a hint of curl giving him a rather severe appearance which contrasted sharply with his engaging personality. His dark eyes had often glowed with mischief, but he had never behaved in an ungentlemanly fashion. No, he had been the perfect husband: dependable, and trustworthy to a fault.

How she missed him!

Feeling trapped in the house they had shared, she got up, set his painting aside, and quickly changed out of her mourning clothes. Sunday afternoons she usually gathered herbs, and, clinging to her routine when all else was in turmoil, she put on a softly faded lavender skirt and blue bodice. After donning her apron and a worn cap, she picked up the basket she kept for such outings and headed out the front door. As she stepped onto the road, her spirits soared, only to plummet as she heard Byron Barclay calling her name.

Grasping the handle of her basket with both hands, she wheeled around and waited for him to catch up with her. "I'm positive I explained that I'd not work with you on the Sabbath, Mr. Barclay. You look to be in perfect health, so you can't have come seeking medical treatment."

"Thank you," Byron replied, as though she had complimented his looks. "I have no intention of asking you to work this afternoon. On the contrary, I thought we might just go out for a walk. I'd like to know something of the town's history and I was hoping you'd share it with me."

Arielle was not even remotely tempted to believe that ridiculous ploy. "You have imprisoned in your stockade a great many men who could explain in intricate detail the history of the town, Mr. Barclay. Now, I would like to suggest that you go back into that town, and satisfy your curiosity there. I have herbs to gather, and no time to waste."

Arielle again started off down the road, but Byron quickly caught up with her. "Colonel Winslow didn't think it necessary to forbid the women of Grand Pré to leave the immediate area, but you are, however, restricted to the town. Now, if you wish to leave to gather medicinal herbs, or to enjoy the last of the summer's wildflowers, then I'll have to go with you."

Arielle again came to an abrupt halt. Her eyes narrowed to menacing slits as her gaze swept over him. He was dressed in blue today, and looked as substantial as ever. "Are you telling me that I'm as much a prisoner as the men you've locked in the stockade?"

"No, of course not, madame. You're not a prisoner at all. You're just restricted from leaving Grand Pré. Unless, of course, you have a suitable escort. I'm volunteering to be one for you so that your valuable work isn't interrupted for lack of supplies."

Certain her intention, if not her words, would be clear, Arielle chose French to damn him to hell for being the interfering bastard he continually was. "I find you personally annoying, and your company nearly intolerable," she then described in English. "Now if you insist upon following me, I can't stop you. But I'll not pretend we are on a pleasant outing when that is so far from the truth!"

Byron waited for her to move on ahead of him, and then followed at an easy pace. He smiled slyly to himself, for he was confident once they reached the woods, he could find a reason to strike up another conversation.

Arielle tried to pretend the afternoon was no different than the previous Sunday's, but she could actually feel Byron watching her. It made her shoulder blades itch, and she wiggled uncomfortably in an attempt to shake off the wretched sensation, but failed. It took nearly an hour to get out past the farms and reach the woods, and by the time she arrived, her head ached from the effort to ignore the persistent Englishman's presence.

She focused her attention on the herbs she had come to find. Several were favorites of the Mic Mac Indians who lived in the area. She feared she might be unable to locate them growing wild wherever she was sent, so as she moved through the shady glades she took seedpods as well as the leaves and stems. It wasn't until her basket was full that she got the inspiration to play a trick on Byron.

Moving behind a thick screen of wild blackberry vines, she bent down and hurried away. When she came to an oak that had invitingly low branches, she hid her basket beneath an outcropping of ferns, and after hiking up her skirt, climbed up where, shielded by leaves, she could watch the forest floor without being seen.

Several minutes passed before Byron walked by, hurrying along, glancing from side to side as though he expected to find her at any minute. Arielle had to cover her mouth to keep from laughing out loud, and when later he began to shout her name, she couldn't stop her giggles. She hoped he felt very foolish for losing sight of her, and would soon go back to town. At long last his voice grew faint and when she could no longer hear him calling, she climbed down, picked up her basket, and, simply enjoying the solitude she had usually found there, she took her time in leaving the woods.

When he had initially lost sight of Arielle, Byron feared she might have stumbled and fallen, but when he found no trace of her in the area where she had just been, he had to face the humiliating fact that she had deliberately eluded him. Frustrated and annoyed, he sat down, and waited near where the path left the woods and became the meandering trail to town. He dozed off, but awakened when he heard someone approaching. Rising quickly, he moved out in time to block the trail.

"Did you find everything you need?" he asked Arielle, smiling, as though she hadn't just played him for a fool.

"Why, yes, I did, thank you," she replied. "But you ought not to leap out at people like that. It's really very rude."

Byron looked down at her and for the first time noticed the soft sprinkling of freckles that graced the bridge of her nose and cheeks. As she tried to slip by him, he reached out to stop her. She saw him incline his head, and was shocked he apparently intended to kiss her, but not so badly outraged that she turned away to avoid the gesture. His lips were soft, quite pleasantly warm, and the pressure he exerted gentle rather than harshly insistent. When he leaned back and regarded her with a quizzical glance, an incredulous daze prevented her from making any coherent comment, let alone a forceful protest.

Byron had acted on impulse, but he had enjoyed kissing Arielle so much that when she did not erupt in a furious fit of bilingual name-calling, he raised his hand to caress her cheek and kissed her again. There was something so enchanting about her hesitant response that he allowed his lips to linger over hers until, overcome by desire, he pulled her close to deepen the kiss and savor her delicious taste more fully.

Her shyness dissolving in a heartbeat, Arielle opened her mouth to welcome a more intimate exchange, and Byron's tongue caressed hers with a slow, enticing motion that banished all thoughts save those of him. She leaned against him, drinking in the heat of his muscular body, for it radiated right through his fine clothes. Lost in his stirring affection, she could no longer consider him an enemy, but now, remarkably, the dearest of friends.

No, he tasted of something far more luscious than friendship.

Equally affected, Byron brought up his other arm to embrace her, but inadvertently tipped the basket in Arielle's hands awkwardly shattering their romantic mood. Her freshly cut herbs rained down on their feet, and as startled as she that what had begun as a chaste kiss had quickly turned so desperately passionate, he bent down to help her refill the basket. "I'm sorry to be so clumsy," he quickly apologized, steeling himself for the blistering tirade he was certain she would swiftly deliver.

Jolted from what had seemed a blissful daydream, Arielle felt her cheeks burning with shame. Bernard's kisses had been teasing and sweet, but never as fiercely arousing as Byron Barclay's and, terrified, he sensed how much she had wanted that second kiss, and dear God, enjoyed it, Arielle concentrated on retrieving the fragile herbs before they were crushed.

"Be careful," she urged, "and get the seedpods, too. I don't know where I'll be going, and I might have to raise my own herbs." As they reached for the same dark-brown pod, their fingertips brushed, and she recoiled with a start as the heat of a delicious thrill shot clear up her arm. She looked up to find Byron's eyes level with hers, and his lips, graced with the hint of a smile, mere inches away.

For one dreadful moment, she was nearly consumed by the reckless desire to kiss him again, but somehow she managed to fight it away and refocus her attention on the last of the scattered herbs. She raked them up, in her haste dirtying her nails with the rich forest soil. As soon as she had reclaimed the last one, she rose and began to back away.

"I'm going home and please don't follow closely."

Arielle then turned and fled down the trail with the rambunctious grace of a fawn. Byron was shocked. After all, they had merely exchanged a few kisses, that didn't mean that he wouldn't let her go without demanding more. She had looked terrified. Not wanting to increase her fears if he had caused them, he again sat down where he had waited and rested his arms across his knees, assessing the situation.

He had gotten the unmistakable impression Arielle had wanted more as much as he. For a prim and proper widow, that must have been an enormous shock, and, being discreet, he would not speak of what had transpired between them that day. No, he would continue to be the perfect gentleman as they conducted their survey, but the next time they were alone, he would remind her in the most sensual way how delightful their first kisses had been.

Upon reaching home, Arielle first separated the herbs, which was a far more troublesome task than usual because of their complete disarray. She then tied them in neat bundles and hung them along the wall to dry. She used a brush to remove the dirt from beneath her nails, but even after restoring her hands to their former ladylike appearance, she didn't really feel clean.

Her head ached with the effort to suppress the memory of Byron's kiss, and, her work finished for the moment, she brewed herself a cup of tea made from the bark of the willow tree and lay down to rest. An arm flung across her eyes, she finally gave in to a lengthy recollection of the Englishman's kisses and then to her own shameless response. She certainly didn't love the man, so why had the brief interlude been so enchanting? she wondered.

Gaetan was just as tall and well-built, and dark rather than fair, he was every bit as handsome, too. His defiant refusal to consider the British as more than vermin had inspired a new respect for him, but never, not even once, had his kisses held such magical sweetness. Nor had Bernard's, she admitted regretfully. She knew of no herb that would instill a hardier dislike for the Englishman than she already held, but why, dear God, did his kisses have to feel so good?

Absolutely mortified that she might not be able to find the strength to refuse him should he press for more, she vowed right then to stop working with him. All she would have to do when he arrived at her home the next day was find the courage to send him away.

Monday dawned bright and clear, and, again dressed in gray, Byron rapped lightly on Arielle's door. He then stepped back to assume a more respectful distance. When she appeared, clad elegantly in black, he greeted her with a warm smile. "Good morning. It's such a beautiful day, I'm hoping your neighbors will be in a far more cooperative mood than they were on Saturday."

Arielle stared at him, trying to remember the excuse she had practiced until late last night. "I won't be able to assist you any longer, Mr. Barclay. Taking the census will simply cut too severely into the time I must allot to those who need me. Now, here are your questions. Please, I beg of you, take Mr. Beauchamp with you today."

Byron took the sheet of paper, but deliberately caressed her palm in the exchange. At his touch, Arielle's fair complexion brightened with a captivating blush, and, certain she was simply too stubborn to admit how much she liked him, he refused to even consider her request. "We've already discussed why you're a far better choice for my translator than he, madame."

Stepping close, he lowered his voice to a soft, seductive tone. "I want to apologize if what happened between us yesterday embarrassed you in any way. I won't pretend that I didn't consider it delightful, but I'd given you my word that there need be nothing personal between us and I feel badly about having broken it. Let me assure you that I will endeavor, and heroically if need be, to avoid any repetition of yesterday's events." Unless, of course, she encouraged them, he wisely did not add.

Merely confused by that gentlemanly promise, Arielle bit her lower lip as she tried to think how best to make herself understood. She dared not admit that just waiting to see him that morning had made her whole body ache with longing. Now that he was there, she felt even worse. "It is simply a matter of where my talents are best used," she finally told him. "I am a *femme sage,* not a translator."

Byron nodded, but did not give in. "Let's attach a note to your door giving the location where we'll be working. Then you'll be easy to find should anyone need you."

Arielle shook her head slightly. "I doubt we can be that precise."

"Of course we can. Now fetch a piece of paper, and write the name of the owner of the last house we visited on Saturday and the direction in which we'll be walking. Leave plenty of room, and each morning you can add another name to inform your friends of your whereabouts."

"Mr. Barclay, please—"

Byron stubbornly refused to acknowledge the cause of her distress. You have already agreed to translate for me, madame, and I'm going to hold you to that bargain."

"Even though you did not keep yours?"

"I've already apologized for that regrettable slip. Now let's go. We could have already visited half a dozen houses in the time we've wasted arguing. Colonel Winslow expects the ships to arrive soon, so we must complete the census without delay."

Arielle did not want to spend another hour with him when it took no more than an accidental brush of his fingertips to arouse cravings she dared not satisfy. She reminded herself that with the whole town facing tragic deportations, an unfortunate attraction to an Englishman was of little consequence. But still it hurt. Her effort to avoid him having failed to convince him, she left the message he had suggested affixed to her door, and carrying their supplies, left with him, but the sunshine of the day did absolutely nothing to lift her mood.

A middle-aged woman came to the door of the first house they visited. Flanked by two daughters, she answered Arielle's questions in a dull monotone while the girls wept. One reached out and spoke to her as she turned to go, and, after making a brief notation on their questionnaire, Arielle assured her she would do what she could about her request. She had become adept at juggling paper, pen, and ink, but not with dealing with the sadness they encountered at every house.

Byron had again remained in the background, but he was curious what the girl had asked.

"She asked to be on the same ship as a young man she admires," Arielle answered, stopping briefly before approaching the next house. "Doesn't Winslow care about separating sweethearts? After all, they may comprise families of the future."

Byron rocked back on his heels. "I suppose we can keep track of sweethearts without too much difficulty. But surely there are some young people who are so popular their names will be mentioned several times. Then there will be complaints unless we place them aboard the same ship with all their admirers."

"That problem is easily solved. The person who is chosen frequently gets his or her choice, rather than the other way around."

"I see. So if a great many men wish to be on the same ship with you, as an example, then I'll just ask you whose company you'd prefer. Is that what you had in mind?"

Unable to abide his openly teasing gaze, Arielle

looked down the street where several woman stood in a huddled group observing their progress through their neighborhood. While it was true that Gaetan Le Blanc was her most enthusiastic and persistent suitor, there was a slight possibility several older gentleman might request her ship. One of the gossiping women was now pointing their way, and fearing whatever she was saying to her friends wasn't good, Arielle turned back to face Byron.

"We seem to be causing something of a stir by standing here talking, so let's just keep on with our work. In answer to your question, I've already told you I'd make my selection of traveling companions later."

As they made their way down the street, Byron kept a mental tally of their successes, which he counted as anyone who responded, whether or not it was politely. More people cooperated than did not, but every fourth or fifth house was owned by someone who thought what he assumed were colorful insults were all he needed to hear. None of the men being held in the stockade could be judged cooperative, which meant they would be dealing with large numbers of hostile passengers. Believing the ships' crews would be able to handle them, Byron hoped he would not be asked to supervise anyone during his voyage home.

He listened, and, still hoping to learn some French, tried to catch a familiar word as Arielle interviewed the next family. Here a young woman who held one baby and had two more barely out of infancy clinging to her skirts looked out at him with tear-filled eyes. Her plight obviously pathetic, Byron tried to smile but that show of friendliness only distressed her all the more and she began to sob openly.

Embarrassed, he turned away and waited for Arielle to complete her list. After that same pitiful scene occurred repeatedly throughout the morning, he had a better appreciation for what the expulsion truly meant to the citizens of Grand Pré, but he reacted with anger rather than sympathy.

"Acadia has belonged to Britain for more than forty years," he reminded Arielle in a harsh whisper. "If only your people had cultivated some loyalty to the Crown, none of this horrendous upheaval would be necessary. We are standing on British soil, and your continued perverse loyalty to France has proven to be an exceedingly costly mistake. I wish you'd remind these women of that the next time they start sobbing."

"Need I mention Queen Anne's promise to respect us as British citizens?" Arielle countered bitterly. "A country which has repeatedly lied to us, ignored us, and treated us with furious contempt does not inspire loyalty! Now I am going home to eat and rest. I shall be ready to work again in an hour, but I will never be ready to listen to your insufferably ignorant opinions again!"

Byron supposed he deserved that rebuke, but it did not change his mind about the collective intelligence of the Acadians, nor the wildly exciting widow Douville.

Five

John Winslow permitted his prisoners to exercise outdoors each day, and while walking with Sophie's husband Jean Doucet, Gaetan Le Blanc kept a close eye on their guards. The colonial troops' frequent outbursts of raucous laughter soon revealed a greater fondness for exchanging rude jokes than for being attentive to their duties. After three days of being treated with the same insulting indifference, Gaetan was anxious to make his plans.

"There are nearly five hundred of us," he stressed softly, "while Winslow has only three hundred men. If we attack together, we could overpower them, seize their arms, and make prisoners of them all."

Fearful of being overheard, Jean cast a furtive glance over his shoulder before remembering they could shout if they wished and still not be understood. Even without the worry of being caught plotting, he remained uneasy. At thirty he was only two years Gaetan's senior, but far more conservative in his attitude.

"Yes, I agree we have the superior numbers, but not all of Winslow's men are on duty at the same time so we couldn't possibly capture them all at once."

Gaetan scoffed at Jean's objection. "Perhaps not,

but we could use the arms of those we had captured first to attack the rest."

Having never fired a shot at another man, Jean was horrified by the violent tactics Gaetan proposed so eagerly. He had to struggle to keep the fear out of his voice. "Do you expect them to surrender without a fight?"

"No, of course not. They're a slothful lot, but that doesn't mean they're cowards."

"Then fighting them might easily result in casualties on our side as well as theirs."

Gaetan came to an immediate halt. Still speaking in a subdued tone, he managed to convey his displeasure. "The British are about to strip us of all we own and cast us to the winds. What are a few casualties compared to that monstrous threat?"

Jean swallowed hard and looked away. He was terrified by the prospect of deportation, but that did not mean he thought rushing armed men was a good idea. "I have Sophie to consider, Gaetan, and our children. Being alive to support them means far more to me than taking part in a brutal fight to salvage our honor."

"Without honor we are already dead!"

His children's smiles vivid in his mind, Jean stood firm. "If your plan succeeds, do you honestly believe Governor Lawrence will allow us to remain here?"

"Yes! We can hold Winslow and his troops hostage, and guarantee our own security with their lives."

Gaetan appeared to be so utterly incapable of seeing the dangers inherent in his plan, Jean finally lost patience with him. "But first you must capture Winslow and his troops, at what could very well be a great cost to ourselves. I admire your daring, Gaetan, but no, I do not want to be a part of it."

Seething with a bitter rage, Gaetan let Jean walk away without hurling insults at his back, but he still believed seizing the initiative was their only true means of survival. Rather than become discouraged by Jean's gloomy attitude, he sought out others whose thinking more clearly matched his own. Like Jean Doucet, most of the married men he approached were cautious, and weighed what they saw as the minute possibility of success against the tremendous risk; but after a tense hour, he had formed a hardy core of followers among the bachelors. Alain Richard, Eduard Boudreaux, and Jacques Mouflet were as brash as he, and equally eager to repay the British for the wrong that had been done them.

By the afternoon, talk of escape was rife among the prisoners, and debate grew heated between the men who believed, as Gaetan, that a glorious death was preferable to being swept from their homelands like trash, and those who swore their only duty was to remain alive. There were others, thoughtful, taciturn men, who were reluctant to take a stand. Gaetan stood back and watched while, spurred by desperation, the number of men on his side gradually grew to a force sufficient to act. Cheered for the first time since his arrest, he began to plan seriously for an attack.

When Arielle arrived at home that noon, she hurriedly scanned the note she had left pinned to her door, but the only message was her own. Too infuriated to cook, she sat down to a cold meal of bread and cheese. Now it seemed ludicrous that she had ever found Byron Barclay attractive, for the beast had the sensitivity of a stone! That he had actually suggested she deliver political lectures to sobbing women about to lose their homes was unconscionable.

Too upset to attend to her chores, she did not wait an hour before returning to work, and when Byron caught up with her, she had already completed the tallies for three more houses. "I really don't see any need for you to follow me around like a puppy," she greeted him coldly. "Why don't you just stand across from the stockade and deliver political tirades while I do the rest of this contemptible survey alone."

Byron had dined on roast duck and several goblets of a surprisingly good Spanish wine at the inn and he had hoped to find Arielle in as improved a mood as he was himself. Now he wondered why he had ever harbored such a ridiculous notion. "I'd prefer to consider any such speeches history lessons rather than 'political tirades,' madame, but I'd require a translator, and because you're busy with this task, I'll have to forgo that pleasure. I'll stay with you. Not that you need to be supervised, but my presence lends the proper authority to the task."

Arielle responded with a defiant glare, and for the remainder of the afternoon, she made a great show of ignoring the Virginian. She did not speak to him as they walked from house to house, nor did she reply to his comments with more than a distracted nod and he soon dropped all pretense of making friendly conversation. That did not prevent her from cataloging his faults, however, but other than his absurd political views, they appeared to be few.

Despite his well-tailored suits, he could not be accused of swaggering. On the contrary, he moved with a relaxed easy gait, as though the streets of Grand Pré were home to him as well. *Not yet!* she thought angrily. He greeted everyone they passed politely, and on one occasion, picked up a small child who had tripped while running by. He had set the little boy on his feet, and ruffled his hair with what appeared to be genuine affection. Amazed to find him capable of such a spontaneous act of kindness, Arielle's frown deepened, but the harder she tried to find fault with Byron, the more admirable his behavior became.

While questioning one woman, she turned, hoping to catch him doing something totally repugnant, but he was merely gazing out toward the bay, enjoying the view. His profile was as handsome as the rest of him, and, disgusted with herself for having such an inappropriate opinion, she made her next notation in an angry scrawl. Then shielding her eyes with her hand, she glanced up to judge the position of the sun, and was relieved it would soon be time to quit for the day.

Noticing the direction of her gaze, Byron feared he had made Arielle work too long. When she completed the list for that house, he suggested they stop while there was still sufficient light for her to find her way home. Then he realized his mistake.

"Wait, I'll walk with you," he called.

Emotionally as well as physically drained, Arielle closed her eyes momentarily to wish him away, but when she opened them, he was still there. "Please, Mr. Barclay. I would like to savor the exquisite joy of walking home alone."

"Fine, then do so, but I plan to arrive about ten minutes later. There's something we need to discuss, and the street's no place to do it."

His expression was completely serious, and yet Arielle didn't believe him. "No," she stated firmly. "I'd prefer we talked in the church."

While a religious setting would certainly hamper any attempt he made to impress her, Byron agreed with a smile. "What a charming idea."

They were only a few minutes away and arrived quickly. After genuflecting gracefully, Arielle slipped into the last pew, and, the Church of England having the same custom, Byron also made the respectful gesture. Flickering candles along the side aisles provided dim light, a subtle trace of incense scented the cool air, and when he realized no one else was present, he thought this might not be such a bad place to talk after all.

"Madame," he whispered, "while I tried my best to hide it, I've been as uncomfortable as you all day. Perhaps I should describe it as being uncomfortably aware of you. I have already apologized for being too forward yesterday, but since you have been so short-tempered with me, I can't help but feel you want more from me."

Arielle had fully expected to find a few people in the church reciting their prayers. She was shocked to find herself alone with Byron and absolutely mortified he wanted to discuss a scandalous incident she thought better left forgotten. She moved over to put more space between them, and held her breath until she was certain he would not also change his position.

"I can't believe you brought me here to discuss yesterday!" she hissed.

"Madame, you are the one who suggested we meet here, not I. Now please, tell me what it is you wish me to do and I'll gladly do it. Returning to Virginia, or giving up the census aren't options, however."

"I deplore confrontations," Arielle countered. "But I can not abide your smugly superior attitude. Now please, just leave me alone."

"We're already alone," Byron pointed out. He reached for her hand, and, bringing it to his lips, tickled the length of her lifeline with the tip of his tongue before placing a kiss in her palm. Then he drew her index finger into his mouth. After writing all day, she tasted of ink but that scarcely spoiled his fun.

Arielle tried to withdraw her hand, but Byron had too firm a grasp on her wrist and, conscious of their sacred surroundings, she dared not yell an objection. She despised him, she knew she did, and yet, when he touched her, she didn't feel the slightest twinge of revulsion.

Despite his appealing appearance and charming affection, he was the wrong man. This was most definitely the wrong place and the glorious response welling up in her breast was a damning wrong as well.

Byron saw Arielle's lashes flutter, and her gaze grew so muddled that for a jarring instant he feared she was about to faint. "Madame?" Now rather than nibble at her fingers, he slapped the back of her hand to revive her. "Arielle!"

"I was married in this church," she managed to gasp. "Please don't make me ashamed to come here."

"You've no reason to be ashamed," Byron assured her.

"No! You're the reason!" Certain he would block her way if she tried to leave by the center aisle, Arielle rose, and grabbing up the basket she now wished she had had sense enough to place between them, she used the side aisle to flee. She knew she couldn't keep running away, but for the time being, it was the only means she had to save her virtue and her soul.

Thoroughly dismayed by his continual lack of success with her, Byron slumped back in the pew and fought the horrible possibility that pursuing Arielle Douville was simply a lost cause. Then, realizing he ought to leave before the priest appeared, he bolted through the door at nearly the speed Arielle had departed. John Winslow was just crossing the road on his way home to the priest's house and, fearing he had already been seen, Byron stepped out to meet him.

"How's the census coming?" Winslow asked.

"Well, I didn't expect complete cooperation, and we haven't had it, but it's going fairly well. Madame Douville is a tireless worker."

"Is she? I wouldn't have thought she'd even be civil to you."

Byron laughed. "I said she was tireless, Colonel, I didn't say civil."

"Well, do your best to finish up quickly. There's a tense undercurrent of argument rippling through the prisoners' conversations and escape has to be the subject. I don't have to understand French to notice the change in the men's behavior. I'll make some changes just as soon as I find a way. If it comes to a demonstration of force, can I count on you?"

Byron assured him that he could, but his first thought was of the effect an escape attempt might have on Arielle. She was such a desirable young woman, he couldn't help but believe there must be several young men who would make straight for her house if they were able to break free. One man in particular came to mind.

"I noticed a fellow during the meeting at the church," Byron offered before Winslow could continue on his way. "Tall, with curly black hair and green eyes. He displayed a vicious temper, and if anyone is plotting an escape, I'll bet it's him."

John Winslow nodded. "That's Gaetan Le Blanc, and he's definitely one to watch."

"I'll do whatever I can to help you," Byron repeated. "Whether it's fighting Le Blanc hand to hand, or firing a musket."

"Let's hope it doesn't come to that."

Because he would relish a good fight, Byron bid him good night without echoing that plea.

When Arielle arrived home, she didn't bother to rekindle the fire, nor light candles. Instead, she sat down and hugged her sides, but she couldn't stop herself from shaking. All she knew was that she had to keep away from Byron Barclay and because that appeared to be impossible, she would have to be on her guard never, ever, to be alone with him again.

He had twice proved that he could not be trusted to act as a gentleman should; but how had she behaved?

"Not as a lady!" she wailed. Then, terrified by a sudden knock at her door she fell silent. Fearful the Englishman had followed her home, she wasn't going to answer, but hearing a child's voice, she bolted from her chair to admit him.

"It's the baby, madame," Marc Hébert explained. "She's coughing, and Mother is afraid none of us will get any sleep tonight without more of your cough syrup. I've brought your bottle. May we have some, please?"

"Of course, Marc." Welcoming any task, Arielle quickly refilled the small bottle with the thick blend of onion juice and honey she had found most efficacious. Marc's mother was married to Sophie's brother, Joseph, and Arielle knew the family well.

"Here you are, but just to be certain there are no other problems, let me fetch my basket and I'll come home with you."

Assuring Marc it was no trouble and grateful for the excuse to leave, she not only accompanied Marc home but then stayed to have a bowl of soup after a dose of cough syrup and gentle rocking had helped the baby girl go to sleep. Marc and his three younger brothers joined them for supper, quietly observing their guest with sad, fearful eyes.

Feeling she ought to offer some encouragement, Arielle put down her spoon. "I know you're all good boys; have you been helping your mother while your father is away?" Their heads bobbed in unison. "Good. He'll be very proud of you."

"I've told them we're being sent away, but they don't understand why."

Laure started to sob then, and Arielle went to the young mother's side and hugged her. She wanted to promise that the voyage would be uneventful, and that their new home would be in as beautiful and bountiful a place as Grand Pré, but, fearing it would all be lies, she patted Laure's back, smiled at her sons, and kept still until Laure again found her composure and they could complete their meal.

When it came time for Arielle to leave, Laure insisted Marc walk her home. They had not gone far before the boy began to confide in her. "I heard something today, madame, but I'm afraid to tell my mother." Marc grabbed Arielle's hand to bring her to an abrupt halt. "Pierre Benoit's father was home today, and I heard him say that there's talk of an escape."

"An escape?"

"That's why I don't want to tell Mother, because if our father doesn't escape, she'll be very disappointed."

That was not the only problem Arielle could foresee. She bent down beside the lad. "Marc, you were right not to tell your mother. Most likely it's just talk, but you mustn't tell anyone because if the British learn of it, the men in the stockade could all be punished. We don't want that to happen, do we?"

"Oh, no, madame." Frightened, the little boy choked back a sob. "Would they beat my father?"

"I don't want to even imagine what the British might do, so let's just keep what you overheard a secret." She hugged the boy tightly before straightening up. "You go on back home, Marc, and if you hear any other secrets, come tell them to me rather than your mother. Understand?"

Marc turned and dashed away, and, pained that small children had to worry about whether or not their fathers might be beaten, Arielle hurried home at an equally brisk pace. No longer preoccupied with Byron Barclay, she built a fire and sat staring into the flames. If there truly were plans being made to stage an escape, she felt certain Gaetan would have a hand in them.

"An escape to what?" she wondered aloud. How far could any of the men travel before being recaptured by the British? An escape really made very little sense unless it was a complex plan that involved seizing the ships meant to deport them and transporting the whole town across the bay to Canadian soil. The audacity of that idea made her heart pound, but she knew it was precisely the sort of grandiose scheme Gaetan would propose. Feeling rather proud, she poured herself a glass of brandy, and after lifting it in a silent toast to the handsome Acadian, drank to his success.

Tuesday morning, Byron started out for Arielle's house early and still met her walking toward town. "I wish you'd wait for me to come get you," he scolded. "After all, we're working together, but you'll make it extremely difficult if I've no idea where you are."

Arielle attempted to slip past him, but Byron fell

in by her side. "Did I mention how attractive you are in black?" he asked, reaching out to caress her hand.

"Mr. Barclay, please! If you can't keep your hands to yourself this morning, I'll be forced to go to John Winslow and file a formal complaint."

Amazed that her words did not match what he felt each time they touched, Byron frowned slightly. "As I recall, you warned him of the possibility of rape, but there have been no instances of the crime. Nor, as far as I know, any complaints of his troops' behavior toward the female citizens of Grand Pré. Don't you think you'll look rather silly if you go running to him because I touched your hand? After all, the colonel already has more than enough on his mind."

"On the contrary, because he is charged with the care of the women of this town, he ought to be made aware of how excruciatingly uncomfortable you are making me. If you so much as brush against me again, I shall go straight to his headquarters to complain!"

Byron nodded, but pointed out a complication she had overlooked. "As I recall, the first time you wished to speak with him you required my assistance to get inside the stockade. If you intend to complain about me, I sincerely doubt I'd be inclined to help you see Winslow again."

Arielle straightened up proudly. "Believe me, if I wish to see Winslow, I most certainly will and I won't need your help to do so. Now we can stand here and argue the question or we can continue the census. Which is it to be?"

Byron stepped back and gestured broadly. "Please, madame, I beg you to continue your fine work."

His eyes were sparkling with mischief, making it plain her threat had had absolutely no effect, but Arielle attempted to assume an air of triumph anyway. She walked briskly, and stayed ahead of him each time she moved to survey an additional house. As he had the previous day, his behavior was friendly to all they met in their travels, but more often than not the glances directed her way were darkly accusing.

Saddened by the hostile passersby as well as the nature of her task, by the time they stopped at noon Arielle was even more depressed than usual. She decided to visit the docks. The view of the bay would be soothing, and the fear that she would not have much longer to enjoy the peaceful scene was another excellent reason to go there.

When Byron noticed the direction Arielle was taking, he hurried after her. "You ought to keep away from the docks," he warned. "With the fishermen all in the stockade, they aren't safe."

"My father was a ship's captain, Mr. Barclay, and I'm confident I'll be as safe there as anywhere else."

Having agreed to meet with John Winslow at noon, Byron had no time to argue with her, but he was uneasy all the same. While he took care not to touch her, he did move close. "There may be trouble," he confided, "and you ought not to be wandering around on your own."

Byron dared not make his warning more specific, but as he left her, he hoped John Winslow had found a way to prevent trouble from materializing. He hurried to the stockade and found the colonel and several of his officers in the midst of their preparations to stifle burgeoning problems. While Byron was surprised by Winslow's plan, he could not offer a better one.

"Counting the supply ship on which you arrived," John Winslow explained, "there are now five vessels moored in the mouth of the river. They can be used as prison ships for a week or two, thereby reducing the number of men we have to guard in the stockade. We've one hundred forty-one unmarried men among the prisoners, and I'm going to move them out first."

"When?"

"Tomorrow morning, but I'm not announcing the proposed transfers until then. As you'll be out in the town for the rest of the day, you'll have to take care not to give any hint of our plans. Should you hear even a whisper of an escape attempt, however, let me know immediately."

Byron sat back and nodded thoughtfully as the men continued to discuss how best to move the prisoners through town to the ships, but he was gravely worried that by even vaguely warning Arielle of the possibility of trouble, he had already said too much.

Six

Tormented by fears of what the coming days might bring, Arielle awakened before dawn. Too tired to rise and face the day, she lay trapped in her own misery. Searching for a more comfortable pose, she twisted and turned, but that morning her fine feather mattress seemed full of agonizing lumps.

Closing her eyes, she attempted to form a picture of the bay as it looked at sunrise when a golden sheen sparkled on the water. The mental image was blissfully serene and she tried to relax fully and float on its tranquillity, but just as sleep beckoned invitingly, Byron's warning of trouble echoed in her mind. Jarred awake, she sat up, and with sudden insight realized his warning and Marc Hébert's tale of an escape had to be related.

If only she had paid more attention at the time, but she had been so desperate to shut Byron out of her thoughts that she had not analyzed his warning as she should. Now it seemed painfully clear that the English must know the prisoners had an escape planned, and that meant the Acadians had no chance at all to succeed.

She would have to warn them, but how? Refusing to be stymied for a way to get word to Gaetan, she forced herself to breathe deeply and find a solution. Just then, an image of the priest flashed into her mind. If he asked to visit the prisoners, surely he would not be refused.

Certain he would agree to help her, Arielle got up and made her bed, then afraid it was much too early to visit the cleric, she sat down again on the side. Making a concerted effort to compose herself, she ran her fingertips over the intricate stitches of the quilt. After all, if she fluttered about like a headless chicken, she might attract the attention of Winslow's troops and that would accomplish absolutely nothing.

"But Winslow is staying with the priest!" she muttered in remembrance. Appalled that she had forgotten such an important detail, Arielle got up and went into the other room to start a fire. By the time she had heated milk for hot chocolate, she had decided she would simply have to wait until early mass to speak with the priest and pray that would not be too late to warn Gaetan.

After an agonizing wait, she again dressed in mourning clothes and headed for the priest's home. The streets were usually deserted at that hour, but in the distance she heard the low rumble of male voices. Unable to discern whether the men were speaking French or English, she knew it had to mean something unusual was afoot and quickened her pace. Also drawn by the noise, housewives began to appear, first at their windows, then running from their homes with small children in tow.

As Arielle rushed along, she heard sobbed questions and hoarsely moaned prayers, but no answers until she reached the church and found the prisoners had been moved from the stockade. There, with great commotion, they were being lined up in the open area between the church and the priest's home. Her first thought at finding the chaotic scene was that the escape attempt must had been made and foiled. She cursed her own folly then for not having gotten a warning to Gaetan in time.

As desperate for answers as everyone else, Michelle Mouflet pushed her way to Arielle's side. "What's happening, madame? Are they taking the men away?"

"No, they couldn't be. They promised we'd all go together." But even as she spoke, Arielle feared that as punishment for planning an escape, the men were being sent so far away, their families might never see them again. When the troops began separating the bachelors and shunting them off to the left of the married men, she searched for Gaetan, and swiftly found him.

He was shouting obscenities at a guard who drew back, threatening to strike him with the butt of his musket, but the Acadian stubbornly refused to join a line as he had been ordered. Another of the soldiers yelled a command, and, distracted, the guard moved on without hitting Gaetan, but Arielle feared he had escaped serious injury by mere seconds. He saw her then, broke into a wide grin and waved enthusiastically. She raised her hand and tried to smile, but she certainly didn't want to encourage him to act badly when it was so dangerous.

Threading her way through the earlier arrivals to the front, she called to the closest soldier, "Where are you taking the men?"

Surprised to be questioned in English, he came toward her. "Just out to ships on the river. There's no cause for the women to be upset. The men aren't going anywhere."

Arielle translated his words for the women standing nearby, but, unconsoled, they continued to call to their men, while the little children in their arms wailed pitifully. Wanting to escape the awful din, Arielle tried moving to the side, but at the same moment the frantic crowd suddenly surged, and pitched forward, she lost her footing. She might have fallen and been trampled had Byron Barclay not been standing close enough to observe her plight and avert the mishap.

"You're out rather early, madame," he commented as he pulled her into a protective embrace.

Arielle clung to him only long enough to regain her balance. Then she struggled to break free, but he failed to relax his grasp. "Let me go!" she ordered him.

"No, come with me," he countered, and having the superior strength, he easily directed her toward the rear of the priest's house where they could observe without any danger of being crushed by the crowd. "Now answer me," he then scolded. "What are you doing here?"

Arielle glanced over her shoulder, but a hurried survey of the group of women failed to reveal any angry stares. Still, she wasn't at all certain she hadn't been deliberately pushed. It had all happened so quickly, but she had felt something, a hand or a shoulder, pressed against her back.

Looking up at Byron, she knew there were people

who felt her association with him was ample cause for such hostile action, but she kept her suspicions to herself. "Sunday you insisted I was restricted to Grand Pré," she reminded him. "Am I now forbidden to leave my home?"

"No, of course not, but you didn't answer my question. Why are you here?"

Indignant that he thought he had any right to ask, Arielle looked away, and almost immediately her gaze locked with Gaetan's. His expression was now one of furious contempt, but she couldn't tell if his anger was due to the sorry situation or the fact she was speaking with Byron. Wishing Gaetan could hear just how hostile their exchange was, she turned back toward the Virginian.

"I came to attend early mass, but found this disgraceful scene instead. Why are the men being moved?"

"I think you know why." Byron prayed that she had been unaware of whatever escape plan the prisoners had devised, but at the same time, her continual defiance fed his suspicion that she knew far more than she would ever admit.

"Because the English break every promise they give?"

"No, madame, because there's less chance for the trouble I predicted if they are divided into smaller groups." He studied her face closely, watching for even a slight glimmer of guilt, but her gaze remained steady, and the fierceness of her frown didn't waver. "Are you acquainted with Gaetan Le Blanc?" he asked then.

Sensing that he had asked that question merely to

gauge her response, Arielle replied with deliberate restraint, "Yes, but he's a hostile sort, so I must advise you to avoid him."

Byron glanced Gaetan's way, and found him staring right back. Amused, he began to smile. "For his sake, madame, or mine?"

"His, of course."

Byron supposed he deserved that, but he continued to smile in hopes Gaetan would think their conversation was going far better than it truly was. "It's plain we'll find no one at home to question this morning. Why don't you go on back to your house, and I'll come for you at one o'clock."

"No, I intend to stay here and watch what happens."

"You don't trust me to provide an accurate report?"

"No, I do not." Hoping he would get discouraged and go, Arielle stepped away, but, maddeningly, Byron followed.

"Did Colonel Winslow stage this ghastly display with the sole intention of frightening the women of our town out of their wits?" she asked bluntly.

"No, it's most unfortunate that it's had that effect."

Arielle responded with a skeptical glance, for it was plain to her that Winslow must have wanted scores of hysterical women present in order to better intimidate their husbands. The colonel appeared then and announced that the unmarried men were being transferred to ships for detention. Captain Adams and eighty soldiers came forward to escort them. Winslow's words were promptly translated into French, but when ordered to begin the march to the river, the bachelors, following Gaetan's defiant example, began to complain loudly that they were being separated from their loved ones, and they refused to take the first step.

Standing on tiptoes, Arielle saw Winslow order a squad forward, and, with fixed bayonets, they moved up to threaten the first row of bachelors with a swift death if they did not immediately obey. The young men continued to protest, however, and adamantly refused to leave their families. A stunned hush fell over the crowd as mothers covered their children's eyes, but in the next instant, the small square reverberated with pleas for mercy only the prisoners could understand. Apparently unmoved, Winslow grabbed Gaetan's arm and again ordered him to step forward.

As fascinated by Arielle's cool detachment as he was by Gaetan's heroism, foolish though it might be, Byron slid his arm around her waist. "Come, you don't want to watch this."

"Oh, but I do. I want to see every despicable minute!" While she did not want to see Gaetan killed by a savage bayonet thrust, she feared he would not back down. "They don't believe Winslow," she explained. "They think they're being sent away."

"If you were to reassure Le Blanc of our purpose, would he believe you?"

Afraid that he would not, Arielle shook her head, but in a move that completely astonished her, Gaetan suddenly ceased to resist. He took the first step with a long, aggressive stride. Once he had started to move, the others followed, and the march to the river was begun without bloodshed. Still confused and frightened, the women in the crowd behaved as though the young men were been led off to their executions and intensified their loud wailing.

"Now will you go home?" Byron urged.

"No, I'm going to walk with them." Arielle lifted her skirt and started after the heavily guarded group.

Byron had seen something more than defiance in Gaetan Le Blanc's gaze when he had looked at Arielle, and too curious to allow her to follow the Acadian alone, he joined her.

When they reached the docks, the bachelors, who numbered one hundred forty-one, were separated into five groups and sent out to the supply ships anchored off-shore. Six soldiers were assigned to each vessel to guard them. Having completed his initial assignment, Captain Adams then returned to town with the remainder of his detail, but Byron knew there was still more to see.

"Winslow is transferring another hundred men out to the ships. All we need do is wait here, and you can wave to them, too."

Gaetan had been among the first to be ferried out to a ship, and while Arielle had had no opportunity to wave to him, she understood Byron's remark for the jealous one it was. Not about to debate her loyalty to the men of Grand Pré, she ignored the taunt. "I can't believe Winslow found it impossible to guard unarmed farmers and fishermen in the stockade, but there's no point in our continuing the census if he intends to load women and children on board ships with the same lack of regard for their families that he showed these men."

Byron clasped his hands behind his back. "Madame, the supply ships are being used only on a temporary basis. Transport ships will arrive soon and as I have assured you, passengers will sail in family groups. Our census is vital to that endeavor, and we'll complete it as planned. Because we're unlikely to get any cooperation today, however, I'll be happy to help you pack your belongings so that you'll be ready to leave when the transports arrive."

"How thoughtful. Is that a service you're providing for everyone?"

"No, only you," Byron confided softly.

Arielle met that promise with cool indifference. "I doubt I shall be allowed to take more than a thimble and my herbs, so I have no need of an assistant to pack."

"On the contrary, you'll have a generous allowance for luggage. As will everyone else," he took care to add.

"I'll need only my herbs," Arielle insisted.

"You must have some things you treasure for their sentimental value."

"None too large to fit in my pocket. Now because you have already stated we'll not have to work today, I plan to stay here, but you needn't fear I shan't find my way home."

Byron nodded, but he didn't leave. He remained with her until Captain Adams returned with the second group of prisoners, many of whom were weeping openly. As the men were being loaded into the boats to be rowed out to the ships, he sighed with relief, but another argument soon developed between the prisoners and their guards.

He turned to Arielle. "How many times must they be reassured they aren't being deported?" he asked.

"That's not the problem. They're refusing to eat English rations."

While Byron thought that an outrageous complaint, he stayed out of the discussion, and it was eventually decided that the prisoners would be allowed visits from their families, who would deliver their food each day. He thought the arrangement a totally unnecessary complication, but wisely chose not to share his opinion with Arielle. Wanting to spend more time with her, he finally thought of a reason she would be likely to accept.

"We have enough names to begin making up passenger assignments," he said. "Why don't we spend the rest of today on that? We could work at a table at the inn."

Because that was a public place, Arielle felt confident he would have to behave well, but she really did not want to be seen with him. "If you tell me what size the groups should be, I can do it myself."

As usual, she was proving difficult, but he was ready for her. "No, I really need to work with you on this because the more I learn about the townspeople, the better solutions I'll be able to propose for their problems."

That made too much sense to dispute, and eager for a task to keep her mind off the morning's sadness, even if it involved him, Arielle agreed. "We'll have to stop by my house to pick up the lists."

"That's fine." As they walked back through town to Arielle's home, Byron silently bemoaned the fact he still knew far too little about his lovely companion. If she had known of an escape attempt, she hadn't admitted it, nor had she revealed what her relationship might be to Gaetan Le Blanc. She hadn't wept when she had seen him separated from the others, nor had she begged for his life when he had come close to having his chest pierced by a bayonet. While he could tell at a glance how badly Gaetan wanted her, she had kept her feelings for the Acadian a secret. His only reason for cheer was that, stranded on a ship anchored off shore, Gaetan couldn't provide much in the way of competition.

Once inside, Byron looked down at Arielle, and his feelings too close to the surface to hide, asked what he truly wished to know. "Are you in love with Gaetan Le Blanc?"

"Whatever made you think of him?"

"Just answer me."

Unlike him, prevarication did not come easily and she did not resort to it now. "No, I'm not."

Byron nodded, and as he moved closer, she understood what he wanted. He raised his hand to caress her cheek lightly, and her breath caught in her throat. She turned toward him. He bent his head, and now knowing how delicious his kiss would be, she reached up to meet him. He kissed her very gently, started to draw away, but could not. Instead, he wrapped his arms around her waist and, pulling her close, kissed her with a fervor that would have frightened her had he not already proved himself to be a considerate man.

She put her hands on his shoulders, then wound them around his neck as she returned his kiss with a longing she had not meant to reveal. She closed her eyes, but nothing about Byron Barclay reminded her of Bernard, and she wasn't thinking of her late husband now when she fit so perfectly in Byron's arms. He had the strength to crush her, but held her in an adoring embrace. Relaxing against him, she shyly made it plain she wanted another kiss, and yet another, until her wanton behavior pierced her consciousness and she hurriedly broke free of him.

Amused by her dismay, Byron backed away, kissed her lightly on the cheek, then crossed to the door and put on his hat and coat. "I think we've seen enough of each other for today," he said with a rakish grin. "What do you want to do about tomorrow?"

Arielle didn't know quite what to say. It took her a long moment to realize he was referring to the census, and then she was embarrassed she had thought he was alluding to something more personal. "My conscience compels me to see what has been done to my people on the boats."

In spite of his bitterness toward her people, he was touched by her loyalty. "I'll go with you and make certain you don't have any problems."

Byron took his time walking back to the inn, and once there, it was a simple matter to satisfy the physical cravings Arielle had aroused, but as he lay stretched out across his bed, he still wanted more. Unlike the frivolous young women at home, Arielle was such a serious person, and yet delightfully affectionate at times.

He imagined her lying beside him now, her legs tangled with his, her cheek resting on his shoulder. He ran his hand down the flat plane of his belly, and wished it were her touch that he felt rather than his own. Closing his eyes, he could almost remember the delicacy of her floral fragrance, and thought she must crush the petals of wildflowers to make her own perfume.

"Soon," he whispered in the darkness, and wanting her too badly to believe his wish wouldn't come true, he fell asleep and dreamed of a laughing nymph with long golden hair and a passion for him he was only too willing to indulge.

Arielle started down to the river along with the others going out to see their families. She had rehearsed a polite refusal of Byron's company all the way to the docks but discovered he would accept none of her words as a viable excuse.

"There's a boat ready to take you out there now," he told her. "I'll wait for you here."

Relieved he did not intend to row the boat himself, Arielle thanked him, and then hurried to board the boat which already held three other women. Anxious to see their husbands, they merely nodded to her and, talking among themselves in hushed voices, cursed the British as demons sent from hell. While Arielle knew they were justified in their views, she could not help but turn back toward the shore to search for Byron. He was now talking with a soldier, making which side he was on clear, but she found it impossible to regard him as one of the devil's minions.

When they reached the ship, sailors took the food baskets families had brought them and helped them to climb the rope ladder.

As Arielle was assessing the situation, a coarse yell from another boat filled her ears. "Why don't you come to see me?"

Arielle shook her head, but Gaetan kept calling and waving until the sailor who had rowed her out to the first ship came to her side.

"Orders are to only allow visitors on one ship, but if you want to go to the next one, I'll take you."

Because she was so close, Arielle readily agreed and in a few minutes stood on the deck of Gaetan's ship and apologized to him for not having brought him something.

Now that Gaetan had succeeded in enticing her onto his ship, his mood darkened and he lowered his voice to a threatening whisper. "Have you no shame? I saw you yesterday and you were with one of Winslow's men. Do you think the British will treat you any better than the rest of us if you sleep with them?"

Too shocked to dignify his accusation with a response, Arielle turned away, but Gaetan grabbed her arms and slammed her against the rail to prevent her escape. "Answer me," he hissed. "Is he a good lover? Do you beg him to make love to you the way you never did me?"

Appalled Gaetan would ask such disgusting questions, Arielle looked for a sailor or soldier to help her break free of his grasp, but Alain Richard and Jacques Mouflet were standing behind Gaetan, facing away, their broad shoulders forming the perfect screen. Clearly they intended to aid Gaetan, and no one else was aware of her plight.

"How dare you!" she cried. "Let me go!"

"Why, so you can return to the Englishman's bed? I would sooner see you dead than his whore!"

Terrified that he would vent his hatred of the British on her, Arielle began to struggle, but shoving his knee between her legs, Gaetan kept her pressed against the rail. He caught her chin in a bruising grip and kissed her with such brutal abandon his teeth sliced her lower lip, leaving her mouth swollen and bloody. Still not satisfied that he had marked her as his own, he began to fumble with the thick folds of her skirt. The more she twisted and fought him, the more aroused he became, and he would have raped her right there had the ship's captain not begun walking their way. Alain shouted a hoarse warning, and not wishing to be caught, Gaetan had to step back in an attempt to make it appear he and Arielle were merely having a friendly chat.

The instant Gaetan relaxed his grasp, Arielle bolted from his arms and, dodging between Alain and Jacques, she dashed for the rope ladder. Hurling herself over the rail, she slid down it into the waiting boat. Astonished by the speed of her descent, the sailor who had been waiting to row her back to shore sat gaping until he saw her tears and realized how urgently she wished to depart. Grabbing for the oars, he began to row with short, choppy strokes that sent the boat skidding across the water.

Refusing to look back up at Gaetan, Arielle faced the shore, but knowing Byron would be waiting for her was no comfort.

Was what she had done so wrong? She agonized. Had she not agreed to take the census, she would not have spent so much time with Byron. She would not have kissed him, and would not now fear that Gaetan might be right. Maybe she was no better than Byron's whore.

Dear God, what was going to become of her?

"Please," she called to the sailor, "don't take me back where the others are waiting. Let me off at the next dock."

Straining at the oars, the sailor nodded, but when they reached the shore, he was quick to offer advice. "I wouldn't go back out to that ship if I were you. I don't know what happened, but it's plain it wasn't good."

"No, it wasn't." Arielle took his hand, climbed from the boat to the dock, and then, too ashamed to face Byron, fled. She knew he would expect her to work on the census, but she couldn't. Not today, and maybe not ever again. When she reached home, she took her own advice, barred both doors, and then flung herself across her bed and wept for the love that had flavored Byron's kiss and now knew she dared not taste again.

When Byron saw the sailor who had taken Arielle out to the ship again loading visitors at the dock, he called to him. "Bring the young woman dressed in black back with you. She's helping me with a survey and we're late getting started."

The sailor first helped an elderly woman into his boat and then walked over to Byron. "I already brought her back, sir, but she was crying and got out at the next dock."

"Crying, why?"

The sailor shrugged. "Most of the woman are crying."

Byron had already noticed that, but their sorrow

didn't explain Arielle's tears. He questioned the sailor at length, and upon learning Arielle had visited a second ship, he checked its list of prisoners and grew thoroughly disgusted when he found Gaetan Le Blanc's name. Arielle had sworn she didn't love the man, but at her first opportunity had gone to visit him.

Infuriated, he left the docks and started for Arielle's home where he intended to make it plain that until they finished the census, her days belonged to him. That she had lied about her involvement with Gaetan was too obvious to mention, but he had been warned, and now knew her delicious kisses were flavored with lies.

Seven

Byron strode up to Arielle's door, pounded on it with a vicious rhythm and, when she did not respond immediately, he struck the weathered wood a final fierce blow. He tried the handle, but the door was securely barred. While it was possible she had gone to tend someone, he doubted a patient could have summoned her at such a convenient time. Intending to see her without delay, he circled the house to enter through the rear, but as he passed by her bedroom window he heard the sound of anguished weeping.

Startled, he stopped, and Arielle's heart-wrenching sobs dissolved his anger in an instant. Rather than simply avoiding him, it was plain some terrible tragedy had befallen her and he did not want her to have to face it alone. He continued on around to the back door, but it was also barred. He cursed under his breath, and, thinking Arielle too distraught to hear his knock, much less respond, he went back to her window. He was about to rap on the glass when the intensity of her weeping lessened noticeably, then began to gradually grow faint. Her tears must have exhausted her Byron surmised, and she was falling asleep. Byron couldn't bear to disturb her.

He leaned back against the house, and drew in a

deep breath. He would much rather have held Arielle in his arms, and soothed her pain with kisses, but he was sadly afraid he had contributed to the cause of her distress. When he had arrived, he had believed the Acadians fools for not supporting the British when they lived on English soil, but now that he had come to know some of the people, he could better appreciate their situation as mere pawns in the battle between England and France.

Perhaps he was no better than a pawn himself. Shaking his head, he wondered what could have transpired between Gaetan and Arielle to upset her so badly. Was she afraid the fool was going to get himself killed? he wondered. Or did she miss him so terribly, a brief meeting had brought a flood of tears? Now afraid he had interfered in her life with the same destructive force the British were using to sweep the Acadians from their land, he walked back out to the road. Unable to continue the census without Arielle, he had nothing to occupy him in town. The docks were awash in miserable women who would only remind him of her, so he chose the opposite direction and headed out toward the woods. He hoped he could find some peace there, but doubted it was even possible.

An hour later, Arielle awoke with a start. She sat up, and at first thinking someone must have come seeking her advice, she went to investigate, but there was no one waiting outside. She closed her door and leaned back against it. She knew she ought to be out compiling names, but after the horrible confrontation with Gaetan, she didn't feel up to the task. She didn't want to have to offer excuses to Byron, either.

Hoping he would not be too angry with her for shirking her duties for a day, she changed out of her mourning clothes into the comfortable skirt and bodice she wore for trips to the woods. Tying a worn apron around her waist, she picked up a basket, and, hoping to avoid the Englishman should he be coming her way, she left by the rear door. She passed through her garden, then turned out onto the road when she was certain she wasn't being followed.

The day was warm, and the tangy, overripe scent of autumn hung heavily on the air. Quickening her step, she knew she might not have many more opportunities to gather herbs and Byron had proved to be such a distraction on her last outing that she had missed several of her favorites.

Eager to supplement her supplies, she chose the first path entering the woods, and had nearly filled her basket before reaching a small sunlit glade. She bent down to pluck a sprig of mint and looked up to find Byron sitting not ten feet away. He had discarded his hat and coat, but in his shirt-sleeves he was no less attractive, and the sadness of his gaze made it impossible for her to turn away.

"I didn't feel up to working with you today," she blurted out.

Byron rose and walked toward her. "I understand. I didn't feel like working today, either." He wanted to take her in his arms and erase the sorrow in her eyes as he buried his own deep within her, but taking care not to frighten her away, he took her hand and led her back to the comfortable spot where he had been resting.

"Just talk with me a while," he invited softly.

His touch was so gentle compared with Gaetan's that while Arielle knew she ought to refuse, she didn't really want to. She sat down and set her basket aside. "This is a lovely spot. I'll try and remember it."

"I'd much rather you remembered me," Byron replied, and when she turned toward him, he was shocked he had not noticed the change in her appearance at first glance. Her lower lip was swollen, and when she dipped her head slightly, the bruises left by Gaetan's fingers were clearly visible along the smooth skin of her jaw.

"My God," he whispered. "What happened out on that ship?"

Mortified by Gaetan's abusive handling, Arielle just shook her head. She knew Byron had the power to punish Gaetan, but she feared that would only feed the flames of the firebrand's hatred.

"I ought not to be here with you," she murmured, but she made no move to leave.

Hoping that was not the answer to his question, for he really did not want to believe her association with him had caused her earlier distress, he leaned over and peeled away her cap. Her hair was secured atop her head with a single comb, and a gentle tug removed it and sent her pale golden tresses tumbling down over her shoulders in the glorious silken stream he had imagined. A light breeze ruffled the ends of Arielle's hair, and sent the subtle fragrance of her perfume swirling toward him. It was one of life's few perfect moments, and while he longed to savor it, he knew he ought not to let it pass into memory without wringing out every bit of pleasure it held.

His grasp now confident, he reached for Arielle and pulled her across his lap. He took care not to press against her bruised lips, but instead to drink deeply of the honeyed sweetness of her mouth. He longed to feel the swell of her breast cupped beneath his palm, but not wanting to risk frightening her away, contented himself with cradling her against his chest. When she pulled away the ribbon that had secured his hair at his nape, he did not pause to encourage her with words, but, lying back, drew her down into the grass.

Echoes of Gaetan's bitter taunts had sounded when Arielle had first come upon Byron, but now that he had touched her, kissed her, made her feel precious once again, she heard only the sweet music of the forest and the longings of her own heart. She ran her fingers through Byron's hair, fondly caressing the silver streaks at his temples as well as the dark golden tips. The fine linen of his shirt was soft, and the pleated silk stock easily removed. She unbuttoned his waistcoat, and slid her hand inside his shirt. His chest was covered with coarse curls whose springy resilience invited the caress she gave most willingly.

She felt the steady rhythm of his heartbeat beneath her fingertips while her own pulse quickened with each successive kiss. When his hand at last strayed across her breast, she did not push him away as the nipple hardened, but instead leaned closer, coaxing still more from the wonderfully affectionate man.

Too lost in passion to retain his caution, Byron slid his hand under Arielle's skirt. Her legs were long and slim, her lace-trimmed drawers scarcely a barrier to his wanderings and he began to apply gentle pressure as his fingertips crept up her thigh. Parting her legs, he teased her with a slow circling motion meant to make her crave an even more intimate touch. He had never wanted a woman so badly, and yet he dared not give in to his own needs until he had shown her how easily he could satisfy hers.

Bernard had been a very tender lover, gentle and sweet, but while he had often stirred longings within Arielle for something she could not name, he had never fulfilled them. Now, as Byron's touch grew increasingly bold, she was filled with a desperate longing to possess the secret that had always eluded her. Afraid he would stop while she had only a hint of that rapture, she clung to him, urging him with her kiss and caress to share all that he knew of love.

She shuddered with delight as his fingertips brushed across her bare stomach. Sorry she had on so many layers of petticoats, she dared not risk breaking his enchanting spell to toss them away but eagerly raised her hips to help him discard her drawers. He used her own wetness then to ease the smoothness of his magical caress. Probing, sliding, dancing across her senses he created a piercing sweetness that did not merely lead her toward ecstasy, but enveloped her in its fiery splendor.

His kiss muffled her cries of joy, but as he moved over her, into her, the delicious sensation began to swell within her again. She arched her back, and, moving with him, took up his slow cadence, then, increasing it to a thundering beat, leaped with him into rapture's realm

When he finally could, Byron rolled over and brought Arielle up on top of him. As he pressed her cheek against his shoulder, and fanned her hair through his fingers, Arielle was vaguely aware that she had just fulfilled the darkest of Gaetan's suspicions, but she did not feel as though she had done anything wrong. Raising up slightly, she looked down at Byron and found his expression as delightfully satisfied as she knew her own had to be.

She waited for him to say something, anything, to encourage a bond beyond the physical magic they had shared, but he responded only with a sad, sweet smile. Embarrassed that she had apparently expected too much, she lay back down, nestled against him, and kept still. After all, they had only known each other six days, so perhaps it was too soon for him to make poetic declarations of love. Then the sudden realization they might be parted before he became so inspired drenched her in a cool wave of apprehension.

Pushing away from his embrace, she got up slowly, and not wanting to don her drawers with him watching her, rolled them up and hid them beneath the herbs in her basket. She wound her hair atop her head and replaced her comb and cap. Byron sat up and rearranged his clothes, but she warned him away. "No, please don't get up, not yet. I want to go back into town alone."

"It's early. You needn't leave me yet."

A sly twinkle filled his eyes, and Arielle could readily imagine why he wanted her to stay. She still felt lightheaded and weak in the knees from the joy they had shared, but she needed to get away and think about what it had meant to her, since apparently it had meant so little to him. "No, I must go home, someone might need me."

Byron rose with an easy stretch. "I need you," he assured her with a devilish grin.

"I'm sorry, but I really must go." Unable to match his flirtatious mood, Arielle turned away, but as she recrossed the glade, she feared that in one afternoon she had found and lost the only treasure worth having. Once hidden by the trees, she hurriedly pulled on her lingerie. She smoothed out her skirt and adjusted the fit of her bodice, but she could still feel the warmth of Byron's loving deep inside.

Her thoughts jumbled she entered her home, washed away what remained of Byron's scent and sat down in the rocking chair Bernard had bought to rock the babies they hadn't had. It was a sturdy but comfortable chair, but she had only herself to soothe with its gentle motion. She knew she wasn't the first woman to follow her heart and grasp for fleeting pleasure, but, having done so, she now wanted far more than one glorious afternoon. But did Byron want the same? She closed her eyes, and, remembering the sweetness of his smile, hoped that even if he had not said so, he did.

Byron walked in slow circles as he waited in the clearing, his thoughts as muddled as Arielle's.

He was infuriated anew to think Gaetan Le Blanc would mistreat such a dear young woman. While Arielle hadn't named her assailant, Byron was positive it had been Le Blanc. Finally deciding he had given Arielle sufficient time to return home, he pulled on his coat and cocked his hat at an angle. He used the walk into town to plot how best to teach Le Blanc a lesson, and by the time he arrived at the docks, he had what he wanted to say well in mind. Lacking a translator, he intended to make an emphatic statement without words.

The same sailor he had spoken with that morning rowed him out to Gaetan's ship. Byron introduced himself to the captain, described the nobility of his purpose, and received the gentleman's enthusiastic approval. He began a slow tour of the deck and found Gaetan standing in the stern with three other young men. Not worried about being outnumbered, Byron walked up behind Gaetan, tapped him on the shoulder, and when he turned around, Byron slammed his fist into the Acadian's chin with such brutal force the young man's knees buckled and he fell to the deck where he lay in a heap quivering like underbaked pudding.

A sailor was swabbing the deck nearby, and Byron gestured for him to bring his bucket of water. Readily understanding the reason for the summons, the sailor came over, and with one exuberant fling, emptied his pail and drenched Gaetan. The Acadian gagged, coughed, and sputtered, but when he tried to get up, his feet slipped on the wet deck and he remained sprawled in front of Byron. Warned not to interfere by Byron's fiercely determined frown, Alain Richard, Eduard Boudreaux, and Jacques Mouflet backed away, leaving Gaetan to face being humiliated alone.

Lacking the patience to wait for Gaetan to rise on

his own, Byron bent down, grabbed the front of his shirt, and hauled him to his feet. Then, yanking him close, Byron announced the reason for his visit as loudly as he could. "If you ever touch Arielle again, I'll kill you!" Certain he had made his point, he released the dazed Acadian. Gaetan made a clumsy grab for the rail in an effort to catch himself, but again slipped on the wet deck and fell.

Disgusted, Byron turned his back and left the ship. He did not once look back to see if Gaetan was watching him, but he could feel the hatred coming from the prisoners and knew the Acadian was probably cursing him with every filthy word he knew. That didn't faze Byron; he had just wanted to make certain Arielle was safe from the obstreperous young man's anger, and he was now confident that she was.

Wanting to continue their rounds, Byron went out to Arielle's house the next morning. As he approached, he saw a word scrawled across her front door in whitewash, but it was in French, and he had no idea what it said. Testing the paint, he found it still damp. Afraid whatever message the painter had left could not possibly be complimentary, he would have removed it himself before Arielle saw it, but just then she opened her door.

Arielle's smile froze on her lips as she read the freshly painted insult. "I'm so sorry," she then apologized.

"You needn't offer excuses, just tell me what it says."

Dreadfully embarrassed, Arielle shook her head,

but when Byron took a step closer, she found it impossible to back away. "It says Whore. Please wait, I want to wash it off before we leave."

Byron stood on her doorstep while she fetched a pail of water and a brush, but he promptly took them from her hands. "No, this is because of me, so I'll do it."

Arielle was touched he wished to be helpful, but that scarcely erased the pain of the insult or the fear that it was deserved. After the kindness she had shown everyone, this was a tragic way to be repaid, and yet the British were clearly the enemy so how could her neighbors be wrong? she agonized. "The whole town is badly frightened; ordinarily our people would never be so mean." Then she noticed he had scraped the skin from his right knuckles since she had seen him last. "How did you hurt your hand?" she asked.

"I had a disagreement with someone."

Whoever had slapped the word on her door had used only one coat of whitewash and Byron rinsed it off easily. He set the water and brush aside, but he doubted either of them would soon forget the epithet. It wasn't difficult to trace its source. "Does Gaetan Le Blanc have a large family?" he asked.

"No larger than most. His parents are dead, and he has no brothers, but he does have three married sisters, and nieces and nephews. Is he the one with whom you had the disagreement? Are you saying that he's behind this?"

Byron had not planned to reveal that he had seen Gaetan, but he wouldn't lie to her. "Yes. If anyone's calling you filthy names it's because of your association with me. I told Gaetan not to bother you again, and this is undoubtedly the result. He must have had another visitor yesterday afternoon and told them what to do, because I doubt this was something one of the fine ladies of Grand Pré would have thought of on her own. It looks as though I'll have to speak with Gaetan again."

"Oh no, absolutely not, you mustn't!"

"I'm not going to let the man insult you, Arielle. He didn't get away with bruising your face and upsetting you so badly yesterday, and he'll not get away with inciting this type of disrespect, either."

While Arielle was gratified by how swiftly Byron had come to her defense, she was more afraid for him than herself. "No, please don't go out to see Gaetan again. It's early, so I'm sure no one noticed anything on my door except you and me. Let's just forget it ever happened."

Exasperated, Byron shook his head. "I'll not back down on this, Arielle, you're much too important to me."

Arielle licked her lips. Her mouth still felt slightly swollen, but she didn't know if that was Gaetan's fault, or his. "That's very kind of you, but—"

"Kind?" Byron lowered his voice. "How many times must I explain kindness has nothing to do with my actions where you're concerned? While I was raised to treat everyone kindly, that description doesn't begin to describe what's happening between us."

"And just what *is* happening?" Arielle asked shyly.

"I have no gift for tender poetry," he complained,

"so I'll not risk ruining whatever we have by giving it a name."

Arielle could think of only one name: love, and, puzzled by his refusal to use the word, she made no attempt to coax it from him, and said instead, "Come inside and I'll put some salve on your hand."

"No, you needn't bother."

"It is no bother. Come in."

There was an insistence to her tone that brooked no argument and after looking down the road to make certain they weren't being observed, he followed her into her parlor. He took a chair at her table, she fetched a small jar from her basket, and, taking the place beside his, began to smooth a cool cream into his torn skin. "That feels good, or maybe it's just your touch."

Arielle had meant only to provide medicinal care, but when their eyes met, she wondered if she hadn't really wanted to invite him to come inside where they could be alone again. It was a delectable prospect, but her spirits dampened by the insult painted on her door, she knew she dared not delay their departure. Giving his hand a final pat, she rose, replaced the lid on the jar, and put it away.

"I need to put the note on my door," she recalled absently, and she did that before picking up the basket filled with their survey materials. "I'm ready, shall we go?"

Byron got to his feet and came toward her. "We'll have to be more careful," he whispered, but after tilting her chin with a fingertip, he gave her a slow, teasing kiss that made caution exceedingly difficult to recall.

Arielle's breath caught in her throat, and if Byron had not taken her arm to lead her toward the door, she might have remained where she stood all day. "You make a very poor enemy," she said. He turned then, and as his gaze darkened slightly, she realized that was only true for her, for surely he was the very worst of enemies for Gaetan. Still smarting from the way her countryman had treated her the previous day, she was not moved to defend him.

The morning started out uneventfully enough, but where Arielle had initially encountered bitterness and tears, she soon began to find an undercurrent of suspicion directed her way. Women grew slow to respond to her questions, and because she knew Byron did not want her to furnish information on her own, she kept pressing for an accurate count from everyone, but it was never freely given. This was the third day the men were being held on the river and she tried to take that into account, but still, the hostility appeared to be directed at her personally, and that saddened her.

Attempting to maintain the appearance of strangers joined only for a common task, she and Byron parted at noon, but as she ate a simple meal at home, she missed him. All the disapproval she had seen in the eyes of those she had surveyed that morning hadn't erased the memory of the joy she had found in Byron's arms, and if she encountered it again, she vowed she wouldn't let it make her feel guilty.

While Byron could not help but admire the way Arielle conducted the census, he saw how often the menacing looks first directed his way later came to rest on her. In some degree, it had been that way from the start, but now there was a difference. Where once doors had been opened wide, women now spoke to Arielle through a mere crack. The conversations had grown increasingly brief, and often residents disappeared back into their homes before Arielle had finished writing. He was pained that this was such a thankless task for her, but even after losing a day, they were making good progress and would soon complete their work.

He frowned as he sought an excuse to keep seeing her then, but when she did not object to his offer to walk her home, he felt confident they would think of something. He hoped her door hadn't been decorated for a second time, and when they saw only the note she had left on it, they sighed in unison. Arielle removed it, and shrugged slightly.

"I was very busy before you came, but other than a child's cough, I've had no calls."

"You did take very good care of my hand," Byron reminded her.

"Thank you, but after I saw so many falling ill with worry, it's troubling not to be needed."

Seeing she was sincerely concerned, Byron leaned back against her door. "Let's tell each other the truth. Gaetan's problem is jealousy, but even without his relatives adding to your heartache, a great many people object to your working for me. Perhaps things will improve when we finish, but I hope you'll agree to see me. We can be discreet, or at least try to."

"You just asked for the truth," Arielle replied, "so I see no reason to lie to the town. Won't you please stay for supper?"

Byron dimly recalled her mentioning that she liked

to cook when she was home, but frankly he didn't care if she couldn't heat milk. She was bravely ignoring the sentiments of the entire town and he thought it a remarkable display of courage. "You said your father was a sea captain. What became of him?"

Warmed by her memories, Arielle smiled easily. "He was lost at sea, but he had led a glorious life."

"I hope you have some wine so that we may toast him."

"Indeed, I do."

Byron had come to Acadia with the worst of motives, but as he followed Arielle into her charming cottage, making love to her was the only thing on his mind.

Eight

Byron took a seat at the table and did his best to be amusing company as Arielle prepared supper. A ladder placed at the side of the fireplace led to the attic where she stored much of her food, and just watching her climb up and down accompanied by the musical rustle of her petticoats was a treat. At home, the Barclays' meals were prepared outside in a separate kitchen by the cook, Polly McBride, and served in the dining room by her daughters, Catherine and Rosemary. As a child, Byron had sat on a tall stool and watched as Rosemary kneaded bread or made cookies and he could still recall how good her baked goods had tasted fresh out of the oven.

He had not watched a woman prepare a meal in years, and he envied all the evenings Arielle's late husband must have sat at their table and recounted his day while she cooked their supper. He did not really want to think of her being with another man, and yet with the painful insistence of a soldier worrying a wound, he had to know what their life had been. "What sort of work did your husband do?" he asked.

"Bernard was a farmer, but after his death, I sold our farm and moved here to be closer to town. Perhaps that's why moving again won't be so difficult for me as it will be for the others. I've already left behind all that I loved once, and this second time won't be nearly as hard."

Byron sat forward slightly. "You never lived here with Bernard?"

Arielle was working on a floured board placed across from him, and hesitated before looking up from the pastry she was rolling into thin layers. "Didn't I just say that?"

Embarrassed to have revealed how important her response was to him, Byron shrugged and leaned back. "I guess you did. I'm sorry if I seem to be prying."

"No, there's a difference between prying and friendly curiosity."

"Thank you. Just what is it you're making for us?"

"A *sipaille* casserole, or sea pie. It's several different kinds of fish—salmon, bass, cod—layered with pastry and herbs. I hope you'll like it."

"I'm sure I will."

"The only problem is that it takes more than an hour to bake. Perhaps we can begin making ship assignments while we wait."

She crimped the edge of the pastry topping the first layer and sprinkled on fresh herbs to begin the next. He had often admired the beauty of her hands, and the grace of her gestures. The memory of how her fingers had slid over his chest, gentle and yet teasing, made any thoughts of work difficult to hold on to. He picked up a teaspoon, and tapped the bowl against the table in a lively staccato beat, unconsciously signaling his impatience while he still wore a relaxed smile.

"That's one possibility," he finally managed to agree, "but I'm sure we can think of others."

"I've told you before that I won't need help to pack." With an easy competence Arielle built several layers of fish and herbs, then topped the casserole with a final thin pastry sheet, and set the pan over the coals in the fireplace to bake. She dusted the flour from her hands and wiped them on her apron. "I've some peas and carrots, but I'll add those later. Now, shall we see to the ship assignments?"

There was a blossom of flour on her cheek, but thinking it a charming accent Byron didn't ask her to brush it away. What he really wanted was to make love before supper and again afterward, but the innocence of her expression kept him from revealing the carnal direction of his thoughts. "Yes, that's a very good idea." He rose and waited for her to clear away her cooking things and fetch the lists they had been accumulating.

"How many should we assign to a ship?" she asked.

"The transports ought to hold at least two hundred. Let's use that figure."

"Two hundred?" Aghast, Arielle turned to study his expression. "Just what sort of accommodations can we expect?"

It was her use of the term *we* that tangled Byron's thoughts, for he had easily separated her from the rest of Grand Pré in his mind. Now he did not hesitate to make that distinction a fact. "You've been very helpful, Arielle. I'm sure you'll have the best accommodations Colonel Winslow can provide."

"No, I won't accept any special treatment." She paused, waiting for him to argue that *she* was special to him rather than John Winslow, but sadly he did not. "Should we allot people to specific destinations?"

"No, not yet. All we need do is make up preliminary lists. Just place the families in tentative groups. We won't have to make the final copy of their names tonight."

Arielle reviewed the census sheets with a casual glance, then, adding the totals silently in her head, began gathering them into piles. "This isn't going to take long at all," she murmured absently. "We might just as well be sorting buttons, as people."

Touched by her wistful tone, Byron hastened to reassure her. "I haven't forgotten that they're people, Arielle. Winslow hasn't, either. This assignment has been very difficult for him. For us all," he added.

Arielle thought his sympathy misplaced. "Not nearly as difficult as it is for those of us who are being deported, Mr. Barclay. Please try and remember that."

"You haven't called me Mr. Barclay in days," Byron responded with a sly chuckle. "Please call me Byron when we're alone together."

Arielle repeated the name silently, as if trying it out on her lips. Sophie had scolded her for calling him by his Christian name. She hadn't spoken to Sophie that day, nor yesterday, either, and that was most unusual. She wondered if her friend had begun to shun her.

Feeling the warmth of Byron's gaze, she glanced up at him. "Byron is a very nice name."

"Thank you. So is Arielle." He savored the sound as he spoke, making a musical phrase of it. "It's a lovely name. Rather like Melissa."

Arielle was puzzled. "Melissa?" she asked with raised brow.

"My sister. My beautiful sister. My brother Elliott was handsome, too, but an attractive appearance didn't save either of them."

Perplexed by the dark turn their conversation was taking, Arielle probed no deeper and hurriedly sorted through the sheets laying on the table. "Unfortunately, there are a couple of families who don't get along with many people."

"Put them together then."

"No, that would be a disastrous mistake; they despise each other."

"What a pity. Well, let's just place them wherever their numbers fit most conveniently. Then if they complain, or if the other passengers protest having them along, we can explain their assignment was due to a simple numerical process."

"I still say we might as well be sorting buttons."

"Think of them as buttons with faces if you must, but make them human," Byron cautioned.

Arielle nodded, and in a moment had the family lists piled in a neat stack. "There, that's done, but I still doubt the British are truly capable of seeing us as people."

"Arielle . . ." Byron got no further before the need to hold her far outweighed the requirements of his conscience to defend his countrymen. He pulled her into a comforting embrace, enjoying the pungent scent of herbs clinging to her apron as much as the delicacy of the lace trim on her cap. She was a delightfully feminine creature, and yet he believed her to be incredibly strong. When she turned to lift her lips to his, he couldn't disguise how badly he wanted her. He kissed her with a deep, devouring devotion that left her trembling in his arms. Certain he was not rushing her now, he took her hand and led her into the bedroom he had been relieved to learn Bernard had never seen.

He removed her cap and freed her hair. "I want to be able to touch all of you this time," he murmured as he untied her apron. "Your skin is as smooth as cream and just as luscious."

This was what Arielle had wanted when she had invited him to stay, and she smiled and kissed his palm, silently encouraging him to undress her, then slid his coat off his shoulders. He had such handsomely tailored clothes, but she scattered them about her bedroom without regard to their cost. When she peeled away his shirt, she marveled at the toughness of his lean, muscular build. She bent down to lick a leathery nipple, and felt him flinch.

"You don't like that?" she asked.

"No, I like it very much."

Arielle raked her nails down his chest, her touch sure but gentle. "You said you didn't plant tobacco yourself, but you're as muscular as a laborer. Why?"

"You're forgetting that I've been a soldier, Arielle, and I've seen and done things that burned away whatever softness I may have once had. If I have a muscular build, it's because I've earned it."

"Like the sadness in your eyes."

"I've earned that, too," Byron exclaimed, and with

his next kiss he drew her down onto the feather bed. He nuzzled her neck and twisted her hair into silken ropes. He longed to bind her heart as easily as he wrapped his wrist in the blond coils. After drinking in more kisses he refocused his attention on the ties and lace and petticoats that still hid her figure. When at last he had stripped her bare, he nibbled at her breast, teasing the pale-pink crowns into rosy peaks. He brushed the slight growth of his beard across her tender skin, marking her with his own intimate brand before kissing her again.

Byron's warmth felt so good to Arielle that she rubbed against him, reveling in the contrast of his hair-roughened body to the lissome softness of her own. She wound her arms around him, and, again flinging away the ribbon tie, sent her fingers through his hair. She could readily imagine how blond he had been as a child, but thought the silver accents he had now immensely appealing. She licked his earlobe, then pulled it through her teeth. She wanted to taste all of him, to devour him with loving kisses and make him a part of her that could never be lost.

When he rolled away to discard the last of his clothes, she propped her head on her elbow to unashamedly observe and was pleased to find his body as magnificent as his fine clothes made it appear. His shoulders were broad, and his chest covered with a handsome spray of curls. His stomach had a rippling flatness, while his hips were narrow and his arms and legs perfectly proportioned. When he returned to the bed, she slid away from him, and, turning, spread kisses over the taut muscles of his belly.

"You like this too, don't you?" she breathed into his navel.

"Arielle!" Byron gasped, but her next kiss stole not only his breath but his reason, and he grabbed for her hair, again coiling it around his wrists as living chains. Enslaved by desire, he gave himself up to her wanton kisses until the need to possess her became too great to suppress. He reached for her arms, and in a single fluid stretch brought her up beside him. He kissed her lips as he raised himself over her, and, seeking the end of her tender torment, he probed her depths with a single knowing thrust.

Now joined, he shifted slightly to align their bodies and bring her the same ageless thrill he sought. Her eyes glowed with a seductive fire, luring him on and, spurred by her joyous eagerness to love him, he began to move with a deep, driving lunge. The resulting friction created a glorious heat that radiated clear through him and into her, releasing a grateful gasp that kept him feeding the flames of her passion until they flared into ecstasy.

Delaying his own release had intensified his pleasure, and when it at last burst forth, he collapsed in her arms. Dazed, he feared if making love felt any better, his heart would surely burst. The risk of dying in Arielle's embrace was not at all daunting, however, and although sated for the moment, he began to plan how best to please her the next time, and the next.

Arielle refused to think. She wanted only to feel Byron's weight, and savor the lingering bliss of his loving. As before, he had touched her so deeply the memory would live forever in her soul. She combed his hair through her fingers and, inhaling his scent, let it wash through her senses. The faint traces of a soap spiced with cloves was a heady reminder that she had invited a rich man to her bed, and an Englishman at that, but, pleasure erasing any shame, her happiness was untarnished by guilt.

It wasn't until the savory aroma of the *sipaille* casserole began to fill the bedroom that she was inspired to move. "Our supper is almost ready," she whispered enticingly. "I need to get up and cook the vegetables."

Reluctantly Byron moved aside to allow her to rise.

After donning her nightgown and apron, Arielle left him to dress while she saw to the promised vegetables. Other than her husband, Gaetan was the only other man with whom she had shared her meals. While he was the very last person she wanted to dwell upon tonight, as perverse as always, he kept intruding on her thoughts.

His suspicions had sent him into a rage. What would the reality of her affair with Byron inspire? She could imagine an even more furious tantrum should Gaetan learn the truth, but, held prisoner, he would be unable to lash out at her as he had before. She had not loved him, though, nor ever pretended to harbor more than the regard one friend feels for another, and he had had no right to treat her badly.

When Byron finished dressing and joined Arielle, he was surprised to find her expression mildly troubled. She had left him with a playful smile, and he hoped she had not already come to regret being with him a second time. He waited for her to speak, but it wasn't until after she had served their supper and sat down with him that she raised her wine goblet. "I believe we were going to toast my father."

"Yes, what was his name?"

"Jean-Claude Leger."

"To Jean-Claude Leger, who must have been a remarkable man to have produced such a beautiful and courageous daughter."

Arielle took a sip of her wine. "Thank you for the compliment, but I don't feel especially courageous."

Byron took a bite of the *sipaille* casserole and moaned in delight. "This is absolutely delicious! We never have anything this good at home."

Arielle sampled a bite, and thought she was lucky not to have overcooked the dish when he had again distracted her so thoroughly. "Thank you, but as our men complained, the English have little appreciation for the elegant preparation of food. You didn't answer my question. Why do you think me courageous?"

Byron finished another flavorful forkful before replying, "You've chosen to see me as a man, rather than an enemy, and anyone would regard it as a courageous act."

"No, you're wrong. Gaetan would call me a traitorous whore, and most of the town would agree. It's only you English who would be more generous, and because my decision benefits your cause, that's not surprising."

Alarmed by the darkness of her mood, Byron laid his fork aside. "No one is going to call you filthy names, Arielle. Not Gaetan, nor anyone else, and I won't let you refer to yourself in disrespectful terms, either."

"I thought we had agreed to speak the truth."

"Yes, of course, I don't prefer lies, do you?"

The peas were fresh from her garden, and Arielle rolled them into a bright-green heap before scooping some up on her fork. Bursting with flavor, they tasted of the warm sweetness of home. "No, but two people can often see a situation in different ways. Each reports the truth as he sees it, but they could both be wrong."

"In that case they're simply mistaken, not liars." He waited while she replenished their wine, then reached across the table to take her hand. "I can imagine how painful it must be to see your town destroyed, and I am sincerely grateful that you don't blame me."

Arielle gave his fingers an affectionate squeeze before withdrawing her hand. "Since Bernard's death, I have lived not merely on the edge of town, but on the edge of life in Grand Pré. I'm sorry for what's happened to the others, for their heartache and pain, but having suffered a far more severe loss than that of a town, I can't really share their distress. My life has already been shattered into so many jagged fragments that being relocated will cause only a few small cracks in what's left."

Byron understood the isolation she was describing, for he had felt the pain of loneliness himself, as well as heart-wrenching grief, when Melissa and Elliott had died. Still, tragic though they were, he doubted the deaths of his brother and sister could be as devastating as the loss of a beloved spouse. Saddened to think he might never touch Arielle's heart, Byron again envied Bernard. "You must have loved your husband very dearly."

Arielle nodded, and then unable to complete her sad commentary, she finished eating her supper with slow, methodical bites. When she glanced up and found Byron had also finished, she feared she was being a poor hostess. "Would you like more?"

Byron's first impulse was to say how much he wanted more of her, but her downcast mood called for a gentlemanly reserve. "Your supper was superb, so I don't need anything more in the way of food, but I definitely want to spend more time with you."

Craving far more of him, Arielle cocked a brow. "Only time?"

"We have agreed to tell the truth, haven't we?" When she responded with a delighted smile, he again reached for her hand. "First let's put everything away, and then—"

"No, let's make love again first."

"It would be very rude of me to argue with the routine you follow in your own home."

Without letting go of his hand, Arielle rose, and came around to his side of the table. "Very rude, and anyone can see you're a gentleman."

Byron was tempted to use her argument and point out that Gaetan would certainly describe him in different terms, but wanting to be the only man on her mind, he kept silent. He pulled her down on his lap, and kissed her until they were both so dizzy from lack of breath they had to seek the comfort of the bed. Once stretched out on it, their mood turned playful, and with teasing kisses and gentle tickles they began a lengthy prelude to another deeply satisfying act of love.

In an effort to safeguard what little might now be left of Arielle's reputation, Byron returned to his inn before midnight, but this time sated by pleasure, he had splendid memories rather than only amorous hopes to fill his dreams and he enjoyed the deep, untroubled sleep of a truly happy man.

Gaetan Le Blanc had neither sleep nor dreams that night. Too proud a man to bear the previous day's public humiliation in silence, he lay awake, his jaw still aching, plotting revenge with his confidants, Alain, Eduard, and Jacques. "We need a boat," he whispered. "Then we can escape this accursed ship and make our way into town. I'll find the Englishman, stuff his mouth with his dirty socks, and carve him up into such tiny pieces, they won't be enough for Winslow to identify in the morning."

While none knew Byron Barclay's name, they all understood which Englishman Gaetan meant. Huddled close in their misery, their imaginations supplied endless bloody schemes. They despised all the British, and took a fiendish delight in devising cruel ways to punish this particularly abhorrent man.

A fisherman like his friends, Eduard Boudreaux's brown hair was still streaked by the summer sun, and in an attempt to avoid the glare off the water, his blue eyes were narrowed in a permanent squint. Tall and lean, he was such a good-natured individual that no one had ever noticed he was not truly handsome. Ordinarily, he liked to play practical jokes on his friends, but captivity had made him surly. "Castrate him first," he suggested. "Then hack him to bits."

Stretched out beside him, Alain Richard finished a noisy yawn before offering any advice. The smallest of the four, with brown hair and eyes, the sharpness of his features lent him a ratlike appearance. He had a cynical bent even on his best days, and this was definitely not one of them. "No," he argued, "first gouge out an eye, but leave the other so he can watch the mutilation."

At nineteen, Jacques Mouflet was the youngster of the pack. He shared Alain's dark coloring, but he was of medium height and build. His charming smile and ingratiating manner made him popular with women, but when the occasion arose, he could be as cruel as any man. "Don't treat him so gently," he cajoled. "Let's set him afire."

Amused by that stirring show of hatred, Gaetan forgot about his jaw, began to laugh, and then winced as a sharp pain tore up the side of his head. He feared the Englishman had come close to breaking his jaw, and it was small comfort that he had failed. Gaetan was sure it was only because he had been caught off guard, and he had no doubts about his ability to triumph in a fair fight, especially in one with such a despicable opponent.

"If I have my way, I may do all three," he told them, "but mark my words, I will teach the Englishman who is the better man."

"And Arielle?" Jacques asked, then fearing he had let slip how much he admired the pretty widow, he coughed and lowered his voice. "What will you do with her for bedding him?"

Gaetan responded with a derisive snort. "I don't believe she is. I merely accused her of it to chase the thought from her mind."

Alain disagreed. "I think you chased her right into the Englishman's arms. Why else would he have come after you?"

Not having considered that question, Gaetan remained quiet for a long while. "I don't doubt that he wants her; any man would. There was blood on her lips when she left here, perhaps a bruise on her cheek, and he must have seen them, but that does not mean he has seen any more of her."

Thinking Gaetan had made a joke, Jacques laughed, but Gaetan promptly leaned over and punched his shoulder to silence him. "I didn't mean to insult you," Jacques quickly apologized.

"Good. See that you don't make the same mistake twice. Arielle was a faithful wife, and she is a virtuous widow. If we hear otherwise, it will only be because the Englishman has spread the rumor to taunt me."

Because Jacques also wanted to believe Arielle was a chaste woman, he did not argue with Gaetan's prediction. Alain, however, poked Eduard, who nodded. They both believed there was a kernel of truth behind the gossip, and knew if the Englishman had succeeded with Arielle when Gaetan had not, then their friend might truly use their suggestions to make him pay in blood and screams.

Arielle had gotten up when Byron left. She had kissed him a last time at the door, then tidied the kitchen before returning to bed. Her sheets smelled of cloves now, and, tossing her nightgown aside, she wrapped herself in Byron's scent before closing her eyes. She knew she ought to be sleepy, but instead, she was filled with a sparkling exuberance that made it almost impossible to lie still.

She had enjoyed the warmth of Bernard's presence, the calm, steady assurance of his love, but she had never known the rapture in his arms that she found in Byron's embrace. Byron's elegant manners, fine clothes, and the polish of his language marked him as a rich man. That he was English and she Acadian was a small difference compared to the vast discrepancy in their place in society.

After all, she was a simple farmer's widow, and the daughter of a sea captain who smuggled more cargo than he ever carried honestly. Byron might be attracted to her, perhaps because she was the only woman in Grand Pré who understood English, but she had no delusions that his fascination with her would last. How could it? Was she a woman he could take home and proudly introduce to his parents? She might be pretty and bright, but she was completely unsuitable as a wife for a gentleman from Virginia and she thought too much of Byron to force him to say so.

Arielle took what joy she could from the moment. With any luck, she would spend several more rapturous nights in his arms, but she knew there was no hope she would become his wife. Their meeting had been by chance, and their eventual parting was a certainty; but while they were together, Arielle promised herself not to weep for what could never be.

Nine

Not having meant to neglect Sophie, Arielle went to see her Saturday morning before beginning her rounds with Byron. She rapped lightly at the front door, and when there was no answer, she assumed Sophie must be in back tending her garden. Hurrying along the path worn in the faded grass, she turned the corner of the house so quickly she nearly kicked over a pail that had been carelessly left in the way. Halted by shock and dismay, she couldn't believe what she had found.

It was an old, weather-beaten oak bucket Sophie's children might have used for play. That had plainly not been its last use, however, for the whitewash drying in the bottom still held the ends of an old brush mired in its soggy crust. Arielle had not looked for the culprit who had painted the insult on her door, but that it could have been Sophie hurt worse than being called a whore. Their homes were close by, and hoping another vicious artist had tossed the pail around the side of Sophie's house as she had run away, Arielle picked it up and carried it to the back door.

Sophie was standing at the edge of her garden, the baby balanced on her hip while her older children saw to the watering. She noticed Arielle out of the corner of her eye and turned toward her, but when she saw the bucket in her friend's hand, she gasped as sharply as Arielle had upon finding it. Flustered only momentarily, she called to her children.

"I need to speak with Arielle. You all go on in the house and we'll finish later." An obedient brood, the two little girls and their brother stopped their work and headed toward the back door. Sophie handed the baby to her six-year-old daughter, and when the children were all inside, she crossed her arms over her ample bosom and adopted a surly tone.

"You found the whitewash, so I won't deny what I did. Maybe it was cowardly, but it was the fastest way to make you see the whole town's calling you wanton. Everyone knows the Englishman was at your house again last night. Have you no shame?"

It took a sincere effort on Arielle's part to try to understand Sophie's anger, but it was difficult not to see it as self-righteous meddling and she had not come for a lecture. "I know you were upset when I first began working with Mr. Barclay." She had been careful not to call him Byron. "But if you had had the opportunity to come to know him as I have—"

Sophie sent a hurried glance over her shoulder to make certain none of her children were peeking out the door before she interrupted in a vicious whisper, her features distorted with scorn. "He's an Englishman and that's all I'll ever need to know. Gaetan is one of our own, and he loves you, but you wouldn't even consider marriage with him. Then some British scoundrel arrives, and you couldn't lure him to your bed fast enough. Don't be so stupid as to believe he'll take you home to his fine house. He won't. He's just bored, and when he has his fill of you, he'll discard you."

Having heard more than enough, Arielle hurled the incriminating bucket toward the side of Sophie's house where it landed with a thud that echoed her racing heartbeat. She took a step toward Sophie, but her former friend moved back, leaving the distance between them unchanged. "I thought we were true friends who cared about each other, but you're so quick to judge my actions and brand them as sinful that I can't believe we were ever close. I know Byron won't take me back to Virginia, but it doesn't matter. Whatever he gives me here will be enough."

Outraged that Arielle would reject her sound advice, Sophie raised her fist and shook it. "You're not only behaving like a whore, you are one! No Englishman has the wealth to buy my virtue!"

"I've not sold myself," Arielle denied, for indeed, she had given her heart and her body most willingly, "nor done anything of which I'm ashamed. I shall miss you." Sickened by the blistering encounter, she turned away, and, walking with her head down, her eyes blurred with tears, when she reached the road she nearly collided with Byron just as she had the first time their paths had crossed.

He reached out to catch her arms. Arielle looked away to hide her tears, but he wasn't fooled. "What's wrong? Tell me what's happened?"

Arielle shook her head, for there was no way she was going to give life to Sophie's accusations by repeating them. Every harsh word had scraped her soul, but she wanted to share only pleasure with Byron, not pain. Sunlight fell across her face, drying her tears, but she had no intention of ever revealing why she had shed them.

Clearly Arielle was miserably unhappy, and while Byron knew he ought to escort her home and offer comfort there, he could not wait. "Come here," he urged, and he drew her into a warm embrace. He waited for someone to hurl a stone at his back. He held his breath, ready to shield her while he absorbed the shock, but if they were observed, no one rallied a crowd to object.

There was only the gentle whisper of the morning breeze and the shrill cry of the gulls who had strayed from the river. He was greatly relieved he had not disturbed the peace of Grand Pré after all. He took Arielle's hand and walked her back to her home, then followed her through the door and leaned against it.

"You needn't tell me the exact words, when it's plain you're being criticized for associating with me." He paused then, trying to sound noble rather than deeply disappointed. "If it's too difficult for you to continue seeing me, then I'll find a man who can help me finish the census. I want to do what's best for you, Arielle, and if knowing me is turning everyone against you, then I'll remove myself from your life. But I can't pretend that I won't be sorry."

Arielle put her hands over her ears to block out the hideous echoes of Sophie's taunts. She didn't want to believe Byron had tired of her when being with him had come to mean so much to her. Dropping her hands, she slumped against the edge of the table. "I know I'm not as sophisticated as the young women you must know at home, but I do have my pride. If you've merely satisfied your curiosity and grown bored with me, I'd rather you didn't lie and say you're leaving me for my own good."

"Leaving you?"

The words had left his mouth in an explosive rush, and Arielle feared she had made a costly blunder. "Yes, I know, we were never together in any significant way so you can't be leaving me. You'll just no longer be seeing me; that's what I should have said."

Byron was positive he had just made a public demonstration of how much she meant to him and he couldn't understand why she doubted what he believed to be his unabashedly high regard for her. He wanted to grab her and shake some sense into her, but forced himself to remain at the door.

"If I sounded shocked, it was not because of your choice of words, Arielle, but because I don't understand how you can even imagine that I'd ever tire of you, or desert you for any reason. You mean far too much to me. Can't you taste it in my kiss, or feel it when I make love to you?"

Arielle swallowed hard and brushed away a fresh burst of tears. "I'm sorry if I've insulted you, but I discovered who painted my door and it was the very last person I would have expected. Nothing is as it should be anymore."

Byron waited, the suspense agonizing, but when Arielle came toward him, there were no answers in her gaze. For one terrible moment he feared he had lost her, but then she slid her arms around his waist and snuggled close. He breathed a grateful sigh as he dropped his arms around her. "There isn't a man alive who would ever grow bored with you, Arielle, not a one, and certainly not me."

The horrible confrontation with Sophie would have left her shaken all day had Byron not appeared. Now, she drew strength from his embrace, and knew even if Sophie's anger were not the worst she faced, she would survive. She lingered only a moment longer before stepping away.

"We need to get started with the census. There's not that much more to do and—"

"Arielle," Byron reached out to draw her back into his arms. "I can still find a man to do the survey, if you'd rather not continue. Working with me, and seeing me can be two entirely different things if you like."

Regretting her momentary lack of courage, Arielle was adamant when she broke away. "No, I always finish what I begin and the census will be no exception."

That Arielle had spirit as well as beauty was something Byron had known from the start, but he had never guessed how much he would come to admire her. Again dressed in black, she was a beauty, and Byron found it difficult to maintain a discreet distance as they walked through town. He waited outside each dwelling as he had before, but at times Arielle was invited inside where she could write more comfortably while he was left outside on the walk. They were never parted for long, but by noon, the strain of projecting a disinterested pose, when it ran counter to his feelings, was beginning to tell on him.

"Thank God tomorrow is Sunday," he whispered before they went their separate ways to eat.

"Are you a religious man?"

"No, I didn't plan to observe the Sabbath in church, Arielle, but in the woods with you."

He winked, then turned away, leaving her holding the last of the morning's lists and unable to reconcile the joy he brought to her when the rest of the town despised him and all things British. She watched him walk away, his stride long and sure, an optimistic young man moving through what would soon be the ashes of Grand Pré with the easy command of the conqueror. She moved far more slowly, and grateful to find a request for a visit on the sheet she had tacked to her door, she fetched her basket of remedies and spent the noon hour tending Anne Guidry, an elderly woman who was so profoundly deaf, she had not heard the gossip about her.

The afternoon passed quickly, and when sunset neared, Byron whispered a promise, "Go on home. I'll have supper at the inn tonight and come by later. It may not stop the gossip, but at least we can't be accused of flaunting our involvement."

Understanding now that his only concern was protecting her, Arielle nodded and went on her way. There were no more requests for calls on her door, and she felt certain Anne's had been a fluke. There were no babies due any time soon, and if the malicious gossip followed her to her new home, she doubted anyone would consult her for herbal cures. Perhaps there was no point in even taking her herbs along with her.

She paced her parlor with the same lonely, distracted step that had become a habit when she had first moved there. She had lived alone only briefly between the time of her mother's death and her marriage, but she had not enjoyed it then and she most assuredly did not enjoy it now. Two years of widowhood had not made the solitary evenings pass any more swiftly, and she hoped Byron would arrive soon.

She knew she ought to eat, but had little appetite, and was satisfied with plums and cheese. She bathed, then suddenly sleepy, donned her nightgown, and curled up on her bed to wait. There had been far too many nights when she had lain awake dreading the new day, but tonight her thoughts were of Byron, and so pleasantly sweet, she soon drifted off to sleep.

After enjoying another scrumptious meal, Byron left the inn. Now familiar with the streets of Grand Pré, he headed down toward the docks to confuse anyone who might be observing him and then swung back on a side street to make his way to Arielle's. He approached her house from the rear, and when she failed to instantly answer his knock, he opened the door and peered inside. A fire was burning low on the hearth so he knew she had arrived home safely. Thinking she might have been called out again, he let himself in, then noticed her basket of remedies on the table and discounted the idea.

At home, the young women awaited callers dressed in their finest gowns, and he wondered if perhaps she might still be preparing for his visit. He hoped she had not gone to a great deal of trouble, because he did not want her dressed at all. The door leading to the bedroom was open, and when he looked in and found Arielle asleep, he was at first disappointed.

Had she been so unenthused about seeing him that she had not even bothered to stay awake?

Meaning to wake her, he took a step toward the bed, but Arielle's expression was blissful, and the hope she was dreaming of him stilled his anger. He had allowed her little sleep the previous night, and she had put in yet another day of hard work trudging the streets compiling the tedious census. Ashamed that his first thoughts had been disparaging ones, he began to peel off his clothes. He took care to be quiet as he slipped off his shoes so as not to disturb Arielle, but as soon as he was completely unclothed, he crawled over the end of the bed to join her.

Beginning with her toes, he spread feathery kisses along the bottom of her foot. She flinched and changed positions slightly, but didn't wake. He licked her ankle, but got only the same result. Now taking the challenge of awaking her more seriously, he shoved the hem of her nightgown up out of his way, and sent his fingertips dancing along her calf. This time she murmured softly, and, inspired, he moved his hand up her thigh. Tonight, her skin was lightly scented with lavender rather than wildflowers, and he pressed his mouth to the pale flesh of her inner thigh.

Arielle responded with a languorous sigh and, flinging her arm wide, rolled over on her back. Thinking she would open her eyes and speak to him, Byron hesitated, but the deep, easy rhythm of her breathing was unchanged. Propping himself on his elbows, he watched her sleep for a moment, but her enticing pose soon lured him past his original purpose. He didn't care whether she was asleep or awake, he had to taste all of her.

Moving up to better position himself, he combed the nest of blond curls between her thighs. He teased her first with his fingertips, then spread her feminine folds and pressed an adoring kiss against her inner lips. He felt her hand brush his hair, but no longer satisfied with merely awakening her, he sent his tongue wandering through a delicious valley of desire. He had never even been tempted to take his passion for another woman this far, but now Arielle's own delectable nectar made him crave still more. He licked, and lapped, tickled, and nibbled until she was writhing in his arms, tilting her hips to encourage his eager flurry of intimate kisses.

He felt her straining toward the rapture he had coaxed so lovingly, but not wanting her to find it alone, he spread himself over her. He entered her with a quick, shallow thrust and quickly withdrew. She opened her eyes to look up at him, and, glazed by desire, her gaze held an intoxicating aqua glow. He lunged forward, piercing her deeply, but again withdrew to leave only the soft tip of his manhood pressing against her most sensitive flesh. She pushed down against him, but he forced himself to wait until his whole body cried out for release and he could no longer control his need for her. Then, his way eased by her inviting wetness, he slid deep inside her.

Beyond any conscious choice now, he felt the pulsating heat of her fiery inner core surround him, drawing him down into a soul-searing ecstasy that demanded more of him than he had ever given. The exquisite torment carried him to the heights of ecstasy, then drained him of desire, yet unable to abide being apart after he withdrew, he held Arielle tightly clutched to his chest.

"I thought you would be a light sleeper," he remarked when his breathing at last resumed its normal pattern.

"I am." Glorying in his warmth, Arielle hugged him closer still.

"Not tonight you weren't."

Arielle licked her lips, then realizing that he hadn't kissed her mouth, she raised up to kiss him. It was a long, slow kiss that all but blurred her memories of how the evening had begun, but she kept to her vow to be truthful. "I heard you open the back door," she confessed.

"You were only pretending to be asleep?" Dismayed but not the least bit disappointed at how her ruse had ended, Byron gasped her wrists and pinned her beneath him. "Is this what I can expect from you?"

Expectations implied a future, and knowing they did not have one, Arielle could not reply in words, but instead chose a subtle roll of her hips that was so enticing, Byron completely forgot the subject was deception rather than desire. When he lowered his mouth to hers, she welcomed his kiss, and grateful for each precious minute, again led him into the earthly paradise known only to lovers.

Byron returned to the inn to sleep, and, awakening alone on Sunday, Arielle had to remind herself his visit had not been an erotic dream. She got up and dressed in the mourning attire she had worn all week, but her mood was no longer the defiant, angry one that had originally dictated her choice of the elegant black velvet and taffeta clothes. She felt only a buoyant giddiness that kept bringing a most inappropriate smile to her lips.

In little more than a week, she had been swept from a maelstrom of despair into a glorious calm centered in Byron's generous affection. That she had no one with whom to share her joy, save Byron, tugged at her conscience, but failed to dim her happiness.

She usually walked to church with Sophie, Jean, and their children. Fearing as bitter a reception from the rest of Grand Pré as she had gotten from her old friend, she left home early, and was one of the first to arrive at the church. She took her place without having to face anyone who might wish to comment on her behavior, but throughout the service she felt an uncomfortable sense of being watched and overheard more than one hushed whisper that included her name.

At the conclusion of the service, she left through a side door and rushed away rather than give anyone an opportunity to confront her.

Once back home, she changed into the lavender skirt and blue bodice she usually wore into the woods so as not to attract any notice when she left home carrying her basket. Today, however, rather than being empty, the deep wicker basket was filled with bread, cheese, and a flask of wine.

Byron slept far later than Arielle, and the church service she had attended had already let out before he left the inn. The day was another glorious autumn treat and he took it as a sign of continued good fortune. Eagerly looking forward to spending the afternoon with Arielle in the woods, he was badly disappointed when a soldier overtook him less than half a block from the inn.

"The first transport's arrived," the breathless soldier announced, "and Colonel Winslow needs you down at the docks, sir."

Hoping all that was needed was an update on the census, Byron went with the soldier. Women waiting to visit their menfolk again crowded the docks and several minutes passed before he got his first glimpse of the schooner, *Incentive.* While it reached Grand Pré safely, its peeling paint and patched sails scarcely made it appear seaworthy. Feeling he ought to complain in the interest of the women Arielle and he had surveyed, he looked about for John Winslow. As he had expected, the colonel wanted to know how much longer he would need to complete his census.

"Possibly a day, no longer for the town, and another for the outlying farms," Byron replied, "but I'd not ship my family's tobacco in that decrepit vessel."

John Winslow looked equally pained. "It appears Governor Lawrence hired whatever ships he could find, and while this one won't offer luxurious accommodations, I fear none of the others will, either. Don't share your dismay at the quality of this ship with the Acadians as we'll have to send the first group off by the end of the week regardless of what they think of it. I want everyone out by winter, and

I can't allow anyone to complain about his assignment."

Byron had made no promises to anyone but Arielle, and he certainly wouldn't risk her life by assigning her to such a sorry schooner. He hated to force anyone else to sail on it, either, but Winslow had made it plain luxury wasn't a concern to him. Byron was about to argue luxury wasn't the issue when a sailor from the newly arrived schooner approached him.

"Are you Mr. Barclay, sir? I have a letter for you if you are."

Surprised that anyone would wish to write to him, Byron took the letter and was about to slide it into his pocket to read later when he saw the return address. It was from home, but the writing looked like that of his cousin Alanna, rather than his mother or father's. Perplexed, he tore open the envelope. "Will you excuse me a moment, this is from home and—"

"Of course. Take your time. I'll probably be here all day."

Byron carried the letter to the end of the dock where an overturned barrel made a passable seat. Fearing the worst, he hurriedly scanned the neatly written page and his suspicions were immediately confirmed. His posture slumped under a burden of sorrow; he reread the letter more slowly, but taking it a word at a time was no easier. A painful burning filled his chest and he sat a long while staring at the letter, although the words were blurred by unshed tears.

In the wake of his sister and brother's deaths, he had left home to escape the wretched gloom that had spread over the plantation. Now he was being called back home. His family was begging him, pleading with him, to return and he could not say no. When he finally remembered the plans he had made with Arielle, the thought of her waiting for him alone in the woods broke his heart. He folded the letter, slipped it into his pocket, and went to inform John Winslow of the situation, but as he left the docks, his feet were so heavily weighted with dread he doubted he would reach the woods before sundown.

Arielle had expected to find Byron waiting for her, and when he still hadn't appeared after she had gathered more berries than they could possibly eat, she began searching for herbs. By the time she had finished, she was too hungry to wait for him and cut herself a hunk of cheese and broke off the end of the small loaf of rye bread. She was often paid in foodstuffs rather than money, and it occurred to her that if she had no more patients requesting her care, she would have to begin providing for herself.

She had looked forward to an afternoon of playful loving, but without Byron to distract her from the coming deportations, her thoughts grew dark indeed.

She sat alone under the old oak, picking at the food she had expected to share and wondering why life had to be so endlessly sad. As a child, when her father had been home, she had had wonderful bursts of happiness, but when he was away, she had frequently gone several days without a laugh or even a smile. The light had left her mother's eyes after her father's death, and all too soon she had succumbed to what Arielle would always believe had been a broken heart.

Then Bernard Douville had come calling, and softly spoken of love. He had known what she needed to hear, and had provided the only true security she had ever known, but then, like her father, he had been taken away. Now, she found herself alone again, waiting for a man who might never arrive, and could not stay forever when he did.

Fearing she would not be fit company for him should he appear this late, she wrapped the remains of the cheese, and tore the bread into tiny morsels she scattered about for the birds. She took a sip of the wine, then laid the flask on the berries and herbs. Doubting there would be time for other picnics, she started for home, but her step no longer held the gaiety of her excited arrival and her cheeks weren't flushed with anticipation.

Byron saw Arielle coming toward him in the distance. He recognized her easily from her faded clothes, and, knowing how badly he must have disappointed her, he hurried along the path to meet her. At first he merely lengthened his stride, then seized by a desperate eagerness to see her, he broke into a run.

Startled by the jarring haste of his approach, Arielle remained where she stood. When Byron got close enough for her to make out his features, she could tell something was wrong.

Byron heaved a sigh as he reached her, then removed his hat and wiped his forehead on his sleeve while he caught his breath. "I'm so sorry to be late, but I've had dreadful news from home."

Arielle took his hand, led him into the tall grass at the side of the road, and pulled him down beside her. She opened the flask and handed it to him. "It's only wine, but it should help to calm you."

Byron regarded her sympathetic gesture as patronizing and reacted badly. "It's not a *femme sage* I need, Arielle." Unmindful of how deeply that sarcastic comment had hurt her, he tipped his head, and poured the rich, red wine down his throat. "My father had a stroke, and apparently a severe one, the day after I left home. A letter with the news just reached me. I told Winslow we could finish the census in another two days. The first transport has arrived, and I'll have to be on it when it sails, assuming it does not sink at the dock under the weight of its human cargo."

Arielle sat with folded hands, her pose attentive. She was as badly shaken as Byron but for an entirely different reason. She had not truly expected him to invite her to come home with him, but to hear him say that he would have to leave without any regard for her feelings was so cold, she now wondered how she could have been so foolish as to have expected anything more thoughtful.

At last noting her downcast expression, Byron reached out to pat her knee. "I'm sorry for being so curt with you. It's just that my family has withstood so much misfortune the last couple of years that I don't see how we can survive anymore."

That he did not have a particle of understanding

for her pain was something Arielle could no longer excuse or ignore. "Welcome to Grand Pré, Mr. Barclay. We positively thrive on misfortune here, but obviously you haven't noticed." On that subtle note, Arielle rose and, with an angry stride that bounced the topmost berries from her basket, started for home alone.

Ten

Amazed by the hostility of Arielle's reaction, Byron decided she must have been far more disappointed that he had been late to meet her than he had first realized. He was positive he had apologized, though, and provided a compelling excuse not only for his tardiness but also for the darkness of his mood. Her complete lack of understanding annoyed him.

He knew he ought to go after her, but couldn't summon the strength to rise, let alone counter the sharpness of her savage wit. He took another long drink of wine and leaned back on his elbows. For all he knew, his father might already be dead. He had expected tender concern from Arielle, rather than the contemptuous disregard for his feelings she had shown.

He pondered their disastrous exchange at length, but did not alter his original conclusion that disappointment on her part had colored her reaction to his news. Had they been together when he had received the letter, he was positive she would not have deserted him. After another drink of wine, he was convinced he could tame Arielle's temper, and forced himself to consider what he might find when he reached Virginia.

While he had been engaged in Braddock's tragic campaign, his cousin Alanna had been cast out of the family for marrying a Seneca brave. Not that his parents would have accepted an Indian under the best of circumstances, but Alanna had wed the man who had fathered Melissa's son. The situation at home had to be desperate indeed for his mother to have forgiven Alanna for what she and his father had seen as horrendous disloyalty to Melissa's memory and a hideous blight on the family honor. His mother was devoted to his father, though, and sadly, with two of her children dead, and her only surviving son away, she must have had little choice about summoning her niece and Hunter to help care for him.

Byron withdrew his cousin's letter from his pocket to confirm the details, but he had not been mistaken in his first reading. Alanna and Hunter had moved back to the plantation, along with the Indian's son, Christian, whose very existence Byron's parents had denied. That had to mean his father was even more badly incapacitated than Alanna described. He refolded the letter with shaking hands, slid it into the tattered envelope, and replaced it in his pocket. Surely one of the most important letters he would ever receive, he intended to save it.

At the moment, however, it was his relationship with Arielle that needed saving. He pushed himself to his feet, but exhausted by dread, he lacked the energy to overtake her. Instead, he made his way slowly back into town. When he reached her house, he knocked politely at the door, but as was so frequently the case, there was no answer. He went around to the back, and when Arielle again failed to respond to his call, he was relieved to find the door unbarred, and went in.

The basket of berries and herbs sat on the end of the table, and he left the now-empty wine flask she had given him beside it. A hurried glance into the bedroom revealed only an empty room. He walked in, circled the bed, and was on his way out when he noticed the miniature on the dresser. It was a delicately rendered painting of an intense-looking young man whose steadiness of gaze readily conveyed an admirable depth of character.

Certain it must be Bernard, Byron took care to return it to its place. He was surprised Arielle's husband hadn't been a more handsome man, but clearly she had adored him. He wondered if she would ever show him the same devotion. Covering a wide yawn, he looked longingly at the comfortable bed, and, unable to resist the lure of a few minutes sleep, he kicked off his shoes, removed his hat and coat, and stretched out on it. He was sound asleep before he considered just how irritated Arielle would be to find him there.

Too distraught to remain at home, Arielle had gone to see a friend whose baby she had delivered not long ago and stayed to help her prepare *sagamite,* a thick soup made from ground corn flour flavored with dried fish and peas. She enjoyed her visit, for among the conversational topics was not a word about what many considered Arielle's blatant indiscretions. Not wanting to strain the growing family's ability to provide food, she excused herself before they sat down for supper and returned to her own home.

She saw the flask as soon as she came in the back door and knew Byron had been there. Surprised that she could still feel his presence, she stood by the table a long moment, and then the shiver of a premonition sizzled down her spine. Alarmed, she tiptoed into the bedroom, and, appalled to find Byron sound asleep on her bed, she picked up the pillow that wasn't cushioning his head and walloped him with it. Rudely awakened, he raised his hands to fend off her blows, but that didn't slow the furious lambasting.

"This is still my home!" she shouted. "You can't take it yet, damn you, not yet!"

On her next downswing, Byron grabbed the pillow and yanked it from her hands. Not amused by her vicious if ineffectual assault, he aimed a glancing blow at her hips before flinging the pillow aside. He reached for her hands, and, yanking her forward, drew her down across him. Livid, she struggled to break free, but holding on tight, Byron rolled over to pin her beneath him. He locked his fingers around her wrists, then propping himself on his elbows, looked down at her.

"I haven't confiscated your house," he began, "but we have something important to settle and I simply fell asleep waiting for you."

Arielle resorted to French to tell him exactly what she thought of him for invading her home uninvited. She then went on to curse every Englishman ever born, from King George II down to the most insignificant pauper in his realm. By the time she had completed her vindictive tirade, she had burned off the worst of her anger, but even after she had fallen silent, her expression remained fiercely displeased.

"Whatever that was about, I'm sure I didn't deserve it," Byron argued. "Now, I've apologized once for missing the afternoon we'd planned and I'll do so again if that will soothe your hurt feelings. I am sincerely sorry to have left you waiting alone in the woods, and I promise you I'll do my best to avoid disappointing you ever again."

That Byron so misunderstood the cause of her distress completely baffled Arielle. She could understand why he had been late and forgive him, but she could not accept his making plans without any regard for her feelings. "I'm not a mere button," she declared, "even one with a face!"

She was the one who had likened making up the passenger lists to sorting buttons, not he, and Byron did not understand why she would mention such a thing now. The fullness of her breasts welling up at the top of her bodice was a terrible distraction, but it was plain the weight of his body was having no amorous effect on her. Despite his initial startled dismay, he found her spirited defense of her home wildly exciting, and hoping she could feel his arousal through the thickness of her skirts, he ground his hips against hers.

"Tell me what it is you want, Arielle, and I'll gladly supply it."

Arielle felt his virile hardness, but passion wasn't what she craved. "Get off me, you arrogant oaf, and get out of my house," she responded in a venomous whisper.

If there was one thing Byron had learned as a soldier, it was when to make a strategic retreat, and he did so now. He released her wrists, then moved off the bed. "If you won't accept my apology, then I don't know what else to do. It appears you'd prefer your own company later tonight, but I'll expect you to work with me tomorrow and Tuesday to finish the census. I'll call for you in the morning." Not waiting for a reply he feared would be negative in the extreme, he carried his coat and hat outside, and put them on there.

"Damn." His earlier fatigue forgotten, he strode off toward the docks where he intended to ask the captain of the *Incentive* for a tour. While he was certain exploring the schooner wouldn't be nearly as diverting as crawling over Arielle's luscious body, for the moment it appeared to be far safer.

Arielle remained on her bed with both her heart and conscience aching badly. All she had wanted from Byron was a show of regret at their parting or a sweetly worded promise to remember her fondly. That he didn't care enough about her to do either left her awash in shame. She still wasn't ready to admit Sophie had been right about Byron, because the days and nights they had truly shared had been glorious.

He had brought a delicious taste of forbidden love, but he had also taught her a valuable lesson. The next time she gave her heart, it would be to a man like Bernard, a kind, decent, honest man who would have a higher regard for her happiness than his own. She looked over at Bernard's tiny portrait and, missing him terribly, a tear rolled down her cheek and soaked into the pillow beneath her head.

* * *

Byron spent the first of the week with a silent companion who did little more than acknowledge his presence when he arrived at her house in the morning. John Winslow found them a wagon and team to survey the outlying farms, but even on what might have been idyllic jaunts, Arielle remained maddeningly aloof. Just a glance of her profile as they rode along made him wince with desire, and when their work was finally complete, and she handed over the last of the names neatly assigned to passenger lists, he responded with a polite reminder that they had yet to agree on how she was to be paid.

"I thought I'd made it clear I'd not accept money from you," Arielle contended. "Not for the census, nor anything else."

With the last of their work in hand, Byron had no reason to return to her home, but he had no intention of allowing her ill humor to dictate his future. "I do recall a mention of thirty pieces of silver, but I'd hoped you'd changed your mind. It's always helpful for a woman to have money of her own, and you've certainly earned it."

Infuriated with his obstinate inability to understand even the most straightforward of statements, Arielle lowered her voice to a threatening whisper. "If you persist in your demeaning attempts to give me money, I'll throw it in the street for the children to fetch. Now, good day."

She slammed her door in his face, and, frustrated that no amount of consideration had softened her insufferable defiance, Byron carried their lists straight to John Winslow. He had already discussed the severity of his own situation, and the colonel knew how anxious he was to leave.

"It's all here," Byron stated. "We've counted everyone, even a newborn babe, and assigned them a place among relatives. Choose any group you like, and I'll recopy the list and post it so the passengers can begin preparing to leave. I imagine there will be quite a commotion when the names are first read, but I've no idea how to soften the harshness of the deportations."

"Neither do I." Winslow perused the lists, searching for a single name. "Here, let's send this group first. Gaetan Le Blanc is causing more problems aboard ship than he did in the stockade and I want him and his friends gone. From what I've heard, you and he have taken a dislike to each other, so do your best to avoid him."

"Really, sir, I'd rather not travel with Le Blanc."

Winslow sighed wearily and shoved the list toward Byron. "I've already decided not to listen to complaints about assignments, Barclay. You've been an enormous help to me, but other than thanking you, and requesting a commendation from Governor Lawrence, there's nothing more I can do. Now, see if you can't get that list posted before nightfall. It will give the passengers more time to accept their situation, and prepare."

Disappointed, Byron was far too proud to plead. "I'll see to it immediately, sir." He went to the inn, and after sampling their strongest spirits, copied the list of names in his own bold script. At the bottom he added his own name, and Arielle's.

* * *

Wednesday morning, Arielle was gathering peas and beans from her garden when Marc Hébert found her. He had run all the way from his house, and took a big gulp of air before he spoke. "My mother is worried that with you leaving on Friday, she'll not have enough cough syrup for the baby. She wondered if you would tell her what's in it, so we can make our own from now on."

Amazed by Marc's puzzling comment, Arielle set her basket aside and came toward him. "What made your mother think I was leaving so soon, Marc?"

"Your name's on the list posted at the stockade, madame. Hadn't you heard? You're to sail on the *Incentive* on Friday."

Arielle stared at the dear little boy her mother had delivered, her gaze uncomprehending. "Not this coming Friday?" she finally had the presence of mind to ask.

"Yes, madame, but from the looks of the ship, you won't go far."

Marc's big brown eyes were full of innocent curiosity, but Arielle dared not vent her emotions in front of the lad or he would be terrified by her hysterical tirade and repeat it all over town. She took a deep breath, and released it very slowly. "Go home and tell your mother that I'll be happy to share my secrets with her now that she'll no longer be able to call on me. I'll write down the recipe for the cough syrup and see that she has it before I leave."

Satisfied that he had delivered his mother's message and received a favorable reply, Marc scampered off for home, and, seething with a bitter fury, Arielle turned back toward her garden and screamed. Her cry was long and shrill, one that could never be mistaken as a plea for help for it rattled with the bright jangle of her badly frayed nerves. Byron had told her he was leaving without so much as wishing her good luck, and now he expected her to sail with him? Was there no end to the man's arrogance?

Not about to allow the uncaring swine to upend her life, she stormed into her house, rinsed away the dust of the morning's chores, and, wearing her elegant mourning attire with a renewed sense of pride, she made her way to the stockade. There was a small crowd milling about in front of the list Marc had described. When she approached, the women parted, several whispering innuendoes she didn't care to hear, but she caught a harsh phrase about an Englishman and his whore that she had no way to dispute.

She recognized Byron's writing from his original list of questions, and read the names he had transcribed. He had made no changes in the group she had suggested, but she was jarred to find this was the one containing Gaetan's name. Dear Lord, she prayed silently, as the prospects for a truly dreadful cruise presented themselves. She skipped over the remainder of the passengers and when she found not only Byron Barclay's, but her own name at the bottom, she went over to the massive gate. Two soldiers, thankfully not the same pair she had encountered on her last attempt to speak with John Winslow, were standing guard.

"I need to speak with Colonel Winslow, please."

The more ambitious of the pair stepped forward,

drank in her prettiness with a parched glance, and then straightened up proudly. "If it's about the passenger list, he won't see you, ma'am. If your name's on the list, better go on home and start packing."

Although it sounded as though the young man had repeated that same response several times, his tone had been respectful, and Arielle smiled as she backed away. She doubted Winslow was the man to see anyway, and made her way to the inn. Byron was out, but believing he would return for the noon meal, she sat down to wait. Silently rehearsing one approach and then another, she kept herself occupied until the Virginian strode through the front door. She rose and went toward him, but when he appeared to be not merely surprised to see her, but delighted as well, she forgot everything but why she had come.

"I need to speak with you about the passenger list you've posted."

"Fine, let's discuss it while we have something to eat." Taking her arm, he led her into the common room where they found a table near the window. "The food is very good here," he remarked.

Unconcerned about the quality of the inn's fare, Arielle clenched her hands in her lap. "I have something serious to discuss," she warned. "Fearing my departure, patients have begun to request the recipes for my remedies. As one of the few *femmes sages* in Grand Pré, I ought to be on the last ship to sail, not the first."

Byron nodded thoughtfully, then waved for the barmaid. She came to their table, and he ordered roast venison for them both and their best Spanish wine. When she left for the kitchen, he smiled at Arielle. "I seem to recall your complaining that due to your association with me, people were no longer consulting you. That makes your request, noble though it may be, completely unfounded."

Rather than an easy smile, Arielle saw a pompous gloat and, deeply offended, looked out the window where the women passing by were undoubtedly as troubled as she. How could they not be? she mused silently. "I put my name on the list with the Mouflets. Why wasn't my choice respected?"

"Why?" Byron leaned back in his chair, and wished the barmaid would hurry with their wine. "Has the time we've spent together meant nothing to you?"

"It meant a great deal to me," she replied without glancing toward Byron.

"Then why are you so surprised that I'd want to take you home with me?"

Shocked to the marrow by that presumptuous question, Arielle searched for a sufficiently harsh reply, but before she found one, the barmaid returned with their food. She took a bite of venison before she replied.

"I'm not some exotic souvenir that you can include among your luggage."

"Certainly not," Byron agreed. "Whatever gave you such a ridiculous idea?"

Arielle had to swallow her second bite before she answered. "My ideas are not ridiculous, Mr. Barclay."

Byron shrugged. "Forgive me, I did not mean to insult you, which is unfortunately far too easy to do. Let me rephrase my question. I feel as though I'm being punished, but I've no idea of what crime I've been convicted. Would you please tell me?"

Perplexed, Arielle swirled a carrot slice through the savory gravy and chewed it slowly. "Perhaps you are simply unaware that women are not pretty pets who can be led here and there. We have feelings, Mr. Barclay."

Infuriated by what he saw as a deliberate, and unwarranted, attempt to aggravate him, Byron took a sip of wine in hopes of cooling his rapidly rising temper, but its numbing warmth failed to have the desired affect. He leaned forward. "I'm aware of a great deal where you're concerned." He lowered his eyes to the delicate black lace edging her bodice, then met her gaze with such a hungry stare that she was forced to look away.

"I know you, Arielle, and how to arouse the most delectable feelings in every splendid inch of you."

Arielle scooted her chair back slightly so she could leave the instant she finished her reply, but she forgot to lower her voice and spoke so loudly everyone in the inn was privy to her outrage. "I will not be ordered about like some pathetic whore eager to do your bidding, not here, nor in Virginia!" Like a startled raven, she bolted and fled past the gaping soldiers who had entered the inn for the noon meal, struck the door with both hands, and, once outside, disappeared into the crowd on the street.

In all his life, Byron had not been the focus of a public spectacle and he did not enjoy the uncomfortable role now. While he had lost his appetite, he remained in his seat, and, behaving as though nothing untoward had occurred, he finished his meal, and what remained of Arielle's before he left the inn. That he would be the butt of all manner of scandalous jokes that evening embarrassed him badly, especially since he had done his best to shield Arielle's reputation. He was not the sort of man to bow to public opinion, however, or ridicule, if it ran counter to his principles.

He had found something so precious with Arielle that he considered her worth whatever pain it took to recapture her heart. Attributing her current distaste for him to an understandable fear of leaving home, he went down to the docks, and while he still did not like the looks of the *Incentive,* his eagerness to sail away from Grand Pré made him blind to her more obvious faults. He looked out toward the ship where Gaetan Le Blanc was being held and shook his head. If he had his way, he would see that the belligerent young man made the whole voyage in chains.

It was now Wednesday afternoon, and the *Incentive* was scheduled to sail Friday morning. When she returned home after the horrid confrontation with Byron, Arielle cast a hurried glance around her kitchen. She had inherited a full complement of stockpots, stewpans, pie dishes, and utensils from her mother, but lugging them all with her now seemed ridiculous. She would have no one to care for in her new home but herself, and, setting aside only one kettle and her favorite utensils, she put the rest of her cookware on the table.

The Mic Mac Indians had been allies of the Acadians and had been good to her. Knowing how dearly the Indians had to pay in furs for iron kettles and the like from traders, she wanted them to have the things she could no longer use. She borrowed the Héberts' small wagon, loaded it with her discards, and, taking Marc along for company, pulled it out to the woods and left her things for the Mic Mac to find.

"You're just leaving your things here, madame?"

Marc obviously did not approve, but Arielle ruffled his hair and laughed. "The Indians need pots to cook in, too, and if I leave them in my house, some English soldier will just steal them, so isn't it wiser to give them away?"

Marc grabbed the handle of the wagon and started it rolling back toward the trail. "It will be dark soon. Do you want to bring them anything more tomorrow?"

"I don't know. I might. Will you come with me again if I do?"

"Yes, of course." Marc walked along with his free arm swinging in a wide arc, his brow furrowed with concentration. They went a long way before he found the courage to speak. "If you're just giving things away, my mother has always admired your rocking chair."

"Has she? Would you take it to her then? It would save me finding someone else to take it."

"I didn't mean to beg, madame. You mustn't tell her that I asked you for it."

"You're a wonderful son, Marc. When we reach your place, I'll ask your mother if she would like to have the rocking chair, and we'll let her decide. After all, I may have other things she would rather have."

Because Arielle lived very simply, she hadn't really thought that much about her things, but now that Marc had mentioned the rocking chair, she began to wonder if she didn't have some more useful items others might treasure. There was a nice pair of candlesticks, extra linens, all manner of things she discovered once she began a thorough mental inventory. What she couldn't give away, she would bring out to the Mic Mac, for they might be able to use her goods to trade with other tribes if they did not want the things themselves.

By early Friday morning, Arielle had her precious herbs carefully wrapped and her clothing packed. The few household articles she wished to take fit into her one remaining kettle. She carried everything outside and loaded them in the Héberts' wagon she had again borrowed. She covered her belongings with the beautiful blue-and-white quilt, slipped Bernard's miniature into her pocket, and was ready to go.

While she waited for Marc to appear, she took a last walk through her home, Sophie's vow to leave nothing for the British ringing in her ears. She had spent far too many lonely days and nights there to feel all that sad about leaving, but still, it had been home. She lit a roaring fire in the fireplace, lit a candle, and used it to set the bedroom curtains on fire. As the flames crept up the sheer fabric, she turned to the bed to ignite the drapes and canopy.

Leaving the bedroom engulfed in flame, she

turned her attentions to the parlor and soon had savage tendrils of fire dancing up the walls. When she left her cottage for the last time, she closed the door on countless forgotten dreams and watched it burn without the slightest sense of regret. Lured outside by the smell of smoke, neighbors who had ceased speaking to her left their homes to watch in awed silence. One or two came running with buckets of water, but when Arielle waved them back, they understood the blaze was a deliberate act, rather than a terrible accident.

A chorus of whispers swept the crowd, and then a shout of approval rang out, followed by more cheers. Frightened, Marc Hébert ran to her side, and she bent down to talk with him. "With your fine help, I gave away all that I could, and I refuse to leave anything behind for the British. Now let's go. As I no longer have a house, I certainly don't want the *Incentive* to sail without me."

They had just started pulling the wagon when Byron raced up the street. Horrified by the sight of the women and children gleefully applauding as Arielle's house burned, he was about to yell the obscenities he believed they deserved when he saw Arielle coming toward him, silhouetted against the flames. There was no sign of distress in her expression, only a joyous calm that he was certain early martyrs had shared. In an instant he understood why.

"You did this yourself, didn't you?"

"Yes, I most certainly did. If you've come to tell me I won't be sailing with you after all, it will be most inconvenient."

Byron handed Marc several coins, and took the

handle of the wagon himself. "No, I came to help you take your things down to the dock. I'd not have left you behind."

Arielle would have responded had Sophie not stepped out her door. She hoped now that they had mere seconds left to spend together, her old friend would reach out to her and hug her good-bye. She stopped to wait, and smiled, but Sophie merely spit in the dirt and turned away.

Disgusted by that show of disrespect, Byron reached out to take Arielle's hand. "Come on, let her be. She doesn't deserve a good friend like you."

"Since when have the people of Grand Pré gotten what they deserve, Mr. Barclay?"

"Not now, Arielle, please. Just come along with me. I promise you won't regret it."

"Not regret it? But Mr. Barclay, I already do."

Byron tightened his hold on her hand and vowed to make her change her mind, and soon.

Eleven

When Byron and Arielle reached the docks they found them in an even worse state of confusion than on the day the men of Grand Pré had been transferred onto the supply ships. The departing families had been reunited with their menfolk, and while there was rejoicing in that, like the iridescent rainbows on soap bubbles, the happiness sparkled only briefly, then burst and evaporated into the gloom that hung over the crowd. There wasn't a single soul who wished to leave his home, while those being left behind had come to bid a tearful farewell to the lifelong friends they doubted they would ever see again. Frightened by their mother's tears, children began to wail, and grown men wept in each other's arms.

There were only a few who, like Arielle, projected a stoic calm, but the sorrow reflected in their eyes was just as heartbreaking. Marc Hébert had followed them to retrieve his family's small wagon once it had been unloaded, and he stood at Arielle's side, his dark eyes wide. He had envied the first group to sail, for it had seemed like an adventure to him, but now that he was confronted with such a miserable spectacle, he knew he had been very wrong.

"Where are you going, madame?" he asked.

"I don't even know," Arielle confessed sadly, and turned to Byron. "Where are we being sent?"

"The *Incentive* is bound for Boston, but you and I are going on to Virginia."

Arielle could not abide the relaxed confidence of his manner. She reminded herself that, unlike the rest of them, he was going home, but the fact he had simply assumed that she would accompany him still gnawed at her insides, doubling the pain of her departure. Surrounded by people beset with a far greater tragedy, she did not complain aloud. After all, there would be time before they reached Boston to refuse Byron's unwanted hospitality so emphatically he could not possibly believe she would accompany him anywhere, but for now, she simply looked away and hoped he had the intelligence to discern just how disgusted with him she truly was.

Her eyes swept the anguished crowd and came to rest on Gaetan. He was talking with his sister, Julienne, while her son, Stephan, hugged his knee. He was standing close, not offering comfort to the sobbing woman or terrified child but intently conveying a message that, from the depth of his frown, appeared to be of vital importance. A few steps away, Alain Richard and Eduard Boudreaux were talking with their relatives. Arielle cursed the fact she had put the belligerent trio together, but at least their fourth member, Jacques Mouflet, would sail on another ship.

Unconsciously, Arielle moved closer to Byron. He might be spoiled, as she assumed all rich men's sons invariably were, and misguided where she was concerned, but she felt safe with him. She continued to watch Gaetan, and was dreadfully sorry she had remained involved with him over the last year. While she had not done anything to encourage his advances, she certainly had not discouraged them, either. She had put him off with excuses when she should have simply had the courage to tell him he ought to pursue another woman. When he glanced toward her, she was frightened clear through and hurriedly turned away.

The gentle breeze ruffled Arielle's lacy cap, and she raised her hands to make certain it was properly secured. Craving any sort of a diversion, she cast her attention toward the *Incentive* and quickly came to the same disconcerting conclusion as Byron. A captain's daughter, she knew exactly how important it was for a ship to be kept in good repair.

"How can the owner of the *Incentive* have such little pride in his ship that he does not keep her painted or supplied with unmended sails?"

"I've spoken with her captain, Robert Fitzpatrick. He's just purchased the ship and plans to use what Governor Lawrence is paying him to refurbish her. He has no shortage of pride, simply a lack of funds. He impressed me as a competent sort. I took the precaution of touring the vessel, and while she's not pretty, she's sound. Believe me, I'd not have allowed anyone to sail on her if she weren't. We'll arrive in Boston in a few days and I'll secure passage on a far finer ship to take us on to Virginia. There's Fitzpatrick now. Come with me and I'll introduce him."

Leaving her belongings with Marc for the moment, Byron took Arielle's arm and guided her through the crowd. The captain greeted Arielle with a slight bow, and then promptly ignored her.

"You and the lady ought to board now, Barclay, and remain in your cabins until we're under sail. From the looks of this pathetic scene, quite a few people might bolt, and if Winslow has to fire on them, you don't want to run the risk of being hurt."

Arielle was positive the captain had used the word *cabins,* and cheered by the fact she would have her own, she relaxed slightly. "Surely Colonel Winslow won't fire on an unarmed crowd filled with women and children."

Fitzpatrick dismissed Arielle's comment with an impatient shake of his head. "I didn't say I'd recommend it, ma'am, but it might happen. Now it's time to start boarding." He then leaned close to Byron to whisper a final comment before moving away. "Lock the bitch in her room."

Appalled, Byron would not even consider it. He could tell from the curiosity lighting Arielle's glance, she wanted to know what the captain had said, but he would not repeat it. "Fitzpatrick thinks you're very pretty," he said instead. "Come on, I'll show you to your cabin, and then I'll bring your luggage."

Now that the moment to depart had finally arrived, Arielle refused to look back. She had known both great happiness and desperate sorrow in Grand Pré, and she could scarcely imagine what she would find in Boston, but she had no intention of going any farther. From what she had heard, it was a large city, and because she spoke English, she was positive she could lose herself in it and escape both Byron and Gaetan forever.

"I still don't like the looks of the *Incentive,*" she confided softly. "Most of our men are fishermen, and they can't trust her seaworthiness, either."

"Then trouble seems likely. We better take Fitzpatrick's advice and remain in our cabins until we're underway." Byron led her up the gangplank and onto the two-masted vessel. The captain and crew were quartered below deck in the aft, and while he had expected Arielle to need help descending the ladder, she surprised him by moving down it with an agile step.

"I'd forgotten that your father was a ship's captain. Did you sail with him often?"

"Never, but I used to play on board his ship, and it was a far finer vessel than this."

Byron wondered just how far her memories had strayed. "The weather's clear, Arielle. Despite the tragedy that befell your father, you needn't worry we'll be lost at sea."

He was the one who worried her, not the voyage, and she regarded him with a skeptical glance. "That possibility doesn't worry me at all."

"Good, now this is your cabin, and mine is next door. Fitzpatrick expected to have a few British passengers, so these were already set aside for whomever wished to book them."

Arielle surveyed the narrow cabin and was surprised it smelled of oily furniture polish rather than mildew. The linens on the bunk appeared freshly laundered but there was so little space, she thought it fit for no more than sleeping. "Where are the others going to be staying?"

Byron tried to find a way to soften his description

of their wretched circumstance, but could not. "The cargo hold has been modified to accommodate them."

"How, into cabins?"

Byron rested his arm against the doorjamb. "No, they'll be quartered together."

"They'll be provided with bunks at least?"

Byron wasn't even tempted to stretch the truth when he knew she would probably visit the other passengers to see for herself. "No, there isn't room for bunks. I'm afraid there's not even enough room for everyone to sleep at the same time."

"What?"

Byron looked away, obviously ashamed and Arielle understood why. "It sounds as though we're being treated no better than slaves, although I've no idea why I expected better."

Byron sighed unhappily. "That's overstating it, Arielle. This is a voyage of mere days rather than months, and while less than ideal, the conditions aren't nearly so harsh as you imagine."

Arielle clenched her fists tightly at her sides. She knew she ought to refuse the use of a cabin and take her place with the others, but then she would have to contend with Gaetan again, and her dread of him outweighed her guilt at receiving special treatment. She truly had only one choice, and, reluctantly taking it, she entered the small cabin, sat down on the bunk, and folded her hands in her lap.

"I appreciate your having arranged for separate quarters for me," she offered grudgingly. "It will make the voyage much less awkward."

Byron didn't explain that had there been a cabin

spacious enough for them both, they damn well would have shared it.

Arielle sat primly on her bunk until Byron closed the louvered door, then her courage deserted her and her posture slipped into a dejected slump. She remembered seeing her father off from the very same dock. Her mother had always smiled and waved until the sails of his ship disappeared out in the Bay of Fundy, but she had always wept copious tears once they reached home. Her father had never known how terribly her mother had missed him, but she supposed they were together now in paradise. At least she hoped they were, if God allowed smugglers in heaven.

She heard the rattle and clank of the carts being hauled up the gangplank, and felt the ship dip lower in the water. She tried to distract herself by rehearsing her next conversation with Byron, but he returned with her luggage long before she had found words forceful enough to make her need for independence clear.

"You had so few things that I brought them all. I think there's room to stow them all in here."

Arielle shrugged, rose and made a halfhearted attempt to find a place for everything but the lockers failed to hold it all. "I doubt I'll be entertaining in here, so there will be no harm in leaving the kettle and quilt out."

Clutching the precious quilt, she looked very small and lost. Byron wished he could think of something encouraging to say that wouldn't sound stupid or trite. "I'll try and bring Marc on," he finally ventured. "He wants to tell you good-bye."

"Oh, no, I'd quite forgotten him. Wait, I'll go back up on deck, and—"

"No, it's bedlam up there. Wait here and I'll bring him."

A long time passed before Byron returned with Marc, and before she could thank him, he threw himself into her arms. She hugged his sturdy little body and knowing he also had a fine mind, she was certain he would be a credit to his parents regardless of where he was raised. She savored his warmth, and then gently pushed him away.

"I wish I had something to give you . . ." she began.

"Oh, but you have, madame. You gave us that fine rocking chair and Mother says we will take it with us no matter what has to be left behind. I will remember you always, and someday, we may all meet again. I pray that it will be here in Grand Pré."

"Yes, that's a lovely thought. Someday, and I hope soon, we may be able to come back and reclaim everything that was stolen from us. Now give your dear mother a kiss for me." Arielle kissed his cheeks, and then turned him toward Byron. "Now hurry home, so she doesn't worry."

Byron took Marc's hand and closed her door on the way out. Arielle returned to her bunk and finally gave in to the tears she had been too stubborn to shed on the dock.

Gaetan sat in a corner of the hold, his knees pressed against his chest. Eduard and Alain were seated on either side of him. It had taken so long to load the ship it had not sailed until noon. It was now three in the afternoon, and Gaetan had had enough.

"Are we men, or poor lambs being led to slaughter?" he asked.

"Men," Alain and Eduard replied in unison.

The hold was dimly lit and poorly ventilated through the open hatch. It was uncomfortably warm, the aroma of sweat and despair mingling in the stale air. Women and children were still sobbing, while the men were either trying to quiet them or cursing just as loudly. Even after the humiliation of being confined first in the stockade and then on a supply ship, even after the anguish of losing everything he held dear, this was the most miserable day Gaetan had ever endured, but he had no intention of allowing it to end with that distinction.

"As soon as darkness falls we'll seize the ship," he predicted confidently. "There are knives aplenty among the utensils the women brought on board. We'll slit the throats of the soldiers guarding us and toss their bodies over the side. We'll then take the captain and crew hostage. There are a dozen among us who can captain this ship better than the fool who allowed her to fall into such sad disrepair and a great many more to serve as crew."

He paused then, and lowered his voice slightly to savor his plan. "I want Arielle's Englishman kept alive. We'll amuse ourselves with him later."

Alain and Eduard again offered inventive ways to torture him, and Gaetan nodded appreciatively at every one. "Nothing must happen to Arielle, though," he reminded them. "She must be protected."

Knowing better than to insult the lovely widow within Gaetan's hearing, the bloodthirsty pair simply murmured their consent.

While being held on the supply ship, Gaetan and his friends had wiled away many an hour rehearsing just such an attack. Although their plan to escape from the stockade had been thwarted, it was there that they had learned which men would help, and which would remain cowering in the hold until the deed was done. Now ready to do it, Gaetan began sending a whispered order to those he trusted. So as not to frighten the women and children, his words requested only time on deck for fresh air, but the conspirators all recognized it for exactly what it was and were ready to obey a more explicitly violent command.

Byron rapped lightly on Arielle's door. "Captain Fitzpatrick would like us to join him for supper," he confided. "Can you be ready in ten minutes?"

Awakened by the sound of his voice, as Arielle sat up, she knew by the gentle rolling motion of the ship that they had left Grand Pré. She had not wanted to go up on deck and watch the Acadian coastline fade in the distance, but now she was sorry she had not even known when it had. She went to the door and opened it only a few inches.

"I'm really not hungry. Just have him send me the bread and gruel he'll serve the others."

Annoyed by her sarcasm, Byron grew curt. "Your friends are being provided with adequate rations, Arielle, not prison fare. As for us, we'll dine with the captain, and that's final. Now, stop acting like a child and get ready."

Arielle slammed the door and leaned back against it. If they were going to have a battle of wills, then she supposed it might just as well begin now as later. During her nap, her cap had been knocked askew allowing several tendrils to brush her neck in enticing disarray. Unmindful of their seductive effect, she didn't bother to redo her coiffure or don her best cap, and when Byron next appeared, she greeted him far more firmly.

"I think it's time to end your pretense that we're traveling together when we're not. I'm not your mistress, and I don't wish to take my meals with you."

Byron didn't dispute her analysis of their situation, for he had never considered her his mistress. Instead, he reached his hand into the cabin, grabbed her wrist, and pulled her along behind him down the companionway to the captain's cabin. He rapped lightly at the door, and hearing a word of welcome, drew her inside with him.

"Madame Douville is unaccustomed to travel," he explained, "so I hope you'll excuse her less than perfect appearance. But I'm certain she'll be a charming dinner companion for us both."

Byron was glaring at her, daring her to disobey, but Arielle refused to surrender meekly. "The truth is, I don't want any part of your hospitality, Captain, and I have no intention of being charming with either of you."

Ordinarily a taciturn man, Fitzpatrick was so amused by Arielle's spunk that he broke into a deep, rumbling chuckle that sounded as though it had been borrowed from a much larger man. "A woman with spirit as well as beauty! How extraordinary! I insist that you join us." He motioned toward a chair, and Byron scooted Arielle into it.

Fitzpatrick took his own seat, and with a great flourish spread his napkin across his lap. "We're having roast chicken," he announced, and when in the next instant a light knock was heard he called out and the cook's helper entered bearing a heavily laden tray.

The young man served them plates heaped with slices of an expertly roasted hen, along with steamed potatoes and carrots. He offered a basket of bread and a cup of butter, then poured them all a tankard of ale. He stood back a moment to allow the captain to comment if he had another request, but when Fitzpatrick merely nodded his approval, he returned to the galley.

Arielle looked down at her plate. The aroma wafting up from the chicken was heavenly, but Acadians did not regard potatoes as fit to eat unless starvation was imminent. "Do the British actually like potatoes?" she asked.

The slight wrinkle to her nose made her disdain clear, but Byron thought her criticism of the food extremely rude. He was about to say so when the captain began to recite a lengthy blessing thanking God not only for the delicious meal but requesting a safe voyage. He had just murmured amen when a jarring thud resounded up on deck.

Fitzpatrick glanced up, but when after a brief wait there was no repetition of the noise, he took a bite of chicken. "A water barrel must have broken loose," he commented before sampling his potatoes. "Think nothing of it. The crew will relash it to the rail."

Arielle glanced over at Byron who was also enjoying his meal, but she doubted what they had heard had been caused by a loose barrel. "That wasn't a rolling sound," she argued, "but more of a thump, as though someone had fallen."

The captain cut another slice of chicken breast. "While generally agile, a sailor occasionally falls, my dear. I'm sure he got up."

"I am not your 'dear,' " Arielle pointed out.

"Merely a figure of speech, dear lady," Fitzpatrick responded with a decidedly insincere smile.

The next sound from above was most definitely a thump, followed by a deck-raking slide. "Another barrel?" she asked. "Or have all your crew suddenly become clumsy?"

Fitzpatrick rolled his eyes upward, but, as before, the sound had come and gone so quickly that he was not at all certain exactly what he had heard. "Mr. Barclay mentioned your lack of travel experience, Madame Douville, but I trust you'll soon become accustomed to the sounds of a ship at sea. The constant din is all quite natural to us, but I assure you, you've no reason to become alarmed by a thump or two."

Arielle stared at the captain as he continued to eat with complete nonchalance. He was behaving as though he had bales of cotton in the hold rather than people who did not want to be there. She was about to point out the foolishness of his pose when it occurred to her the telltale sounds might well have been caused by clever Acadians rather than careless sailors.

She took a sip of ale to steady herself and hoped she had not already said too much. She ate a bite of carrot and then one of chicken, but, her apprehensions growing, she was unable to sample more of the appetizing meal. She took a slice of bread, and, picking it apart, appeared to be eating while the men cleaned their plates and drank a second tankard of ale. She wished she knew what was happening up on deck and, glancing toward Byron, managed a shy smile. He smiled back, and she was relieved to think he did not suspect a thing.

"Tell me, Mr. Barclay, do you enjoy chess?" Fitzpatrick inquired.

Not wanting to neglect Arielle by being drawn into lengthy games with the captain, Byron was about to say that he did not when the door to the cabin flew open and Gaetan Le Blanc came striding in holding a pistol in each hand. Sickened that he hadn't investigated the ruckus up on deck, Byron raised his hands.

Gaetan gestured with his pistols, and the startled captain raised his hands, too. The Acadian then gave a sharp order and nodded for Arielle to translate.

It was one thing to suspect something odd was afoot, quite another to be confronted with it. Shaken, Arielle rose slowly and gripped the back of her chair to steady herself. "He says if you resist him in any way, you'll go over the side."

Hatred lent Gaetan's green eyes a yellow glow, and Byron's first thought was that they were dead no matter what they did. It was only the fear that Arielle might be shot by accident that kept him from leaping from his chair and tackling the surly Acadian. Undaunted, he looked him in the eye. "And if we don't resist?"

Arielle conveyed his question and waited for Gaetan's response. "He says you'll live to see another day."

That wasn't at all comforting, and Byron sent the captain a warning glance at the same time Arielle added a thought of her own. "Gaetan's rage is justifiable, but I'll do what I can to see you're treated better than we have been."

"How considerate of you," Byron replied just as Gaetan hit him with the butt of a pistol. His vision blurred, then cleared as Arielle came to his side and pressed his napkin against the gash in his forehead.

"Get away from him!" Gaetan cried.

"I'll not allow you to beat him!"

"I'm going to rip him to bits, but not tonight. Tear the captain's sheets into strips and tie them to their chairs, and hurry up about it."

"Not unless you promise me you'll not hurt them."

While Byron was unable to follow their conversation, he was amazed Arielle would stand up to Gaetan when the man looked as though he would just as soon shoot her as not. "Better do as he says," he whispered.

Gaetan raised his hand to strike Byron again, but Arielle stepped between them to block the blow. "Stop it!" she cried, "or you'll show yourself to be no better than the British."

Gaetan laughed at that comparison. "Chérie, I am much worse. Now tie them as I asked you to."

Arielle yanked the top sheet from the bunk and used a knife she found in the captain's desk to cut through the hem. She then ripped off a dozen strips and, beginning with the captain, tied him securely to his chair. Gaetan slipped one pistol through his belt to free a hand to check the tightness of the makeshift bonds and nodded his approval.

Arielle then went back to Byron. "I didn't know anything about this," she assured him.

Blood was still dripping down his face, and when Arielle again tried to stem the flow he could feel her hands shaking. It was plain to him she spoke the truth or else she would not have questioned Fitzpatrick's description of the sounds they had heard. He was thoroughly disgusted with himself for not understanding what they had heard when clearly she had.

When she bent down to tie his ankles to the chair legs, he tried to move his feet forward slightly to provide some slack, but Gaetan saw what he was doing and called a warning. Arielle looked up at him, her eyes brimming with tears, and Byron couldn't understand why. "Isn't this what you wanted?" he whispered.

Arielle rose, again putting herself between him and Gaetan before she replied. "You would fight to the death for your plantation. How can you expect any less from us?"

Unable to reply, Byron just shook his head, but it was plain he failed to see the parallel.

Now that the prisoners were securely tied. Gaetan began a thorough search of the captain's cabin. He found another pistol, and some ammunition. He joked with Arielle as he tossed the items into a pillowcase. "Clearly the captain believed the few soldiers Winslow sent to guard us were enough. Did he think he had only women and children on board?"

"Do you want me to ask him?"

Gaetan turned, reached out to grab her arm and drew her close for a savage kiss he did not end until he was good and ready. Even then, he kept a tight hold on her. "No. That is all he and your Englishman need to know. You're mine now, Arielle. You may have made the wrong choice before, but I forgive you. We were meant to be together. Why else would God have placed us both on board this ship?"

"It wasn't God who made up the passenger lists, Gaetan."

The Acadian's glance grew stern. "Fate, coincidence, whatever, we are together at precisely the time that we need to be. You can be proud of me, Arielle, as you never could be of an Englishman."

"I *am* proud of you," Arielle readily admitted. "You have the courage of ten men. Please take hostages if you must, just don't kill anyone."

Gaetan shrugged. "You're too late for that plea. Several are already dead, and these two will be next if you don't do exactly what I say."

Arielle straightened her shoulders proudly. "Am I your prisoner, too?"

Amused by her question, Gaetan responded by giving her another ravishing kiss. "You'll never escape me now, chérie. Soon you won't even want to."

Arielle wiped her mouth on the back of her hand. "I want Byron kept alive."

"Good, so do I, for as long as possible."

His smile gave a sinister meaning to his words and

Arielle shuddered. "Not kept alive to suffer inhuman tortures. I mean, unharmed in any way."

"Too late, chérie. Now it is time that I got what I want." With that vow, Gaetan laced her fingers in his and led her from the cabin.

Arielle turned back to shake her head, a final warning for Byron, but he saw only the woman he adored leaving with his worst enemy and nothing more.

Twelve

After following Arielle inside her cabin, Gaetan sneered in disgust. "This is as crowded as the hold. Someday I will build you a magnificent house with more rooms than you can count."

He released her with a shove that sent her stumbling toward the bunk, then glanced out into the companionway. "The *Incentive* is ours now and I'm needed on deck. Can I trust you to stay here, or must I assign a man to guard you?"

Arielle slipped her hand into her pocket and grasped Bernard's miniature. She prayed that her late husband would hear her silent plea for help and just touching his portrait gave her a burst of hope. "Where would I go?"

Gaetan shook his head as though she were being impossibly silly. "Right back to your Englishman. But if I find you with him, I will slit his throat and use your dress to sop up the blood." He watched a sheen of terror brighten Arielle's eyes, and, cupping her chin, leaned over to kiss her. When he pulled away, she looked no less fearful, while he felt a leaping surge of joy and broke into a wicked grin.

"Stay here. We have much to discuss, but it will have to wait. I'll come back when I can."

He drew her door closed on his way out, and Arielle was again left to deal with the same fright and sorrow that had filled her when they had sailed—only now the torment had been magnified tenfold. She understood Gaetan's anger so well and could not fault him for despising the British, but she could not excuse wanton murder. She gagged, and, fearing she might lose what little supper she had eaten, took several slow, deep breaths to control her distress.

Once her stomach was properly settled, she swung her legs up on the bunk and got as comfortable as she could in order to consider what the next few hours might bring. However Gaetan had managed to commandeer the ship, he had saved the unwilling Acadian passengers from being scattered across the English colonies like seeds borne on the wind. She knew the people in the hold had to be rejoicing, and she supposed she ought to be, too, but she no longer felt as close to them as she once had. She felt only sad, and desperately frightened that her affair with Bryon had put his life at risk. She would not allow him to suffer on her account and, certain Gaetan could not be moved by tears, she resolved to match his strength with a show of such fierce will that he would have to respect her demands.

If he shouted, she would yell right back, and if he tried to beat her again, she would respond with such blistering defiance that he would soon learn just how little his superior strength won him.

"I should have been warned!" Fitzpatrick decried.

"Yes, you should have, and I'm afraid I'm partly to

blame because I knew Gaetan Le Blanc might cause trouble—"

" 'Might cause trouble!' The man may have slaughtered my entire crew, and you dismiss it as merely causing 'trouble'?"

Byron yanked on the crude ropes that held him, but they showed no sign of weakening. "No, of course not. Losing control of the *Incentive* is a catastrophe, but there's no point in wasting our time bemoaning it. We've got to find a way to take her back."

"For all we know, we're the last two Englishmen alive."

"I doubt it. Le Blanc isn't stupid, and the value of holding hostages won't be lost on him."

Fitzpatrick snorted. "Didn't you see the look in his eye? The man's a killer. They're all dead I tell you; and we sat right here, heard two of them fall, and did nothing!"

"Clearly that was a mistake, but—"

"This is all about that woman, isn't it?"

"Arielle? No, it's not about her. The Acadians simply had no other way to protest their deportation, but don't despair. When we don't arrive in Boston on schedule, Governor Shirley will undoubtedly suspect a revolt and send troops to rescue us."

When Fitzpatrick's response was another derisive snort, Byron ceased mouthing wasted words, attempting to focus the captain's attention on the obvious need to escape their bonds. He tugged, yanked, twisted, and pulled, fighting every minute rather than allowing his mind to fill with images of what might be transpiring between Gaetan and Arielle.

Fitzpatrick watched Byron struggle but made no effort to emulate him. "Fool, you'll never get free."

Gaetan walked through the door before Byron could answer Fitzpatrick. He noticed the food left uneaten on Arielle's plate and after a lazy perusal, picked up a drumstick. He tore off the meat with a raffish bite and then flung the bone aside. He sampled the ale, wiped his mouth on his sleeve, and picked up a piece of bread. Relishing the conqueror's role, he bit through the crust and chewed it slowly before approaching Byron. Elated by the reversal of their circumstances, he regarded the Englishman with a sly smirk.

Byron knew Gaetan would not understand anything he said, but neither that fact nor fear of punishment was a sufficient cause to remain silent now that Arielle had left the cabin. "I intend to have Arielle," he announced proudly, "and you can't stop me."

Because Byron's mention of Arielle's name prompted the worst of responses in Gaetan, the Acadian didn't need to understand the rest. He clenched his fist and slugged Byron so hard, he knocked him unconscious with a single blow. Proud of himself, he took another swig of ale before turning toward Fitzpatrick, an unspoken challenge in his glance.

Unwilling to follow Byron's example and bravely encourage abuse, the captain shook his head.

"Good," Gaetan responded, grabbing another piece of chicken on his way out. "At least one of you is obedient."

* * *

Gaetan noted the change in Arielle the instant he opened the door to her cabin. Somehow in the two hours he had been away, her demeanor had changed from shy apprehension to bold confidence. Still seated upon her bunk, she was glaring at him now, her defiance as open as that of the Englishman she prized. Startled, he paused before he walked in.

"A pout does not become you, chérie," he chided.

Arielle sat perfectly still, making her response all the more chilling. "I am way beyond a pout, Gaetan. I am outraged. Please go. You are no more welcome in my cabin than Byron Barclay was."

Gaetan came forward rather than retreating and sat by her feet. "Do not pretend Barclay was unwelcome here when everyone in Grand Pré knows how eager you were to have him share your bed."

"No one knows anything."

Gaetan had expected her to weep and beg, to offer delights he had only imagined in exchange for Byron's life. To find her so coldly unconcerned annoyed him. "What was he doing at your house if he was not your lover?"

Arielle continued to return Gaetan's insulting stare with icy calm. "I don't have to justify my behavior to you or anyone else. I'll tell you only that whatever happened between Byron Barclay and me is over. I didn't ask to be on this ship any more than you did, and I would have gone no farther than Boston."

Gaetan wrapped his hand around her ankle. He expected her to flinch or pull away, but she ignored his touch as though it were the insignificant brush of a child's hand. Disappointed, he removed her slippers and began to rub her feet, but even that familiarity drew no response. "You were quick to beg me not to harm him. Are you now saying you don't care what happens to him?"

"I care about all the people on board. I don't want any of them abused in any way."

"Even me?"

"Yes, of course. I don't want you to come to any harm, either."

Gaetan took a deep breath, then let it out slowly. "You must have felt the ship change course. We're sailing back up the Bay of Fundy, but we'll seek a haven in New Brunswick rather than Acadia. We'll sight land by morning and the families who wish to flee to Quebec will be free to go. Those who wish to remain with me and fight will be most welcome to stay. As for the crew of the *Incentive,* they will be given a choice. Either they may become willing workers in establishing a settlement or they may seek a place in heaven."

"Am I to be given a choice?"

Gaetan laughed and gave her foot a tender squeeze. "I've made it for you, chérie, but unlike your Englishman, I know how to show you the proper respect. As soon as I can locate a priest, we'll be married."

"I won't marry you."

This cold, seething rage of hers was disturbing to Gaetan. "I've already made it plain that I have made your choices for you, Arielle. Don't fight me on this. We are a well-suited pair and our marriage will be a happy one."

Arielle looked down at his hands. Had Byron been rubbing her feet, she knew she would feel a delicious

IF YOU LOVE READING MORE OF TODAY'S BESTSELLING HISTORICAL ROMANCES.... WE HAVE AN OFFER FOR YOU!

LOOK INSIDE TO SEE HOW YOU CAN GET 4 FREE HISTORICAL ROMANCES BY TODAY'S LEADING ROMANCE AUTHORS!

4 BOOKS WORTH UP TO $23.96, ABSOLUTELY FREE!

tingle all the way up her legs. With Gaetan, she felt only revulsion. "We're ill-suited in the extreme," she argued. "You're hot-tempered and wild, with more courage than sense. While those faults might serve as assets when fighting the British, they won't make you a fine husband."

Rather than being insulted, Gaetan laughed at her description. "And what about you? You are just as hot-tempered, chérie, and for a once-proper widow to take an English lover was definitely wild. No, I am right, we are exactly the same, and a perfect match."

He rose, and stretched out an arm to prop himself against the bank of lockers opposite the bunk. He glared down at Arielle, so desperately eager to make her his own he could taste the sweetness of the kisses she had always denied him. "Before the sun sets tomorrow, you're going to beg me to marry you, and because I love you so dearly, I will agree, but you'll have to pay a price for my consent. I'm sure you know what it is. Think about it tonight. You'll either wear my ring, or the memory of the Englishman's blood will forever stain your hands. I know you'll make the wisest choice."

"You bastard!"

"Be careful. Neither you nor the Englishman will profit from insults. You must do your best to keep your future husband happy. Put away that black gown. I want to see you wearing pretty colors again."

Arielle controlled the fury that leapt within her soul until he had left the cabin. She doubted she would sleep at all that night, but it would not be because she was debating her choices when, in truth, she had none. She withdrew Bernard's portrait from her pocket and traced the edge of the gilt frame.

She had been proud to be his wife, but the prospect of taking a second husband filled her with a numbing sense of dread. To be forced into marriage would make a mockery of the vows, but her happiness was a small sacrifice compared to Byron's life.

Gaetan escorted Arielle up on deck the next morning. A thin blanket of fog floated above the water and hid the shore, but in the distance she could hear the sound of waves breaking against rocky cliffs.

"We're near the mouth of the St. John River," Gaetan answered Arielle's unasked question. "That would be too obvious a harbor, however, so we'll sail farther north before making for land. The coastline is riddled with coves and inlets. So it won't be difficult to find a good place to put ashore and build a fortress."

They remained at the rail and in moments, the sun had burned off the fog leaving the tree-lined coast in full view. A dense pine forest extended down to the water, and Arielle knew it would be home to plentiful game. The men could hunt and fish, and by next spring have ground cleared for crops, but even with abundant wood to build shelter, she feared surviving the winter would be a difficult challenge for them all.

"Does everyone agree with your plan?"

Gaetan eyed her with a taunting gaze. "They do now. I will admit there were some who were afraid at first, but now that we've taken the ship, they've come to believe we can succeed at whatever we try."

"Even the men with families?"

"Yes, especially them. They can build a home for their wives and children here without fear they will be ridiculed or treated as criminals as we surely would have had we meekly allowed ourselves to be taken to the British colonies."

Gaetan rested his arms on the rail. "No, this is the ideal place for us, chérie. If we had to leave Acadia, then this was the best place to come. With wood so plentiful, we can build our own ships and continue the fight against the British. We'll have to take care of ourselves for now, but in the spring, we'll send someone to Quebec to volunteer whatever service we can provide to put an end to the British scourge."

Arielle had only recently referred to the British in the same way, but that did not mean she wished to join Gaetan's band of rebels. She had dressed in blue, her only concession to his demands, but Bernard's miniature lay nestled in the bottom of her pocket where she could touch it for comfort whenever she needed. There had been two hundred passengers, two hundred and two with her and Byron added. She tried to remember the names on the list, then had to resort to scanning the faces of the others on deck.

"How many able-bodied men do you have?" she asked.

Concerned about her motives, Gaetan shook his head. "We'll manage."

"The majority of the passengers are women and children, with a few elderly couples. You might plan to use the sailors as laborers, but are there enough Acadian men to support the settlement you envision?"

"We'll attract others," he assured her.

"To what, your Acadian colony with English slaves?"

Amused, Gaetan laughed at her fears. "Yes, I like that idea. It sounds wonderful to me."

Foolhardy was the word that leapt to Arielle's mind. She glanced over her shoulder, searching for the one face she wanted to see, but there was no sign of Byron. Two little boys ran by, their laughter a welcome sound, and she sighed softly. "You'll have to be especially good to the children, Gaetan. We can't lose any of the children."

That she was looking toward the future rather than the past pleased him and he slipped his arm around her waist to give her a hug. When she pulled away, he yanked her back. "Must I remind you that you must be especially good to *me,* chérie? Or do you want to see your lover dead?"

"When did you become so bloodthirsty?"

"When the British invaded our land." Gaetan released her, but stayed close. "I will be a fine husband for you, Arielle, but I am nothing like Bernard. He was a good man, but cautious."

"Had he been as cautious as you imagine, he would still be alive."

Gaetan shrugged. "Perhaps."

"Are there Indians living here?"

"Do not worry, if there are, they will be friendly like the Mic Mac, rather than the murdering Iroquois who killed Bernard."

"How can you be sure?"

"I've sailed this bay for many years. I've spoken with other fishermen and trappers. Believe me, there are no accursed Iroquois here. You'll not be widowed twice, Arielle. Put those fears aside."

Arielle could sense just how eager he was to renew their confrontation over Byron and deliberately thwarted his attempt to bait her. She looked out at the forest, and wondered if the friendly Indians Gaetan imagined were watching them. It was an eerie possibility that brought a shiver to her spine.

"Are you cold?" he asked.

"No," she replied. "Just uneasy."

"We all are," Gaetan admitted. "But we'll feel better in a day or two when our newly won freedom is assured."

Arielle did not respond, for she had never felt less free.

Byron and Captain Fitzpatrick had been left tied to their chairs all night. At first light, Alain Richard had appeared to set them free. Armed with both musket and pistol, he had allowed them to relieve themselves and to stroll the deck for a few minutes before he marched them back to the captain's cabin and gave them cold biscuits and ale for breakfast. The whole time he had watched them with the eager attention of a cat observing a bird, and once they had eaten their meager repast, he had Fitzpatrick tie Byron to his chair and then tied up the captain himself.

As soon as he had left them, Fitzpatrick again began to complain about everything from Governor Lawrence's promise of an easy voyage to the damage he feared was being done to his ship. Byron had awakened with a stiff neck and terrific headache. Uninterested in listening to Fitzpatrick's litany of woes, he had soon heard more than enough.

"Blame your own greed for getting you into this and shut up," he ordered. Raising his voice had made his whole head throb, but, satisfied the captain had understood him, he went on to a more vital concern. "I missed much of last night. Did you feel a change in course; do you have any idea where we are?"

Insulted by Byron's curt demand, Fitzpatrick was reluctant to reply, but having no one else to talk to, he soon did. "We're sailing up the Bay of Fundy, thank God. I had feared they would head on out into the Atlantic, make for the Saint Lawrence River, and take us into Quebec. My guess is that they want to remain close to Acadia. Like every man, they have a natural fondness for home."

The mention of home filled Byron with a tormenting sense of loss. "I was on my way back to Virginia," he revealed. "My father is ill and I'm needed at home. I can't stay here."

"I do not see any other choice at present."

"I'll find a way," Byron assured him. He did not want to think of Arielle's having to suffer, and hoped Gaetan was treating her well. He rolled his head around in a circle to loosen the stiffness in his neck, but the effort proved too painful to continue. Sad and sore, he sat waiting for the opportunity to confront Gaetan, hoping he would still have the strength to do so when it came.

* * *

Having planned and carried out their successful liberation, Gaetan met with no objection to his naming a sheltered cove as his choice for their base. Well aware the tides in the Bay of Fundy had a range of nearly fifty feet, he stood at the rail discussing the problems the changing shoreline would present with the other fishermen among them while the farmers listened attentively. Unconcerned about tides, Arielle slipped away from the group.

No longer the sobbing waifs who had set sail from Grand Pré, the children scampered around the deck, dodging the masts and leaping over coils of rope. Not nearly so resilient, their mothers and grandmothers huddled in the stern, talking in hushed voices and fearing they had traded one set of worries for another. Arielle had not the slightest interest in joining them. Longing to make certain Byron was safe, she glanced toward the stern but dared not risk sneaking down to the captain's cabin to see how he had fared.

She was as eager to drop anchor and go ashore as Gaetan, but only because she hoped he would allow his prisoners time to exercise so she might send Byron a smile if nothing more. She turned to find Gaetan staring at her over the head of a farmer, and couldn't find even a hint of a smile for him.

After Gaetan and a small party had taken lifeboats ashore and found the terrain surrounding the cove perfect for their purposes, he arranged for all the Acadians to go ashore where he proceeded to present what he was certain would be an amusing bit of entertainment. At low tide, there was a wide expanse of beach, and plenty of room for the contest he planned to stage. He sent Alain and Eduard back to the *Incentive* to bring Byron.

"I thought we ought to settle matters between us immediately," he told Arielle. "I'm going to prove which of us is the better man, and then your Englishman's fate will be up to you."

Arielle had to summon strength she had not known she possessed to meet his level stare. "This is an absolutely senseless waste of time," she countered. "I have no interest in the man, other than what as a Christian woman I would naturally feel for anyone."

Gaetan shrugged. "Don't watch then. I'll tell you later what happened, as he certainly won't be able to."

Gaetan didn't wait for Arielle to reply, but walked down to meet the lifeboat holding his most prized captive. He waded out, and although Byron's hands were bound, he handled him far more roughly than was necessary to help him out. He then prodded him on up the beach to where Arielle stood. He pulled a knife from his belt and gestured with it.

"Tell him we're going to fight, and if he wins, he may have you."

While Arielle was elated to see Byron, she was shocked by the bloody gash on his cheek and she could tell by the way he was holding his head that he was even more badly hurt than he looked. "He's already been beaten," she argued. "You can't ask him to fight again."

"Nonsense," Gaetan responded. He reached out to trace a line across Byron's jugular vein with the tip of his blade. "He's young and strong. A few bruises haven't harmed him. Now tell him why we're fighting so we can begin."

While she was loath to repeat such a stupid request, Arielle did, but she made her own bias clear in the telling. "Gaetan insists upon fighting you, and I can't talk him out of it."

Encouraged by the fact she was standing well away from the Acadian, Byron responded with a grin. "I'll be happy to fight him with whatever weapon he chooses. Are you the prize?"

Arielle glanced up at Gaetan, who looked anything but pleased by the fact Byron was flirting with her. "That's what he says, but don't believe him."

Byron turned toward Gaetan and held out his wrists. "Cut me loose," he offered, "and I'll kill you with my bare hands."

Understanding Byron's gesture if not his threat, Gaetan slit his bonds, then handed his knife to Alain to hold. He stepped back to remove his shirt and waited while Byron took off his coat, waistcoat, and shirt. He was surprised by the Englishman's well-muscled physique, but hid it beneath a contemptuous frown.

Seizing an opportunity to incense his rival, Byron handed his clothes to Arielle, and brushed her cheek with a light kiss. He then turned to Gaetan, and, raising his hands, gestured for him to come forward. His headache forgotten, and the stiffness in his neck only a minor hindrance, he backed away, luring Gaetan to follow his lead. The shoreline was strewn with stones worn smooth by the tides, and he moved with cautious agility to avoid tripping.

Accustomed to using brute force rather than the

strategy Byron displayed, Gaetan went for him with a wild lunge. At the last instant, Byron jumped aside and slammed his fist into the back of Gaetan's head as the Acadian roared right past him. Dazed, and shocked by his own clumsiness, Gaetan wheeled around and came back for Byron, but again the Englishman refused to stand still and easily avoided his second blow.

Not about to fall prey to Byron, Gaetan stalked him, moved in slowly, and rather than risk missing with a punch, he threw his whole body against him in an effort to knock him off his feet. Byron twisted free, and slammed a vicious chop to Gaetan's ear. His head ringing, Gaetan tried to shake off the pain, but while the Englishman was proving to be a far tougher opponent than he had anticipated, he still had every intention of beating him senseless.

While the Acadians cheered Gaetan on with great, leaping enthusiasm, Arielle stood silently clutching Byron's clothes. She did not want to watch the gruesome spectacle, but she could not make herself turn away. Gaetan had a searing lust for revenge that kept him coming after Byron long after another man would have tired and grown slow. He absorbed blows without blinking that would have toppled lesser men and finally managed to knock Byron off-balance with a bruising lunge.

Byron pushed against the Acadian, but slipped on a stone, and both he and Gaetan went down in the damp sand. They rolled over and over, a jumble of flying fists and feet. The Acadians' cheers soared to deafening levels as they urged Gaetan on with hoarse cries for blood, while Arielle held her breath in numbed horror. At last Byron gained the upper hand, and, seated astride Gaetan's waist, he drew back his fist to strike a crushing blow.

Reaching out, Gaetan grabbed up a stone, and before Arielle could shout a warning to Byron, the Acadian had slammed the fist-sized rock into Byron's temple. The sound of flesh tearing against bone rang loud and blood sprayed the Acadian's arm and shoulder as Byron fell limp across him. Gaetan shoved him away, and, with a triumphant shout, leaped to his feet and raised both hands above his head.

Sick clear through, Arielle dropped Byron's clothes and rushed to him. He was unconscious rather than dead as she had feared, and she ripped off her apron to stem the flow of blood from the gaping wound in his head. Gaetan would have none of it. He grabbed his knife from Alain, and, shoving Arielle aside, he drew the tip of the blade down Byron's chest to his navel, leaving a thin bloody trail.

"Give me your answer, chérie. Either you marry me or I'll gut your lover like a fish and leave his entrails as a feast for the gulls. Which is it to be, marriage to me or death to him?"

Her apron bright with Byron's blood, all hope of resistance died in Arielle. "Just keep him alive," she begged, "and I'll marry you."

Gaetan turned to Alain. "Take the bastard back out to the ship and tell the captain to tend him. If he dies, it will be God's will." He then reached down to yank Arielle to her feet and with the appreciative crowd still cheering, he led her into the trees.

Thirteen

Arielle stumbled and nearly fell, but Gaetan took no note of her distress. He stomped through the forest, the thick layers of pine needles that carpeted the ground muffling the angry thud of his footsteps. He kept going until they were well past the danger of being seen or overheard by those left in the cove. He then pushed Arielle up against the rough trunk of a spruce and kept his hands on her shoulders.

"I let that man live out of respect for you," he swore, "and for no other reason. Do not give me any cause to regret it."

Still bare-chested, he was wearing Byron's blood like war paint, and, sickened, Arielle had to look away. Hitting Byron with a rock had not been fair.

"You had to cheat to win," she replied.

"Cheat?" Gaetan scoffed at her accusation. "He could just as easily have picked up a stone as I, chérie. Do not fault me for being more resourceful."

"It wasn't a fair fight," Arielle still insisted.

Gaetan pulled her forward slightly, then slammed her back against the spruce. "You have already given me your word. Don't try and go back on it or I won't complete my half of the bargain."

Rebelling at his rough treatment, Arielle grew all

the more hostile. "Why would you want a woman you have to force into marriage?"

Gaetan leaned close to kiss her, but Arielle quickly turned her head and his lips brushed her cheek rather than her mouth. He checked the impulse to slap her, and spoke in a warmly seductive tone. "You know that I love you, Arielle. I would do anything for you."

"No, that's a lie. If you loved me, you would respect my wishes and never demand that I marry you against my will."

Gaetan moved still closer and nibbled her earlobe playfully. "You will soon want me for a husband, Arielle."

"Never," she swore.

Gaetan sank his teeth into her earlobe. He felt her stiffen, but she refused to cry out her pain. Disgusted that she was no easier to control than before, he released her and drew away. "Is this what I can expect from you even after we're wed?"

When Arielle glanced away rather than answer, Gaetan shrugged. "Then you give me no choice about finishing off the Englishman now. Come on, let's go back to the ship. I will toss him overboard before he comes to, and he will drown without even noticing."

"No!"

Gaetan had already taken several steps away, but hesitated and came back. "I thought the terms of our bargain were clear. I spared the Englishman's life in exchange for your hand in marriage. If you are not going to make any attempt to be an agreeable wife, then I might as well kill the man."

Again Gaetan turned away and Arielle ran after him. "No, wait!" she cried. In a frantic attempt to stop him, she grabbed his arm, but as she pulled him to a halt, she saw only the blood on her own hands. It was caked beneath her nails and had streamed through her fingers staining her pale skin with crimson trails. Horrified, the anguished cry she had stifled when he had bit her earlobe tore from her throat in a torrent of hideous shrieks.

Terrified that he might have driven Arielle mad with his threats, Gaetan wrapped her in his arms and forced her mouth against his bare chest to muffle her shrill screams. Despite her temper, he knew her to be a gentle soul, and genuinely afraid he had broken her spirit with the worst of results, he sank to his knees and drew her down with him into the pine needles. He pulled her across his lap, and when at last her piercing cries dissolved into choked sobs, he rocked her as though she were a frightened child.

"I won't harm him, chérie. I won't," he crooned. "I will be the best of husbands, you'll see. I love you more than any Englishman ever could. You're mine now, and you'll be mine forever."

He held Arielle so tightly his arms soon began to ache, but he wouldn't let her go. She was so precious to him, and he dared not take her back to the cove until he had soothed the torment he knew he had caused her. He sat with her for more than an hour, and when she finally looked up at him, all trace of madness had left her eyes. Her expression was now one of profound sorrow, but relieved by that improvement, he did not demand a smile.

"Come, we must go back to the others." Gaetan

rose and helped her to her feet. "We will never speak of our bargain ever again," he promised. "You will become my wife and our children will never suspect how one-sided the love was in the beginning."

Arielle watched Gaetan's lips move, and understood he was babbling on about marriage, but she did not really hear his words.

"You'll let Byron live?"

Annoyed that she doubted him, he again turned cross. "Yes, but you must tell me what he did to inspire such devotion."

Arielle could not explain why it was so much easier to love one man than another. "Love is a mystery," she replied, "and better left as such."

That she could speak of loving a stranger, and an English one at that, broke Gaetan's heart. He framed her face with his hands, and, putting his anger aside, kissed her tenderly. "You'll soon come to love me, Arielle. I promise you will."

Arielle relaxed against him, but the tears that trickled down his chest revealed far more about the depth of her love for Byron than she would ever admit aloud.

When they at last reached the cove, the tide was coming in and most of the Acadians had already returned to the *Incentive.* They rode out to the ship in the last lifeboat, but rather than taking Arielle to her cabin, Gaetan led her into the captain's. She cast an anxious glance around the spacious quarters, but all trace of Fitzpatrick was gone. Gaetan had insisted upon washing her hands in the bay after he had cleaned himself up, but just rinsing away the gore hadn't erased her memory of what she had seen, and, unbearably sad, she sank into a chair at the table.

"What have you done with the captain?"

"I had Alain move him down to the hold. He'll have his crew for company, and help care for your lover. You'll be staying here with me until the settlement is built. I'll fetch your things and bring hot water for a bath. Then I want you to sleep until time for supper. I mean to take very good care of you, chérie. I want you to be happy."

Arielle did not look up as he went out the door. She leaned back in her chair and tried to talk herself into the necessity for living up to the bargain she had made, but her ravaged feelings made coherent thought impossible. She knew what she had to do, but her mind refused to even remotely approach how to go about it. Her sorrow was simply too deep.

Gaetan made two trips to bring her belongings, and after the second, spread her quilt over the captain's bunk. "I found a nice copper tub. It will be an improvement over the old wooden one you had at home."

Arielle remained in her chair, silently observing as he brought in the tub and carried hot water from the galley. He found the captain's soap and towels, and when everything was ready, turned toward her, looking far more pleased with himself than she thought he had any right to. When he took her hand to help her rise, she met his gaze easily.

"Aren't you going to leave?"

"No, why should I? You'll soon be my wife, and there's no need for any secrets between us. It would give me great pleasure to watch you bathe."

Feeling trapped in his embrace, Arielle wondered if she would ever grow accustomed to it. She felt smothered rather than loved, and remained tense, her pose awkward until at last he released her. "Must you take your own pleasure at the expense of mine?" she asked.

Gaetan's eyes narrowed slightly. "Do not test my patience, Arielle. You know I'm not a patient man."

"I don't know what you are anymore."

"Your servant. Your slave."

"I have no need of slaves. Please go."

Gaetan opened his mouth to object, ready to insist that he would damn well have what he had bargained for, but Arielle's downcast expression made such a demand seem barbaric and he leaned down to kiss her cheek before backing away. "Bathe, then, and rest. I will try and remember that we'll have a lifetime together."

It wasn't until he was gone that Arielle realized she had dug her fingernails so deeply into her palms that she had drawn blood. She hurriedly shoved her hands into the warm bathwater and then shook them dry. She did not trust Gaetan to leave her alone for long, and trembled with dread as she removed her clothes.

She was no innocent virgin who had no idea what to expect from a man. Indeed, her mother had been far too wise and sympathetic a woman to have let her grow up in the complete ignorance of men as so many girls did, so she had faced her wedding night with a delicious excitement rather than fear. If making love with Bernard had not been as beautiful an experience as her mother had described, it had at least been warm and sweet.

As she slipped down into the bathwater, a blissful calm replaced the tension in her limbs and she sighed softly. Closing her eyes, she leaned her head back and let her mind drift to the sunlit afternoon when she and Byron had first made love. The ecstasy they had shared would remain one of her most precious memories. It was much too soon to forget Byron, and, crowded with fond memories of him and Bernard, there was no room at all in her shattered heart for Gaetan.

The water was losing its heat, and knowing pursuing old dreams would only increase her pain, she straightened up, and then leaned forward to wash her hair. She was already beginning to yawn, and left the tub as soon as she had rinsed her hair. Wrapped in one towel, she dried her hair on another, and then after donning a fresh camisole and drawers, she climbed upon the captain's bunk, snuggled down into the familiar folds of her quilt and fell asleep.

Sorely tempted to help Arielle bathe, Gaetan could think of only one distraction intriguing enough to divert his attention from the lovely young woman. He grabbed a lantern, and taking Eduard Boudreaux with him, went down to the hold to see Byron. Unlike the other captives, the badly injured man had not been bound hand and foot, but lay unconscious at the bottom of the ladder where Alain had dropped him. Gaetan bent beside him, and after listening to the wounded man's shallow breathing for a moment, he glanced up at Eduard.

"How does he look to you?"

Eduard shook his head. "I don't think he'll last the night."

Torn by a thirst for vengeance that made him long to see Byron dead, and the equally strong need to keep him alive to control Arielle, Gaetan had to force himself to think clearly. For a man used to relying on his intuition, rather than pondering alternatives, this was a difficult choice, but because his desire for Arielle outweighed his lust for revenge, he decided Byron had to be given the best chance to survive.

He dared not allow Arielle to tend Byron, for that would only make her all the more attached to him. He looked around for a suitable substitute. He straightened up, went to the captain, pulled a knife from his belt, and cut the man's bonds. He pointed to Byron. "Do what you can for him," he ordered in French.

Fitzpatrick rose, and shifted stiffly to loosen his muscles before he approached Byron. He knelt at his side, and swiftly came to the same dreary conclusion as Eduard. "I'm a ship's captain, not a physician, but I—"

While Gaetan could not comprehend Fitzpatrick's words, the whining tone of his voice clearly projected the man's fears. Gaetan reached down to grab the captain by the scruff of the neck and jerked him to his feet. Relying on volume to convey his message since he had no one to translate, he yelled, "Keep him alive!" When the captain's dark eyes widened in terror, he was certain he had been understood.

He had Eduard fetch a bucket of water and rags and waited as the captain washed the blood from Byron's face and neck. Once that grisly task was finished, Fitzpatrick gestured as though he were pulling a needle through cloth, and Gaetan sent Eduard back up on deck to borrow sewing gear from one of his sisters. When his friend returned, he set the lantern down beside Byron's head and took a perverse delight in watching Fitzpatrick repair the bloody gash in his rival's head. If Byron survived, his hair would cover the scar, and, disappointed he had not disfigured the handsome young man, Gaetan vowed to ruin his looks if they ever fought again.

It would have been a simple matter to kick the unconscious man in the face and shatter his nose and front teeth, but Gaetan deemed such brutality unnecessary when Byron was already so gravely injured. When the captain finished his handiwork and snipped the thread, he had Eduard collect the sewing equipment and fetch drinking water for the prisoners. He handed the captain the cup, and enjoyed making him hold it while each of the captives drank his fill. He nodded toward Byron, but while Fitzpatrick lifted his head and tried to coax him into taking a sip, all the water trickled down the wounded man's chin.

Gaetan shrugged off Fitzpatrick's questioning glance and turned to Eduard. "See that the captain watches him closely. I don't want him to die of neglect." Leaving his friend to stand guard, he went back up on deck. As he rounded the bow, the happiness radiating from the faces of the Acadians leaning against the rail made his chest swell with pride.

The families that had left Grand Pré heavily burdened with grief were filled with optimism now, and he basked in the warmth of their grateful smiles. He had believed not merely in the desperate imperative of regaining their freedom but the possibility of it, too. He had had the courage to act where others were too frightened to think, let alone plan, and now that he was openly acknowledged as their leader, he knew it was because he had earned that right.

Preferring to sleep on the deck that night, the men had begun dismantling the sails and were stretching ropes between the masts and rail to support the canvas and create tents of varying size and design. Admiring their ingenuity, Gaetan paid them compliments, but insisted a path be kept clear so they could all still traverse the deck and go below without difficulty. Not that he planned to visit the imprisoned crew often, but he did want them watched, and closely.

Lonely for Arielle, he brushed away the hands that reached out to offer congratulatory pats and went below to the cabin he intended to share with his reluctant fiancée. He was pleased to find she had followed his suggestion to rest, and, after lighting the oil lamps, turned their wicks down low to provide a dim illumination that wouldn't disturb her. He removed the water from the tub, then carried it up on deck where anyone else who wished to bathe might use it. He returned with the few belongings his sisters had brought for him, and after tossing Robert Fitzpatrick's clothes out into the companionway, stored them in lockers.

Arielle's skirt had slipped off the chair where her other clothes lay, and as he picked it up, he felt the weight of an object in one of the pockets. Curious, he withdrew Bernard's portrait, and was shocked to discover that not only had he had to drag her out of the arms of her English lover, she was still clinging to her late husband as well. Tired of the competition from a dead man, he was about to carry the miniature up on deck and fling it over the side when he realized it would prove far more valuable in striking another bargain.

Delighted with his own cleverness, he hid it at the back of the locker containing his shirts and left to bring some of the soup the women were cooking for supper. When he returned with a kettle, he placed it on the table and then went back for bowls and spoons before turning up the lamps and waking Arielle. "Come, chérie," he coaxed. "We have not shared supper in too long, and I insist that you join me tonight."

Arielle had been sleeping so deeply that she needed a moment to recall just were she was. She sat up, and, after only a brief survey of the unfamiliar surroundings, she remembered how she had come to occupy them. Gaetan had placed her clothes on the foot of the bunk, and, grateful that he had his back turned while he filled their bowls, she got up and pulled them on. As she smoothed out the folds of her skirt, she immediately missed Bernard's miniature. Thinking that it must have fallen out of her pocket, she bent down to look for it before putting on her stockings and shoes.

"Have you lost something?" Gaetan asked solicitously.

"Yes, Bernard's portrait. It was in my pocket, and now it's gone."

Gaetan replaced the lid on the kettle before turning toward her. "Could you have dropped it in the woods?"

Heartsick that she might have lost it, Arielle sat down on the edge of the bunk. "I don't know. I suppose I could have. I'm afraid I'll never be able to find the place we went though. Could you?"

Gaetan came forward to take her hands and pull her to her feet. "I understand how precious Bernard's memory is to you, chérie, and I will find your missing miniature even if I must crawl through the whole forest on my hands and knees."

His smile held a touching sincerity, and Arielle squeezed his fingers slightly as she crossed barefooted to the table. "I hope that such an effort proves unnecessary, but I would greatly appreciate your help in finding it."

"Consider it found, beloved. Now I'm afraid we have only pea soup tonight, but it's flavored with ham and will at least be filling."

Arielle looked down at the thick soup, and thought of the crew. "What are you feeding the prisoners?"

"If you're worried about your lover, he's alive, if not feeling all that well, so I doubt he'll want much for supper. The rest of the crew will have the same meals we do. After all, I can't expect them to fell trees and construct a fort without nourishment."

Arielle wanted to hear more about Byron, but when Gaetan took a spoonful of soup, and then another, she realized he had said all he would. Because a show of interest might only prompt him to abuse

Byron all the more, she forced herself to sample the soup, too. Warm and rich, it tasted of home, and she finished her bowl almost as quickly as Gaetan.

Gaetan had led Arielle to the table before she had donned her cap, and he reached over to entwine his fingers in her hair. "You washed your hair for me," he remarked with a wide grin. "Perhaps now that you've agreed to marry me, you don't find the prospect of sleeping with me unappealing."

Arielle put her hand over his in an attempt to pull free, but he refused to let go. His green eyes sparkled with a teasing light, but she was in no mood to appreciate his light-hearted flirting. "I simply wanted clean hair," she explained. "I didn't know when I'd next have the chance to bathe."

"You my bathe whenever you wish," Gaetan promised. "Whatever you need, I'll provide it. You need only ask. Now kiss me."

Using her hair as a golden leash, Gaetan pulled her close, and when she raised her lips to his without objecting, he thought his patience was beginning to pay off.

When he chose to be gentle, as he was now, his kiss was not unpleasant, but Arielle felt not even a faint glimmer of affection, let alone the thrill of love. She did not fight him, but she did not respond with any enthusiasm, either. She just waited, holding her breath until he drew away.

Disappointed by the meek acceptance he knew he had demanded, Gaetan left the table to bring a bottle of brandy he had found while cleaning out the captain's lockers. "I think we ought to celebrate our freedom." The cabin's only beverage containers were pewter tankards, but he was certain they would do. He poured a small amount of brandy in his own, and twice as much in hers. He handed a tankard to Arielle and raised his.

"To a new life," he proposed.

Arielle tapped the lip of her tankard against his and took a sip. Not used to drinking anything stronger than wine or ale, she wrinkled her nose and shuddered. "That's awful."

"I think it's delicious. Try another sip, and I'm sure you'll agree."

Arielle knew Gaetan was trying to get her to be so drunk she would not object to his amorous advances. The chance to become too drunk to be aware of how they spent the night had a definite appeal, but after a second sip, her stomach lurched painfully. She set her tankard down with a thud that sent droplets of brandy flying over the rim and grabbed her waist.

"What's wrong?"

"I don't know. Perhaps it's the brandy, but I just don't feel well. I think I'd better lie down."

Arielle's face had grown so pale, Gaetan instantly believed her. He left his chair and offered her a hand to reach the bunk. "I seem to recall your telling me quite recently that you were never ill."

Arielle remembered her comment well. "That was the day you were arrested." The same day she had met Byron. She closed her eyes, swung her legs up on the bunk, and curled into a tight ball. "It seems like so long ago."

"It was little more than two weeks, chérie, not that long at all."

"No," Arielle murmured sleepily. "So much has happened since then. Too much."

Her hair had fallen across her eyes in a silken stream and Gaetan swept it aside and leaned down to kiss her cheek. Finding there was room enough, he sat down beside her and rubbed her back as he had that afternoon. "You are a sensitive young woman, and this has been a very trying day for us all. Your basket's here. Tell me what to mix and I'll prepare a remedy for you."

Arielle shook her head, for she had no potions to cure a broken heart. "Neither of us got much sleep last night," she reminded him in a lazy whisper. "Aren't you exhausted, too?"

"No, I'm far too happy to be tired. This has been the best day of my life. I've wanted you for so long, chérie, and—" Overcome with emotion, he paused to find words pretty enough to express his true feelings. Then, embarrassed by his inability to do so, he leaned down to kiss her again, but she was already sleeping soundly.

He straightened up, and, dismayed that he had had the woman of his dreams within reach only to have her again slip away, brought an anguished moan to his lips. "Patience," he cautioned. He took a deep breath, and, resigned to waiting another day to sample more of Arielle's affection, he covered her with her quilt, returned the kettle and dishes to the galley, and went up on deck where the chill of the evening breeze only partially cooled his ardor.

Ducking under the ropes supporting the canvas shelters, Gaetan strolled the deck offering everyone hope and praise. The night was clear, the heavens bright with stars, and he considered it the best of omens. They might have been driven to the opposite side of the Bay of Fundy, but they were still close to Acadia, and they would soon feel at home.

Alain leaned against the rail at Gaetan's side and folded his arms across his chest. "I thought you would have better things to do tonight than admire the stars."

"I do," Gaetan promptly agreed, "but there will be plenty of time for Arielle later."

"I would not waste what time I have now," Alain advised with a sly chuckle.

"That's the difference between us," Gaetan exclaimed. "I prefer to savor the possibilities for a while."

Alain considered Gaetan's response for a long moment, and then let out a low whistle. "You've obviously thought of a possibility that I'd overlooked. You're wise to wait until you're certain Arielle is not carrying the Englishman's babe."

Incensed by that piece of unwanted advice, Gaetan moved away from the rail, but he had to shove his hands into his pockets to keep from wrapping them around his friend's neck and squeezing every bit of life out of him. "Don't ever mention that man to me again. I won't have you speaking his name in the same breath with Arielle's. Do you understand?"

Alain didn't need to see Gaetan's face clearly to feel his rage. "Forgive me. I meant only to compliment you on your cleverness."

"I'd prefer loyalty. Now, see that someone is guarding the prisoners better than we were guarded. I want to be free more than one day."

* * *

Robert Fitzpatrick had been at sea for all his adult life, and because disagreements between sailors often turned violent, he had sewn up many a gruesome wound. In his opinion, the gash in Byron's scalp had been more bloody than deep, and upon close examination, he felt certain the young man had suffered only a concussion. He covered him with his own coat, and cradled his head in his lap.

Lost in a painful haze, Byron drifted in and out of consciousness. He felt the hardness of wood rather than the comfort of a fine mattress supporting his back, and choked on the stale air, but the agony tearing his thoughts kept him from complaining aloud. All he could manage was an occasional moan, and not recognizing the voice that responded, he felt very lost and alone. He opened his eyes, but finding only a disappointing darkness, he closed them and sank down into the unceasing pain.

Fourteen

It was the unaccustomed feel of the weight of Gaetan's arm curled around her waist that awoke Arielle shortly after dawn. Startled, she gasped in surprise then remembered how they had come to be together. She had not gotten up again after lying down after supper and she was still fully clothed, as was Gaetan. The compact bed was barely wide enough for two, and he had wrapped himself around her to make the best use of what little space they had. While she had not felt him join her in the bunk, she doubted he had been with her long, for surely they would have been so crowded she would have been jostled awake long before this.

Tears welled up in Arielle's eyes as she imagined herself waking up in Gaetan's arms every morning for the rest of her life. She tried to blink them away but failed, and they trickled down her cheeks and soaked her pillow. No price would have been too high to pay for Byron's life, but she did not know how to conceal her overwhelming sorrow. She could not cry all the time, nor could she pretend a happiness she did not feel.

Burdened by the fears and doubts she could not assuage, she could not lie still, but when she attempted to slip off the bunk without waking Gaetan, he immediately tightened his hold on her waist to stop her.

"Where are you going?" he asked.

"Nowhere. I just wanted to get up."

Gaetan raised up slightly. "Don't. Stay with me instead." He kissed her forehead, her temple, her cheek, then nuzzled the warm curve of her neck. "How do you feel?"

The slight growth of his beard tickled terribly, and she had to fight her natural impulse to draw away. "All right. At least I think I do."

"Good." Again stretching out behind her, Gaetan drew Arielle closer to his chest. She did not resist his move, but rather than relaxing against him as he had hoped she would, she was merely limp. He wanted to make love to her so badly. He ached to feel the softness of her bare skin against his own, but at the same time, he wanted her to give her love freely as she had to Bernard and the Englishman. That she would stubbornly withhold it pained him badly.

He propped his head on his elbow so he could study her expression. "What is it about me that you find so objectionable?" he asked. "Why don't I please you?"

Arielle glanced up at him. Uncombed, his dark curls dipped low on his forehead giving him a boyish appearance that didn't match the insolent set of his mouth. With his dashing good looks and unusually charming grin, he ought to have had an equally attractive personality, but sadly he was demanding rather than considerate. He was angry with her more often than not, and she did not want to provoke him again by reciting a list of his faults. Instead, she tried to smile.

"Our temperaments are very different, Gaetan, but that really doesn't matter anymore, does it? We're together, and there's no reason to emphasize our differences when we ought to be striving for harmony."

Confused by her conciliatory tone, Gaetan did not pursue his question. He laced her fingers in his and brought her hand to his lips. "I want us to be as close as a man and woman can possibly be. A man has every right to expect that from his wife, doesn't he?"

"Yes, he does." Arielle also believed a woman had a right to certain expectations, but love and tenderness had had no place in their bargain. She had made a simple trade, as though they were dealing with horses rather than human lives. She could feel Gaetan watching her, and when the force of his gaze made her so uncomfortable, she did not know how she was ever going to be a real wife to him.

He leaned down to kiss her, and, caught by surprise, she again failed to provide an affectionate response. Before she could offer an apology, or promise to try to do better, he released her hand and, bringing his knee up into the small of her back, shoved her right off the bunk. As she rolled over the side, she barely managed to catch herself in time to remain upright.

Moving out of his reach, she grabbed the back of a chair at the table for support. "You have such little regard for my feelings, I doubt you have even the vaguest notion of what love truly is. I promised to marry you, and I will, but I'll not allow you to mistreat me."

Gaetan swung his legs over the side of the bunk and stared at her coldly. "You'll not give me orders," he countered darkly. "You'll do as I say."

Arielle turned her back on him, and her silence was as eloquent a protest of his insufferable domination as any she could have spoken aloud.

Gaetan jammed his feet into his shoes. He started for the door, but then turned back and pointed at her. "I will give you exactly one month before I take you as my wife. That's time enough for you to appreciate the consequences of defying me, and for me to be certain our first child isn't an Englishman's brat!"

He slammed the door on his way out, and certain he would not be back for a long while, Arielle slid into the chair. She had been badly shaken by that furious outburst, but as she went over it in her mind trying to find a place where she could have changed its bitter outcome, she realized Gaetan had unwittingly given her a sliver of hope. He had mentioned children, and this had not been the first time. He apparently assumed they would have babies, but she had not conceived in three years of trying with Bernard.

She sat up straight and forced herself to think rather than simply fret. If she convinced Gaetan that in all probability she was barren and would never give him a son, maybe he would refuse her for a wife.

She decided to wait to talk with him about it until the end of the month he had given her. The possibility she might have conceived in the few times she had been with Byron was extremely remote, but she could use that to her advantage, too. After all, if she had been with two men, and could give neither a child, why would Gaetan want her? She had faint hope that the ploy would work on the belligerent man, but it was at least a start, and with thirty more days to consider her options, she might think of another excellent reason why she would make the worst of wives. By that time, Byron would surely have recovered from his injuries, and be able to defend himself. At the very least, he would know better than to trust Gaetan to wage a fair fight. Feeling as though she had been given a reprieve mere seconds before her execution, she rose intending to prepare for the day, but a sudden wave of dizziness sent her back to the bunk.

At high tide, the ship was rocking gently in the water, but, unaccustomed to sleeping anywhere but her own bed, Arielle assumed it was only the latest wretched confrontation with Gaetan that was making her ill. She would get up later and make some chamomile tea, but for now, she said a silent prayer for Byron and fell asleep.

Captain Fitzpatrick had slept nearly as fitfully as Byron and awoke feeling ill-used and sore. The hold was dry but musty, and the sunlight streaming in through the open hatch caught him in the eye with a painful glare. He squinted and tried to move without jostling Byron too badly. When his eyes had adjusted to the morning light, he looked for the guard and found him leaning against the ladder. His body was striped by shadow, but it didn't hide the musket in his hands.

"We all need to get up and walk about," he called.

The Acadian guard did not respond.

Fitzpatrick glanced down at Byron. The young man was breathing easier, and with only a slight shake, came awake. "Well, you're still with us after all. I'm afraid most of my men bet against your recovery. You must be thirsty. Here, let me get you a drink."

Although the captain took care to ease Byron's head off his lap very gently, the Virginian was assailed by such excruciating pain that he cried out. He had never had such hideous dreams, but now that he was awake, he felt even worse. The captain pressed a tin cup to his lips, but Byron choked on the water. "Wait," he begged, and after drawing a breath to steady himself, he was able to take a drink.

"My head feels as though it's on fire. What happened?"

"Damned if I know," the captain replied. "You were taken ashore, and brought back unconscious. I had to sew up a gash in your head, but I think you'd already lost a lot of blood before you were brought back. Can't you remember what happened?"

Byron doubted there was an inch of his body that didn't ache. He ran his hand over his bare chest, and wondered what had happened to his clothes. "My head hurts too much to think," he replied in a hoarse whisper.

"Well, we're all curious," Fitzpatrick explained. "Maybe they plan to beat all of us."

Hazy memories of a fistfight hovered on the edge of Byron's memory, but he couldn't recall who had been involved. Since he had obviously lost the bout, he knew he must have been one of the combatants, but he could not name the other man. He had never had trouble recalling his past, and now to find a piece of it missing was deeply disturbing. Before he had time to worry about his present situation, however, two men came down the ladder. Their faces were vaguely familiar, but he couldn't name them.

Alain and Eduard moved along the line of bound seamen and soldiers. They freed only one at a time, and then sent him on up the ladder before cutting the next man's bonds. When only the captain and Byron remained, Alain reached for the captain's arm.

"Where are you taking us?" he asked.

Alain gestured toward the ladder with the butt of his musket.

"You can't leave Mr. Barclay alone down here, he's too weak to even sit up. He needs looking after, and food."

Neither understanding nor caring about the captain's complaints, Eduard grabbed him by the arm and started him up the ladder, but Fitzpatrick turned back to Byron.

"I'm sure we'll all be back soon. Don't lose heart."

Byron let his head roll to the side with the gentle motion of the ship. At first the noise from up on deck seemed a constant hum, but gradually he began to distinguish individual sounds. There was the staccato beat of children's running feet, an occasional burst of their playful laughter, and sweetly feminine voices calling back and forth. Where were the men? he wondered. It was as though he were lying in the basement of a crowded house, eavesdropping on the residents but unable to join them.

He watched the sunlight move across the hold, and knew the day was passing, but he dozed off so often, he lost all track of time. He knew there was somewhere he had to be, but had forgotten why. Wherever that place was, though, he was positive it was far more comfortable than the *Incentive*'s hold.

Thirsty, he fumbled with the cup, and had to struggle for several minutes to raise himself and scoop up a drink from the bucket of water Fitzpatrick had thoughtfully left at his side. When he finally managed it, he was inordinantly proud of himself. Hoping to feel better, he tried to relax and let his body float with the ship, and gradually his pain began to lessen. Encouraged, the next time he wanted a drink, he sat up too quickly, and instantly a bolt of white-hot pain seared through his brain. The tin cup slipped from his hand, and he didn't awaken again until noon when Gaetan shook him.

"I've brought you some food," the Acadian announced.

Byron looked up, not recalling the man's name, but certain they weren't friends. He had not understood Gaetan's words, but the bowl of soup he held out to him was message enough. He tried to prop himself on his elbow, but when Gaetan put the soup down in front of him, he found he couldn't hold onto the spoon. His knuckles were scraped and swollen, and his hands simply refused to work as they should.

Gaetan had not really expected to find Byron so badly incapacitated and grew concerned. He pulled a hunk of bread from his pocket, broke off a piece, and after dipping it into the broth, pointed it toward Byron's mouth. "Eat," he coaxed. "I need you alive."

Byron was too sore to be hungry, but recognizing

the need for food, took the bite Gaetan offered and chewed it slowly. Not having eaten in more than a day, his stomach contracted painfully and he closed his eyes to force away the resulting wave of nausea. In that dark instant, he saw his path clearly, and when he again looked up at Gaetan, he made his expression completely blank. He accepted the bread the Acadian pushed toward him without so much as a flicker of protest. He ate with the gentle obedience of a dog, but all the while he was planning his next move, and the next.

By the time Gaetan had fed Byron the meager meal, he was deeply troubled. At first he had thought the Englishman was simply in pain, but now he feared Byron's injury had affected his mind, for he spoke not at all and his eyes were without their former sparkle. He had known one man who had never fully recovered from a severe beating and he was afraid he was looking at another. Appalled by that possibility, he carried the empty bowl to the ladder, then looked back at his prisoner in an attempt to convince himself that all he had promised Arielle was to keep Byron alive.

Still, he did not know what he was going to tell her. By the time he had returned the bowl to the galley, however, he had decided she would be better off not knowing what had happened to her former lover. He would continue to report that Byron was alive, but nothing more.

After Gaetan had gone, Byron lay back, stretched his arms wide, and took in a deep breath. He had never felt worse, but at least he could still think. It had grown very quiet up on deck and he supposed everyone was eating. There could not possibly be enough rations stowed on board to feed more than two hundred people all winter, so the Acadians would have to hunt and fish to prepare for the cold months ahead. Maybe that was where the men had gone, to search for game. He hoped it was plentiful, because he was going to need more than watery soup if he was going to lead an escape.

Even flat on his back, and aching all over, Byron began to smile. Gaetan had succeeded in taking control of the *Incentive*, but he intended to take it back.

When the captain and the others returned at sundown, he quizzed the man at length.

"We spent the day felling trees," Fitzpatrick explained. "They're building a stockade to encircle their settlement."

Byron knew he had been ashore, but couldn't remember anything about it. "Near the water?"

"No, inland, so it will be hidden by the trees. They chose a clearing, and we were put to work extending it." He mopped his forehead on his sleeve. "I've never worked so hard in my whole life. Had they had whips, I feel certain they would have beaten us, but fortunately no one did."

Byron insisted the captain describe the day in more detail, and then, his curiosity satisfied on all but one point, he changed the subject. "Did you see Arielle?"

Fitzpatrick shook his head. "No. Several women brought stew and bread for us at noon, but she wasn't among them."

"And you didn't see her on deck when you came aboard just now?"

"No, but then, I wasn't looking for her."

"Well, tomorrow, look!" Byron fell silent as a guard appeared, then another carrying a kettle of thick corn chowder. They were all given bowls, but no spoons, and half a loaf of bread. Byron took his time, and ate so slowly, all the others finished long before him. He played with his bread, eating some and breaking the rest into tiny bits he laid out in a row and slammed flat with the heel of his hand.

"My God, man, what are you doing?" Fitzpatrick asked.

Byron replied in a low whisper, "I want our guards to think I've had all the sense knocked out of me. The more pathetic I look, the easier it will be for us to escape."

"Escape!" Fitzpatrick quickly glanced over his shoulder to make certain the guards weren't listening, then remembered they wouldn't understand his outburst even if they were. One was watching Byron play with his bread, but his companion was looking the other way and the captain relaxed slightly. "How are we going to manage that?"

"I don't know yet, but if the Acadians can do it, then we surely can."

When Byron glanced toward him, Fitzpatrick wasn't at all certain his battered friend *hadn't* had all the sense knocked out of him, but he grasped for the faint hope the young man offered. "I used my life savings to buy the *Incentive,* and I'm willing to do whatever I must to save her."

Byron nodded, and continued to flatten bits of his bread.

* * *

More than a week passed before Arielle saw Byron again. Gaetan had not confined her to her cabin, but neither had he rescinded his order that she not seek out the Englishman. He had provided terse reports on the slowness of the injured man's recovery, but they had been grudging and without detail. Believing Byron was still convalescing in the hold, she was startled to find him among those returning with the work party that had gone ashore that morning.

Elated that he was well enough to help build the settlement, she left the child whose skinned knee she had just finished tending to dip below the ropes supporting his family's tent. She rounded the forward mast, and approached the entrance of the hold. After all, Gaetan certainly could not accuse her of sneaking off to see Byron if the Englishman just happened to walk by her while she was on deck.

He was the last out of the lifeboat, and moving more slowly than the others on deck. Arielle was shocked by the way his badly soiled pants and shirt hung lose on a newly gaunt frame. Unkempt, he obviously hadn't shaved or combed his hair since he had been taken captive, but even thin and filthy, he still looked good to her.

She dared not step too close, but certain she would catch his eye, she was badly disappointed when he failed to look her way. Not wanting the moment to pass without at least a glance, she waited until Byron had reached the hatch and risked whispering his name. He turned toward her, and she smiled, the love she could no longer hide lighting her face from within, but he looked through her rather than at her. His expression was faintly puzzled, as though he had heard her speak but couldn't locate the source of the sound.

Arielle was standing no more than five feet away, and to receive a blank stare from Byron rather than the same joyous smile she had given him brought an anguished cry to her lips. Her spirits crushed, she turned and fled for the rail. Two more lifeboats were returning from shore, and Gaetan was in the last. Sick with anger and fear, she still knew better than to confront him on deck where he would consider such behavior as unbefitting the role of loyal wife she had promised to play. She retrieved her basket, then went to her cabin to wait for him to join her for supper as he did each night.

She sat on the bunk, and unable to accept the only reasonable excuse for Byron's disinterested glance, she twisted her hands in her lap and fought to ignore the tears stinging her eyes. His appearance had changed so greatly she had scarcely recognized him. But the deeper truth of their brief encounter was far more shocking: his body might have recovered from the abuse he had suffered at Gaetan's hands, but not his mind.

"He didn't even know me!" she sobbed, and no longer able to hold back her tears, she cried for the man she had lost. Then to add to her pain, she began to blame herself, for if she had not become involved with Byron, Gaetan would never have made him a target for his rage. Byron would still be whole and fit, rather than the pitiable creature she had seen shuffling along the deck.

When Gaetan at last came through the door, handsomely groomed and wearing clean clothes, she flew at him and pounded his chest with both fists. "You lied to me!" she screamed. "I saw Byron. He'll never be well!"

Gaetan caught her wrists and yanked her close. "How could you have seen him? I told you to stay away from him. Do you think you can disobey me without having to pay the price?"

Arielle fought to break free, twisting and writhing but he refused to release her. Finally, her strength sapped by the unrelenting tragedy her life had become, she stood still, but far from defeated. "I saw him when he came back from shore, and he didn't even know me."

Gaetan relaxed his hold, drew her close, and rested his cheek against her cap. "I'd hoped you'd never find out," he finally admitted. "Perhaps in time—"

"No," Arielle sobbed. "Time won't heal that kind of wound. His mind's gone."

Hoping to put an end to her sorrow so she would begin to think of him, Gaetan swung her up into his arms and carried her to the bunk. He sat down, keeping her cradled in a warm embrace. "I fought him for you, chérie, and he would have killed me had he been able. You mustn't hate me just because I won."

Arielle didn't hate him. She just wanted to be free of him. The rest of the passengers treated him like a god for delivering them from the dread of deportation, but his touch sickened her, and she sat stiffly on his lap, like a beautiful child who is passed around by eager relatives when all she wants is to be left alone.

"The settlement is going well," Gaetan assured her. "We'll move the tents in a few days, and I know being on land will lift your spirits. The forest is very beautiful, and while I've not found Bernard's portrait as yet, I'm sure that I will."

Arielle didn't reply. She still had three weeks before he demanded more from her than silent obedience, but the painful ache that filled her chest and clogged her throat would never be gone by then. Utterly devoid of hope, she did not hear a word he said. Instead, she longed for the sweet release of death, for surely oblivion could not be as painful as serving a life sentence in Gaetan's arms.

Shunning Arielle had been the most difficult thing Byron had ever done, and now, seated in the hold, he felt her pain as deeply as his own. He had steeled himself against the torment of seeing her, for he had known he could not greet her with the enthusiasm he felt and continue to act docile and confused with his guards. He had known precisely what he would have to do when he saw her, and had done it, but he had not dreamed how badly it would hurt.

He could still hear the slight catch in her voice as she had called his name. Despite the argument that had been raging between them when Gaetan had commandeered the ship, her expression had told him how much she still cared. To have been unable to claim and return that devotion was worse torture than being made to work harder than a slave.

Exhausted, his legs were drawn up, his arms resting across his knees. Their guards would soon bring their supper, but in the meanwhile, he was confident they would be left alone. He turned to Fitzpatrick, who sat next to him.

"Several men went hunting today. More might go tomorrow. That improves our odds for escape. We haven't enough men to take everyone captive again, so as soon as the families have been moved off the ship, we'll seize her and sail away."

Fitzpatrick raised his brows and let out a dejected sigh. "Didn't you see what's happened to the sails? They'll be useless spread out all over the deck as they are now."

Byron had noticed the Acadians' forest of tents, but he waved the captain's objection aside. "At high tide we can weigh anchor and drift out of the cove on the current. We can rerig the sails long before we reach the Atlantic. Or, if you don't care to keep the *Incentive,* we could always escape in a lifeboat."

Fitzpatrick snorted in disgust. "I'm not leaving here without my ship."

"Fine, then we agree."

The captain complied with a reluctant nod, but as he and Byron continued to plan their escape, the young man's ideas began to sound better and better. "You've not mentioned Arielle," he pointed out. "How does she fit into your plans?"

Byron hesitated a long moment before replying. "I prize her more highly than you do this ship. I won't leave here without her."

"That may complicate things considerably."

"I don't care. There's no point in escaping if I have to leave Arielle behind."

Fitzpatrick opened his mouth to tell Byron love had turned him into a fool, but doubting his opinion would matter, he chose not to make the effort. He could smell the savory aroma of pea soup as the guard started down the ladder with their supper, and licked his lips. He would never say a good word about the men of Grand Pré, but he had to admit their women could certainly cook.

As they worked the next day, Byron watched the Acadians more closely. The ring of spruce that formed the stockade was nearly complete, and construction would soon begin on cabins. While he was at work burying the base of the last of the trees that had been felled to create the circular wall, he repeated the escape plan silently in an endless chant.

He didn't want a fight that might cost them the lives of any more men, nor did he want to endanger the lives of the Acadian women and children. High tide came at midmorning and late at night now, and the longer he thought about it, the more prudent a late-night escape seemed. He braced the trunk of the spruce with his shoulder as three seamen packed dirt into the trench to secure it. This was the hardest physical work he had ever done, but he relished every precious second, for with each beat of his heart he felt himself growing stronger. They might not escape tonight, but they would soon, and he would be ready.

Fifteen

"It may take more than a day to transfer the tents to the stockade," Gaetan said, "but I want to have a celebration tonight. Everyone needs it."

Arielle remained seated on the bunk where the dizziness that had continued to plague her each morning wasn't quite so severe. Attributing her discomfort to the strain of her unsettling existence, she had not bothered to look for a deeper cause. That it seldom lasted long had convinced her it was nothing serious.

"We do have a good reason to celebrate," she agreed without enthusiasm. "Is there something I can do to help prepare?"

Searching his mind for a suitable chore, Gaetan frowned slightly. "You might ask my sisters if they need any help moving."

Arielle nodded, for his sisters were sweet young women whose company she enjoyed. "How long will you be gone?"

Gaetan came close to kiss her cheek. "I hope to shoot enough game this morning, then we'll have the afternoon to roast the meat. Why, will you miss me?"

"I just wondered if I ought to move our things is all."

"No, we'll stay on board until our cabin's finished. Another few days and our first house will be ready to move into, but until then, I'd rather not sleep in a tent."

"I would rather not, either, but don't you have to set an example?"

Gaetan rubbed his hand across his brow. "I've set us free, and begun our new town. That will have to be example enough for now." Arielle was looking down at her tightly clasped hands, and Gaetan had no idea what she was thinking, but she looked far from happy and that pained him.

"Our house will be twice the size of your old one," he boasted, "and in another year or so, I'll build us another. You'll be happy here, chérie, if you just give it a chance."

She knew he was too proud to beg her to give him a chance, but she doubted she would ever be happy again. The thought of Byron being made to work on a house she would share with Gaetan was painful to contemplate. She rested a while longer after Gaetan left, and then wanting to have her own things in order before she volunteered her services elsewhere, she looked through the lockers in the captain's cabin.

Although Gaetan had not continued to share her bunk, he had left his belongings there, and when she came to a stack of rumpled shirts, she took them out to fold. Tangled in a sleeve, Bernard's miniature slid out with them and struck her toe as it fell. Astonished, she picked it up and held it to her heart. That the precious portrait had not been lost all this time but was right there in her cabin brought forth first a furious anger, and then an icy wave of disgust.

Would Gaetan ever have given it back to her? she wondered. The fact he had put it away where it would be safe rather than hurling it into the bay made it seem likely that he did intend to return it someday, obviously at his own convenience. Saddened that he had lied to her, she felt the chains of their reprehensible bargain tightening around her. Everything was wrong, every last thing, but how could she escape him without betraying the promise she had made to save Byron?

Byron was working on the second cabin being built inside the stockade. He had quickly learned how to notch the ends of logs to make them fit together so closely mud could scarcely be forced into the cracks between, but he never stopped watching what took place around him. When he saw Gaetan lead a hunting party off into the woods, he could barely contain a triumphant shout. He looked up, searched for Captain Fitzpatrick, and when he found him sharpening an ax nearby, he caught his guard's attention, raised the tool he had been using and, gaining permission to sharpen it as well, walked over to the captain.

"Gaetan just left with six men. While conditions aren't ideal, this might be the best chance we're likely to have to escape and I'm taking it."

Fitzpatrick straightened up and pretended to test the sharpness of his blade. They had discussed escaping so often he did not shout over the pounding of his heart about the need to reconsider, but simply nodded. "I'll pass the word."

His men often sang sea chanties while they worked and, knowing their guards could not follow the words, he began one with a haunting chorus that cautioned silence, stealth, and the speed of the wind. He nodded as his men glanced his way, then shared the message with what was left of the contingent of soldiers who had originally been assigned to guard the Acadians during the voyage.

The men worked a few minutes longer, then on the last note of the chanty, they attacked the guards they now outnumbered. Fast and brutal, each knew better than to allow any of the guards to fire his weapon and bring the hunting party running back to shift the advantage to the Acadians once more. Some skirmishes were more violent than others, but, caught by surprise, the Acadians were quickly subdued without any suffering permanent harm.

After the prisoners' hands were tied, they were marched into the first completed cabin. Byron left two of the colonial soldiers to guard them, and ran back to the shore with the newly freed men. Not wanting to display the arms they had just recovered and give away their plot, they hid the weapons among the shrubs bordering the cove.

"We'll have to get the women and children off the *Incentive* as quickly as possible," Byron told Fitzpatrick. "They were all packing up to move, so it shouldn't be difficult. I'll ask Arielle to translate for us." Ashamed of how he must look, he bent down to wash the grime from his face and hands.

"I wouldn't trust her not to warn her people," Fitzpatrick said.

"I'll not ask her to betray them, merely to explain what must be done. Now, let's go. We've been ferried back and forth so many times, I doubt anyone will think it odd when we return to the ship early. In fact, let's just help the women pack and bring them ashore. There's no need to frighten them."

Fitzpatrick appeared aghast. "You mean not tell them we're taking back the ship?"

"Yes, let's see how much we can accomplish before they have to be told."

Fitzpatrick wavered a moment, then seeing how Byron's proposal would eliminate panic, he agreed and turned to give such an order to his men. Inspired by their leader's confidence, the English seamen and soldiers piled into the lifeboats and rowed out to the *Incentive.* The tide had yet to crest, but each knew they had no time to waste if they were to make good on their escape. When they reached the ship, they climbed aboard, and then, with smiles and polite gestures, began coaxing the women and children into the boats.

Byron hurriedly scanned the faces of those on deck, but Arielle wasn't among them. He patted a little girl who clung to her doll, and then sprinting past her, went below to the captain's cabin. He rapped lightly at the door, and, having no weapon, prayed she would go along with his plan by choice.

When Arielle swung open the door and found Byron standing in the companionway, she stepped backward so quickly she stumbled and nearly fell. He reached out to catch her, and then, after satisfying himself that she had been alone in the cabin, quickly shut the door. His gaze was intense, his voice urgent.

"We're taking back the *Incentive,* and I need you to tell the women it's time to go ashore."

Arielle didn't know which was more astounding, the nature of his request or that Byron was in full possession of his faculties. She focused on the most obvious question. "When I last saw you, you seemed not to know me and I feared—"

Taking her hand, Byron led her from the cabin. "Yes, I know what you thought and I'm sorry, but we've another problem at present. I will explain later."

Arielle dug in her heels and pulled back with sufficient strength to stop him. "What have you done with Gaetan?"

Byron's eyes narrowed slightly. "Do you really care?"

"Yes, of course I do!"

"He's off hunting, and if we hurry, we can get away without bloodshed. If we delay, then he may very well return and begin hunting *us.* I hope to move the women and children to shore without their realizing what's happened. I don't want to risk any of them getting hurt. We need to hurry so we can sail on the high tide. If we delay too long and the tide goes out, we could run aground right here in the cove. If that happens there will be a battle over possession of the *Incentive* that will cost both sides too many good men. Now, will you help me or not?"

"You want me to take your side against my own people, is that it?"

Although distressed by her choice of words, Byron

had no time to argue the point. "I'm asking you to *protect,* not betray them. I don't want to see any of them hurt. We're in command again and I can march the women and children up the beach screaming and crying or quietly anticipating moving into new homes. Now which is it to be?"

Her conscience pained her for not siding with the Acadians, but she had been so badly troubled by her bargain with Gaetan that she simply could not. She clutched Bernard's portrait briefly, then nodded. "I'll do what I can to inspire everyone to hurry, but if they become suspicious, I don't know what we can tell them."

"You've solved your own problem," Byron pointed out. "Don't allow them to become suspicious. Tell them all they need now are their belongings, and that we'll send the sails so they can rebuild their tents once they're all ashore."

"You don't intend to actually allow them to keep the sails, do you?"

Byron shook his head. "Not a one."

Arielle glanced away, for the prospect of lying truly appalled her, but she supposed it was a minor point when Byron's purpose was to keep the women and children out of danger. Her choice made, she shrugged off her doubts and followed Byron up on deck where the sailors and soldiers were carefully dismantling the tents while their former residents stood by and watched.

The Acadians seemed not to have noticed that the Englishman was without guards, and she hurried to distract them before they did. She asked the women at the ends of the stretch of tents to stack their belongings nearby to be the first to be loaded in lifeboats. She smiled and cajoled, endeavoring to create the mood of cheerful anticipation Byron had wanted. Gaetan had announced his intention to provide game for a feast, and a reminder of that expected treat was enough to get everyone moving more rapidly.

Within fifteen minutes of Byron's arrival, the first of the lifeboats was filled with women and children clutching their cherished possessions. In another few minutes, the next group set out for shore. Arielle waited at the rail, waving, and trying not to feel like the traitor she feared she was. It was only the knowledge that her former neighbors were a lot better off here than being deposited in the English colonies that kept her smiling.

Occasionally Byron noticed a woman wearing a puzzled frown or a perplexed stare, but he rushed in each time to create a distraction and keep the movement to the shore flowing smoothly. He had underestimated the time that would be required, and when the final group had been lowered to a lifeboat, the tide had already crested and begun to ebb. Alarmed, he turned to Arielle.

"I've got to go back and get the men we left standing guard. Don't let Fitzpatrick sail without me."

He scrambled over the side and dropped down into the crowded boat before Arielle could respond, but she kept a close watch of the scene on shore, praying the whole time that Byron's scheme would work. Fitzpatrick came to her side and she sent him a worried glance.

"Your Byron is one of the bravest men I've ever

met," he commented calmly. "Let's just hope he makes it back with the rest of our men."

Arielle had no idea how long it had taken to off-load the ship. Too long, perhaps, if Gaetan had found game right away. While she hadn't visited the settlement, she could easily imagine Gaetan and his hunting party approaching from one direction while Byron raced through the forest from the other. "He wasn't armed," she worried aloud.

"I know." The captain turned away to begin the preparations to sail. The canvas tents that had been stacked in broad heaps now had to be returned to their original purpose, and he ordered his men to hurry up about it. "I'll begin weighing anchor the instant Byron gets back to the shore," he confided, but the sound of gunfire in the distance put his plan in jeopardy.

Arielle's fingers were a ghostly white against the mahogany rail, and she had to bite her lower lip to keep from crying out. The sailors had been unloading the last of the things from the lifeboats and the scene on shore had been one of orderly progress until that moment. Now the women began to call to their children, and others, having a firm hold on their little ones, fled into the woods. The sailors simply threw down the goods they had transported with care, littering the cove with every manner of domestic item from iron kettles to rocking chairs.

Using their lifeboat as a shield, two sailors waited for Byron and the two missing soldiers while the other lifeboats returned to the *Incentive.* The explosive boom of musketfire was coming closer, and, straining to see while wanting to look away, Arielle was nearly faint with worry. Behind her, sailors were struggling to rerig the ship, and the hopes to sail without bloodshed grew dimmer by the second.

After an excruciatingly long wait, Byron and the two soldiers he had left at the stockade came barreling out of the trees. One slipped and fell, and Byron stopped to grab him by the arm to help him rise while the other man ran on to the waiting lifeboat.

Arielle heard the captain give the order to weigh anchor and the clank of the chain as it was drawn up, but she could hear the shouts from shore just as clearly. With the tide flowing out, the expanse of beach had grown wider, lengthening the dash from the cover of the trees to the unprotected lifeboat. Slowed by the dampness of the sand, the fleeing men moved at a torturous pace and did not reach the water before Gaetan and his men burst out of the forest.

Arielle watched in horror as Byron and his companions leapt into the lifeboat, but had it been rowed by a demon they could not have outdistanced the flurry of musketfire aimed their way. Having kept their weapons, the two soldiers Byron had relieved returned the fire, then ducked down with the others to reload, leaving only the sailor rowing the lifeboat fully exposed. Terrified, his strokes were short and choppy, and he managed to propel the boat by mere inches as Gaetan and the Acadians paused to reload. To make matters worse, with her anchor raised, the *Incentive* began to drift toward the bay, making the efforts to reach her side all the more difficult.

Arielle screamed as a spray of blood shot up from the lifeboat and the sailor at the oars slumped over.

Shoving him aside, Byron took his place, and, pulling with desperate strokes, hurried their pace. Their only defense, the soldiers kept firing, but using the household goods heaped on shore for cover, the Acadians reloaded without risk of being hit. It was a horribly uneven contest, with seven armed men battling two, while Byron kept rowing toward the *Incentive* in a heroic attempt to escape further harm.

The boatload of men could not waver from their course and, fearing the worst, Fitzpatrick returned to Arielle's side. "Come away," he urged. "You don't want to watch this."

Arielle pushed him aside and leaned over the rail to yell Byron's name. She was looking right at him when a musketball tore through his arm. Rising up, the remaining sailor grabbed the oars, and with the soldiers now alternating their fire, he gradually drew the lifeboat out of range. The challenge then was to reach the *Incentive,* and when he tired, one of the soldiers took a turn at the oars, then the other. When at last they came close enough to be thrown a rope, the weary men could barely hang on to it.

Praying Byron's wound was not mortal, as she waited for him to be brought on board Arielle cast a last look toward the shore where Gaetan stood shaking his fist. Their eyes met, and, sickened by the hatred she saw directed her way, she was positive she had made the right choice. The sailor who had taken the first turn at the oars was dead, and his body was laid to the side. Byron climbed over the rail, pale and bloody, but very much alive.

"Help me get him to my cabin," Arielle begged.

"That's my cabin," Fitzpatrick reminded her, "but I don't mind him using it for today."

"We'll use it as long as we damn well please!" Arielle screamed.

"Let's not argue," Byron whispered. Weak from exertion and loss of blood, he would have been content to rest on the deck, but Arielle wrapped both arms around his waist to help him remain on his feet. They nearly fell descending the ladder, but managed to stumble into the captain's cabin without causing either of them any harm. Arielle eased him down onto the bed, then ripped away what was left of his shirt.

Relieved to find the musket ball had passed cleanly through his upper arm, she hastened to reassure him. "The ball missed the bone, and once I stop the bleeding, all you'll need is rest."

Feeling dizzy, Byron reached out to grab her apron, and she cradled his head against her bosom while she called over her shoulder to Fitzpatrick. "Look through the lockers; Gaetan's shirts are there someplace. They'll make good bandages. Hurry, I don't want him to lose any more blood."

"He can't have all that much left," Fitzpatrick mumbled as he fetched a clean shirt.

Arielle grabbed it out of his hands and, folding it lengthwise, wrapped it tightly around Byron's bicep to stem the flow of blood still oozing from his wound. "Thank God it is your left arm rather than your right," she offered encouragingly, "so you won't feel awkward while it heals."

Byron closed his eyes, and sighed deeply. "I wish the other man had been as lucky."

"Yes, so do I," Arielle agreed. She turned again to seek help from Fitzpatrick. "Pour him a brandy, please. It will ease his pain."

The captain found little left in the bottle, but poured it into a tankard as asked. "Here you are. Better sip that, Byron."

Byron got a shaky grip on the pewter tankard and drank the fine brandy in a single blazing gulp.

Arielle caressed his hair, and drew back when she felt the row of stitches Fitzpatrick had taken to close his head wound. She would remove them while he slept. "I didn't appreciate the trick you played on me. Letting me think you were little more than alive was unspeakably cruel."

"It had to be done." Byron gritted his teeth and waited for the numbing warmth of the brandy to ease the agonizing pain in his arm. "I had to make Gaetan believe I was no longer a threat. It worked, and our guards got careless. If only we had been a few minutes quicker, we would have gotten away without anyone suffering any harm."

Byron's words were becoming slurred, and Arielle eased him back on the bunk. "There, just close your eyes and rest." She sat down beside him to keep the pressure on his crude bandage. "I'll be here when you wake."

"Promise?"

"Yes, I promise," but as she said the word she recalled the promise she had made to Gaetan and shuddered. "What's going to happen to the Acadians?" she asked.

Byron didn't reply, and Captain Fitzpatrick just shrugged, and after mumbling something about setting a course, left her to tend the wounded man alone.

Awakened by a tempting aroma, Byron glanced toward the table where Arielle was eating her supper. She was spooning fish chowder from a bowl with such deep concentration she failed to notice he was awake and he enjoyed watching her so much he did not remedy the situation.

She had elegant manners, and ate with silent bites. She broke off small bites of bread and chewed them thoroughly before again picking up her spoon. She took an occasional drink of ale from a tankard, and then set it aside gently. Her actions were as graceful as the finest of ladies back home in Williamsburg and he did not doubt that he would be the envy of all his friends when he introduced her.

His thoughts drifting toward home, he prayed that despite the unexpected delay in his return, his father was still alive. He couldn't bare to think that he wasn't, for his poor family had sustained too many losses in the last year to bear another. Deeply depressed by that thought, he raised his hand to wipe the threat of tears from his eyes.

Noticing his gesture, Arielle left her chair immediately and sat down on the edge of the bunk. She felt his forehead, and smiled when she found his skin cool to the touch. "Are you in pain?" she asked.

Byron tried to smile. "I'm free, and I have you back. Whatever minor discomfort I feel really doesn't matter."

Arielle drew back slightly. "You have the *Incentive*

back, and I happen to be on board. That's the extent of your good fortune."

Byron would have laughed had he felt well enough to stand the jarring any show of mirth might cause his arm. "If you wanted to stay with Gaetan, you should have spoken up sooner. I doubt that I can convince Fitzpatrick to take you back now."

"Stop teasing. I've no desire to go back, but what will happen to the settlement we were building? Will you send soldiers to attack it?"

Byron laced his fingers in hers. "When we reach Boston, I'll have to provide a full report of our voyage to Governor Shirley, but Gaetan's no fool. He won't remain at the stockade we built. He'll go deeper into the forest, or up the coast and I doubt Shirley will care what happens to him and his followers. They're out of Acadia, and that's all he wanted."

"You make it sound as though he considers us vermin."

Byron drew her hand to his lips. "No, not at all, but can't we stop dividing people into your camp and mine? I want you to be happy in Virginia—"

Arielle pulled her hand from his. "And if I'm not?"

"You will be," Byron assured her. "I've told you my family owns a beautiful plantation and you'll be welcome there."

Arielle could scarcely believe her ears. "Do Virginians usually bring their mistresses home to meet their parents?"

Byron couldn't help but laugh at that question, and the resulting pain was almost worth it. "You're not my mistress, Arielle. A mistress is merely a pretty diversion, and you mean much more to me than that."

Arielle waited for him to describe his feelings in more depth, but sadly he did not. Disappointed, she looked away. She felt queasy, and gripped the side of the bunk to steady herself. "This has been such an awful day, and I really don't feel up to discussing the future. I'll get you something to eat, and we can make plans another time."

"I'm not hungry. Go ahead and finish your supper."

"I'm not hungry, either."

Byron edged over slightly. "Then come to bed."

Arielle was growing accustomed to his beard. Growing low on his cheeks, it was a handsome accent to his features and made him resemble a frontiersman rather than the wealthy man he was. Still, she hesitated to lie down beside him again. "I think I ought to sleep elsewhere," she argued.

Byron frowned slightly. "No, you dare not leave me alone when I've been so severely injured. What if I start bleeding again, or become feverish and there's no one here to tend me?" He reached out his hand.

Gaetan had grabbed for her, never coaxed her so invitingly, and in spite of her best intentions not to join him, Arielle placed her hand in his and let him draw her down beside him. Unlike the one occasion upon which she had shared the bunk with Gaetan, she and Bryon fit together perfectly.

"I didn't sleep with Gaetan," she blurted out.

Immeasurably relieved, Byron gave her a hug. He could not imagine how she had escaped that ordeal, but didn't want to hear the details. "Good. I'm sorry that I had to make you believe I'd forgotten you. I didn't mean to be cruel."

Arielle snuggled against him. "I'll forgive you if you agree to saying good-bye to me in Boston."

"Never," Byron swore. "Why would you even consider staying in Boston?"

"It's as good a place as any."

Saddened by her wistful tone, Byron pulled himself up slightly. He had survived a brutal beating, and had the Acadian who had wounded him been a better shot, he would be dead. As he saw it, he had earned the right to keep the woman in his arms. "This has been too difficult a trip for me to go home alone, Arielle. I won't even consider it. Besides, at the rate misfortune has befallen me of late, I need a woman with your talent at healing by my side."

"You must have physicians in Virginia."

"Yes, and fine ones, but I want you."

Arielle waited for a tender explanation of why he held her in such high regard, but, again, it wasn't forthcoming. Ceasing to expect it, she repeated her preference. "You'll be fine, Byron, and I'd really rather stay in Boston."

Byron gave her another possessive hug. Having lost a dear brother and sister, he dared not speak of love for fear of losing Arielle, too, but he could offer something else instead. "I don't feel up to fighting with you about this. Just come home with me and if you aren't happy there for any reason, I'll take you on to New Orleans. The people are French, and their ways can't be all that different from the people of Grand Pré! You'd make friends far more easily there than in Boston."

"New Orleans sounds impossibly far."

"I'm not giving you an option. You needn't worry about the trip. You'll love Virginia and never want to leave."

Arielle closed her eyes. She could feel the wind filling the sails and lifting the *Incentive* over the waves, but she refused to allow her spirits to soar. There was only now, this blissful moment when she lay in Byron's arms and, savoring it fully, she dared not dream of anything more. "I can't make any promises," she whispered.

Byron pulled her closer still. "I don't need promises," he assured her, for not knowing what he would find at home, there were none he could confidently give in return.

Sixteen

Within two hours of the *Incentive*'s arrival in Boston, Byron had made his report to Governor Shirley. Anxious to reach home, he then arranged passage for Arielle and himself to Newport News on the first ship bound for Virginia. While they waited for her to sail, they took separate rooms in a comfortable inn near the Common. Their first afternoon there, Byron lay down to take a nap, but too restless to remain in her room, Arielle went out to stroll the spacious park.

She had hoped once they reached Boston and she could again walk on solid ground her health would return to normal. Instead, she felt even worse. Not only was she dizzy but nauseated as well. She had delivered too many babies not to recognize such a classic symptom of pregnancy, but uncertain of Byron's reaction, she dared not share her suspicions. Instead, she would continue to brew herbal remedies to settle her stomach and hide any lingering distress until she had a better opportunity to assess his feelings. She loved Byron and would have rejoiced at the idea of having his child had he only loved her.

But Byron never spoke of love.

At unguarded moments on the voyage to Boston, his features had relaxed in a mask of such terrible sadness that she knew he had to be dreading what he might find at home. He was obviously devoted to his family, and she was certain he would always miss his brother and sister. With his father gravely ill, and not yet fully recovered from an excruciating ordeal himself, she would not dream of burdening him further with the responsibility of a child.

Enjoying the fresh air and wide lawns, if not her turbulent thoughts, Arielle tarried so long in the Common that Byron was deeply worried by the time she returned to the inn. "You should have left me a note so I'd know where you had gone," he chastised. "I was afraid you'd gotten lost."

Arielle shrugged. "I'm sorry you were worried. I will not run away. Is that what you feared?"

She had accurately guessed his concern, but Byron stubbornly refused to admit it. "No, I didn't think you'd simply disappear, but from now on, please let me know when you're going out. I'll try and go with you."

"You lost a great deal of blood and need to rest."

Hating the weakness he had yet to overcome, Byron shook his head. No more than you. Now, come on up to your room. The innkeeper summoned a seamstress and she'll be here soon."

Arielle remained on the stairs. "Are you ashamed of my clothes?"

"No, not at all. They were perfect for Grand Pré, but now you're going to Williamsburg. You'll need something more sophisticated there."

Despite his reassurance, Arielle feared she had surmised the truth. "I may put on more elegant clothes," she warned, "but I'll still be Acadian."

"I've no intention of trying to hide that fact, Arielle. Now come on up to your room and we can talk about what you'll need so we won't keep the seamstress waiting later while we argue. She'll have little enough time as it is to complete your wardrobe before we sail."

Arielle continued on up the stairs, but she doubted she could gather much enthusiasm for new clothes, for no matter how expertly they were tailored, in a few months their fit would no longer be superb.

Although Arielle tried to be patient and understanding, Byron's mood remained dark, creating an uncomfortable tension between them which marred the voyage to Virginia. It wasn't until they reached Newport News and he hired a small boat for the journey up the James River that his spirits finally began to lift. This homecoming an anxious one, he stood in the bow, eager for a glimpse of familiar sights.

"Look!" he called. "That's our house on the hill."

Although Arielle had known Byron's family was wealthy, the sight of their impressive brick mansion left her too awed to speak. Set on a rise that provided a splendid view of the river, it was surrounded by colorful gardens and verdant lawns that sloped gently to the family docks.

It looked like a palace to Arielle and she was extremely grateful for the new wine-colored silk gown Byron had provided. Self-conscious, she reached up to adjust the ribbon bow on the matching bonnet. She would have been far more comfortable in a gown she had brought from home, but understood without

Byron having to tell her why it was important that she look her best. Regardless of how she looked, though, she doubted such a grand house would ever seem like home to her.

As soon as their boat had tied up at the dock, Byron took Arielle's hand to escort her to his door, but she hung back. "I think you ought to go first," she suggested. "With your father so ill, your mother might be upset that you've brought home a guest, and I don't want to risk displeasing her."

Byron had spent the time in Boston resting and eating wholesome food in an attempt to return home in as robust good health as when he had left, but he still didn't feel strong enough to scoop up Arielle in his arms and carry her across the lawn as he would have liked. Although he had not felt up to making love, he had kept her with him each night. Still, he could feel her pulling away and he didn't know how to bring her back. He reached out to stroke her cheek.

"I realize conditions are far from ideal, but I'll not leave you out here on the dock like some poor homeless waif. This is my home as well as my parents', and whomever I bring here will be welcome. Now, let's hurry, I'm sure my mother expected me to arrive long before this and I don't want to keep her waiting any longer."

Ashamed to cause a delay when he had stated his need for haste in such thoughtful terms, she took his hand. They made their way along the path toward the gracefully columned portico framing the entrance of the imposing residence. If Arielle wasn't nearly out of breath from the combination of excitement and dread when an Indian burst through the front door and came running toward them, she would have responded with a terrified shriek rather than a pathetic wail.

Amused by her cry of alarm, Byron dropped her hand and strode into the savage's welcoming hug. "You needn't be afraid," he assured her. "This is Hunter, my cousin Alanna's husband."

Rather than Hunter's engaging grin, Arielle saw only an Indian brave with fierce black eyes and couldn't stop trembling. He had tied his thick ebony mane at his nape like a white man, but wore fringed buckskins and moccasins. There was a knife in a beaded sheath attached to his belt. Eyeing the weapon fearfully, she wondered how often he had used it to spill white men's blood. Sickened, she took a step back, then glanced over her shoulder to make certain the boat they had taken from Newport News was still there in case she had to flee.

Hunter appeared to be nearly as startled as the lovely widow Douville by their unexpected encounter. He listened attentively as Byron said her name, and then gave a mock bow. "I am pleased to meet you, madame."

Byron turned slightly, but Arielle immediately ducked behind him to hide. He moved again, but failed to catch her hand and pull her out in front of him. Beginning to lose patience with her antics, he stood still. "Whatever is wrong with you?" he asked, then in an appalling flash of insight, he knew.

"Oh, God, I'm sorry. I didn't think." He looked back toward Hunter. "Her husband was killed when a band of Iroquois attacked him and his traveling companions."

Hunter had to peek over Byron's shoulder to address Arielle. "Where did it happen?"

"Near Quebec, wasn't it?" Byron called to Arielle, and she confirmed his guess in a breathless murmur.

"I've never been there," Hunter assured her. "I am Seneca, and while we are part of the Iroquois league, our home is in the west."

Arielle heard Hunter's calmly spoken explanation, but it didn't even come close to alleviating her fears. "I want to wait here," she begged.

"Fine," Byron agreed. "I'll have Hunter wait with you."

"No!"

"Then come inside with me." Byron winked at Hunter, but the Indian understood Arielle's fears, while unfounded, were too real for jests. "All Indians are not alike, madame. My wife's family were murdered by the Abenaki, and she does not blame me." He stepped around them, then called over his shoulder, "Go see your father. I'll fetch your luggage."

Arielle was sorry she had ever complained. "Of course," she replied; he responded with only a curt nod.

Having sighted their boat from an upstairs window, Rachel Barclay met them at the front door. Thrilled by her son's return, she scarcely noticed Arielle before she threw her arms around his neck. Sharing her enthusiasm for his return, he lifted her off her feet in a joyous one-armed hug. Then, remembering Arielle, he put her down.

He quickly introduced the young woman, taking special care to identify her as *Madame* Douville, a widow. "I made her acquaintance in Grand Pré," he explained, "and because she was forced to leave when I did, I invited her to come home with me."

Rachel mistook Arielle's hesitant smile for a futile attempt to project an innocence she was positive the Acadian beauty did not deserve. "How dare you bring a Frenchwoman here?" she asked coldly.

"Mother, please," Byron begged. "I meant no disrespect; Arielle was born on British soil, and ought to be considered a British citizen just as we are."

Not impressed by that argument, Rachel responded with a rude laugh. "If anyone believed that lie, she would still be residing in Grand Pré. The Acadians are French, and that's why they're being sent into exile. I won't have their miserable kind in my home."

Rachel was blonde and blue eyed. Still slender at forty-one, she usually had an angelic appearance and radiated tranquillity, but the fire in her soul was unmistakable this day. She crossed her arms over her bosom, and, lifting her chin proudly, forcefully barred the front door.

Knowing Byron must be as horribly embarrassed as she, Arielle hastened to set things right. "Mrs. Barclay, please forgive me for intruding at such a difficult time. I've no desire to stay where I'm not wanted, so I'll bid you a good day." She turned away, only to find Hunter approaching with Byron's satchels. Shrinking back, the fact she had nowhere else to go was painfully clear. Sensitive to her apprehension,

Hunter set the bags down on the walk and went back to get the rest.

Byron slipped his arm around her waist and drew her close. "This is my home as well as yours, Mother, and I say Arielle will be welcome here for as long as she likes. Now, let's not create a scene out here on the porch. I want to see Father immediately. How is he?"

Rachel glared at Arielle, silently challenging her to cross the threshold. "There's been no change since the night he suffered the stroke. He sleeps most of the time, and even when he's awake, he's not truly with us."

Remembering the vigorous man his father had been, Byron did not want to accept such a sad description. "Won't he get any better?"

At last Rachel focused her attention on her son, and she did not like what she saw. "You look as haggard as you did when you returned from Braddock's campaign, but with rest and good food, you'll soon be fit. As for your father, Dr. Earle says it's a miracle he's lived this long. There have been several days when I didn't think you would get here soon enough to see him a last time."

"Well, I'm home at last and I'd like to see him. Arielle can wait in the parlor."

Rachel weighed his request, and, while reluctant to admit the Acadian, she finally stepped aside. "I'm doing this for your father, you understand, not for you, or her."

Byron looked from his mother's determined frown to Arielle's bewildered expression and knew he had been remiss in not anticipating his mother's hostile reaction. "The Acadians are being dispersed throughout the colonies, and for them to have any chance of successfully rebuilding their lives, they'll have to be treated with compassion rather than scorn. It's to our advantage to welcome them. They're hard-working people who will be a credit to any town."

Rachel remained openly skeptical. "Perhaps I misunderstood your intention. Did you bring Madame Douville here to work? If so, I'll find a place for her in the laundry."

"Arielle is my guest," Byron emphasized once again, "not a potential employee."

Rachel simply shrugged, and, reentering her house, started up the stairs without making any provision for Arielle's comfort.

Disgusted by that snub, Byron led Arielle into the parlor. "I'll just be a minute, then I'll help you get settled."

"Don't rush on my account. Take your time and have a nice visit."

From what his mother had said, Byron doubted it would be an enjoyable reunion, but he brushed Arielle's cheek with a kiss and left her alone in the splendidly decorated parlor.

Despite being surrounded by soothing shades of blue, she was unable to sit calmly and wait for his return. Instead, she perused the room, admired the paintings, and, pausing at a window, enjoyed the lovely view of the James River.

While Hunter had been insulted by Arielle's fear of him, he had overheard enough of the conversation between Byron and Rachel to feel sorry for her. Before carrying the first of their luggage upstairs, he paused in the parlor doorway. "When Alanna brought me home and introduced me as her husband, Byron's father tried to shoot me. Your welcome was a warm one compared to mine. Don't despair, I'll call my wife and she will be kind to you."

Amazed to find an Indian offering sympathy, Arielle nodded slightly, but cautiously remained on the far side of the room. She ran her fingers along the edge of a highly polished cherry-wood table and wondered if she ought not go back to the docks. After all, the boat would soon be returning to Newport News, and in such a huge port, she would surely be able to find a way to reach New Orleans.

"And then what?" she wondered aloud. Pass herself off as a very recent widow, and when her child was born, let everyone assume her late husband was the babe's father? That was no more appealing a prospect than having to face Rachel Barclay again. She had had such a placid life in Grand Pré, and now look what had become of her. Her eyes were filling with tears by the time a young woman carrying a child appeared.

"Hello there," she called as she swept through the door. "I'm Alanna, Byron's cousin." She paused to shift the dark-haired little boy to her other hip. "You've already met Hunter, and this is our son, Christian."

Arielle could not help but stare at the bright-eyed boy. He had his father's straight black hair and dark eyes, but his skin was a soft golden shade rather than bronze and his smile had an enchanting sweetness that mirrored Alanna's. "He's a handsome child," she remarked. "But isn't Christian an unusual choice of name?"

"For an Indian's son, you mean?" When Arielle nodded, Alanna gave the boy a loving squeeze, then placed him on his feet. He laughed, and, holding on to the table Arielle had admired, began to toddle around it. "Yes, indeed it is, but he's named for my brother who died in infancy, so we consider it an appropriate family name."

"I'm sorry if I sounded rude."

"No, you weren't rude at all. Hunter and I realize we're an unusual pair and we don't mind answering questions." She gestured toward the settee. "I can see why Byron brought you home. You're lovely. Sit down with me so we can get acquainted."

Arielle moved to the settee, but she found it easier to watch Christian's efforts to master walking than to return his mother's curious gaze. "How old is he?"

"He'll be a year old next month, on November eleventh."

"He's a fine boy."

"Yes, I like to think so. Your accent is very charming. Would you like some tea, or something to eat?"

Arielle shook her head. "I fear I'm intruding, and I don't want to trouble anyone."

Alanna frowned slightly. "This is a large home and we have ample staff to serve our needs. How could you be any trouble? Would you like me to show you to your room? There's time for you to rest before supper if you'd like."

"I think I ought to wait here for Byron." Feeling horribly uncomfortable, Arielle clasped her hands tightly in her lap and wished Byron would hurry back. She smiled shyly at Alanna, who bore a slight resemblance to Byron, but her features were sweetly feminine. "I shouldn't have come here," she blurted out.

Alanna caught Christian's hand as he began a trip around the settee and set him off in the opposite direction so he would not bother their guest. "Byron would not have brought you home had he not cared for you. Do you have feelings for him as well?"

Alanna's gaze was warmly sympathetic, inviting the sharing of confidences, but Arielle did not know how to respond and was quiet for a long moment. "I grew up in Grand Pré," she finally began, "and was perfectly content there. I feel lost now, but Byron is more to me than a mere refuge."

"Yes, I'm certain he is. As for my aunt Rachel, I hope you'll forgive her rudeness. She adores John, and to see him reduced to a pitiful shell of the fine man he once was is extremely difficult for her. She lost two children in the last year, and she had not even begun to recover from that grief when John fell ill."

Rather than being reassured, Arielle spirits sagged even lower. "Yes, I know how difficult her life has been, and I'm afraid I'm only adding to her sorrow." She glanced toward the stairs again, longing for Byron, and at the same time fearful that he might take his mother's side and send her away.

Byron remembered his father as being tall and lean, a handsome man who wore fine clothes with a careless elegance. He'd favored wigs to his own hair and had owned several, but the gaunt figure lying in the bed showed no sign of being concerned about his appearance, or anything else. He lay staring up at the ceiling, his mouth slack, and his skin, too loose for his wasted body, hanging in limp folds along his jowls.

Had Byron not known this was his parents' bedroom, he would not have recognized his father. He turned toward his mother, but she shook off whatever questions he might have and nodded toward the bed, encouraging him to move closer.

"I'm home, Father," he greeted him, but John Barclay gave no sign of having heard him. Byron had to swallow hard to rid his throat of a painful knot, but then he gave a brief account of his trip to Acadia. "The countryside was very beautiful, and the people industrious farmers and fishermen. I brought an Acadian woman home with me. We got to know each other while conducting a census. Her name is Arielle Douville, and when you're feeling better, I'm certain you'll enjoy meeting her."

Rachel moved to her son's side. "You mustn't tire him. Come back later and visit with him again."

Having no assurance his father would be more alert later, Byron squeezed his withered hand. "I'm home for good," he promised. "We'll be able to talk often." He left the bedroom, but, horribly depressed by what he had found, he lacked the energy to rejoin Arielle in the parlor. There was a padded bench on the landing. He sat upon it and leaned back against the wall.

Rachel made certain her husband was resting comfortably, and then renewed her argument with Byron.

"This is one of his good days," she insisted. "He requires more exhausting care than an infant, and Alanna, bless her, helps me all she can. Do you think your Frenchwoman will find a household devoted to an invalid's care amusing?"

Drained of all emotion, Byron failed to react to his mother's taunts. "Arielle is a midwife, and proficient in herbal cures. She's used to treating the sick and she'll provide excellent assistance, if you'll just give her an opportunity."

Rachel put her hands on her hips and leaned forward slightly. "Dr. Earle is a fine physician, and I'd prefer to rely on his advice rather than some Acadian herbalist. I can only imagine what foul-tasting remedies she might prescribe. How you could have taken up with a Frenchwoman after fighting them the last two years is beyond comprehension. Did you find her so beautiful you couldn't remember how hard you'd fought the French the last two summers? Or even worse, that their heathen allies shot Elliott? How could you have overlooked something so damning as that? Such disrespect for Elliott's memory is appalling."

Byron looked up at his mother. He couldn't deny that he despised the French, and with just cause, but he could never hate Arielle. "She's a fine woman regardless of her heritage, and I want her made welcome here."

"Then you will have to see to it yourself, for I'll do no more than tell the girls to set an extra place at the table."

"Fine, that's a start."

Rachel responded with an angry glare and returned to her husband, but Byron still lacked the will to go downstairs. In a moment Hunter appeared carrying some of Arielle's belongings, and he felt a sudden kinship with the Iroquois brave. "Things couldn't have been easy for you here."

After placing the bags on the landing, Hunter sat down on the top step. "Your mother needed Alanna, and knowing she would not come here without me, she had no choice about accepting me. She seldom speaks to me, though, and then it is usually just to tell me to get out of her way. As for Christian, she has warmed to the boy, but that's only because he is too good-natured to understand her refusal to love him. I spend my time in the fields. While the men consider me a poor substitute for John, they've learned to do what I say."

"I hope you'll stay. I could use your help as much as my mother needs Alanna's. Elliott and I always expected to run the plantation together, you see, and it will be awfully hard for me to do it without him."

"I can't take his place."

"No, I don't expect that of you. Just stay as long as you're able, and do what you can."

Hunter nodded and rose. "Where should I put your woman's things?"

Byron would not upset his mother further by having Arielle share his room, although that was what he truly wanted. The guest rooms on the third floor were all comfortable, but not nearly close enough to suit his tastes. His brother's room was across the hall from his own, and the best choice from his point of view. "Put her things in Elliott's room, please."

Hunter stopped to really look at Byron and saw the

same signs of weariness and strain Rachel had observed. "What really happened to you in Acadia?"

Byron shook his head. "My trip wasn't nearly as uneventful as I want Mother to believe, but I'll have to tell you about it another time." He rose and stretched. His left arm ached from his shoulder to his fingertips and he flexed his hand slowly in hopes of easing the pain, but got no relief. What he needed was one of Arielle's potions, and he started down the stairs hoping her herbs would be the first thing she unpacked.

Arielle leapt to her feet when Byron reached the bottom of the stairs. Then, feeling foolish, she apologized to Alanna. "I've enjoyed talking with you, but I need to unpack, or make plans to go elsewhere."

Christian came toward him, and Byron bent down so he would not have to pick up the youngster. "He's grown a lot while I was gone."

Beaming, Alanna followed the little boy and gathered him into her arms. "I swear I can see a change in him every day. I can hardly wait for him to start talking. I just know he'll say wonderfully clever things."

Byron straightened up slowly. "Yes, I'm sure he will." He then offered his hand to Arielle. "Come upstairs, I want to show you your room."

Arielle licked her lips, smiled once again at Alanna and her son, and then accompanied Byron up the stairs.

Byron pushed open the door to Elliott's room, and, taking her hand, led her inside. While the room had been cleaned as often as the rest of the house, the air was stale, and he opened the two windows facing the garden. "There, that's better. This was my brother's room. I'm just across the hall."

Arielle surveyed the handsomely decorated room. The walls were painted in a deep terra-cotta while the ceiling and woodwork were a sparkling white. The furnishings were of beautifully carved fruitwoods, and the four-poster bed looked very comfortable. "What is your mother going to say about my using this room?"

"I really don't care. The guest rooms on the third floor are just too far away."

Arielle sat down on the edge of the bed, and found it felt as inviting as it looked. "I don't really understand what my place is to be here. Your mother dislikes me merely because I'm Acadian. If she knew how intimate our friendship is, she might throw you out with me."

Byron collapsed into a wing chair by the window. He ran his hand over his eyes, then relaxed completely. "I think we can be discreet. She may suspect we're close, but I don't plan to flaunt our friendship in a way she'll find offensive. I know you wouldn't do that, either."

Arielle glanced over his shoulder at the cloudless sky. "I can be discreet for the time being," she promised, "but I can not remain indefinitely as a guest in your home. Don't expect that of me. I have my own life, and I must find a way to live it again."

Byron closed his eyes. "I want you to look in on my father tomorrow. Perhaps you can suggest something to help him."

Embarrassed that she had failed to inquire about

the man, Arielle hurriedly agreed. "Of course. How does he seem to you?"

Byron just shook his head. "I hardly recognized him."

"Only God works miracles, Byron. Don't ask one of me."

"Just come here and kiss me. That's all the miracle I need." Arielle removed her bonnet, smoothed her hair, and then crossed the room. She felt so completely out of place that it wasn't until her lips met Byron's that she remembered why she had come to Virginia with him. One kiss was not nearly enough for either of them, and when he pulled her across his lap, she snuggled against him and wished with all her heart that she would one day be more than a guest in his home.

Seventeen

Until that overcast afternoon, Byron Barclay had never really believed anyone could die of a broken heart. The flowers he carried had wilted on the ride into town, but it was a heavy burden of grief that had drained the pride from his posture. Shadows criss-crossed the narrow lane forming an intricate web and, suddenly recognizing the strange pattern as an evil omen, he quickened his pace and hurried toward his sister's grave.

Melissa Barclay Scott was buried on a gently sloping rise. It was a lovely, peaceful place, but Byron had never appreciated its beauty and associated it only with the pain of loss. He carefully divided the limp bouquet and placed half upon Melissa's grave. She had been a young woman of remarkable beauty, and no elegantly carved marble headstone could ever convey her spirited charm. Come spring, Byron intended to plant flowers all around her grave, and his brother Elliott's, as well.

To have lost them both was a tragedy Byron could barely comprehend, let alone accept bravely. Now his father was clinging to life with only a tenuous grasp. There would be three graves to visit then, but Byron struggled to suppress that grim eventuality.

He dropped the remainder of his meager floral tribute on his brother's grave and choked back the tears he was too proud to shed. The three of them had been so close. As the eldest, he had always felt responsible for them, and their tragic deaths had diminished his world immeasurably. He would never stop loving, or missing, them.

"I hope you're together," he whispered, "and that we'll meet again one day." He bowed his head and began to pray, his thoughts a rambling confusion of joyful memories and the agonizing pain of loss, but before he had even touched upon the peace he had sought, he heard a familiar feminine voice calling his name. Angered by the intrusion, he wrapped his aching heart in an icy veil, and, pretending a composure he did not feel, turned around.

Sarah Frederick had been so excited to find Byron there she had lifted her skirt and broken into an ecstatic run, but his darkly forbidding stare brought her to an awkward halt. She loved him with all her heart, but she had seen him show more warmth to a stranger. Jarred by disappointment, she recalled too late where they were.

"How thoughtless of me," she murmured. "Whenever Robin and I come into town, we always stop by Elliott's grave, and I was so thrilled to see you that I didn't realize you wouldn't share the feeling. When did you get back from Acadia? We've been praying for your safe return."

Byron managed a slight nod that took in Sarah's younger sister, Robin, as well. Dressed in stylish autumn gowns of blue and rose, the pretty pair provided a poignant reminder of the carefree days of his youth, but he was now a grown man, and in no mood for the frivolous pastimes they had shared.

"Thank you. Your prayers were answered," he replied without revealing just how arduous his journey had been.

He had once been amused by the not altogether unfounded speculation that he would one day wed Sarah, while their friends had wagered Elliott would take Robin for his bride. Had their families' adjacent plantations been consolidated through marriage, the prosperous estates would have further enriched the fortunes of the already wealthy owners. Now Elliott had no need of a wife, and, except for fond memories, Byron had no feeling for either of the attractive brunettes. They were undeniably sweet, but their futures held no more meaning to him than his own.

Robin knew just how desperately her sister had missed Byron, but it was painfully clear he had not missed her a bit. Embarrassed that he had greeted them without enthusiasm, she brushed by him and knelt to place the roses she had brought on his brother's grave. "We've called on your mother several times since your father's stroke," she informed him. "His illness must have been a dreadful shock. I know it certainly was to us."

"Shock does not even begin to describe the depth of my reaction. It was fortunate that Alanna and Hunter were here to help my mother cope."

Sarah shuddered. "That Indian always frightened me."

Furious at her comment, Byron's glance took on a menacing gleam. "I'd be as dead as General Braddock had he not saved my life last summer. If that were not enough, he's married to my cousin. That makes him family, and if you dare speak another word against him, I'll slap your head right off your shoulders." Certain he had made his intentions excruciatingly clear, Byron skirted the walk, cut across the grass, and strode away.

Devastated their chance encounter had gone so badly, Sarah debated several options, including doing nothing, but she wanted Byron too badly to wait for him to come to his senses and apologize. Seizing the initiative, she again gathered up her skirt and ran after him. She caught up with him just as he reached the gate.

"Please wait a moment," she begged.

The last remnants of the fine manners his parents had instilled were all that saved her from another strongly worded insult. "What is it now?"

Sarah forced a smile despite the sharpness of his tone. "It's no wonder you're cross with me. I should have inquired about your trip. Was the situation difficult in Acadia?"

Byron glanced toward his carriage. "No, things weren't difficult at all, at least, not for me, but I'd like you to meet Madame Douville. She'll tell you an entirely different story." He opened the gate, and gestured for Sarah to precede him. He pulled open the door of his carriage, looked in at Arielle and made the proper introductions.

Sarah had always thought of Byron as her very own, and as she stared into the cool aqua eyes of Arielle Douville she saw not merely a lovely rival, but the end of her most cherished hopes as well. She could barely hear Arielle's softly accented greeting above the pounding of her heart, and as for a reply all she wanted to do was scream.

She looked up at Byron, her heartbreak as bright as her tears. "I don't understand," she mumbled.

Unmoved by Sarah's obvious distress, Byron gave a rueful laugh. "No, I'm certain you understand perfectly." He climbed into the carriage, and, after taking a seat opposite Arielle, closed the door and leaned out. "Thank you for calling on my mother. That was very kind of you."

Sarah had known Byron all her life, but she scarcely recognized this arrogant stranger. The sullen set of his mouth made him look so bitter. They had shared such wonderfully happy times and she couldn't bear to think they might be over. "Am I no more to you than an attentive neighbor?"

Feeling cornered, Byron's temper nearly got the better of him, but he drew in a deep breath, and let it out slowly in an effort to remain civil for Arielle's sake as much as his own. "Don't try and pretend we were ever anything more than good friends, because it just isn't true."

Humiliated that he would speak so callously to her in front of another woman, and a foreigner at that, Sarah thought his response not merely rude but cruel, and she didn't understand what had happened to the once-tender feelings she was positive he had had for her. "I've no wish to be considered a relic of your childhood, Byron, but I've always believed that you enjoyed my company, and that someday . . ."

When she was unable to complete her thought, the confusion dampening her sparkling brown eyes brought a sudden surge of guilt, and Byron lowered his voice to a more considerate level. "If I've somehow encouraged you to dream of things that will never be, I'm sincerely sorry. I promised we'd not be away from home long, so we really must go. It was good seeing you both. Please tell Robin I said so."

He signaled their driver, and the carriage rolled into a wide turn as they started back toward home. Embarrassed by the whole sorry episode, Byron tried to shrug it off. "I know what you must think, but Sarah Frederick and her sister truly are no more than childhood friends," he explained to Arielle. "Elliott and I used to escort them to parties, but that was more out of habit than any serious intention on our parts."

Arielle had seen more than mere friendship in Sarah's tearful gaze. If he could so easily forget a woman he had known all his life, how long would it take him to forget her? she agonized, and feeling as badly betrayed as Sarah, she glanced out the window and, preferring the pastoral scene to making conversation, remained silent all the way home.

Sarah had wanted so desperately to impress Byron, but, dismayed and discouraged, she watched his carriage disappear into a rumbling dust cloud, aghast at how badly she had failed. When Robin finally reached her, she was still trying to comprehend what had happened.

"How could he have brought an Acadian woman home with him? Did I merely imagine that he loved me?" she asked. "Wasn't it ever true?"

Robin's depression over the death of Elliott was as

deep as Byron's, and uncertain what the truth was anymore, she clung to the facts she knew, enumerating all Byron's losses. "I don't think you can fault him for making what must surely be an unsuitable attachment," she concluded. "I doubt that it will last. Just give him time."

"Time? To do what? Forget all about me? I've been patient, Robin. I didn't press him for a proposal before he went to fight with Braddock, or before he left for Acadia, and look how badly he treated me just now."

Having no more advice to offer, Robin listened silently as Sarah continued to bemoan first Byron's neglect and then his betrayal. They boarded their carriage for the short ride down the Duke of Gloucester Street to the shops, but while coming into town had once brought a delicious excitement, nothing held any appeal without Elliott to share in her delight. Sarah, however, could always find a way to spend their father's money, regardless of her mood. Paying little attention to the wares on display in the shop windows, Robin bumped into her sister when she stopped suddenly.

Sarah grabbed Robin's arm. "Good Lord, Robin, isn't that Ian Scott?"

Two English officers splendidly attired in the red coats and white breeches of the Coldstream Guards were approaching, and Robin recognized Melissa's husband and one of his friends. "Yes, it certainly is, and that's Graham Tyler with him. Do you suppose they'll remember us?"

Sarah pursed her lips thoughtfully. "On a day when Byron swears we were never more than friends, probably not, but let's hope they do anyway." Sarah had never been shy, and, desperate for the attention Byron had withheld, she quickly linked arms with Robin and stepped out to block the men's way. "Captain Scott, and Captain Tyler, how wonderful to see you again."

The Frederick sisters had been frequent guests in his late wife's home, and the innocent sweetness of their smiles brought back a flood of painful memories. Ian nodded rather stiffly. "Good afternoon, ladies."

"I'd not heard that you'd returned from England," Sarah said. "We've missed seeing you."

Graham waited for Ian to respond, or for Sarah to turn her attention to him, and when neither event occurred, he brought the awkward silence to an end by mentioning an urgent appointment. He and Ian then continued on their way.

Again distressed, Sarah turned to study her reflection in the adjacent shop window. "Whatever is wrong with me today?" she asked. "Why is it simply impossible to draw a kind word from a man?"

"Don't be silly. Byron's infatuated with his Acadian, and Ian and Graham have somewhere else to be. You mustn't take their preoccupations so personally."

But Sarah most certainly did. "I always liked Ian," she confided.

"Yes, so did I, but he adored Melissa and she's been dead not quite a year. Did you expect him to ask for permission to call on you?"

Sarah frowned slightly as she considered that possibility. "No, not really, but I'd certainly have encouraged him if he had."

"What? After the way you were pining for Byron not ten minutes ago?"

"Maybe a little competition would do Byron good. After all, I don't want him to think I'm sitting at home alone waiting for him to grow bored with that Arielle."

Robin shook her head. "I doubt making Byron jealous would be wise, and most certainly not with his former brother-in-law."

Sarah turned back toward the window and, primping, slipped a stray curl back into place beneath her lace-trimmed cap. Ian had left for England shortly after Melissa's death, and she had promptly forgotten him. It would take some adjustment in her thinking to regard him as a beau rather than her best friend's husband, but he was such an attractive man she didn't believe that change would be terribly difficult.

Robin watched a mischievous gleam fill her sister's dark eyes and reached out to touch her arm. "I know that look all too well. What are you plotting?"

Sarah feigned surprise. "What an absurd question. I don't hatch plots."

"You do so, and I always get punished along with you when they go wrong. It would be cruel of you to pretend an interest in Ian just to make Byron jealous. You'd be much better off concentrating on Byron."

Sarah stared at her sister a long moment. Born only a year apart, they were sometimes mistaken for twins, but as the eldest, she had always been the leader. "How am I supposed to do that when Arielle's living in his house?"

"Well, you're a clever girl and I'm sure you'll think of something."

* * *

Graham and Ian were the last to leave the Raleigh tavern that evening, and when they returned to their quarters, they shared one last brandy before going to bed. "I keep thinking about the Frederick sisters," Graham confided. "Or rather, the quiet one. With Elliott dead, Robin must be desperately lonely."

Ian glared at his friend and slumped down lower in his chair. "There's not a woman alive worth knowing."

Graham winced, uncertain whether Ian had simply made an unfortunate choice of words, or was comparing all women unfavorably to his late wife. Because Melissa had died giving birth to her Indian lover's son, Graham decided Ian could not possibly have been paying her a compliment. He knew better than to mention the tragic circumstances of Melissa's death, however, and continued with his original subject.

"Robin's very pretty, and while she never says much, she appears to be bright."

"Maybe she's just never has the chance to speak when she's around you."

Graham had heard that same complaint from Alanna Barclay, and while he couldn't deny that he had once allowed nervousness to inspire more conversation than was necessary, he believed he now had the impulse well under control. "I'm not nearly as talkative as I used to be," he argued, "and the next time I see Robin I'll make certain she has the opportunity to say whatever she likes. If I didn't know Sarah was practically engaged to Byron Barclay, I'd swear she was flirting with you this afternoon."

Ian responded with a distracted grunt. He usually tried not to think about the Barclays, but, more than a little drunk, he let his mind drift back to the time when he had been part of their family. He closed his eyes, then shared his memories in a lazy monotone.

"There's no question in my mind that Sarah and Robin were in love with Byron and Elliott, but I never gathered the impression either man cared deeply for them. They saw them merely out of habit. Elliott and Alanna were very close, and had he lived, they might have been the ones to wed."

Now Graham was the one who felt uncomfortable, for he could still not utter Alanna's name above a whisper. He'd been enchanted by her, but she had been devoted to Melissa's son and had failed to return his affection. He hadn't realized Elliott had been his rival. "I didn't know."

Ian nodded. "Unfortunately, Alanna shares Melissa's passion for savages." With that bitter pronouncement, he finished the last of his brandy in a single gulp. "Whores, the both of them."

Graham watched his friend haul himself up out of his chair and lumber off to bed, but he remained seated. He wondered how Ian had learned that Alanna had wed Hunter, then decided it really didn't matter. The pair were raising the Indian and Melissa's son and that was all Alanna had wanted.

There were nights, like this one when Graham longed for a woman's company, that he felt more than a twinge of regret for being unwilling to marry Alanna when it meant raising a savage's child. He had loved her, but she hadn't been more then merely fond of him, so it would have been a very bad bargain. Even knowing that, thoughts of her still hurt.

He closed his eyes, and considered the other young women who had caught his interest since he had come to Williamsburg. There had been several, as Virginia was home to a great many beautiful women, but none other than Alanna Barclay had really touched his heart. He had always liked Robin though. She was petite, and possessed a gentle grace he found most appealing. He had been so embarrassed by Ian's silence that afternoon he hadn't been nearly as gracious as he should have. That had been a foolish mistake he wouldn't repeat.

It was high time he put an end to meaningless flirtations and found a young woman to call his own. Robin was most definitely available, and he thought if he were really clever about it, he might even inspire Ian to allow another woman a place in his heart. When he thought of it that way, he decided the Frederick sisters were exactly what both of them needed, and he couldn't hide a satisfied smile as he made his way to bed.

Arielle was still brushing her hair when Byron tapped lightly at her door. She got up from the bed and let him in. "We've something important to discuss," she remarked before turning away.

Byron reached out to catch her hand and drew her back into his arms. "The day was much too long, and whatever you need to discuss can surely wait until tomorrow."

Arielle relaxed in his embrace, but refused to retract her demand. She returned his eager kiss with a languid grace, then placed her hands on his chest. "You promised that if I wasn't happy here, you'd see that I reached New Orleans."

Startled, Byron gripped her shoulders and pushed her back a step. "We've only been home two days. You can't have had time to make your decision yet."

"No, certainly not, but as I mentioned yesterday, I can't just remain here indefinitely. I believe a month will be sufficient time for me to remain here as your guest. By the end of that time, I should know exactly what I want to do."

"A month isn't much time at all, Arielle, especially with my father so ill."

Arielle arched a brow. "I can't base my decisions on the state of your father's health."

"No, of course not, I realize that, but with my attention divided between running the plantation, and his care, I'll have damn little time to impress you favorably."

When he released her, Arielle returned to the bed clad in a ruffled nightgown he had bought for her in Boston, picked up her brush and continued brushing her hair. Long and straight, it fell over her shoulders in a silvery cascade. "You have already impressed me favorably, Byron, don't you know that?"

He sat down beside her and, taking the brush from her hand, tried to hurry her grooming so they could make love. "Well, I certainly hope that I have, but with only a month, you'll undoubtedly feel pressured, and that might force you to make the wrong choice."

Arielle took his hand and brought it to her lips.

"Your mother refuses to allow me to visit your father. She may ask me to leave long before a month is out."

"I'll take care of my mother."

He sounded as though he could handle Rachel easily, and perhaps he could, but Arielle didn't want him to have to. "Did your mother approve of Sarah Frederick?"

Byron gathered the ends of her hair in his left hand and brushed them over his fist. "Yes. Their plantation is just south of ours, and our families have always been close, but convenience isn't the only consideration in choosing a woman." Laying her brush aside, Byron twisted her hair into a gleaming coil he then looped over his hand to draw her close. "We've each had too much sorrow, and we deserve to find happiness together now."

Arielle knew people did not always get what they deserved, but she savored Byron's next kiss, and the next, and would have lured him into giving far more had they not heard Rachel calling his name in a strident tone. "You better answer," she urged.

Reluctant to leave her, Byron rose wearily. "I'll go, but I'll be right back."

"Stay as long as you wish."

Thinking her remarkably understanding, Byron brushed her lips with another kiss and remembered Sarah's constant coy pleas for attention. He was relieved to be rid of her, and his step was light as he hurried down the hall to his parents' bedroom. "Do you need me, Mother?" he asked, striving to keep the irritation out of his voice.

Rachel sighed dramatically. "Yes, I was afraid your father had missed a breath, but he's breathing easier now. Sit with me a while, Byron. I get so lonely spending all my time with your father when he can't even acknowledge my presence. I've been reading to him each afternoon. I don't even know if he can hear me, but it helps to pass the time. Nights are the hardest."

Byron rested his hand on his father's shoulder. John appeared to be sleeping peacefully and Byron doubted his mother had truly needed him. What she wanted was company, and he supposed he owed her that much, but as he sat down beside her, he longed to be with Arielle. He hadn't felt up to making love the previous night, but he wanted her very badly now. Unable to get comfortable, he moved his chair to allow more room for his legs.

"Do you stay up with him every night?" he asked.

"Of course. He would do the same for me."

"Yes, I'm sure he would, but you need your rest, too, Mother. If there's no one here you trust to stay with him, let's hire someone new."

Rachel shook her head. "No, he ought to be with family."

"I'm not suggesting that you ignore him," Byron explained. "All I meant was that you should consider hiring extra help. You know we can easily afford it."

Rachel raised her hand. "Please, let's not discuss the issue any further. I will continue to look after your father for as long as I can." Her lips began to tremble. "My only fear is that it might not be much longer."

Byron reached over to take her hand. It felt surprising small in his grasp, but he gave her fingers a tender squeeze.

"Get ready for bed, Mother. I'll sit with Father a

while longer. I won't go to bed until I'm certain he'll see morning."

"I won't be able to sleep."

"Then lie down and rest."

Rachel stubbornly refused to give in until she could no longer hide her yawns. Then, defeated by fatigue, she kissed her husband and son good night. "I'm glad you're home," she told Byron for the hundredth time. "Don't leave us ever again."

Byron kissed her fingertips, but gave no promises. Left alone with his thoughts, he shifted nervously in his chair and tried to think of ways to amuse Arielle without offending his mother. He wanted to keep her so entertained she would never want to leave him. He could not bear to think she might really want to go on to New Orleans.

"Please God," he whispered. "Don't take her from me, too."

He sat with his father another hour, and then, satisfied John was in no danger of imminent death, he returned to Arielle's room. She was snuggled down beneath the covers, and while he reached for her shoulder, he reluctantly drew his hand away. He had wanted to find her waiting for him as eagerly as he had awaited to return to her, but couldn't blame her for falling asleep. For all she knew, he might have sat up with his father all night.

The soft light of the lamp made her fair hair shimmer with an angelic glow, and while he knew he ought to sleep in his own room that night, he couldn't bear to sleep alone. He undressed, tossed his clothes across a chair and climbed into the bed behind Arielle. He pulled her back against him, and, inhaling the delicate floral fragrance of her hair, decided just being this close to her was almost as good as making love.

Eighteen

Byron awakened as the first rays of dawn licked the terra-cotta walls of Arielle's room with a kiss of flame. No longer able to suppress his need, he coaxed her awake with feathery kisses and soft, lingering caresses. When she turned toward him, her smile warmed him clear through.

"I want you too badly to wait for a more civilized hour," he whispered against the smooth curve of her throat.

Arielle reached up to run her fingers through his hair and pull him close. "You needn't apologize," she assured him. "There's no better way to start the day." Hoping she wouldn't feel ill as long as she remained in bed, Arielle raised up slightly and slipped out of her nightgown. She then flung it toward the foot of the bed with an exuberant toss that brought a deep chuckle to Byron's lips.

"Hush," she scolded playfully. "You should not be in my bed, so you certainly don't want the entire house to know how much you enjoy it."

Byron knew she was right, but made no effort to be quiet as he drew her into a joyous hug. An air of permanent mourning hung over his home, but he felt no sadness when he held Arielle in his arms. He brushed her lips lightly at first, but, intoxicated by her generous affection, he soon began to drink in her kisses with hungry gulps. He wanted her so close their hearts would beat in unison. His caress grew increasingly intimate, circling, delving, invading, until Arielle lay gasping in his embrace, breathlessly urging him to follow his passion for her to a glorious conclusion.

He shifted his weight to enter her more easily, then, enveloped in her throbbing heat, he lay still, kissing her deeply until the stillness itself became agony. Then, anxious to again brand her as his own, he moved with swift, driving thrusts to create the same magical release he had always found with her. Still, he was stunned when it came in great surging waves of joy that left him again too dazed to give voice to his gratitude.

Equally sated by pleasure, Arielle would have been content to hold Byron in her arms all day but all too soon she heard a door close downstairs. The household servants lived in separate quarters on the plantation, but if the first had come to work, the others would soon arrive. She bit her lip to force back hot tears of despair, for she did not want anything to intrude on the blissful moment.

Byron had complained a month wasn't nearly long enough for her to visit his home, but she feared it was longer than she ought to stay. If Byron were ever going to fall in love with her, then wouldn't he already love her now? she wondered. What difference would a month make, except to deepen the scars on her heart when she had to leave.

Byron had also heard the faint stirring downstairs,

but he savored their closeness as long as he dared. As he pulled away, he saw the glimmer of tears in Arielle's eyes and could not understand what was wrong. "Didn't I please you? I was so certain that I had."

Embarrassed that he had caught her in such a melancholy mood, Arielle quickly wiped away her tears. "Of course you pleased me."

When she failed to reveal the cause of her distress, Byron came to the most obvious conclusion. "I know Williamsburg isn't Grand Pré, but it's a wonderful city filled with caring people. I want to take you to church with me this morning. It will give me a chance to introduce you to my friends."

Recalling Sarah Frederick's dismay at meeting her, Arielle sat up and pulled the sheet over her breasts. Still flushed, her nipples were tender and she pulled back slightly. "Do you really think that's wise? From what you've told me, Williamsburg sent a great many volunteers to oppose French settlement of the Ohio Valley, so I doubt anyone will be pleased to meet an Acadian."

Byron leaned over to kiss her. "Well, I was certainly pleased to meet you, and I'll be doubly pleased to have you with me this morning. That's all that truly matters. Put on the green gown for me, please."

He left the bed, gathered up his clothes and, wearing only the bandage on his arm, left her room and crossed the hall to his own. Arielle remained in bed, however, wondering which would prove stronger, Byron's attraction to her, or his loyalty to his mother and friends, whose disapproval would surely pain him regardless of how stubbornly he insisted it wouldn't.

* * *

Sarah had lain awake most of the night, cursing Byron Barclay with every breath. All she had ever been to him was convenient! Humiliated by that realization, she rejected her sister's advice because patience just wasn't the answer. There was no point in giving Byron time to grow bored with his Acadian mistress, for in the unlikely event that he ever did, he would not turn to her. Obviously he didn't see her as a woman, but only as a faded memory.

What she wanted was a man who would value her love and return it. She could remember how sweetly Ian Scott had treated Melissa during her ill-fated pregnancy. He had been patient with her moods, endlessly encouraging, never realizing her child wasn't his. A fine man like Ian had deserved far better. The memory of the sadness in his eyes when they had spoken yesterday evoked a tender response, while thoughts of Byron only provoked dread. The English officer was not only a gentleman, but also a man of means and she had always found his red hair and freckles as attractive as Melissa had.

As a recent widower, it was only natural that he would be depressed, but perhaps all he needed was someone to help him forget his tragic first marriage. Sarah knew she wouldn't need any help in forgetting Byron after the despicable way he had behaved, but what if she pretended otherwise? Inspired, she sat up and hugged her knees. What if she turned to Ian, not with an offer of sympathy but in a request for compassion? After all, she had been betrayed by a

Barclay, and so had he. Wouldn't a friendship between them be natural?

Despite having spent a wretched night, when Robin came into her room, Sarah was smiling and looking forward to the day.

At the close of the Sunday services at the Bruton Parish Church, Graham Tyler thought he had done a masterful job of steering Ian toward the Frederick sisters. It did not even occur to him that Sarah was deliberately leading Robin toward them. Fearing Ian would show his usual contempt for women, he greeted them with enough enthusiasm for two men.

"Ladies, how nice to see you again," he began. "I had thought you couldn't look prettier than you did yesterday, but clearly I was wrong. You're even more lovely today."

Somewhat startled by Graham's effusive flattery, Robin shied away. "Good morning. It's nice to see you again too, Captain Tyler. I hope you'll excuse me, but I want to visit Elliott's grave."

"He was a fine man," Graham assured her. "May I join you? I'd also like to pay my respects."

Robin glanced toward Sarah, who nodded her encouragement. "Why, yes, of course." When Graham offered his arm, she took it reluctantly, for she really didn't want company while visiting Elliott and thought he ought to know it. She glanced over her shoulder at her sister, but Sarah was looking up at Ian with an adoring gaze and provided no help at all.

Graham tried to convince himself her loyalty was

commendable rather than disappointing. When they reached the gradual rise where the Barclays were buried, he stepped back and nodded for her to approach Elliott's grave alone. He turned his back to assure her privacy, and watched the others passing through the cemetery.

Graham took a deep breath, and, enjoying the splendid day, tried to wait patiently. After all, he was positive he could provide much better company than a dead man, if Robin would just give him the chance.

Like Sarah, Robin had expected to join the Barclay family for so long she had no experience entertaining a variety of suitors. To have caught the notice of a handsome British officer was therefore disconcerting. While Graham was wearing a wig that morning, she could recall seeing him without it and knew his dark-brown hair was thick and wavy. His eyes were a clear gray and sparkled with a teasing light.

She found herself smiling in spite of her best efforts not to, for surely Elliott was the only man she would ever love and she ought not to encourage affection she would be unable to return. Then, embarrassed she was perhaps reading more than friendliness into Graham's offer to accompany her, she began to blush.

Because he was so often criticized for being too talkative, Graham had waited for Robin to speak, but when she appeared to be too embarrassed to converse with him, he was at a loss for what to do. Then he had a sudden inspiration. "Would you mind if we strolled around for a bit?" he asked. "Ian desperately needs the company of a gracious young woman like your sister, but he would never approach her on his own. If we could just give them a few minutes to be together, I'm sure it would do him a world of good."

Robin was so grateful she would not have to find a tactful way to discourage Graham's attentions that she wasn't at all disappointed he apparently had no real interest in her. "Why, no, I'd enjoy a walk, and if Sarah can lift Ian's spirits, then I'm certain she will be happy to do so." Relaxing immediately, this time she took Graham's arm without hesitation.

"Do you enjoy reading?" Graham inquired.

"Oh, yes, I most certainly do. Books provide such wonderful company that I never feel really alone when I read. This may sound foolish, but I like to imagine I'm part of the story. Sometimes I pretend I'm the heroine; other times a minor character seems more like me. I hope you won't think me silly."

Graham patted her hand lightly. "No, not at all, in fact, I often do that myself. I like to play the hero's part in my mind."

"You do?"

Robin was looking up at him with such unabashed joy, Graham was positive he had found a way to take Elliott's place in her life. "I've collected so many books since coming to Williamsburg that I've really no more room to store them. I wonder if I might bring you a few that I've especially enjoyed. I don't want to give them away to just anyone."

"Oh, yes, please do. Maybe I have something you'd like to read and we could trade."

It was arranged that Graham would call that very afternoon.

* * *

Ian watched Graham walk away with Robin and tried to think of a compelling excuse to escape Sarah's company. "Miss Frederick," he began.

"Sarah," she leaned close to whisper. "I wonder if I might have a word with you in private, Captain."

Not having expected such a request, Ian wasn't fast enough with an objection and found himself being led away from the crowded walk. Sarah was shapely and smelled sweet, but the part of him that had once enjoyed a woman's company had died with Melissa. When Sarah released his arm, he unconsciously brushed off his sleeve to rid himself of any lingering traces of her touch.

"Captain, you're a man of experience—"

"None of it good," Ian interrupted to say.

"Precisely," Sarah agreed. "That's why I've come to you." She looked down for an instant, and then up at him to show off her long sweep of dark lashes to the best advantage. "I beg your indulgence for a moment. I would ask my older brother for advice, but he's raising a family and has troubles enough of his own. I don't believe he would give my question the serious contemplation it truly deserves."

Before that morning, Ian had never noticed what beautiful eyes Sarah had, and, in spite of himself, he was becoming intrigued by her. "If it's a family matter, shouldn't you consult your parents?"

"No, this hasn't anything to do with my family." After a quick glance around to make certain they weren't being overheard, Sarah again moved close, and in a well-practiced gesture, allowed the fullness of her breasts to brush his arm. "I have always admired you, Captain, and the courtesy you show women. My question is, if a man is as polite as you are in public, but behaves in a disrespectful fashion in private, how should a woman react?"

This was fast becoming the most peculiar conversation Ian had ever had, but he did his best to follow along. "You're speaking of yourself?"

Sarah glanced down shyly, and again batted her eyelashes as she looked up. "Yes, I've already admitted that, haven't I? I should have known better than to try and fool you."

Flattered, Ian straightened his shoulders proudly, and attempted to answer as though he actually understood the completely befuddling interaction between men and women. "If a man behaves badly toward you in private, I see no reason for you to put yourself in that position ever again. Simply refuse to have anything more to do with him."

"He comes from a fine family," Sarah argued.

"That may be true, but any man who would mistreat a woman isn't worth knowing."

Sarah raised a lace handkerchief to wipe away a hint of tears. "Thank you, I appreciate your advice. It's just that when one has feelings for a person, it's sometimes difficult to make wise decisions if they go against our heart's desire. I wonder, could we discuss this matter at greater length another time?"

Melissa had also been petite, but fair, with blue eyes that shone with a radiant innocence she had had no right to affect. Ian saw nothing of her in Sarah, and, genuinely touched by her troubled expression, he heard himself agree without ever giving the decision a conscious thought.

When Graham and Robin returned to the courtyard of the church, he was astonished to find Ian and Sarah standing off to one side, apparently discussing a matter of great importance. He had doubted Ian could tolerate more than a few minutes of any woman's company, but the pair were obviously getting along.

"You see, our ploy appears to be working," Graham pointed out to Robin, squeezing her hand. Can you think of a way to inspire Sarah to invite Ian to accompany me this afternoon? Ian spends far too much time brooding, and the trip out to your place would give him some much-needed exercise."

Eager to help Ian, Robin readily agreed. "Sarah has always been fond of Ian, and so am I. Why don't I just mention that I've offered to loan you some books. Sarah will be sure to ask him to come along."

"I don't know how to thank you."

Embarrassed that what she considered a small kindness would be so greatly appreciated, Robin looked away to hide her blush. "Just bring me the books you promised. That's all I ask."

"I'll fill your whole library if it will help Ian become the man he used to be."

Thinking Graham a wonderfully loyal friend, Robin favored him with a delighted smile, but she still felt sad she would be spending the afternoon with him rather than Elliott.

Because Virginia was an English colony, there was no Catholic church in Williamsburg, and Arielle used that fact to salve her conscience about attending Byron's church. Due to careful planning on his part, they had arrived after most of the parishioners had already entered, thus avoiding any need for introductions. She was greatly surprised to find the Anglican service so similar in format to those she had attended all her life.

Now standing in the courtyard while Byron greeted his friends, Arielle kept expecting the absolute worst. She thought it only a matter of time before an insulting incident occurred.

She knew she might speak Byron's language and wear his people's fashions with the necessary grace, but she didn't for a second feel as though she were really part of the congregation. She managed to adopt an expression of agreeable calm, but it was a fragile façade that would not have withstood close scrutiny. Each time someone approached, she grew more tense.

As she was introduced, time and again she saw welcoming smiles fade into nonplussed stares. The conversations would then abruptly shift to John Barclay's health. When that question had been answered, all pretense of friendliness vanished and the people hurried away only to be replaced by the next set who repeated the same bewildering pattern.

Was this the type of reception she wanted for her child? she asked herself. While she had not expected Rachel to leave John to attend church, she had been surprised Alanna hadn't wanted to come with them. Even if Hunter weren't Christian, she assumed Alanna must be. Believing that wed to an Indian Alanna might be shunned just as she had been that morning, Arielle felt a new kinship with the sweet young woman.

Her attention straying, she noticed Sarah Frederick and the young woman she assumed must be her sister talking with British officers. The sight of the red-coated men sent shivers down her spine and she tightened her hold on Byron's arm. Because he had served in the Virginia militia, she thought he probably knew the men, but neither glanced their way, for which she was extremely grateful. She summoned a smile for the next pair who greeted them, a couple his parents' ages, but, as before, she saw the curiosity in their gazes quickly turn to scorn.

Byron was amazed to discover the state of his father's health drew far more interest than his attractive companion. He introduced Arielle with unabashed pride, and while he saw a mixture of admiration and dismay fill his friends' eyes, he was grateful none dared be as openly caustic as his mother. He also saw Ian and Graham with Sarah and Robin, and hoped the foursome spent so much time together he would never have to speak with Sarah ever again.

As soon as the crowd began to thin, he led Arielle to their carriage. "There, that wasn't such a horrible ordeal, was it?"

Arielle waited until they were on their way home before she responded. "Perhaps not for you it wasn't, but although I'm not used to meeting strangers, it was plain people were shocked by our friendship."

"That's understandable, Arielle, but they'll accept you soon enough."

"You can't force people to like me, so let's not argue about it. Why didn't you tell anyone about your stay in Acadia, or what occurred on the *Incentive*? Didn't you think your friends would be interested?"

Byron had not really expected Arielle to question his decision not to elaborate on his Acadian adventure, and sighed deeply as he considered her comment. "I didn't lie, Arielle. I just didn't provide any details. The reason for not doing so with my mother ought to be obvious, and if I were to describe how Gaetan had taken over our ship to anyone else, it would surely get back to her. I don't want her frightened."

That was a believable excuse, but Arielle didn't think it was entirely accurate. "I think you were protecting me, too."

Byron conceded the point with a slight nod, then moved to her side of the carriage and pulled her into his arms. "You have remarkable powers of insight."

Arielle opened her mouth to ask him to help her find a place to plant the herb seeds she had brought with her, then realized she might not be in Williamsburg long enough for them to sprout. "I wish your mother would let me visit your father," she said instead. "There are no cures for his illness, but I would like to meet him."

Byron had defied his mother by bringing Arielle into their home, and he saw no reason to ban her from his father's room. "Let's wait a few days and give her time to soften. If she doesn't, I'll arrange for you to visit him when she's occupied elsewhere."

"I don't want to deceive her."

Byron met her steady aqua gaze and nodded. "It isn't deception that worries me," he confessed, "but the uncertainty of it all."

Knowing her own heart, Arielle's only uncertainty was if he would declare the depth of his feeling for her before the month elapsed.

Several days passed during which Arielle saw Rachel only when they chanced to meet on the stairs. The woman continued to demand her son's help at odd hours, but Arielle felt sorry for her rather than jealous. Byron, however, soon grew disturbed about his father's care.

"Dr. Earle will be here this afternoon, and I intend to offer to sit with Father so he and Mother can have tea downstairs," he told Arielle. While they're out of the way, I want you to come in and have a look at him."

Arielle pondered his suggestion a long moment. "I asked to meet him, but please remember, I'm a midwife, not a physician."

"Yes, yes, I know, but I don't think it's healthy for him to be cooped up in a dark bedroom all the time. The fall weather's been warm. I think he ought to at least enjoy the sunshine in his room even if he can't go outside, and why shouldn't he have visitors? Maybe he can't respond to them, but I think he'd sense his friends were here and cared about him. You saw how concerned people were about him at church. I know most of them would come see him if they thought they'd be welcome. All I want is an honest opinion. You'll give me that, won't you?"

Arielle hated to refuse him anything. "Yes, but first ask those same questions of the doctor. Your mother will take his suggestions before she will even listen to mine."

Byron slipped his arms around her waist. "Ours," he corrected. "Let's do this together."

As he lowered his head, Arielle met his kiss with the eagerness she always displayed. She would do what she could. They parted and, as planned, she slipped into his parents' bedroom while Rachel and Dr. Earle were downstairs having tea.

The first thing she noticed was the staleness of the air. Without asking permission, she crossed to the nearest window, pulled back the drapes, and opened it wide. "There, that's better already. What did the physician say?"

Byron shook his head. "Mother's been following his instructions, and neither of them see any reason to change them." He turned to his father then, and, the tension leaving his voice, he introduced her. "Come close so he can see you."

Arielle went to the foot of the bed, but John's expression didn't change. His eyes were open, but he didn't appear to see them or hear what was being said. While his features were slack, it didn't take much imagination to see he had once been as handsome a man as his son.

"Good afternoon, Mr. Barclay," she greeted him warmly. Byron gestured for her to come around to the side of the bed and she moved to stand beside him. She took John's hand and squeezed his fingers, but they remained limp in her grasp.

"Your father's color is good," she observed, "and if he's eating and resting comfortably, then I think fresh air and sunshine would definitely do him good. As for visits by friends, I doubt it would harm him."

Byron broke into a wide grin. "I'm going to tell Alanna and Hunter what we think, and the four of us can talk to Mother together."

"That's a good idea, but I think it ought to just be the three of you. I'm merely a guest here, and have no part in your family decisions."

"I want you there."

"Your mother won't, and there's no point in upsetting her before you even begin to discuss your father's care."

Byron would have kept arguing had the determined tilt to Arielle's chin not warned him not to. "Thank you for your opinion then. I'll handle how it's implemented myself."

"Thank you." Fearing Rachel might return sooner than they expected, Arielle bid his father good afternoon and left.

Byron opened another window and sat for a moment on the sill. Just letting more light into the room had raised his own spirits, and he was certain it had been good for his father's as well. "I wish you could tell me what you think of Arielle," he called to him.

He walked over to the bed then, and while he couldn't be certain, he thought he saw a faint smile curving across his father's lips.

Rachel ate her meals upstairs with her husband, but when Byron described the changes he wanted made in his father's care at supper, Alanna and Hunter offered no objections. They discussed the details with optimistic energy and ended the meal with pleasant conversation about the plantation. But as Arielle waited later in her room while Byron spoke to Rachel, she grew increasingly nervous. She doubted his mother would take the changes in the spirit in which they were intended. When she heard the woman's voice clear down the hall, her heart fell.

While she could not make out the words, and did not care to go out into the hall in an attempt to overhear the argument more easily, it was plain to Arielle what was going on. Byron and his mother had obviously not achieved an understanding, and because she was clearly on Byron's side, she felt even further estranged from Rachel. She sat down on the side of her bed, and when she closed her eyes, long-forgotten memories of her parents' arguments came flooding back.

Her father would be away for months at a time, but no sooner had he returned home, than he would begin planning his next voyage with such obvious relish her mother had been crushed. She could actually hear the rise and fall of their voices as they had tried to argue without waking her. She had known only that something was dreadfully wrong. Her mother had screamed, "You love the sea more than us!" and a loudly slammed door had been her father's reply.

When Byron knocked at her own door, she jumped at the sound, then rushed to admit him. "You needn't tell me how it went. I heard."

"No, you don't," Byron insisted. "I told her that we are going to try doing things my way for a change. That means I'm going to hire extra help to relieve us of Father's care, and I'm not going to treat him as though we were already planning his wake. Now that's enough about my family's problems for the evening. It's warm. Let's go down by the river and take a walk in the moonlight."

Amazed by how quickly he could change his mood, Arielle readily agreed, for she would rather stroll in the moonlight any night than listen to the harsh echoes of her parents' fights in her mind.

Nineteen

When Christian took his nap the next afternoon, Alanna joined Arielle in the parlor. Byron and Hunter were busy with plantation business most days, so the two young women had ample time to spend together. Because each genuinely enjoyed the company of the other, their conversations had gone from shyly tentative to relaxed. A knock at the front door caught their attention, and a minute later, Catherine McBride, one of the girls who worked in the house, entered the parlor.

"There's an invitation here for Mr. Byron. I'm afraid he won't see it if I leave it on the hall table. Will one of you give it to him?"

"Yes, of course," Alanna replied. "Please give it to Madame Douville. She'll see that he gets it."

Catherine hesitated, clearly uncertain what to do, but with an embarrassed shrug, finally handed the cream-colored envelope to Arielle.

Arielle waited until the servant had left and then turned the envelope over. "There's no name or address. Who do you suppose it's from?"

"It could be almost anyone. The people of Williamsburg do a great deal of entertaining during October. It's when our courts and general assembly meet for their fall session, and people come from plantations all over the colony to attend the events. You needn't worry, though, Byron wouldn't go to a party without you."

Arielle tapped the envelope against her fingertips. "Don't you share the same friends? Shouldn't there be an invitation for you and Hunter, too?"

Alanna smoothed out her apron, then folded her hands in her lap. "No, not really, but that's rather a long story."

Arielle leaned forward. "I don't want to pry, but Christian will sleep an hour at least, so we've plenty of time for you to tell me whatever you'd care to."

"I've missed having someone my own age to talk to," Alanna confessed rather shyly. "Melissa and I were very close and, like everyone else, I miss her terribly."

"You must have been like sisters. Having been an only child, I envy you."

Alanna grew wistful, for she had had two sisters. Not wanting to depress their guest, she didn't mention the family she had lost. "I wish you could have known Melissa. She was so charming she had lots of friends, and like her brothers, was invited to all the best parties. I've always preferred staying close to home. Melissa constantly encouraged me to go out, but I used to be so shy parties were agony for me. I've gotten better since I married Hunter."

"You've been so gracious to me, I haven't considered you shy at all."

Sincerely pleased, Alanna's smile brightened. "I hope I've answered your question. People just don't expect me to attend parties, so they don't invite me, but I'm not insulted. Hunter would never consent to going with me, and I'd not go without him."

Arielle could readily understand how out of place Hunter would feel at an elegant party, because she would feel equally ill at ease. Not an hour passed that she did not wonder how her friends from home were faring. She knew none could possibly be living in such comfortable circumstances as she and could not help but feel guilty.

To Arielle's disappointment, Byron greeted the invitation with absolute glee. "This is from Roger and Jenny Washburn," he explained to her. "You met them on Sunday. Their parties are always lavish, and I know you'd enjoy it. Jenny included a note urging me to bring you. Here, see for yourself."

There was indeed a postscript to the invitation written in a delicate hand, but Jenny had simply encouraged Byron to bring a guest. "This says nothing about me, Byron, and I think she'd much prefer you brought another woman."

Byron shook his head. "Oh, no, you don't. The party is this coming Saturday night, and you're going with me. You're the one who detests arguments, so if you want to avoid one, say yes."

Caught on that point, Arielle took another tack. "If the Washburns' parties are as lavish as you say, then nothing I own is fine enough to wear."

Intending to maintain the upper hand, Byron had a ready solution to that problem. "You and Alanna are close to the same size and I'm certain she'd be happy to lend you a gown."

Arielle threw up her hands in dismay. "It would be insufferably rude to ask her to lend me a gown when she wasn't invited to the party. When the invitation arrived, she told me she's never had much interest in parties, but isn't it more likely that no one will invite her because she's married to Hunter?"

Byron's smile blurred into an angry scowl. "What she said is the truth. She was so painfully shy as a child that most of our visitors didn't even realize she could speak." Having said that much, he knew he ought to relate the whole story.

"Apparently my father and his younger brother never got along, so rather than share our home, my uncle Alan moved to Maine. He married a young woman he met there and had four children. Alanna was the eldest, and one day while she was at a neighbor's on an errand, the Abenaki raided her family's farm. She lost her father, mother, two sisters, and baby brother in the space of a single afternoon.

"When she came to live with us, she wouldn't get close to the rest of us, but she tagged along behind Elliott for at least a year, and he never complained. She simply adored him, and he must have felt the same about her." Byron turned away to hide his tears. "He was that thoughtful as a child, so you can imagine how fine he was as a man. As for Hunter, there's undoubtedly something to what you said. There's probably not a family in Williamsburg who would entertain him, but that's their loss. Now, the need for a suitable gown isn't really the issue, is it?"

He turned back to face her then, and Arielle fought to express herself in a way he would understand. "No, it isn't. I just don't believe I'll be welcome. There's no reason for you to miss the party, though. Why don't you go?"

If Byron's affection had failed to convince her how important she was to him, then he did not know what would. "We'll go to the party, Arielle. Alanna will be glad to lend you one of her prettiest gowns and next week, we'll have some made especially for you."

Arielle crossed to the window and looked out, again envying the river its peaceful sense of purpose. She could scarcely protest that it would not be proper for him to buy her more clothes when she had accepted the garments he had had made for her in Boston. For that matter, nothing about their friendship had ever been proper. She finally gave in with a distracted nod. She would attend the party, but she could not promise to enjoy it.

The Washburns had lit so many candles, their entire house was aglow with a magical light. As large as the Barclay mansion, and usually as beautifully furnished, for the festivities the furniture had been removed from the parlor and dining room to make room for dancing. As Byron and Arielle came through the front door, the musicians began to play a lively tune. The other early arrivals took up their places to begin a popular country dance, and he led her out among them.

Before Arielle could explain she had not danced in years, she was part of the lively number in which couples moved together and apart with an infectious gaiety that made her breathless. The next tune was a minuet, and grateful for a slower dance she knew, she held Byron's hand tightly as they pointed their toes and began a graceful series of bows. Alanna had not only loaned her a beautiful gold gown but had also brushed her hair into an attractive upswept style. Too blonde to need pomatum and powder, she was a vision of fair beauty.

She did not feel nearly so confident as she looked, however, for despite her satin gown and sophisticated hairstyle, she felt like an imposter at a royal ball. Expecting to be denounced at any second, she tried to concentrate on the music and follow Byron's lead, but there wasn't an ounce of joy in her heart. Her only hope was to survive the evening without disgracing either of them.

Ian Scott was unclear as to how he had let himself be talked into escorting Sarah Frederick to the Washburns' party. He was positive he had adamantly refused to even consider the idea when Graham had first suggested they ought to attend with the attractive sisters, but here he was with Sarah on his arm. He had refused all invitations since Melissa's death, and his first glimpse of the crowded scene filled him with panic, for the last time he had attended such a festive gathering, his late wife had been at his side.

He had expected curious stares, and possibly hushed whispers, but amazingly, the other guests seemed to be having far too good a time to notice him, and gradually his anxiety began to fade. Feeling very foolish then, he reminded himself Sarah had sought him out for romantic advice, and after having encouraged her to look for a new beau, he could not have denied her this wonderful opportunity to do so. Grateful she had no amorous thoughts about him, he glanced around the room, wondering which of the numerous bachelors present might appeal to her.

Delighted to be with the handsome officer, Sarah was positively beaming until she caught a glimpse of Byron and Arielle. She had not thought it was even possible for Arielle to be any more lovely, but the dancing had brought a delicate blush to her cheeks that made her positively radiant. She was not jealous, she told herself in silent praise, but it was awfully hard to look at Byron's smile without shedding at least one tear.

"Please dance with me," she urged Ian.

Ian offered his hand and they joined the couples doing the minuet. He had forgotten, but he had danced with Sarah when he had been courting Melissa, and while he had at first been fooled by her coloring into thinking there was no likeness between her and his late wife, the longer he danced with her, the more distressingly obvious the similarities became.

He watched her closely after they had changed partners and wasn't surprised to see how easily she flirted with the other men present. She had a smile for everyone, an extra squeeze for a hand, and in one case, he was positive she had even winked at a partner. If this was how she behaved when heartbroken over a failed romance, then he did not want to see her in a more carefree mood.

The music changed tempo, and, unable to leave the dance floor without upsetting the appropriate number of men required for the dance, Ian sullenly extended his hand for his next partner. When he glanced down and found Robin looking up at him, he smiled in relief. While he had not spent nearly as much time in her company as Sarah's the previous Sunday afternoon, he had been impressed by her quiet charm. So had Graham, he reminded himself, but when the number ended, he immediately asked her to have a cup of punch with him.

"Yes, thank you. I would be delighted to leave this crowded room for any reason," Robin admitted, then regretting her frankness, she began to blush. She unfurled her fan and waved it briskly. "Please forgive me. I shouldn't have said that. This is a wonderful party."

Amused to find her so flustered, Ian gently eased her through the line at the punch bowl, and as soon as they had been served, on out onto the side terrace. "I can't abide crowds anymore, so I'm not at all insulted to discover you dislike them, too."

Robin took a sip of punch to cover the last of her embarrassment. A heady mixture of autumn berries and spirits, it brought a burst of warmth to her throat rather than the expected refreshing coolness. "I don't dislike any of the guests, you understand. It's just the crush and heat, but perhaps that's because I'm so small."

"You look the perfect size to me."

Robin had spoken to Ian frequently during his marriage, but never alone, and he had not paid her any compliments that she could recall. He had seemed preoccupied on Sunday, but now that he had finished a cup of punch, his gaze was bright with a teasing light. Several more couples joined them on the terrace, and feeling crowded once again, Robin leaned close to whisper.

"As I recall, the Washburns have a lovely fish pond in the center of their garden. Would you like to see it?"

"Yes, I most certainly would." Ian set her cup aside with his, then took her hand.

Laughing as though they were naughty children escaping a dull family dinner, they left the terrace and hurried down the path with a light patter of dancing steps. Scented with roses, the fragrant night air caressed their flushed cheeks, luring them into the heart of the beautifully kept garden. When at last they reached the pond, they found it shadowed by a tangle of water lilies that broke the reflected moonlight into fragmented golden shards. Struck by the beauty of the enchanted scene, Robin sat down on the edge of the circular pond. She raked her fingers along the water sending a flutter of gleaming ripples across the surface and laughed in delighted surprise.

Charmed by the innocence of her pleasure, Ian sat down beside her. When she glanced up at him, and then quickly looked away, he recognized the shy gesture as one she frequently made. Unlike her far more vivacious sister, he knew Robin listened more than she spoke. He understood why she had appealed to Graham, because she reminded him of Alanna, too. Angered that his friend might merely be looking for a substitute for the woman who had spurned him, he wished a suitor for Robin who would appreciate her for herself.

"I was sorry to learn of Elliott's death," he told her. "Although I'm no longer part of the Barclay family, I know how badly he'll be missed. It's good to see you out enjoying yourself. He would have wanted that."

Ordinarily an unexpected mention of Elliott's name brought an immediate rush of tears to Robin's eyes, but knowing of Ian's loss, Robin was able to accept his comment calmly. "Thank you. I like to believe he would want me to have a full life. Now what about you? How was your trip home?"

While Ian usually kept his own counsel, he found it surprisingly easy to confide in Robin. "It was good to see my parents, but visiting England didn't help me all that much. I couldn't escape myself even there, you see."

"I don't understand. Surely you don't blame yourself for Melissa's death."

"No, not for that, but for being fool enough to love her, I most certainly do."

Without conscious thought, Robin reached for Ian's hand. "I don't think love is ever foolish."

Ian could not have disagreed more, but considering the sweetness of Robin's personality, he did not give her the benefit of his far more cynical views. Instead, he squeezed her hand fondly, and cast a silent stare over the water. It was too dark to see more than the surface sparkle. That's all there had been to Melissa, he thought wryly, but dazzled by her glittering reflection, he had never seen her flaws.

Saddened by his bitterness, Robin wished she knew how to assuage it, but, far less sophisticated than her sister, she did not even try. Rather than offer the same sweet hopes for finding happiness with another she so often received, she simply sat with him, quietly enjoying the moonlight. But she truly hoped he would one day find a new love to heal his broken heart.

When Robin heard Sarah calling her name, she immediately withdrew her hand from Ian's and stood so quickly she tripped on her ruffled hem. She might have toppled right into the pond had Ian not leapt to his feet and grabbed her waist to prevent it. Embarrassed he must surely think her clumsy, she thanked him, and quickly turned toward her sister and Graham who were rapidly coming down the path. Even in the pale moonlight, she could see Sarah's brows were knit in a furious line.

"Why are you two hiding out here?" Sarah asked as she reached them. "If the Washburns had wanted guests to tour the gardens, they would have provided lanterns. I certainly don't see any."

Ashamed to think she had thoughtlessly encouraged Ian to wander where the Washburns had not wanted their guests to stray, Robin offered a hasty apology. "We didn't mean any harm, and we've only been away from the party a few minutes."

As astonished to find Ian with Robin as Sarah had been, Graham quickly stepped forward and offered his hand. "Let's go back to the party. There's still plenty of time to dance before supper is served."

Eager to avoid more of the sisterly criticism she had endured all her life, Robin placed her hand in Graham's, but then turned back to Ian. "Thank you for the punch, and your company."

Genuinely sorry they had been interrupted so soon, Ian responded with an easy smile. "The pleasure was mine, Miss Frederick."

Although formal in nature, Sarah was positive that subtle exchange held a wealth of hidden meaning. Too flustered to greet Ian with any of the amusing phrases she had memorized especially for tonight, she walked with him back to the party and then redoubled her efforts to charm him as they began the next dance. When he failed to respond with even half as warm a smile as he had given Robin before they changed partners, she found it nearly impossible to hide her outrage. Left to fume in an agony of curiosity, she had to wait until the musicians paused for a break to speak with Robin. She then hurried her upstairs and demanded an explanation.

All around them in a second-floor bedroom other beautifully gowned women were comparing impressions of the party as they touched up their hair or added perfume. Fearing her sister might create a scene, Robin coaxed her into an unoccupied corner. "We were too warm and went for a walk," she whispered. "There was nothing more to it than that."

"Nonsense. You must have talked about something."

"He said he was sorry about Elliott, and still seemed frightfully depressed about Melissa."

Greatly relieved, Sarah took a step back. "He didn't mention me?"

"No, I'm sorry."

"Yes, so am I. Well, I knew he must still be brooding over Melissa when I began seeing him, so I'll just have to try harder." Dismissing Robin, Sarah turned away and finding an open place at the vanity mirror, began to add a new sprinkling of powder to her hair.

The few people Arielle had not met at church on Sunday all made a point of talking with her now, and after being pushed and pulled through dances she could not even name, let alone claim to master, the string of new faces was a confusing blur. She repeatedly used the gold lace fan that matched her gown to conjure up a stream of air, but when at last she could no longer tolerate another moment in the crowded house, she made a frantic plea in Byron's ear.

"I simply can't breathe. May we please go outside for a moment?"

Finding the makeshift ballroom too close himself, Byron was happy to oblige her. They moved out onto the terrace, where he hoped Arielle would feel better, but no sooner had they stepped outside than he heard someone mention his name.

"What's happened to the Barclays?" Robert Malone asked. "They've got a bastard, a savage, and now Byron's brought home a French whore!"

The comment was met with uproarious laughter. Deeply insulted, Byron crossed the terrace to confront the man who had served with him in the Virginia Militia. He tapped him on the shoulder, and when Robert turned, Byron hit him in the mouth with a vicious blow. Hurled back against his companions, he wobbled on shaky legs, but thanks to a circle of steadying hands, remained on his feet.

Byron scanned the group. There were two others with whom he had fought, and three more who were thought to be gentlemen, and he was disgusted with them all. "Do any of the rest of you have the courage to make such a damning comment to my face?"

Silhouetted in the doorway, Arielle prayed none of the men would strike Byron. When the group backed away en masse, half-dragging, half-carrying their dazed spokesman, she was too frightened to feel relieved.

"I'd like to go home now, please," she begged Byron when he returned to her side.

Byron pulled on his cuffs to adjust the fit of his blue silk coat, and hoped Robert's mouth would be the same vibrant shade in the morning. "I don't think we should let their kind influence our decisions."

Robert was now leaning over the railing retching into the roses, and Arielle felt nauseated herself. "I understand the purpose of standing up to bullies, not tonight please. I'm simply not feeling up to it."

"Why didn't you tell me earlier if you weren't feeling well?"

Exasperated with him, Arielle attempted to still sound pleasant so she would not be regarded as a shrew as well as a whore. "Other than being too warm, I was fine until a few minutes ago but that sorry spectacle sickened me. Now may we please go before I begin feeling any worse?"

There had always been an admirable toughness to Arielle, and certain she would walk out of the Washburns with her head held high, he offered his arm, and after bidding their host and hostess good night, escorted her home. They climbed the stairs together, but Arielle bid him good night at her door.

"I need my rest tonight."

Byron understood that subtle request and brushed her cheek with a tender kiss. "I had hoped that you would enjoy the evening."

Arielle found a smile for him. "I enjoyed being with you."

Cheered the party had been successful in one regard, Byron gave her another light kiss and waited until she had closed her door behind her to enter his own room. He was far more disappointed in the way the evening had gone than he would ever have admitted to Arielle, but he wanted so desperately for his friends to like her and he could see them dismissing her the instant he spoke her name. She might be lovely, but they saw her as French and despised her on principle. Why had he tried to fool himself that their reactions would be more generous? he wondered.

He lay awake for a long while hoping that what he wanted for himself would not continue to be a torment for Arielle.

Too excited to wait until breakfast to hear about the Washburns' party, Alanna rapped lightly on Arielle's door, but one look at the Acadian's pale complexion warned her this was no time for a chat. "I'm sorry for disturbing you. If you're not feeling well, I'll have some breakfast sent up on a tray."

Arielle was still in her nightgown, and the mere mention of food made her stomach lurch. "No, please don't. I'm just tired and I'd rather rest."

As Arielle made a hasty return to bed, Alanna saw something far more disturbing than fatigue. Rather than retrieve the gown she had loaned her and leave, she sat down on the foot of the bed.

"Hunter and I are expecting a second child," Alanna announced. "With John ill and Rachel so terribly upset, we decided not to mention our good news just yet." Before Arielle could reply, Alanna raised her hand. "Before you offer congratulations, I want you to know that while I'm past it now, there were so many mornings when I awoke looking as queasy as you that I can't help but wonder if you aren't keeping a secret, too."

Huge tears welled up in Arielle's eyes, for she liked Alanna too much to lie and the truth was painful. "Please don't tell anyone of your suspicions. We each have good reasons for our secrets, and I'll not share yours. Please don't reveal mine."

"Hunter knows," Alanna confided. "Does Byron?" When Arielle glanced away, Alanna was positive he did not.

"You must tell him today," she urged.

Arielle shook her head. "He doesn't love me, and I'm going to ask to go on to New Orleans."

"You can't be serious! Of course Byron loves you. He wouldn't have brought you home if he didn't."

Arielle closed her eyes for a moment, and when she opened them, her gaze was clear. "He enjoys my company, Alanna, but there's a difference between that and love. That's why I had to leave him."

"Without telling him he's going to be a father?"

"Please, don't make it sound like a betrayal. It's my only choice."

Alanna rose, took a few steps away from the bed and then having come to a decision, came back. "How much do you know about Melissa?"

"Nothing really, other than that everyone was heartbroken by her death."

Alanna crossed her arms under her bosom in a vain attempt to hold back the grief that was still unresolved. "Melissa had an affair with my husband, then, apparently terrified she might have become pregnant, she wed Ian Scott, a British officer she had been seeing. She had a difficult pregnancy and died giving birth to Christian. I'll never forget Ian's rage when he found out Melissa's son wasn't his. He felt his whole marriage had been a lie, and Hunter felt betrayed.

"Melissa's lie damaged not only her memory, but the whole family as well. If you won't tell Byron now, this very morning, then I swear to you, I will tell him myself. I won't be party to a lie that will break Byron's heart the way Melissa broke Hunter and Ian's."

Alanna had survived unspeakable horrors and had a fiery strength as a result. She had defied convention to wed an Indian, and Arielle knew better than to dismiss her threat when clearly she intended to carry it out. She forced herself into a sitting position.

"I'll tell him," she bargained. "Just give me an hour or so to decide what to say."

"No, the truth doesn't require elaborate preparation. I'll give you time enough to brush your hair, but that's all. You ought to trust Byron, Arielle, he'll not disappoint you."

Alanna left before Arielle could open her mouth to beg for additional time. Frantic, she threw back the covers, then, weakened by a rolling wave of nausea, she had to lie back down. She really didn't care if the truth was best. She would rather die than tell it.

Twenty

Arielle wanted to be anywhere but trapped in bed when Byron arrived and through sheer force of will, managed to rise and cross to the comfortable wing chair placed near the window. She had grabbed her hairbrush from the dresser on the way, but after a few desultory swipes, ceased the effort to groom her hair. Alarmed that she had felt too poorly to brew the tea that had restored her health other mornings, she lacked the energy to wipe away her tears. She had been mortified to hear herself described as a whore, but the insult of the previous evening did not begin to compare to the painful humiliation she felt now.

Having to admit the truth would be like begging for an offer of marriage, and had Byron wanted her for his wife, he would have proposed marriage on his own. She had an option, however, and when he knocked at the door, she called for him to come in, determined to take it.

Byron had been delighted by the summons to Arielle's room, but he was understandably shocked to find her looking so far from her best. Seeing the moisture on her cheeks, he was certain he knew the cause. "I shouldn't have left you alone last night knowing how upset you were."

"What happened last night really doesn't matter."

"Well, of course, it does. I won't allow anyone to treat you in a disrespectful fashion, Arielle, and I'm sure you'd have no use for me if I did."

Arielle gripped her brush more tightly. "I know you're a gentleman, Byron, that's what makes what I've got to say all the more difficult."

Byron knelt by her side. "After everything we've been through, you ought to know you can tell me anything."

His expression was filled with precisely the kindness Arielle had come to expect from him, but she did not want to take advantage of his generous nature. Looking away, she focused on the cloudless sky, and spoke in a halting whisper. "Bernard and I hoped to have children. We wanted them desperately, in fact, but when I failed to conceive in the three years we were wed, I assumed I would never have a child. Now I find I was mistaken."

It took Byron a moment to understand what Arielle was saying, but then he broke into a wide grin. He would have whooped for joy but reined in the impulse when he realized her downcast mood made it obvious she didn't share his delighted surprise. He did a quick bit of mental arithmetic before straightening up.

"How long have you known?"

Arielle studied her shaking hands. "It must have happened the first time we were together, but it wasn't until after we reached Boston that I began to suspect what I had assumed to be seasickness had another cause."

"By my reckoning, the first time we made love was

a little over six weeks ago." Byron paused, for while he thought he was a good judge of character and truly knew Arielle, he was still dismayed that he had not really known his own sister. He tried not to judge Arielle by Melissa's shameful standard, but the temptation was simply too great.

While he had not asked, Arielle had assured him she had not slept with Gaetan. Had that merely been part of a clever ruse? he wondered. Confined to the stockade, Gaetan had not provided any competition for her affections, but for all he knew, Arielle could already have been carrying the firebrand's child when he met her. No matter how he analyzed this sudden announcement of Arielle's, the echoes of Melissa's tragedy still rang loudly in his mind.

Disgusted with himself for harboring such evil doubts, he tried not to be harsh with her, but, unwittingly, irritation crept into his manner. "If you've known since we reached Boston, why have you waited another three weeks to tell me?"

Startled by the raw edge to his voice, Arielle risked looking up only briefly. Byron had sounded elated at first, but now that he had had a moment to adjust, he looked far from pleased, and while her heart fell, she couldn't blame him. "I didn't want to trouble you with needless worries. I thought I might be feeling unwell merely because of the strain of leaving home."

"Now I see. First you believed you were suffering from seasickness, and then homesickness. That's your excuse for not confiding in me sooner?" Before Arielle could form a reply, Byron recalled her insistence to be able to go on to New Orleans should she so desire. "Wait a minute. When you set a limit of a month on your visit, you must have already known about the child, didn't you?"

Unable to respond to that damning question, Arielle nodded.

"I'm sorry, I don't understand. Were you just so confused to find yourself pregnant you weren't thinking clearly? Was that the problem or is there something more to this?"

Arielle wished she had had more time to plan her side of this conversation, but she was so depressed she doubted it would be going any better even if she had been able to prepare. "No, I wasn't confused."

"Well, I certainly am." Byron moved toward the window. "You'll have to forgive me, but my sister behaved in a truly despicable fashion, and I'm afraid I'm finding it difficult not to let memories of her cloud my judgment."

"Alanna told me about Melissa," she volunteered. "I really don't see any similarity in our situations. Do you honestly believe that I'd trick you into accepting another man's child?"

"I certainly hope that you wouldn't."

Infuriated that he could even imagine her capable of such duplicity, Arielle pressed down on the arms of her chair, but lacking the strength to rise, had to remain were she was. Livid, she spit out her words in a blistering staccato. "I've no wish to trick you or force you into anything. You promised to see I reached New Orleans, and that's all I want. I'll raise my child there, and you need never fear you'll be embarrassed by either of us ever again."

Blocking that absurd vow with his body, Byron put

his hands over hers and leaned close. 'You're not going anywhere, but I'm going to church. I'll bring the priest back with me and we'll be married this afternoon. People may refer to Melissa's child as a bastard, but I'll be damned if I'll allow them to say that about mine. Have Alanna help you dress, and if you're too ill to come downstairs, it won't matter. This room will be as good as any for our wedding."

Recoiling in dread, Arielle leaned into the padded back of her chair. "How can you accuse me of lying about the father of my child in one breath and then demand that I marry you in the next?"

"Let's not quibble over the lack of poetry in my proposal, Arielle. I'm telling you we'll be married this afternoon and we need never again discuss the circumstance that prompted our haste."

Byron caught her mouth in a bruising kiss that he didn't end when he felt her stiffen. He kissed her as though getting married was precisely what he wanted to do, but in his heart, he was as badly confused as she.

Byron returned with the priest as promised, but he had completely overlooked the complication his mother would present. He found her waiting for him at the front door. Her fury was etched plainly on her delicate features, and she did not moderate her tone in deference to the priest.

"Hasn't our family borne enough tragedy without your taking that French trollop as your wife?"

"Arielle may have French ancestors, but she's no

trollop, and I won't permit you to insult her ever again."

"It's not your place to give me orders!"

"When it comes to my wife's happiness, it most assuredly is. I regret the fact Father isn't well enough to attend the wedding, but I'm hoping you'll want to be there."

"I would rather leap off the roof!" Rachel spun on her heel, ran up the stairs, and when she reached the bedroom she shared with her husband, she slammed the door hard enough to jar the whole second floor.

Shocked by that show of ill temper, the priest nearly dropped his prayer book. "Perhaps you would like to postpone the wedding," he suggested fretfully.

"Certainly not. My fiancée has her heart set on marrying me this very day." Byron showed the priest into the parlor, asked Catherine to fetch him some tea, and then went upstairs to check on Arielle. Before he had time to knock at her door, Hunter appeared.

"Alanna told me you want to get married, and I want to be your best man," he announced.

Byron was ashamed he had not thought to offer the brave that honor. "I'm sorry. I should have asked you before I left for town. My mother's refused to attend the ceremony, but I know that won't influence your decision."

Hunter broke into a wicked grin. "Your mother and I do not agree on anything but loving Alanna. Do you have the ring? Alanna said I'm supposed to hold it."

"Oh damn. I didn't even think of that. Does Alanna have Melissa's jewelry?"

Hunter stepped back. "No, don't use anything of hers, not even for a day."

"You're right. Well, since you've agreed to be best man, what do you suggest?"

Hunter responded with a sly grin. "I'll ask Alanna to find a ring. Now, go back downstairs; the wedding will be in the parlor."

Byron returned to the priest. "They'll be with us in a moment," he assured him.

"Perhaps I ought to speak with your mother," the priest offered. "It's a shame to see a family divided on what should be a happy occasion."

"You needn't bother. I want you to join us for dinner, and before you leave, perhaps you could say a prayer with Mother for my father."

Reluctantly convinced he could do nothing more, the priest nodded, then, struck by the unusual wedding party descending the stairs, he stared with mouth agape. Byron turned to see what had startled the cleric, and found Arielle approaching on Hunter's arm. It had not even occurred to him to provide her with an escort since she had no relatives present, but even clad in fringed buckskins, Hunter looked as proud as any father ever could. And Arielle had chosen to make the most of their wedding and borrowed another beautiful gown from Alanna. The neckline and sleeves of the lavender satin dress were adorned with exquisite white lace shot with silver threads. She had again styled her hair atop her head and added silver combs. She moved with the regal grace of a princess and when she glanced toward Byron, her gaze held an unwavering pride that made him sincerely regret not having greeted her startling announcement with more compassion.

Alanna, dressed in a shimmering rose gown, came forward to whisper a request, and when Byron nodded, she smiled at the priest. "Will you wait just a moment please, our household staff would like to attend."

When Alanna had mentioned inviting the servants, Arielle had expected only a few, but in came the housekeeper, and the McBride sisters, who served as maids, along with their mother, Polly, the cook, and their brother Andrew, who drove the Barclays' carriage, and an assortment of others ranging from the laundress to the cooper.

When the priest told Byron to take her hand, Byron was concentrating too hard on the wording of the vows to notice the chill of it. He was serious about the promises he made, and sincerely hoped that regardless of this wretched start, he and Arielle would be happy. Hunter slipped him a gold wedding band, and, relieved that he had the proper token, he slipped it on Arielle's hand.

When the ceremony drew to a close, he gave her as passionate a kiss as he dared in front of a priest and roomful of servants, but her response was cool. He hid his disappointment by thanking the priest, and then with his arm draped around her waist, turned to accept the congratulations of the odd assortment of guests.

After they extended their best wishes, and finally filed out, an awkward silence filled the parlor.

Byron was obviously ill-at-ease, but knowing she was

the cause, Arielle had no way to make things easier for him. She glanced toward Hunter, who smiled, and she realized that for the first time, she wasn't afraid of him.

Alanna returned with Christian, whom she balanced on her lap during dinner, and his happy laughter kept the meal from lapsing into too many embarrassed silences. Each time Arielle glanced the baby's way, she wondered at the joy she saw reflected in his eyes and hoped her child would be just as happy. She herself had felt numb since that morning, and prayed she would not have to spend the rest of her life proving herself to a husband who had not wanted her.

After they finished eating, Byron led her down to the river where they had walked in the moonlight not too many nights before. When they came to a romantic spot, he pulled her into his arms. "I'm sorry I didn't put more planning into our wedding. You deserved something so much nicer and—"

Arielle raised her fingertips to his lips. "I had one beautiful church wedding, so you needn't have any regrets about today because I've not missed anything. I'm sorry that you couldn't share the ceremony with all your family and friends."

"I didn't miss them," he assured her. "Let's go into town tomorrow and I'll buy you another ring. I want you to have one of your own."

Arielle drew away slightly. "This is my own ring," she explained. "When Alanna mentioned one was needed, I unpacked the one Bernard gave me."

Byron saw the gold band not as a symbol of their marriage, but as another blasted reminder of how much she had loved another man. He was ashamed to be jealous of a dead man, but he could not overcome the uncomfortable sensation. "Well, in that case, we are definitely going to replace it first thing in the morning. You're my wife now, and I want you wearing my ring."

While Arielle rebelled inwardly, she kept her thoughts to herself. Unable to stifle a wide yawn, she hurriedly apologized. "I didn't sleep well last night. I'd like to go up to my room and rest."

Byron took her hand as they started back toward the house. "I understand, but tonight I expect you to share my bed."

"Is that going to top the list of my duties?"

Byron stopped and pulled her around to face him. "There are absolutely no 'duties' involved in our marriage, Arielle. We may have had no choice about marrying today, but that doesn't mean the decision was ill-advised. I want us to be happy."

Arielle listened attentively as Byron spoke of his hopes for their life together, but not once did he mention love, and that was the only word she wanted to hear.

Byron had given Arielle more than what he considered sufficient time to prepare for bed, and fearful of another confrontation, he had gone stomping into her room only to have her greet him with what he considered an enchanting smile. Rather than berate her for her defiance, he scooped her up into his arms and carried her to his room. He sat her down on his bed, then yanked off his shirt.

"It's a damn good thing I'm strong enough to carry you, but if I weren't, I would have slept in your room. This is our wedding night, and I sure as hell wouldn't have missed it."

Arielle watched him undress. Sorrow still weighed heavily on her heart, but that didn't diminish her admiration of him. When he joined her in his bed, she displayed none of the shyness of a new bride, but instead the tantalizing grace of a vixen. Her kiss was warm, then hot, as the passion each provoked in the other burst into flame. Her nightgown was quickly lost and then the bedclothes were scattered.

Arielle clung to Byron as he laved her breasts with adoring kisses. Tautly muscled, his lean, powerful body was glorious to the touch and she wanted still more of him. While Byron might not have wed her willingly Arielle vowed to make him such a contented husband he would never stray.

Lost in a maze of desire, Byron had no thoughts at all save those of again pleasing Arielle. She was so wonderfully responsive and giving. His hand slid over the soft hollow of her stomach. It was too soon for her incipient motherhood to show, but he knew he would be very proud when it did. He buried himself deep inside her and shuddered through a joyous climax that left him drained of all feeling save those he had for her. After making love until dawn, they slept so long they did not reach town to purchase another wedding ring until late in the afternoon.

Graham Tyler heard the news of Byron's marriage before Ian, and his first concern was for Sarah

Frederick. "I think we should visit Robin and Sarah this very afternoon," he urged. "You and I may know the Barclay brothers had no real interest in them, but Byron's marriage will still provide a shock. I'd rather we tell them than that they hear about it from an unsympathetic source."

Ian was not even remotely tempted to accompany Graham. "I'm not going out to the Frederick place ever again. Sarah asked my advice, and I've given it. I can't do anything more for her."

"I'm sure what she really wanted was your company, Ian, and I can't believe you didn't enjoy hers."

What Ian had enjoyed was his last conversation with Robin, but knowing how fond Graham was of her, he did not reveal that he liked her, too. Unlike his late wife, he was a man of honor, and would not compete with a friend for a woman. "You were mistaken. She reminds me too much of Melissa."

"How can she possibly remind you of Melissa? She doesn't look anything like her."

"It isn't a matter of appearance, but of attitude. She's a manipulative little flirt and I've had enough of her kind to last me an eternity. Don't try to change my opinion of her. If and when I decide I want a woman's company, I'll find my own."

Since Ian's return from England, Graham had frequently seen him in intractable moods, but this time Ian had actually stated a reason for the bleak state and, convinced his friend truly disliked Sarah Frederick, he ceased pestering him about her. He hated to visit the Fredericks' with bad news, but it was a convenient excuse for an impromptu call and he didn't want to miss it. Hurrying off to saddle his horse, he hoped he would arrive in time for tea.

Robin saw Graham coming up the walk and called to her sister. Sarah rushed to her side, then drew back. "Where's Ian?" she asked petulantly.

"I'm sure Graham will tell us, but you mustn't sound disappointed he's come alone. He's a very nice man, and quite good-looking, too, in case you've not noticed."

"I've noticed," Sarah admitted. "I just happen to prefer Ian." Not really caring why Graham had come to call, she let her sister welcome him to their home and ring for tea. Distracted, she paid little attention to the conversation after Graham mentioned Ian had been busy with the payroll. She ate a tiny cake and sipped her tea, but made no comment until Graham revealed the news of Byron's marriage to Arielle.

Tears flooding her eyes, Sarah turned to Robin. "You see how much good patience would have done me?" Unable to hide her heartbreak, she fled the room.

"I was afraid that was going to happen," Graham confessed. "I had hoped Ian would come with me to console her. According to him, Byron never cared as deeply for Sarah as she did for him."

Robin found that impossible to believe. "He actually said that to you?"

Suddenly realizing he was on dangerous ground, Graham tried to retreat. "Well, he lived in the Barclay home for nearly a year, Robin, so he had an opportunity to get to know Byron well."

"Byron was away fighting most of the time Ian lived there."

"Oh, was he?" Graham swallowed hard. "Yes, I suppose he was, but still, Ian had ample opportunity to talk with him." Robin still didn't look convinced, and Graham suddenly realized without Ian's continued interest in Sarah, he might have difficulty courting her alone. Attempting to set things straight, he tried the truth for a change.

"I'm afraid I've done your sister a terrible disservice," he said.

"You're saying the strangest things today, Captain. Whatever do you mean?"

"I've been using Ian as an excuse, and while I did want him to take an interest in Sarah, it was the fact that I wanted to call on you that brought us here that first time."

"I thought you wanted to trade books."

"I would have used any excuse to visit you." Embarrassed he might look a fool, Graham spilled out his intentions in a tangled rush. "I don't do all that well with women, you see, and I wanted so badly to impress you, that I hoped if you thought we were together in order to help Ian regain his optimistic outlook on life you might come to like me without feeling any pressure to do so. But now Ian's refused to see Sarah again, and I don't want you to stop seeing me."

Robin slumped back in her chair. "First Byron's gotten married, and now you say Ian isn't interested in Sarah, either?"

"Oh, please don't tell her I said that about Ian. When he doesn't call on her anymore, I'm sure she'll find someone else. If there's another officer she's mentioned, perhaps I can bring him along the next time I come to see you."

The day had seemed quite ordinary until an hour ago, and now Robin knew she had two very serious problems. The first was Sarah, who was already undoubtedly crying her eyes out over Byron, and would soon learn she had no chance to win Ian Scott either. The second was dear Graham Tyler, and his affection for her.

"Captain, I think it would be best for all concerned if you and I did not see each other again. I do like you; but I don't have romantic feelings for you. What you need is a woman who's free to fall in love and I'm still in love with Elliott, and may always be."

Graham wasn't ready to withdraw gracefully. He rose and, taking Robin's hands, drew her to her feet. "You say you like me and that's enough for now. I want to go on seeing you, Robin. I won't let you throw your life away on Elliott when it was Alanna he loved, not you."

Had the earth opened beneath her feet and swallowed her up, Robin could not have felt a stronger rush of fear and crushing dread. "No, that's not true. Elliott loved me!"

Graham wanted to console her too badly to back down. "It is true," he insisted. "Ian told me how close they were. Had Elliott lived, they would have been the ones to marry."

Robin swayed in Graham's arms. She clutched the wide lapels of his jacket and shook her head as hot tears of shame coursed down her cheeks. "No, you're lying. I was the one Elliott loved."

Graham pulled her close. "Elliott loved you about as much as Byron loved Sarah. Can't you understand that?"

"I loved him!" she screamed, and, tearing herself from Graham's arms, began to back away. "I can't see you again. I won't. Please go away and don't ever come back."

"Robin!" Graham started after her, then stopped. He had told the truth, expecting it to set her free to love him, but now he wished he had cut out his tongue instead.

"I don't know anything more about love than Ian," he cried unhappily as he mounted his horse, and, looking forward to getting drunk with his best friend and forgetting about women entirely, he galloped back into town.

Twenty-one

Sarah had taken to her bed before Graham left the house, and past noon the following day, showed no sign of leaving it anytime soon. Robin donned her riding habit, then looked in on her.

"You're going out?" Sarah gasped through a hiccup. "Where could you possibly have to go that's more important than being here with me?"

"I'm going into town."

Sarah plucked a fresh lace-trimmed handkerchief from the stack on her bed and blew her nose. "Alone? You never go anywhere alone."

Robin had begun to think that was definitely part of the problem. "I'm certain I'll be safe from all threat of harm in midafternoon, and Mother's here if you need company." As Robin pulled the door closed, Sarah's startled expression gave her a new-found sense of satisfaction. The sisters were so similar in appearance new acquaintances often got their names confused, but they were two separate people, and Robin felt fully competent to venture out on her own.

She rode her sorrel mare into town and went straight to the barracks where the British troops were quartered. Without dismounting, she asked to speak with Captain Scott, and a grinning soldier ambled off to find him. Robin was well aware of the fact she was probably making a complete fool of herself, but it was a small price to pay for the truth. When Ian appeared, she had intended to apologize for interrupting his duties, but he looked so happy to see her that she promptly forgot to do so.

"Good afternoon, Miss Frederick. I'm sorry I wasn't able to visit you yesterday with Graham."

"You needn't be, I've seldom had a worse afternoon, and Sarah would judge it no better. Did Graham tell you the subject of our conversation?"

Graham's horse was saddled and tied to the nearby rail. Rather than continue to discuss what he feared was an intensely personal matter, Ian mounted the bay gelding and gestured for the soldier who'd summoned him. "I'm going to escort Miss Frederick home. Tell Captain Tyler I've borrowed his horse."

"That really isn't necessary, Captain. If you'll just answer a question for me, I can find my own way home."

"I'm not worried you'll become lost," Ian stressed, "only that we might lack the privacy we need here."

Robin wasn't worried about making a scene, but she appreciated Ian's offer of privacy and turned her mare to ride along beside him. "Could we please stop just outside town? Graham told me you didn't plan to call on Sarah anymore, and if you come home with me, she'll misunderstand."

Graham had been unusually quiet the previous evening, and now Ian began to suspect it was out of guilt rather than what he had assumed was merely fatigue. "Certainly, if that's what you wish." They continued down the street, and while Ian noted the admiring glances sent Robin's way, she appeared to be completely oblivious to them.

She watched the road rather than flirting with him or passersby, and Ian again thought her company most agreeable. He urged her to continue past the edge of town but after a few minutes, led her into a secluded grove of cottonwood trees. He slid from his saddle and then helped her down from hers.

"There, this is much better," he exclaimed, and with a reluctance that surprised him, he released his hold on her narrow waist. Embarrassed he might have inadvertently revealed his growing affection for her, he took a step backward and clasped his hands behind his back. Tall and slim, his red coat, white breeches, and high black boots made him a dashing figure, but like Robin, the attractiveness of his appearance did not concern him.

"Now we don't have to worry about being interrupted."

Too restless to face him squarely, Robin moved away, her steps muffled by fallen leaves. "I'm not in the habit of luring men away from their work in the middle of the day, Captain. I really meant to take only a minute of your time."

Ian nodded. "I understand."

"Good, then I hope you'll also understand that your answer to my question is of vital importance to me."

Pleased to be with such a sincere young woman, Ian found it easy to be gracious. "Ask me whatever you wish."

Because Byron's recent marriage made his feelings

plain, she dispensed with asking about him and her sister in favor of pursuing her own need for reassurance. "Graham told me you were of the opinion Elliott was in love with Alanna rather than me. Is that true?"

"Dear God in heaven, did Graham actually say that to you?" Ian took a step forward, then halted when Robin's eyes widened in dismay. "Of course he did, or you'd not have asked me such an outrageous question, would you?"

"That's scarcely an answer, Captain."

"Let's take a walk."

Robin shook her head. "I would prefer we stayed right here, and that you gave me a simple yes or no."

Ian struggled to extricate himself from an impossible position. "What Graham repeated was no more than drunken speculation that I refuse to dignify with discussion." He offered his hand. "Come with me. We can talk as we walk."

That a fine man like Ian Scott would admit to drunken speculation was a jolt, but Robin unaccountably found herself reaching for him. She was wearing forest-green kid gloves that matched the green of her dress, and they disappeared into the warmth of his hand. He adjusted his stride to the shorter length of hers, and while she was grateful he was being so considerate, she feared he was only putting off telling her what he knew she did not want to hear. Steeling herself for an awful blow, she bit her lip and tried not to give in to tears as Ian began speaking.

"Melissa was ill during most of our marriage, and I spent so much time catering to her whims that I saw very little of the rest of the family. I took scant note of what Byron and Elliott said or did and at no time did I ever discuss you or your sister with either of them. That Graham would repeat a remark that was flavored with more bitterness and brandy than sense is unforgivable, and I intend to take it up with him."

"Oh, please don't."

Ian drew to a halt but kept ahold of her hand. "No, I must. It was cruel of him to make you doubt what you know to be true, and he'll have to pay for it."

Robin's heart was pounding so loudly in her ears, she wanted to be certain she had understood him. "You really don't know how Elliott felt about me?"

The delicate arch to her brows gave away the intensity of her hopes and Ian was quick to reassure her. "You knew him far longer and better than I did, Robin. Trust your memories, and don't ever let anyone else's thoughtless remarks tarnish them."

Ian's manner was sincere, and his hazel gaze lacked any hint of subterfuge. Relieved of her fears, Robin at last drew a deep breath and smiled up at him. "Thank you for giving me such wonderful advice, but please don't be too harsh with Graham. I told him I'd not see him again, obviously too bluntly, and that's what prompted him to reveal your comment. He wouldn't have done it had I not hurt his feelings."

Ian felt the breeze across his cheek before it ruffled the leaves at their feet, but the afternoon was still warm and he didn't want it to end. He softened his voice slightly in hopes of masking his feelings. "He's very taken with you. Why don't you want to see him?"

Robin opened her mouth intending to provide the same excuse she had given Graham, but standing so close to Ian brought a delicious excitement that caught her by surprise. She had always liked him, but had never been alone with him until Saturday night. She recalled the short time they had spent together as the best part of the whole evening. Embarrassed, she felt the warmth of a bright blush flood her cheeks.

"I told him that I still cared for Elliott, but I realize now that was only partly true. Oh, I do still love him, and part of me always will, but there's someone else, too."

Caught off guard, Ian couldn't hide his disappointment. Dropping her hand, he took a step away and took up a nonchalant pose against the nearest tree. "If you prefer someone else, then you did the right thing in asking Graham not to call. Whoever this other man is, he's very lucky. I can't help but envy him."

Ian began to brush the fallen leaves with his toe. It was a distracted gesture, but Robin wasn't put off by it. She wished she had Sarah's easy way with men, then suddenly was grateful that she did not. She approached him slowly. "I was talking about you," she admitted.

Ian's head came up with a jerk. He stared at the dark curls peeking out from beneath the brim of Robin's hat, then at the radiant darkness of her eyes. It was the generous curve of her lips that caught his attention next and he again offered his hand. "Come here," he ordered in a husky whisper.

Robin moved into Ian's arms with what she feared was unseemly haste but his kiss, unlike any of the chaste exchanges she had had with Elliott, made her shudder with delight and she ceased to worry over whether or not her behavior was proper. When he swung her up in his arms to seat her atop a convenient branch, she laughed easily with him. Their mouths were at the same level now, and Robin wound her arms around his neck as he made his second kiss even better than his first.

Breathless with the first rush of desire she had ever known, Robin folded Elliott's memory away with the most precious times of her childhood, for now that Ian had shown her how it truly felt to be a woman, she no longer needed her first sweetheart. As eager for Ian's kisses as he was to give them, she clung to him, welcoming the slow thrust of his tongue with a sense of wonderment and joy. When he finally drew away to catch his breath, she reached for his lapels to pull him back.

Ian grabbed her hand and brought it to his lips. "I'm sorry, I didn't mean to rush you like that, but it's been nearly a year since I held a woman in my arms. I hope I didn't frighten you."

"Not at all," Robin responded with a burst of giggles. "I like you even more than I thought I did."

"Good, then you won't mind if I come to call on you?"

At first thrilled by that prospect, Robin's expression filled with concern when she remembered her sister's current agony. "What are we going to do about Sarah. I couldn't bear it if she blamed me for taking you away from her."

Ian removed her hat to spill her dark brown curls over her shoulders. "I was never hers," he argued. "She asked my advice, and somehow I ended up escorting her to the Washburns' party. I was hoping she'd meet a man she liked there, but I had no interest in her myself." As if to prove his words, Ian kissed Robin again, a long, slow, luscious kiss that left him draped against the tree. "I want to court you properly, Miss Frederick, and I don't want you to have to choose between your sister and me."

Robin sighed. "Byron's marriage broke her heart, and I know she's so fond of you. Could you wait a while before you pay me any calls? Sarah wants so badly to have a beau and I'm afraid she would see our happiness as a betrayal."

Not at all pleased to be asked to wait after suffering through a year of humiliation and loneliness, Ian could not agree. "I'll take care of this," he promised instead. "I know a man who would be perfect for Sarah, and I'll see he visits her before the week is out."

Robin watched his slow grin widen. He had a wonderful smile and she was so glad to see him use it. "Tell me his name."

"No, I want it to be a surprise." Grabbing her waist, Ian plucked her from the branch and set her on her feet. "The first of a great many very pleasant surprises I hope to provide. After all, you certainly surprised me today."

"I fear I was shamefully bold," Robin murmured as she pushed her hair up under her hat.

"No, my dear, you simply spoke the truth, and that's such a rare trait I hope you never lose it." Ian held her hand as they walked back to their horses, and then sent her on her way home wearing a smile as wide as his. He then started back into town with one intention in mind. He was going to give Graham Tyler a choice: he could either suffer the worst beating of his life for revealing a confidence that could have broken Robin's heart or he could promptly switch his affections to Sarah and save himself considerable pain.

Graham was no coward, but feeling that he truly did owe Sarah Frederick an apology for involving her in his failed attempt to win Robin's love, he chose to call on her rather than fight his best friend. Badly troubled, he doubted he could muster the necessary eloquence to impress Sarah, but he hoped she would at least accept his words as sincere. Assuming she could have any man she wished, he also doubted she would encourage him to return, but he would have fulfilled the conditions Ian imposed simply by visiting her once, and, straightening his shoulders proudly, he knocked at her door.

The Fredericks' housekeeper admitted the officer, then went upstairs to Sarah's room. "There's a Captain Tyler here to see you, Miss Sarah. What shall I tell him?"

"There must be a mistake. Hasn't he come to see Robin?"

"No, miss, he said your name."

Robin had been seated by the window reading aloud to her sister, and while at first puzzled by Graham's request, she quickly guessed what Ian had done. She carefully marked her place in the novel, then laid it aside and came to the bed. "I've asked Graham not to call on me anymore. He's very nice, but just not the man for me. If he's asking to see you, then I imagine it's because he truly wants your company."

"You turned him down, so now he's interested in me?" Sarah murmured dejectedly. "That's scarcely flattering. Why hasn't Ian come to call?"

Robin didn't know how to answer the question about Ian without upsetting Sarah, so she ignored it for the moment. "Graham and I had an interesting discussion or two about books, but we really had nothing else in common. He's such an enthusiastic individual, really far too gregarious for me, and I know I would have begun to bore him in another week or two. You, on the other hand, have the perfect temperament for him. Why don't you see him? I'm sure if you spent some time together, you'd really like him."

"If he thinks so highly of me, then why didn't he call on me first? I don't want to be anyone's second choice," Sarah countered defensively.

Robin watched Sarah twist a damp handkerchief into a knot and refused to allow her to do the same to her life. She turned toward the housekeeper, who was still waiting at the door. "Please tell Captain Tyler that Sarah will be with him in a few minutes."

"But that's not true!" Sarah cried.

"Oh, yes, it is." Robin nodded to the housekeeper, who hid her smile as she closed the door. "Now, you're going to get up out of that bed and put on your prettiest gown. We both know Byron was your first choice, and Elliott was mine, but neither of us saw our dreams come true and if we don't want to die bitter spinsters, then we're just going to have to set our sights on someone new."

Shocked that Robin was showing so much initiative, Sarah let herself be rolled out of bed, but it took her nearly half an hour to look presentable enough to go downstairs and greet her guest. As she entered the parlor, she found Graham standing at the window. He'd come without his wig, and she was surprised by how attractive his wavy, dark-brown hair was. He had broad shoulders, narrow hips, and when he turned to face her, she blushed at how shamelessly she had been appraising his well-proportioned physique.

He wasn't Byron Barclay, that was certainly true, but he was handsome nonetheless, and when he smiled at her, she ceased to care how many times he had called on her sister. She took a place on the settee, poured him a second cup of tea and one for herself. "I'm sorry to have kept you waiting, Captain, but since you were here the other day, I'm afraid I've not been at my best."

Graham returned to his chair. "Which is all my fault, I know. That's why I'm here, to apologize."

A wave of disappointment crested in Sarah's heart, just below the level of tears. "Oh, I see. Well, that was very kind of you," she murmured softly.

Sarah had been smiling so prettily when she had first come in, and the change in her mood wasn't lost on Graham. "I'm afraid I've just done it again. I mean well, Miss Frederick, I honestly do, but nothing I say ever comes out the way it should. You must think me tactless in the extreme, and perhaps I am, because no matter how hard I try, I never make a good impression."

Flabbergasted he would make such a damning admission, Sarah stared in dismay as Graham continued to bemoan his failings. She had been so intrigued by the challenge of winning Ian's heart, she had not paid much attention to Graham, but listening to him now, she felt a sympathetic kinship and warmed to him immediately. When he paused for a breath, she was eager to speak.

"I know exactly what you mean," she offered encouragingly. "Sometimes I want to be liked so badly that I'm afraid I try too hard. Then the chance for a harmonious friendship is lost. When you came here alone the other day, it was because Ian didn't want to see me again, wasn't it, rather than that he was busy?"

Now knowing better than to tackle such a sensitive subject, if not much else, Graham pulled out his handkerchief and mopped his brow. "I can't speak for Ian, Miss Frederick."

Sarah responded with an anguished wail. "You see, that was an incredible blunder. I never should have mentioned him. Robin pointed out the importance of compatible temperaments to me a few minutes ago and I'm afraid Ian and I aren't anything alike. He's become such an introspective man, and here I am, babbling on about nothing as usual. I probably hurt his ears."

"I don't think you're babbling," Graham was quick to argue. "I think you're making perfect sense. I'm afraid I owe you another apology, though. You see, I did so want Ian to find happiness that when we met you and your sister in town that day, I thought since there were the two of you, and the two of us, that we might enjoy spending time together. I didn't know either of you well enough to realize that Robin was better suited to Ian, and I hope you won't think me too forward, but after this conversation we've had today, I think you and I are a much better match."

Graham wasn't spouting lines Ian had demanded, but completely sincere. He was charmed to finally find a young woman who was so much like himself, and prayed he had not behaved like too great a fool for her to like him. He took a sip of tea, and his hand shook so badly his cup clattered noisily as he replaced it on the saucer.

Sarah watched the nervous young man without a single disapproving thought. "I'd like the opportunity to get to know you better, Captain. Do you have time for a walk by the river? I'd like to hear about your home and family."

Graham sprung from his chair with an enthusiastic leap. "I can stay as long as you like. What I mean is, I'd like to stay a while longer. I don't wish to impose."

Sarah rose and, after donning a wrap, led him out the front door. "You aren't imposing at all. In fact, the whole afternoon would have been an utter waste had you not arrived. Now, do you really believe Ian and Robin might be suited to one another?"

Graham already knew Ian wanted Robin, and he summoned every bit of tact he possessed in an attempt not to reveal it. "Yes, I think they would. Do you suppose you could encourage your sister to take an interest in him? He deserves every happiness after what Melissa put him through."

Sarah nodded thoughtfully. "I've always had considerable influence over Robin, and I'll try my best to nudge her in Ian's direction. She assured me they were merely too warm to remain inside at the Washburns' party, but I wasn't entirely convinced that was true."

Graham had had his own suspicions that night, but he nodded as though he were just now considering what might have transpired. "You may be right," he agreed. "They may already like each other, but let's just step out of their way, and allow them to find each other on their own."

"Absolutely not," Sarah exclaimed. "This is far too important a matter to be left to chance. I will speak to Robin this very day."

Graham took Sarah's hand. "Of course, you're the expert when it comes to your sister." Enjoying a rapport he had never found with another woman, he began what he soon feared was too rambling a description of his parents and sisters, but to his immense relief, Sarah didn't seem bored at all.

Rachel Barclay had heard Byron's arguments so many times she covered her ears when he began to recite them again. "Yes, I'll readily admit I'm tired, but I refuse to have incompetent strangers tending your father."

"Perhaps we've been going about this all wrong. We've plenty of people here on the plantation whom Father knows and trusts. Why don't we select several, and hire someone to cover their jobs when they're with Father?"

Rachel immediately opened her mouth to object, and then realized Byron's latest suggestion was so sensible she really could not find one. The trouble was, she did not want to relinquish her husband's care to anyone. "The Fredericks will be here soon. Let's talk about this after they leave. I don't want to be upset when they arrive."

Determined to settle the matter of additional staff before sunset, Byron agreed to postpone the discussion until later, but he had not anticipated just how poorly the Fredericks' visit would go.

Not wanting to crowd the bedroom, he had waited downstairs with Arielle, but the pair were not upstairs more than five minutes before they came hurrying down again. Esther was sobbing and Robert looked badly shaken. Sighting Byron and his bride, they stopped abruptly.

Byron went out into the foyer to greet them. "Won't you stay and have tea with us?"

Esther dabbed at her eyes. "I'm sorry, no. We had no idea your father was so badly incapacitated. I don't believe he even recognized us."

Robert wasn't nearly as tall as Byron, but he drew himself up to his full height to address him. "Perhaps it's a blessing John doesn't know what's going on in his house, but with war with France a certainty in all our minds, he would never approve of your ending a lifelong friendship with my daughter to take a wife from our enemy's camp.

"What are you going to do tell your friends in the militia when you're asked to serve again? Will you choose your wife's side, or ours? No," he scoffed, "you needn't answer that. It's plain you've made your choice, and it's the wrong one." He turned to his wife. "Come, dear. John didn't know us, and while I have nothing but sympathy for Rachel, I no longer wish to associate with what's left of this once proud family."

Out of respect to Robert Frederick's age, Byron did not tear into him the way he had Robert Malone, but his hands twitched restlessly at his sides, for he was sorely tempted. He tried to clear his mind of the distasteful encounter, but when he turned back toward the parlor, he found Arielle standing in the doorway. It was plain in the stillness of her pose that she had heard every damning word.

"I'm sorry. I wouldn't have put you through that for the world. I was counting on them as my parents' friends to be civil to us both."

Arielle shook her head sadly. "I can't understand why when your own mother dislikes me so."

Although her tone wasn't hostile, she was posing the question of loyalty and Byron knew he owed it first to her, not his mother. "I'm going to put an end to that behavior today," he announced confidently as he strode toward her. "I'm going to use people here on the plantation to help her with Father, and I'm going to insist, no make that *demand,* that she begin treating you as a daughter. I want her to show more respect for Hunter, too. There are going to be some changes here, Arielle, and I apologize for not beginning them sooner."

He took her arm to draw her back into the parlor, and Arielle rejoined him on the settee. She smoothed the skirt of one of the pretty gowns he had had provided, and then, as always, spoke her mind. "You've dressed me fashionably and not criticized my manners as lacking, but people don't see me for the person I am. I half expected Mr. Frederick to claim I'm endangering the righteous citizens of Williamsburg."

Leaning forward slightly, Arielle gripped her upper arms as though she were chilled. "I don't want to see war between our countries, but if it ever comes, I want you to know I won't spy for either side. You have my promise on that, Byron. I won't betray you, or my people."

"I'd not even suspect you of it," he assured her. "Had I thought you'd ever wish me or my family any harm, I'd have left you with Gaetan."

Arielle shuddered. "Please, I don't want to think of him. I do pray his little colony is safe and thriving, but I'm glad to be away from him.

"I'd rather hear you say you were glad to be with me."

Arielle straightened her shoulders. "Don't you know that I am?" she whispered seductively, "or must I take you upstairs and prove it again?"

Byron knew Arielle well enough to know she wasn't a tease, and a slow curl of desire began to wind around him. It would be several months before her pregnancy advanced to the stage he would be unable to indulge his passion for her, but wanting to enjoy now what he would have to forego later, he rose and drew her to her feet. "I promised to set everything right here, but it can wait an hour or two."

Not surprised that he would accept her invitation so readily, Arielle moved close as they started up the stairs. Her world had been small in Grand Pré, but now it had narrowed even more. Studying her husband's profile, she hoped she could give him sons who resembled him so closely no one would ever recall they had an Acadian mother. She would not forget her origins, however, but she feared her children would never appreciate their value.

Twenty-two

November 11, 1755, was Christian's first birthday, and Alanna and Hunter would have liked to have celebrated the occasion, but it was also the first anniversary of Melissa's death and Rachel forbade any mention of a party. She had finally consented to having the household servants spend an hour or two each day with John while she saw to the many obligations she had neglected during his illness, but until that Tuesday, she had not once left her home. She saw the prospect of venturing away from her house as abandoning her spouse, and would not have left him for any reason less vital than a memorial visit to her only daughter's grave.

Dressed in black, she instructed Catherine in an insistent tone, "Byron and I will only be away an hour or so, and John should be asleep the whole time. If he does awaken, please tell him I'll be with him shortly so he doesn't fret."

"Yes, ma'am, I will. We'll get along just fine, ma'am," she assured her again. Catherine truly believed that, too, and looked forward to being paid to just sit. As soon as Rachel had left, she sat down in the room's most comfortable chair. In a moment she began to yawn, and before her mistress had been away a quarter hour, she was fast asleep.

Rachel had left the bedroom door ajar, and as Arielle walked by, she was so alarmed by the rasping sound of John's breathing she hurriedly entered the room to investigate. As she had feared, he was in dire straits, for while he was fighting to fill his lungs with air, his skin had already taken on an ominous bluish cast. She propped him up against his pillows and shouted to Catherine. The girl sat up with a start, and then nearly fell in her haste to rise.

Arielle had seen enough cases of heart failure to know John was dying, but there was no reason to frighten him or Catherine by speaking her opinion aloud. "Alanna and Hunter are outside on the lawn with the baby. Go and get them. Tell them it's urgent and to come at once."

Stifling a pitiful wail with her fist, Catherine fled the room. Arielle took John's hand and held it tightly. He was a dozen years his wife's senior, but still only fifty-three. Arielle closed her eyes for a moment, then found the words of comfort she had previously spoken only in French.

"You've nothing to fear, John," she began confidently, seeking to inspire the same trust she had won at home. "The next world is even more beautiful than the one you've known. Free of all earthly sorrows, paradise will surround you with endless joy. All the loved ones you've lost will be there to welcome you. Elliott and Melissa are waiting for you, and tonight you'll dance together with the angels."

Arielle continued to weave the same serenely imaginative tapestry of heaven she had created for the dying residents of Grand Pré until Alanna and Hunter appeared at the door. The Indian held his son, and nodded for his wife to go on in alone. Alanna approached the bed cautiously, for the sight of her uncle's distress was painful to watch. She envied the calmness of Arielle's manner, and tried her best to emulate it.

Elliott had died in her arms, but death had taken Melissa so suddenly there had been no time to say good-bye. Not wanting to have the same regret with her uncle, Alanna recalled all the love he had shown her, and thanked him now. She smoothed back his hair and kissed his forehead, and, with a last untroubled sigh, John Barclay closed his eyes and died.

Alanna straightened up. "He's gone."

Arielle folded John's hands across his chest. "Yes, but he went very peacefully, and I hope Rachel will take comfort in that."

Hunter had remained at the door. "I'll wait for her and Byron downstairs. She already despises me, so there's no danger she can hate me more for delivering such sad news."

As he left, Catherine peered around the door weeping loudly. "What am I going to do, Miss Alanna? Your aunt told me to watch your uncle, but I fell asleep."

"Come in and be quiet," Alanna ordered. "Mrs. Barclay and Byron must be told before anyone else learns of John's passing."

"Rachel is going to take this very hard," Alanna predicted. "John was her whole world."

"There was a time when Bernard Douville was mine," Arielle recalled fondly. Leaving Alanna seated beside her late uncle, she moved to the chair Catherine had occupied and sat back. "I'll wait with you until Rachel and Byron get home. I'd bathe the body, but I believe Rachel would rather tend John herself."

Wanting to be strong for Rachel, Alanna fought back her tears. "Too many of the Barclays have died."

"There's Christian, and the hope of two more children come spring," Arielle stressed optimistically. "The Barclays will survive."

With the addition of Seneca and French blood, Alanna wondered just how much of the Barclay heritage would remain. "We've now had two deaths on Christian's birthday. It has to be a very bad omen."

"I don't read fortunes," Arielle replied, "but I'd not dwell on the coincidence in dates if I were you. Christian is a bright and handsome child, and I believe his luck in life will continue to be good."

Hoping Arielle was right, Alanna remained silent until they heard the carriage coming up the road.

As the carriage rolled into the yard, Byron saw Hunter standing on the steps. The Indian gave the striking impression of a soldier standing a vigil. Believing Hunter would take up such a stance for only one reason, he was nearly overcome by a turbulent mixture of curiosity and dread. He bounded out of the carriage without waiting for Andrew to open the door and lower the steps and hurriedly approached him.

Not wanting to alarm his mother, he whispered his question. "Has something happened to my father?"

Cradled against Hunter's shoulder, Christian was fast asleep, and the Indian patted the little boy's back lightly as he replied. "He's dead, Byron. There was nothing we could do."

Byron stared at his friend, knowing the death of his father ought to cause an agonizing pain, but at the same time feeling only an immense sense of relief, for the invalid he had visited daily had borne only a slight resemblance to the vigorous man who had raised him. He drew in a ragged breath, and then went back to the carriage for his mother. She was still weeping over Melissa, and he had to coax her out very gently. He then put his arms around her and gave her a loving hug.

"Father's gone," he murmured against her cheek.

Rachel first grabbed for his arms to steady herself, then, horrified, drew away. "No," she sobbed through a fresh torrent of tears. "John would never leave me all alone like this."

"You're not alone, Mother," Byron reminded her. "Our home is filled with people who love you."

"No," Rachel swore. "John can't be gone, he can't!" She tore herself from Byron's embrace, and had Hunter not stepped aside, she would have shoved him out of her way as she bolted through the front door. Screaming John's name, she raced up the stairs, but as she came through the door of their room, she saw Arielle and recoiled as though she had been struck.

"What are you doing in here?" she shrieked. Wheeling around, she found Catherine and vented her grief on the terrified maid. "I gave you specific orders to call on your mother or Alanna if there was any trouble. How dare you disobey me? Was Arielle here when John died?"

Flinching under that caustic onslaught, Catherine could barely manage a nod before defending herself in a hoarse rush. "Everything happened so quickly, Mrs. Barclay. There wasn't time to think."

"Get out!" Rachel ordered, and Catherine fled. Then Rachel turned on Arielle, her features contorted in a vicious mask and her words dripping with venom. "I didn't want you anywhere near my husband when he was alive, and I won't have you in his room now. I don't even want you in my house. You may have bewitched my son, but I see you for the conniving creature you are. Get out of my sight and leave me to bury my husband in peace."

Byron had followed his mother up the stairs and immediately put a stop to her insults. "That's enough!" he ordered sharply. "If Arielle's here, then it's because she was needed, and as my wife, she'll live in our home just as long as I do. Show some respect for Father's memory and stop behaving like a vindictive shrew."

Appreciating Byron's effort to control his mother's hysteria, Arielle caressed his arm as she slipped by him. "Thank you, but it will be easier for everyone if I go." She went on downstairs, and having no desire to remain in a house where she wasn't wanted, bolted out the back door and ran across the lawn to the path leading down to the river. She passed one bench and then another before finally pausing to rest.

She was not surprised Rachel behaved badly, but Arielle was not without empathy, and, understanding her mother-in-law's terrible grief, forgave her. She leaned back in an attempt to clear her mind and enjoy the view, but soon found John's death had affected her far more profoundly than she had first realized.

Shaking, she gripped the wooden bench and rocked back and forth slowly. She did not doubt her feelings for Byron, but it was going to be hard to bear Rachel's hostility. She closed her eyes, and, badly depressed, might have remained there until dark had she not been assailed by an eerie sense that she was no longer alone. She looked around, expecting to find a fieldhand, or someone who had business along the river but there was no one in sight.

Unable to shake the uncomfortable sensation that her privacy had been breached, the serenity of the river no longer held any appeal. Rising, she walked back toward the house, but dread weighed down her every step. She knew she had done nothing, other than simply being herself, to incur Rachel's wrath, but that was a small consolation. She was reminded of how bitterly Sophie Doucet had opposed her association with Byron, and since her arrival in Williamsburg, disapproval was coming in blistering waves.

"Byron and I should never have met," she sighed under her breath, but knowing that sentiment was too late to prove useful, she promptly cast it aside. Hunter was still on the front lawn with Christian, and now wide awake, the baby started her way. She knelt down to catch him in a warm hug, then looked up at his father.

"How can you stand living here?" she asked.

Hunter knelt beside her, and, laughing happily, Christian began to play with the fringe dangling from his father's sleeves. "I love my wife and son," he replied. "What anyone else chooses to think of me doesn't matter."

Impressed by the clarity of his perspective, Arielle nodded. "I shall have to cultivate your point of view," she hoped aloud. "What are you going to tell Christian about his mother?"

Pained, Hunter looked away. "I don't want to tell him anything, but Alanna insists that someday he be told the truth. She'll have to do it, though; I can't."

Arielle ruffled Christian's hair. "He has to know, Hunter. Everyone else does, and to keep such vital information a secret would place him at a serious disadvantage."

"Yes, I know, but it will not be easy."

"You'll do what's best for your son," Arielle assured him. "I just wish there were a way to ease Rachel's bitterness. It colors not only her life, but all our lives as well."

Hunter straightened up and swung Christian into his arms. "Pity her, and forget," he advised. "It's getting too cold. Let's go in the house."

Arielle followed him, but she had to force herself to climb the stairs. The door to the master bedroom was closed, and, relieved she could pass by unseen, she went into Byron's room to wait for him. She slept there each night, but still thought of the room as his, and the one across the hall as Elliott's, rather than hers. She supposed they would have supper sometime that night, but she lacked any interest in changing her clothes to prepare for it.

Byron entered a short while later, and found Arielle curled up on the bed. She wasn't asleep, but she looked as tired as he felt. "I'm sorry for my mother's rudeness," he said sincerely.

Arielle sat up. "Your mother's moods don't concern me. It's you I'm worried about. You've lost your father, and you mustn't ignore your own grief in an effort to alleviate your mother's."

Byron sat down beside her and took her hand. "You're very wise Arielle, but when I first got home, I felt as though I'd already lost my father. I didn't want to see him linger any longer in a twilight world where he couldn't speak or even lift his head. It's a blessing he's gone."

Arielle wrapped her arms around him. "Yes, that's true, but it doesn't mean you won't miss him."

Byron nodded, and when the effort to deny his pain became too great, he gave into tears. The people he loved were disappearing from his life with frightening frequency, and he clung to Arielle as he wept, determined not to lose her as well.

The day of the funeral, Arielle put on her mourning clothes, but, out of consideration for Rachel, chose not to go into town to attend the church service. Respecting her decision, Byron left with his mother and Alanna. Hunter took Christian out for a ride, and with all the servants away at the funeral, Arielle roamed the empty house imagining it as it must have been in far happier times.

While Arielle enjoyed living in such comfortable surroundings, she could not help but miss the true warmth of the cozy little houses of her Acadian friends. Their dwellings had been lit with the love and laughter that was so often missing here where tragedy shadowed every corner.

After the funeral, friends began calling to express their condolences and, again absenting herself, Arielle went down to the river. She studied its rippling current and tried to find comfort in its ceaseless race to the sea. She longed for a similar sense of determination but until Williamsburg truly became home to her, and she was not certain it ever would, she feared she would always be fighting the current rather than flowing along with it. Again, rather than peace at the river's edge, she felt uneasy.

She listened for the sound of someone approaching, but nothing could be heard above the James River's steady, roiling hum. She rose to search the foliage bordering the water, and, finding it dense enough to hide a dozen men, backed away from the bench. Fearing she was allowing the dark mood of the day to color her perceptions, she turned toward the path leading back to the house and in the next instant stepped right into Gaetan LeBlanc's outstretched arms.

"Gaetan!" she gasped. "What are you doing here?"

Grabbing for her wrist before she eluded him, the Acadian pulled her close for a welcoming kiss. She failed to respond, but having surprised her so, he wasn't insulted. "I've come for you," he breathed against her ear. "Did you think I'd let you go so easily?"

"But how—?"

Gaetan searched her expression in vain for the joyous glow of love he had hoped to see. "I knew your lover's name, and that he came from Virginia. A rich man is easy to find. But how I got here is not nearly so important as the fact you are coming with me. I have a boat. It's as ugly as the *Incentive,* but it will take us to New Orleans. Come with me now, you needn't tell Barclay good-bye."

Arielle tried to think quickly, for she did not want to arouse the fury of Gaetan's temper anymore than she wanted to leave. "How long have you been here?" she asked. "Have you been watching the house?"

Gaetan's eyes brightened with pride. "I would have spoken to you the other afternoon, but you left before I could reach you. "Now we are together I'll no longer have to hide and spy on you." He slid his hands down her arms, and then took her hand. "Come, we must go."

Again taking care not to anger him, Arielle resisted him, but only gently. "No, wait, there's something you don't know."

"Later, we can talk all night."

"No, we've got to talk now. Your suspicions proved correct, you see. Byron and I are married and we're going to have a child."

Gaetan's whole expression changed to mirror his rage and he again yanked her close. "Where did you marry him?"

"Right here, in his house."

"In a Catholic ceremony?"

Even knowing what his argument would be, Arielle did not lie. "No, the priest was of the Anglican faith."

"Then you are not truly wed," Gaetan insisted. "As

for the babe, I know you'll give me others, so if your first isn't mine it won't matter."

Arielle clenched her fists, but he responded to that defiant gesture by tightening his hold on her wrists. "I won't go with you, Gaetan. I married Byron because I love him and I'm staying here. Go on to New Orleans and make a new life for yourself. You don't need me."

"What do you know of need?" Gaetan countered aggressively. "Have you lain awake each night thinking of me? When you finally fall asleep do you dream of me? Do all your best memories and hopes for the future concern me? Is all the love in your heart only for me?"

Arielle looked away. "I don't love you, Gaetan. I want only good things for you, but they can't include me."

Undaunted by her denials, Gaetan swept her up into his arms and carried her on up the path to a *bateau* he had hidden in the reeds. He shoved her into the bottom and took up the oars. "Don't fight me, Arielle, because I won't allow anything to keep us apart now, least of all your ridiculous preference for another man. You belong with me and we both know it." He then described Englishmen in the vilest of terms, cursing them for invading Acadia and damning them all to the most miserable fate he could possibly imagine.

Desperate to escape him, Arielle sat up, and for an instant debated throwing herself into the water. But her black gown was so heavy she feared she would sink like a stone. She might very well have chosen to risk drowning rather than remain with Gaetan, but she refused to put her unborn child in such terrible danger. She searched with a frantic gaze for someone near the shore who might come to her rescue.

Facing the stern, Gaetan did not share Arielle's view of the river, and, not wanting to give away her intentions, she forced herself to adopt a passive expression. She was keenly alert, however, and when she saw two British officers standing on the Fredericks' docks, she waited until the *bateau* was even with them to scream a frantic plea for help. Gaetan responded with a flash of fist and, knocked unconscious, Arielle fell forward and lay slumped across his knees.

Startled by that sudden show of brutality, Ian Scott and Graham Tyler continued to watch as Gaetan adjusted his course to take the *bateau* farther out into the river. Ian's hands were clasped behind his back, giving him the appearance of being completely unmoved by the sorry spectacle while Graham grew badly agitated.

"I didn't recognize the man," Graham exclaimed, "but the woman looked like Byron Barclay's bride. I caught a glimpse of her at church one Sunday. Could that possibly have been her? Come on, let's ride over to the Barclays' and see what's going on."

"You already know," Ian scoffed. "John's funeral was today and the house will be full of friends eating their fill and offering sentimental platitudes for comfort."

Ian had refused to attend his former father-in-law's service, but wanting to see Robin later, had agreed to wait at the Fredericks' home for the family's return. While Graham could understand Ian's distrust of the Barclays, he wouldn't permit his friend to ignore the act of violence they had just witnessed. "That may very well be true, but if Byron's bride has been kidnapped, then we've got to save her."

"I can't imagine why her welfare should be our responsibility."

"My God, man. We've been stationed in Virginia to preserve order, and I for one intend to do it. If you're too proud to set foot on Barclay land, then take one of the Fredericks' *bateaus* and see where that pair are bound. Well, go on, get moving or I swear I'll report you for not simply shirking your duty, but for cowardice as well."

Knowing Graham had a tendency toward the melodramatic, Ian shrugged off his threats. "For all we know, that was merely a woman who resembles Byron's wife. If her husband chooses to mistreat her, it's extremely unfortunate, but it's not an appropriate concern for the king's officers."

"Do you hate the Barclays so much you've lost your ability to think? It doesn't matter who that woman was. She called for help and I intend to give it. Now you can either follow her, or go to the Barclay place for more men, but don't misjudge me. I intend to see it costs you your career if you just stand here and do nothing. What if Byron had been the one to hear Robin call for help, and he just turned away? What would you do to him?"

Ian had a ready answer. "I'd kill him."

"And you'd be well within your rights," Graham agreed. "Don't give Byron an excuse to kill you."

Ian stared at his friend, for there had been a time when he would have welcomed the opportunity to court death. He had Robin now, though, and such a risk wasn't worth taking. "All right, I'll follow them, but if I end up going all the way to Newport News, I'm going to expect you to come get me."

"Consider it done." Graham tore up the rise toward the house where he had left his mount. Superbly trained, he had yet to see combat and as he rode to the Barclays' he envisioned himself leading a daring rescue that would win him instant fame.

Still unconscious, Arielle moaned as Gaetan transferred her from the *bateau* to the deck of the single-masted schooner he had stolen in Boston Harbor. Waiting for his return, Alain Richard and Eduard Boudreaux moved out of the way as he carried her below, but as soon as Gaetan had lain her on the bunk, they urged him to leave. He glanced over his shoulder, and refused.

"The sun will set soon, and then we'll go."

"Did anyone see you take her?"

Gaetan sat down on the edge of the bunk and rubbed Arielle's hand between his as he nodded his head in the negative. "Downstream we passed two British officers, but they simply stared."

Eduard and Alain exchanged a worried glance. "We left the others to help you find Arielle, but we'll lose our freedom as well as her if we're caught tied up here on the riverbank."

"We'll not be caught," Gaetan swore convincingly. He leaned over to kiss Arielle's cheek and then straightened up. "Luck has been with us this far, and it won't desert us now. Nothing can stop me now that Arielle and I are together."

"Perhaps not, but I do not think we ought to tempt fate by waiting here a moment longer."

"Like a phantom we sailed up the river before dawn, and we'll make our way back down after dusk," Gaetan emphasized darkly. "You two worry more than half a dozen old women; now leave me be."

Once an honest fisherman, Eduard was sick of intrigues. "We'll wait until dusk, Gaetan, but no later."

Gaetan turned to regard him with a stare so threatening Eduard immediately withdrew and returned to the deck, and not wanting to argue with Gaetan alone, Alain followed. Gaetan then leaned forward and unbuttoned Arielle's bodice. He brushed his fingertips across her bare skin and sighed with contentment.

"You have made me wait too long, Arielle," he whispered, "but tonight the waiting is over, and you'll be mine at last."

Arielle heard Gaetan's words, but they seemed to be coming from a long way off. Blurred with the memory of men in red coats, his promise held no meaning, and she slipped under the painful waves that filled her head and sank deep into herself where love was not always paired with loss, and dreams really did come true.

Twenty-three

Arielle's eyelids fluttered, then opened. Gaetan was seated by her side, but, confused by the strangeness of her surroundings, she surveyed the dingy cabin with an anxious glance. Her quarters on board the *Incentive* had smelled of polish, but the odor here was an unpleasant mixture of sweat and rot. She had to swallow hard to bolster her courage before speaking. "This is wrong; you know it is."

The Acadian shook his head. "No, for the first time in a long while everything is right. Don't try and convince me that you have been happy stranded among our enemies. The look on your face when I first saw you down by the river, and again today, was not the peaceful repose of a happy woman, but instead the image of heartbreak and loneliness. The Barclays' house was full of people today, but you wandered away. If you were as content with your English husband as you insist, you would have been at his side."

There was too much truth in Gaetan's observations for Arielle to deny them. Instead, she defended Byron. "His father died, so naturally he's devoting his attentions to his mother for the time being."

Unconvinced, Gaetan cocked his head. "If your

husband prefers his mother to you, then you have married the wrong man."

"It's not a matter of preference," Arielle insisted, "but of duty. A son ought to comfort his mother at such a difficult time."

"While his wife wanders the riverbanks in search of love?"

Arielle did not recall Gaetan ever being so perceptive, and the change in him made her all the more uncomfortable. "I wasn't looking for love. I was merely getting away from the crowded house for a while. I hadn't intended to stay long."

Gaetan leaned down to kiss her, and when she turned to avoid him, he framed her face with his hands to force her to look up at him. "Even if your Englishman does adore you, that may not mean anything to his family and friends. You are merely a beautiful stranger to them and they'll crowd together to keep you out.

"The struggle between England and France may have begun in the Ohio Valley and spread to Acadia, but it won't end there. They'll continue to battle for dominance in the world. I don't want to see you caught in the middle. You're coming with me, where you belong, and when the real fighting begins, you'll thank me for not asking you to take sides against your own people."

"I've already told Byron I won't take sides."

Gaetan laughed at her vow. "Your side was chosen for you at birth. You've French blood in your veins, and you should be proud. Do the Barclays make you feel proud, or like an outsider?"

That Gaetan could describe her life so accurately

stunned Arielle. It also made it impossible for her to dispute his predictions of what lay ahead.

She laced her fingers in Gaetan's and tried again to make him understand. "You must find a woman who'll share your life willingly. You can't demand love, nor force it from someone who cares for another."

Rejecting that unwanted advice, Gaetan leaned close. "You've been widowed once, Arielle, and it could easily happen again."

Rather than displaying his fiery temper, Gaetan's manner held an icy menace that frightened Arielle even more. He had come close to killing Byron once, and she did not want him to try again. "If you so much as touch Byron, I'll not speak to you ever again. Don't make the mistake of thinking that if I'm widowed, I'll fall into your arms because it will never, ever, happen."

Gaetan noted the sincerity of her expression, and then discounted it. "You'll never see him again," chérie. He may live to be a very old man, but he'll do it without you."

"No. You're the one who's going to be alone, because I won't stay with you." Gaetan drew back his hand to slap her, but Arielle didn't flinch. "Only cowards hit women," she insisted, "and I used to think you were brave. What's happened to our people who were on board the *Incentive*? Have you simply abandoned them?"

Distracted by her question, Gaetan dropped his hand. "No, they moved inland. The hunting's good, and they'll prosper. There were other men capable of leading them; they didn't need me."

"Then you can cut all ties to the past, go on to New Orleans, and begin a new life."

"I've already begun that life, chérie, and, believe me, I intend for you to share it. Now I must go up on deck and get us underway. Don't do anything foolish, or the next time I leave you alone, I'll be forced to tie you to the bunk."

Arielle glared at him, and the minute he left her, she began to search the seedy cabin for a weapon to use against him. It might be hours before Byron noticed she was missing, and then he would have no idea where she might have gone. Positive she would have to save herself, she knew there had to be something she could use to force Gaetan to set her free, and while the sparsely furnished cabin was only dimly lit by a single rusty lantern she wouldn't stop looking until she found it.

Ian Scott could not row fast enough to overtake Gaetan's *bateau*, but he did draw close enough to see him tie up alongside a battered schooner. Heading for cover along shore, the officer watched as two men appeared to carry the woman on board, then, not wanting to alert them to his presence, he sat back to wait for Graham to return with Byron.

He was well aware that there was a distinct possibility Byron's bride wasn't missing. In that case, he supposed the challenge of rescuing the woman who had called to them would fall upon Graham and him. Unarmed, he doubted the force of their words would have much effect, and he hoped Graham had sense enough to borrow a musket or two from the Barclays.

Just thinking of the Barclays brought a painful lump to Ian's throat, and he wished he had remained in town rather than at the Fredericks so he would not have become involved in this ridiculous rescue in the first place. Damn! he wished he had been able to stay in England, but he had felt even more sad and empty there than he did here. He strained to look up river, hoping to see Graham, but there were no boats in sight. It would be dark soon, and, unwilling to spend the night in a *bateau,* he debated rowing back to the Fredericks', but he had never left a mission unfinished. He rubbed his hands together to keep warm rather than abandon his post as lookout.

He sat up as he noticed further activity on the schooner's deck. Two men were struggling to pull the *bateau* up out of the water and, fearing they were preparing to depart, Ian memorized the contours of the boat so he could recognize it later if need be. He glanced over his shoulder half a dozen times before he saw a *bateau* approaching, but in the gathering dusk, he could not make out the occupants. In the next instant, the sails were unfurled on the schooner and, riding the current, it began to draw away.

Cursing, Ian grabbed his oars and strained to match the schooner's pace, but the distance between him and the larger ship continued to widen. Giving up for the moment, he waited for the *bateau* following him to pull alongside. When he saw Graham had brought not only Byron but Hunter as well, he couldn't hide his disgust.

"The woman's on board the schooner," he called to Byron. "Is she your wife?"

Rather than waste the breath he needed to row,

Byron nodded. He reached out to grab the side of Ian's *bateau* and then motioned for Graham to climb in with him. As soon as the transfer was complete, he and Hunter continued to row, their strokes long and sure as, already tired, they raced after the schooner. Ian watched them, then, heaving a weary sigh, picked up his oars and trailed in their wake.

Byron knew it was unlikely they could overtake the schooner, but he had to try. When Graham had first spoken to him, he had refused to believe Arielle could have come to any harm and had wasted precious time searching the house for her. He needed those minutes back now, and prayed with every agonizing stretch for more speed.

"Something's wrong!" Hunter shouted.

Turning to look over his shoulder, Byron saw the stern of the schooner had taken on a strange, luminous glow. "She's on fire!" His terror increasing tenfold, he plunged the oars deep to send them skidding along at a faster pace, but they were still much too slow. Smoke was now billowing from the hold and Byron feared that before he could get close enough to offer aid all on board would either burn to death or drown when the ship sank.

Then Alain abandoned the tiller to fight the flames and the schooner floated along, adrift. Gradually straying off its midriver course, it veered toward the shore. Lumbering now rather than fleet, it began to list toward starboard.

Silhouetted against the red glow of the ship, Byron saw two men, and then a third, but no sign of Arielle. If she was trapped below, she would have no chance to escape the fire. He could hear shouts above the steady rhythm of Hunter's breathing, commands relayed in French, and, even without seeing Gaetan Le Blanc, Byron was positive he was on board.

The violence of their exertion had Byron's left arm aching badly, but Hunter still had the strength to power their *bateau,* and they raced on toward the doomed ship. Ignoring his pain, Byron leaned into the oars, gasping for breath as he struggled to make every stroke count. They were gaining on the schooner, but not nearly as rapidly as the fire.

Then striking a submerged log, the ship angled sharply toward the shore, and, with a shudder, ran aground. Not about to waste that piece of luck, Byron shouted, encouraging Hunter to keep rowing with him and, nearly exhausting the last of their reserves, they finally reached the disabled ship. They aimed for the bow and the second they were close enough to board, Byron caught hold of a rope looped over the side and scrambled up over the rail. The sight that greeted him tore at his resolve, for flames were licking the deck and shooting up the mast. The sails ignited with a fierce popping crackle and sent a shower of sparks into the air. He threw up his arms to shield his face and searched the blistering haze for Arielle.

"What have you done?" Gaetan cried, and, pulling Arielle along behind him, he made for the rail. Alain and Eduard were trying to lower the *bateau* into the water again, but before they could, Hunter came leaping over the side and, with a terrifying war whoop, sent them backing away. That escape route blocked, Gaetan raised Arielle into his arms. He would have dropped her right over the side into the river had

Byron not shouted his name. The instant he paused to search for the Englishman through the dense clouds of smoke were all Byron needed to reach him.

"Put her down!" he ordered. Drawing a pistol from his belt, he gave every indication of meaning to use it.

Arielle felt Gaetan tighten his grasp on her, but, unwilling to serve as a shield, she flung herself toward the rail. Grabbing hold, she hung on. Knocked off balance, Gaetan was forced to release her. He then lunged for her skirt, but missed, and she darted into the bow where, with Byron between them, she was safely out of his reach.

Gaetan stared at Byron, daring him to shoot. Byron, however, did not want to end things so easily. He called to Arielle. "There should be two British officers drawing alongside in a *bateau.* Go with them."

"But what about you?"

"I'll meet you on shore."

"Hurry!" Arielle waved to the officers, and, in a few seconds, sat between them. "Don't leave Byron," she begged.

Ian acknowledged her request with a nod, then rowed her ashore. Once she was standing safely on dry land, he and Graham returned to the schooner, which was now listing at a sharper angle. Unable to get away in their *bateau,* Alain and Eduard dove into the water, but surfaced so close to Ian and Graham they were swiftly caught. Hunter and Byron then appeared at the rail with Gaetan.

"Toss him down to us!" Ian shouted, but Byron waved them away.

With a shove, he sent Gaetan into the river. Handing his pistol to Hunter, he dove in after the Acadian and, coming up through a smoky haze, grabbed Gaetan by the hair and towed him struggling and kicking to the shore. Hunter swung over the side and dropped into Ian's *bateau.* He greeted the startled British officer with a wicked grin, and, taking the oars from him, rowed them to shore.

Wet and miserable, Alain and Eduard were no challenge to guard, but Byron had other plans for Gaetan. The flaming ship lit the riverbank with sufficient light for a fight, and he meant to have it. "Come on, you bastard, I want the chance to fight you again and win!"

Gaetan needed no translation to understand Byron's gestures, and he came forward willingly. He dodged Byron's first blow and came back with a flurry of punishing jabs. Byron withstood them all and undaunted, aimed for Gaetan's face.

Graham and Ian kept close watch on Alain and Eduard, but Hunter moved to Arielle's side. "Don't watch this," he urged. He laid his hand on her arm, but she brushed it away.

"No, I want to see it all," she declared. Arielle had too great a stake in the outcome of the bitter contest to turn her back. She had every confidence in Byron, but, knowing he had just recovered from being shot, she doubted he would have the stamina to fight for long. Having no such handicap, Gaetan fought like a demon, coming back time and again from punches so brutal they would have easily subdued a less aggressive man.

They were so evenly matched, the fight might have

gone on all night, but, having nearly lost Arielle, Byron fought with a vengeance that Gaetan ultimately couldn't equal. Bathed in the fire's eerie light, Byron hammered his fists into the Acadian until at last, too badly hurt to continue, Gaetan slipped on the muddy bank and fell. Byron prodded him with his toe.

"Get up, I'm not finished with you yet."

Hunter walked over to Gaetan and laced his fingers in the Acadian's dark curls to raise his head from the mud. "He's done. Let's go home."

Byron had left his coat on the dock before he had set out after Arielle, and his shirt was now filthy and torn. He took a step backward, staggered slightly, and then found firmer footing. "There should be a house just up the hill. I'll borrow a carriage to take us all home."

Ian came forward. "No one's going to loan you a carriage looking like that. I'll go."

Relieved he would not have to take a tiring walk at the end of such a difficult day, Byron still argued. "They know me, Ian, and, regardless of how wretched I look, they'll not turn me away."

"That may very well be true," Ian replied, "but you've done enough. I'll fetch the carriage."

Hunter called to the officer, "Wait, there may not be time later for us to talk. Melissa wronged us both, and while we may never be friends, we don't have to be enemies."

Ian straightened his shoulders, and, with a resolute frown, shook his head. "All I'll ever want is to see you dead, Indian. Stay away from me."

Hunter watched Ian walk away, and, with a regretful shrug, took his place guarding the Acadians.

"At least you tried to make amends," Byron called to the brave. "Forget him now." He walked to the water's edge, ripped off what was left of his shirt, and scooped up several handsful of water to wash off the blood he hoped was Gaetan's rather than his own. Refreshed, he walked to Arielle, and, taking her elbow, led her a few steps away so their conversation wouldn't be overheard by Graham and the three prisoners. That the Acadians wouldn't understand him didn't matter, he just did not want them listening.

"I'll try and find a way to make this up to you," he began.

"We're all safe; that's all that matters."

"No, it isn't. I should have had the foresight to realize Gaetan might come after you and taken better care of you. I would never have forgiven myself had you been harmed. When I saw the schooner in flames, I didn't think I'd be able to reach you in time."

"I'm sorry to have frightened you, but I didn't know you had had time to miss me and I couldn't think of any other way to stop the ship."

The last flickering embers of the fire lit Arielle's face clearly enough for Byron to marvel at her composure. "You started the fire?" he gasped. "My God, whatever possessed you to do such an audacious thing?"

Arielle shook her head, for if he did not already understand her reason, then nothing she could say would make any sense. She looked toward the bluff over which Ian had disappeared and shivered slightly.

"I hope he comes back soon. I didn't realize he was Melissa's husband. It's a shame he's so bitter."

Unable to stand any longer, Byron sat down at her feet and hugged his knees. "He'll be back as soon as he can, regardless of his mood," he assured her, "and I'm going to have him take Gaetan and his friends into town. They can rot in prison for all I care, but they'll not have another chance to do you any harm."

"I think you should send them on to New Orleans," Arielle suggested.

"No, they'll just come back to cause us more grief."

Arielle knelt beside him and stroked his tangled hair. "Let them go. Gaetan knows better than to come back for me now."

Byron caught her hand and brought it to his lips. "I can promise only to think about it."

"Good, that will do for a start."

With a great gurgling heave, the burnt-out hulk of the schooner rolled over in the shallow water and the last of the fires were extinguished with hisses of steam. It was dark now, and although Arielle was safe, she wondered why she felt so guilty when she knew she had done the right thing.

Two hours later, Arielle had bathed, washed the smoky scent from her hair, and, dressed in a nightgown, sat in bed picking at her supper from a tray. Rachel had greeted their return not with welcoming cheers, but with stern recriminations for Byron for risking his life so foolishly. That Arielle might have suffered during the brief kidnapping did not even occur to her mother-in-law and knowing better than to wait until it did, Arielle had gone upstairs to prepare for bed.

She fluffed up her pillows, but she doubted she would get any sleep that night. The memory of Byron standing on the schooner's burning deck was too vivid in her mind for there to be room for dreams. There was so much that was heroic about him, but it failed to make up for the fact he didn't love her. When she heard his knock at her door, she called to him to enter, but there was no enthusiasm in her voice.

Byron had also bathed, and put on clean clothes, but he did not feel any more relaxed than Arielle. He noted the slight amount missing from her plate as he walked by, and began scolding her as he reached the foot of the bed. "You've got to eat more. If you neglect yourself, you'll be neglecting the baby, too. I should have asked earlier, but are you feeling all right?"

Arielle closed her eyes for a moment to better judge how she truly felt. Her head ached, but that was more from disappointment than any lingering pain from Gaetan's blow. She tried to smile when she looked up at Byron. "We both had a harrowing time, but I don't feel any the worse for it. I imagine you do."

Arielle had made an astute guess, for Byron was sore from head to toe. He sat down on the foot of her bed and leaned back against the corner post. "He's tough, but then, so am I."

"Yes, you certainly are. What are you going to do about him?"

"I haven't decided yet." Byron studied her expression in a vain attempt to gauge her reaction, but her level gaze revealed nothing more than what she had already said. "Frankly, I'm more concerned about what I'm going to do with you."

"With me, why?"

"Perhaps I just don't understand your motives, but maybe I will if you tell me how you managed to set the schooner on fire."

Arielle clasped her hands in her lap and, after a thoughtful nod, attempted to explain what had happened.

"I felt the boat move out into the river, and not wanting to end up in New Orleans, used the lantern to set fire to the tattered bedding on the bunk," she concluded her narrative. "The flames spread very quickly to the rest of the schooner, and then you appeared. You know what happened then."

Byron shook his head. "You risked your life in the bargain, or didn't you consider that?"

"Yes, but like so many times in life, I was presented with a choice. I'll admit it was a desperate one, but I took it."

Byron stood and began to pace up and down beside her bed. "I can recall a time, and quite recently, too, when you were eager to reach New Orleans. I imagine Gaetan must have been shocked to discover you weren't willing to go with him."

Arielle was growing more uncomfortable by the minute and leaned forward to adjust her pillows. "He was simply too stubborn to believe me when I met him down by the river or the whole ugly incident wouldn't have happened."

"What were you doing on the river path in the first place?"

"Must I account for all of my actions?"

Byron noted the pulse throbbing in her throat and was nearly overcome by the impulse to kiss it. Her skin was the color of butter-kissed cream and looked delicious, but for the moment he resisted. "No, of course not. It just seems like a strange place for you to be is all."

"I enjoy walking along the river, or at least I did. It's peaceful, and reminds me of home."

"This is your home now, Arielle." When she glanced away, Byron realized it must not seem that way to her. Then why had she gone to such desperate lengths to stay? This time when he sat down on the bed, he chose the place beside her. A possibility occurred to him, but he did not want to push her into declaring her feelings before she was ready. They had had so many conversations, but now he realized how assiduously they had avoided speaking of themselves. He strove to remedy that mistake now.

"Perhaps you ought to ask me some questions. Would you like to know why I risked boarding a burning ship to save you?"

Byron's face was bruised, and his right eye would doubtless be black by morning, but even badly battered he looked very good to her. "A man is expected to try and save his wife and unborn child."

"Is that what you think I did? Merely what's 'expected' of me?"

"You're an honorable man, you'd do no less."

This time Byron couldn't help himself and he leaned over to kiss her throat. He could feel her pulse quicken beneath his lips, but his was already racing. "I want to make love to you," he whispered.

Arielle raised her hand to press his face close, but she couldn't stop the tears that formed in her eyes. They trickled down her cheeks and splashed onto Byron. He leaned back then, and stared at her with an intensity that hurt her all the more. She hurriedly tried to dry her eyes.

"I'm sorry. I don't know what's the matter with me."

Byron thought back to that afternoon. Surrounded by solicitous strangers, he could easily imagine how lonely she must have felt, and why she had sought the solace of the river. He had been too preoccupied accepting sympathy for the loss of his father to note her disappearance, and he was ashamed of how close his selfishness had come to costing him the person he loved most in the world.

"There's something I should have told you, Arielle."

"It's not your fault, really it isn't," she protested.

Byron pulled her into his arms and kissed away her tears. "Hush, and just listen. When I arrived in Grand Pré, I wasn't merely sick at heart. I'd lost all sense of purpose in my life. I'd survived a horrendous defeat by the French, and not through any skill of my own, but because Hunter had kept me from throwing my life away. I didn't thank him for it at the time, either, and the fight we had was every bit as brutal as the ones you've seen between me and Gaetan. I lost that fight, too.

"I came home so bitter and discouraged I couldn't stay here. So I went to Grand Pré where I thought I'd have a chance to get even with French-speaking citizens if not France itself for the losses we had suffered in the Ohio Valley. I had Melissa and Elliott's ghosts along for company and I really intended to hurt as many people as I could. After all, I couldn't see any way out of my own raging misery, so I was eager to compound your neighbors' tragedy."

Astonished, Arielle leaned back to look at him. "But you were never mean to anyone."

"Yes, and I'm thankful for that, but it was only because I met you within minutes of arriving in Grand Pré. I'd never believed in love at first sight, but one glance of you was really all it took for me to decide I'd not leave Acadia without you."

Arielle held her breath, fearful that she had not heard what she was certain she had. "You can't really love someone you don't know," she argued.

"I agree, all you can know is that the possibility of love exists, and pursue it. I think you'll admit I was relentless in that regard. I didn't give you a chance to escape me, and the first time we kissed, I knew no matter how long it took me to win your heart, the effort would be worthwhile."

"But you never spoke of your feelings."

Byron rested his forehead against hers for a moment. "I'd seen too much death, lost a dear brother and sister, and I was afraid to tempt fate by declaring my love for you. Then this afternoon, I could have lost you, and that I'd never spoken of love would have compounded, rather than averted, that tragedy. I do love you, Arielle, with all my heart, and I hope that someday you'll come to love me, too."

Arielle tilted her head to kiss him, and drew him down into her arms. Bernard had given her the tender warmth of true affection and the security she had lacked as a child, but it was Byron who had awakened her passions and she shared them joyously with him now. She nibbled his earlobes and licked his nipples. She raked her nails across the taut muscles of his belly in an enticing tickle, then, stripping him naked, turned his deep laughter to low moans of surrender as she explored his lean body with tantalizing kisses.

She coaxed him to the brink of rapture with a sure touch and flick of her tongue, creating a need so desperate he yanked off her gown with a single tug. A willing offering to his desire, she welcomed him with a supple grace, and, lost in the magic each conjured for the other, they were reborn in a swirling dance of love that surpassed all that had gone before. Drunk with pleasure, they lay with their arms and legs tangled but their hearts in tune.

Byron ran his fingers through Arielle's hair. He tried to be patient, but he wanted to hear the words too badly to wait another minute, let alone another day. "If you have breath enough to speak, I wish you would."

Arielle propped herself up on her elbow and smiled down at him. She had once thought him an arrogant nuisance, but had changed that opinion long ago. "The first time you kissed me, I knew there was something very, very special about you."

"But you ran away."

"Had I stayed, I knew nothing less than this would have been enough and it frightened me to want you so badly."

Byron wrapped his arms around her and pulled her closer still. "Are you frightened of me still?"

"I love you so dearly I would set fire to a dozen ships rather than leave you."

"I didn't understand—"

Arielle found his lips, and, with a teasing sense of wonder, showed him all he need ever know.

Twenty-four

Byron insisted that Arielle remain in bed for several days to make certain her ordeal had no tragic consequences, but he visited her so often she soon began to enjoy the luxury of enforced rest. One day she finally broached what she feared might still be a sensitive topic.

"You've not mentioned Gaetan. What's to become of him and the others?"

Byron tickled her foot playfully. "Ian and Graham were witnesses to your kidnapping, so I could have left Gaetan and his friends in their custody."

He was smiling, so she knew that he hadn't. "Tell me what you did."

"I told them Gaetan's judgment was clouded by love. Because the Acadians have suffered enough, I tried to convince them to let the three men go on to New Orleans. They objected because there was a stolen ship involved, but I promised to cover the owner's losses. I explained no matter where Gaetan was sent he would cause endless trouble, and confident of that, they agreed to foist him off on the French. He and his friends left Williamsburg this morning with a military escort that will see them safely to Newport News, and on board a ship bound for New Orleans.

You may be assured that I made it clear to them that should they ever return to Virginia, they would be buried here."

That Byron would not only plead for leniency for his arch enemy but also cover the man's debts made a deep impression on Arielle. "I know you did this for me, and I'll always be grateful."

Mirroring her sincerity, Byron caught her gaze and held it. "I did it for all of us, Arielle. Gaetan and I have fought for the last time. If I ever see him again I'm not going to waste a second asking why he's come. I'm going to shoot him and his companions as well."

Arielle couldn't help but shudder. "He won't come back. When he realized I'd set fire to the schooner rather than sail with him, he knew his cause was lost."

"I have to admit it was a convincing gesture, but I don't want you to have to do anything that dangerous ever again. I intend to take much better care of you from now on, and I've spoken again with my mother. She finally understands what's expected of her. I made the same plea again for Hunter as well. I'm tired of watching her walk around him, and I'm certain he is, too. Christian is an adorable child, and he needs his grandmother's love. The makeup of our family may have changed, but it's still our family, and I want it filled with love rather than resentment."

"That's a beautiful thought, but as I've told you so often, you can't force your mother to love us."

"Perhaps not, but I *can* keep insisting that she treat you with the respect she's promised to show. "I've encouraged her to visit friends rather than become isolated, and with a new grandchild come spring, she'll have every reason to make you feel welcome here."

Arielle couldn't hide her doubts. "I keep thinking of how rudely Ian Scott rejected Hunter's offer of friendship. There are people who can harbor resentments their whole lives and I fear he is one."

Byron sat up. "Unfortunately it seems that way, but my mother isn't like him. I wish you could have known her before all the sadness began. Our lives have changed completely in the last year, but that doesn't have to mean the best part of us is lost."

"You are the best part of the Barclays," Arielle exclaimed with an enchanting smile, inspiring her husband to begin a string of compliments of his own. The afternoon passed in a wondrous, loving haze.

Missing her husband terribly, Rachel would have failed to observe Christmas had Byron not insisted she must. Arielle and Alanna decorated the house, planned special menus, and saw to the gifts the Barclays always gave their staff. While it was not the most joyous holiday, Byron gave Arielle a sapphire ring and was satisfied their traditions had been kept alive, and, with the addition of French carols, would grow even more meaningful in the years to come.

The Saturday following Christmas, Robin and Sarah Frederick married Ian Scott and Graham Tyler in a festive double ceremony at the Bruton Parish Church. Rachel had been invited, but no invitations had come for the rest of her family. Observing a year of mourning, the recent widow had had no desire to attend the nuptials, but surprisingly, she was deeply insulted that Byron and Alanna and their spouses had been excluded.

"Esther and Robert Frederick were our dearest friends," she complained at supper the evening of the wedding. "Do you suppose Ian had something to do with the fact that you all weren't asked to their daughters' weddings?"

Alanna reached for her husband's hand, for while Rachel might have failed to notice they weren't invited anywhere, she knew Hunter had. Byron cleared his throat with a sip of ale. "Ian will probably carry a grudge against Hunter, and to a lesser extent the rest of us, to his grave, but it may very well have been Sarah who did not want me there today. I apologized for being unable to consider her more than a friend, but she was far too proud to accept even a politely worded rejection gracefully. I don't envy Graham his choice of wife, but perhaps he truly loves her."

Arielle picked up her goblet for an impulsive toast. "To love."

Byron tipped his goblet in a silent salute before taking a sip, and his mother and Alanna joined him. Hunter, who never drank anything stronger than water, nodded his approval.

"We're going to have an interesting assortment of neighbors," Byron mused aloud. "Perhaps our children will get along better with the Fredericks and their new sons-in-law than we have."

Hunter shook his head, but, unwilling to agree with the Indian's dark prediction, Byron chose to talk about new life instead. He supposed his mother suspected the reason he and Arielle had wed in such haste, but that night struck him as good a time as any to make the formal announcement. "We're expecting our first child in June, Mother, and I hope he, or she, is as attractive and bright a child as Christian."

Rachel stared at her son, and, for a fleeting instant, a look of stark terror filled her gaze, but just as quickly she blinked it away and managed a smile. "It will be nice to have another baby here."

Hunter leaned over to whisper a suggestion to his wife, and, although she blushed, Alanna nodded. "This will be a busy spring," she said. "We're having a child in May."

Rachel greeted that news with equanimity, but Byron could still see a tremble beneath her smile. When he and Arielle went up to bed later, he closed their door carefully to make certain they would not be overheard. "You're an experienced midwife. Can you find a way to reassure my mother that we won't have another tragedy when Alanna's baby is born? Or ours, either, for that matter."

Arielle removed her cap and shook out her hair. "Alanna's healthy, she shouldn't have any problems, but women do sometimes die in childbirth. I can't predict the future, but I promise to do all I possibly can to see Alanna has an easy time. Although with a child nearly due myself then, it might not be all that easy for me."

"I'll make certain Dr. Earle is here for both of you," he promised.

As the chill of winter had given way to the promise of spring Byron felt he had gone a long way toward creating a more compatible family group. In all that time Melissa's fate was never mentioned, but Byron was not the only one who remembered how she had died, and was afraid.

By mid-April, the weather was warm and bright. Rachel began taking long walks in an attempt to burn off the nervous energy that kept her awake at night. The coming birth of a grandchild should have been a joyous event, but she remembered the night Christian had been born with a vivid horror that tormented her even more cruelly as May neared. She missed her husband's calming influence, and prayed constantly that her niece delivered a healthy child at no tragic cost to herself. Once that crisis was safely behind them, she would concentrate her prayers on Arielle, but for now, only Alanna occupied her thoughts.

Alanna, who had witnessed too many tragic deaths for one so young, blocked all thought of childbirth from her mind. She thought instead of Christian, and the half-brother or -sister who would soon join them. At night, when she lay sheltered in Hunter's arms, she felt protected by his strength and her dreams were always sweet.

After attending the births of so many other women's babies, Arielle could scarcely believe she would soon become a mother herself. Consumed with a delicious excitement, she nonetheless kept a close watch on Alanna, for she understood as perhaps no one else did, that problems sighted early could be more easily treated and safely resolved.

She had never had much time to sew, but enjoyed sitting with Alanna and Rachel in the afternoon while they hemmed small blankets and fashioned tiny gowns. She had just completed a seam and snipped her thread when Alanna gave a peculiar little cry. Instantly alert, Arielle looked up. "Are you all right?" she asked.

Alanna nodded, but the look on her face said otherwise, and Rachel, full of solicitous concern, hurried to her side. "I fear you've become overtired. Let's get you upstairs to bed."

"Really, Aunt Rachel," Alanna begged. "I didn't have a pain. It was more of a cramp. Maybe I've just been sitting too long."

Arielle understood Alanna's discomfort. She had to use her arms to push herself out of her chair, but she considered Rachel's advice sound. "That's how labor pains feel when they begin," she said. "Let's all go upstairs now. If you don't feel another one, fine, you can just rest, but if you do, you'll be more comfortable."

Alanna laid her needlework aside reluctantly. "But it isn't May yet."

Rachel helped her niece rise. "Babies often forget to look at the calendar, sweetheart. When they're ready, they just arrive." She glanced over her shoulder at Arielle. "I think we ought to send someone for Dr. Earle, don't you?"

"Let's wait for another pain or two," Arielle advised, but they had no sooner reached Alanna's room than she doubled over in pain. Arielle sent Catherine to fetch Hunter, and the brave came running up the stairs, followed by Byron.

Alanna was seated on the side of her bed looking very pale and afraid. Arielle sat down beside her and took her hand. "I delivered a great many beautiful babies in Grand Pré. You can trust me."

Byron nodded affirmation, but he didn't like the lack of color in Alanna's cheeks. "I'm going to send for the doctor." He started out the door, but his mother followed and caught his arm.

"It's going to happen again, isn't it?" she asked. "That damn Indian is going to kill Alanna, too, and we'll have two of his orphans."

Byron took her arm and pulled her along with him. "That's enough, Mother. I want you to come downstairs and stay there. Arielle has the situation well in hand, and once Dr. Earle arrives, I'm sure he'll reassure you, too. We're not going to lose anyone today."

Huge tears welled up in Rachel's eyes. "I don't want to leave Alanna."

"Do you really think you'll be a help to her if you're hysterical? I certainly don't." Byron escorted her into the parlor. "Stay right here and trust Arielle to manage things until the doctor arrives."

Rachel bit her lower lip. "I'd rather watch Christian."

"Fine, do that, but don't you dare frighten Alanna with your fears." Byron left her still sniffling under that stern warning and after sending Andrew into town, he returned to Alanna's bedroom alone. Hunter was still there, moving around the room in a restless prowl. Arielle had gotten Alanna into bed, but after catching Byron's eye, she glanced toward Hunter and shook her head.

Byron pulled the brave aside. "My mother probably doesn't need any help looking after Christian, but I think you ought to give her some anyway."

Hunter weighed the value of Byron's request, and knowing he was doing a poor job of hiding his own fears, nodded. He gave his wife a reassuring kiss, then left the room. Byron opened a window and leaned out. "This is a beautiful day, perfect for having a child."

"You're not the one having him," Alanna moaned.

"Perhaps not, but I can still appreciate the glorious weather. Now, what can I do?"

Arielle was seated at the foot of the bed, and turned to face him. "There really isn't anything that needs to be done as yet. You needn't stay."

Byron started to object, then simply took the chair near the window to make his intentions clear. "I don't want you to have to rely on one of the servants should you need help."

Before Arielle could argue, Alanna curled herself up in a tight ball. "It's really starting to hurt now," she complained. "I should have said something sooner, but I didn't realize the cramps were pains."

"Are you saying the one you had just before coming upstairs wasn't your first?" Arielle asked.

Alanna wiped away a tear on the bed linens. "No, I'd felt them off and on all day. That was just the sharpest one."

Arielle took a keep breath. "Well, then, this might not take nearly as long as we thought." She gestured for Byron to come close. "Fetch us some warm water. I already gathered everything else we'll need."

By the time Byron returned, Arielle was gently coaxing Alanna, urging her to breathe deeply between contractions and push as they swelled. He placed the pitcher of water on the washstand, and then tried to stay out of Arielle's way. Her voice was soft yet authoritative, her manner compassionate as she wiped Alanna's perspiring brow.

Byron could almost feel Alanna's pain, and yet she had such confidence in Arielle her gaze was trusting. He had known Arielle had a gift for healing, but this was his first opportunity to see how she used it and his admiration for her talent swelled. He did not know how he had had the incredible luck to marry such a remarkable woman, but watching the tender attention she lavished on his cousin, he had never loved her more.

Shutting out painful memories, he watched the ageless drama being played out before him. He didn't feel the tears rolling down his face until Alanna's baby daughter gave her first cry. Exhausted, Alanna slumped back on her pillows while Arielle quickly tied and cut the cord and wrapped the precious infant in a towel.

"Will you hold her a minute, please?" she asked.

Stunned, Byron wiped his eyes on his sleeve and came forward. "What should I do?"

"Just hold her while I finish up here, and then I'll bathe her."

Byron reached out his arms and gingerly accepted the noisy bundle. He had not seen Christian the night he was born and didn't realize babies were so small. Her fists clenched, the babe continued to cry. She had a shock of ebony hair, but he couldn't see her eyes. "I think she looks more like you, Alanna, than Hunter," he murmured. "What's her name?" He held his breath, fearing she would choose Melissa, or the name of one of her sisters. He didn't want to see such a pretty child named for someone who had not had a long and happy life.

"I want her to have a name all her own. What do you think of Johanna?"

Byron tried the name out a time or two. "I like it. It suits her." Arielle took the baby then, and after he had filled the washbasin with the water he had brought, she quickly bathed the little girl. She smoothed out her hair, bundled her up in a small pink blanket, and handed her back to her mother.

"There you are. We'll call Hunter and leave the three of you alone to get acquainted." She removed her soiled apron, gathered up the stained linens, and, rolling them into a discreet bundle, walked to the door. "Come on, Uncle Byron," Arielle teased, "it's time for us to go."

Byron followed his wife out into the hall, still in awe of the miracle of birth, and her. "Why don't you lie down for a while. I'll give Hunter and my mother the good news."

Arielle nodded and Byron started down the stairs. But met Dr. Earle on his way up. "Thank you for coming, but Alanna's babe is already here."

"My goodness, well, I'd still like to look in on her if I may."

Byron showed the physician to his cousin's room and then added a request. "I'd like for you to stop in and see Arielle, too, before you go."

"Certainly. It will be my pleasure."

Byron went on downstairs to summon Hunter and his mother, who was thrilled beyond measure that Alanna had had such a swift and easy delivery. "You can thank Arielle for that," he suggested, and after passing on the family's good news to the servants, he returned to his wife. Dr. Earle soon joined them.

He asked Arielle a few questions, seemed satisfied she was doing well, and then offered a piece of advice. "You're such a pretty thing, my dear. If you'd only lose that unfortunate accent, people would soon forget you're Acadian. Perhaps you don't see the advantage to it, but it will help this child and the others you'll undoubtedly have, if you seem more like us. As for Alanna, well, with that husband of hers, there's no way she can hide what her offspring are."

Astonished at the physician's rudeness, Byron quickly came to Arielle's defense. "I love my wife's accent," he protested, "and I hope she'll teach all our children to speak French. As for Alanna and Hunter's children, I expect them to be treated with the same courtesy the people of Williamsburg have always shown the Barclays."

Thinking Byron's expectations absurd, the physician frowned. "Indeed? Well, I have never delivered a midwife's child. Perhaps when your time comes, madame, you would be more comfortable with a woman who shares your trade than with me."

"That's a distinct possibility," Arielle replied. "Thank you for your time."

Byron just shook his head as the doctor left the room. "I had no idea he would behave so badly. He's been our physician for so many years, I just assumed he shared our views."

"Clearly he does not. Do I really sound so very strange?"

Byron sat down beside her. "No, not at all. You

have a marvelous voice, and a lovely accent. I hope you always sound exactly as you do today."

Arielle leaned forward to kiss him, but the doctor's prejudice had hurt her more than she could say.

Arielle slept fitfully that night, and felt tired all the next day. She attributed it to the strain of delivering Johanna, but Rachel had immediately become so devoted to the little girl, Arielle wasn't called upon to do anything more. She napped in the afternoon and fell asleep early that night, but she awoke long before dawn. Unlike Alanna, she recognized the first stages of labor and immediately awakened Byron.

"This is more than a month too soon," he said in alarm. "I'll go and get Polly."

He took care not to make any noise as he went down the stairs, but his heart was pounding loudly in his ears. In the last few months as Arielle's trim figure had become swollen with his child, he had felt an immense sense of pride. He had rejoiced at the prospect of becoming a father, but now that the moment had actually arrived, his knees were shaking and he hoped he could survive the next few hours without making a complete fool of himself.

All the McBrides were in the Barclays' employ and lived in a house on the plantation. Byron reached it quickly, and rapped loudly on the door. Andrew answered, and quickly went to wake his mother. Polly soon appeared, but hung back and peered at him from around the door.

"My wife's labor has begun. Come up to the house as soon as you're dressed."

Polly brushed a strand of gray hair from her eyes. "You never told me you were counting on me for this, Mr. Barclay. Nobody ever mentioned it to me; not your mother or your wife."

"I'm sorry, that was obviously an oversight, but now that you know—"

Polly started to cry. "I don't work as a midwife anymore. I haven't since we lost Melissa. I can't do it, Mr. Barclay. I just can't. Andrew will go for Dr. Earle."

Byron cursed under his breath. "The baby's a month early or I'm sure we would have had better plans for his birth. We don't want Earle. We want you."

Polly burst into a low, sobbing wail. "Didn't you hear me? I can't do it. There are other midwives in town. Andrew will bring you one of them."

"I'm not going to trust my wife and child to a stranger."

The distraught cook wiped her nose on the sleeve of her nightgown. "Then I guess you're going to have to deliver the babe yourself. There's really nothing to it. Your wife will do all the work."

"That's a damn lie. I was with Arielle when she delivered Alanna's child and she was as much a part of it as Alanna."

Polly began to swing the door closed. "Good, then you know what to do. Good luck."

In that instant, Byron would have fired every one of the McBrides, but he had enough trouble on his hands without taking on their whole clan. He went back to the house, and for a long moment stood outside his mother's bedroom door. She had borne three children, so she would surely know what to do. Finally deciding her emotional state was too precarious to risk calling on her, he returned to his bedroom alone.

Arielle hadn't moved other than to roll the hem of the top sheet into two giant clumps around her fists. "I'm glad you're back, but you needn't stay after Polly comes."

"She isn't coming," Byron revealed, and provided a short summary of their conversation. "Frankly, we're better off without her if she's lost her confidence, but I wanted to ask your permission before sending for Earle."

"No, please don't. I've no respect for the man."

"Then how much respect do you have for me, because it looks as though we're on our own."

Arielle took a deep breath and exhaled slowly. "I have tremendous respect for you, but if this proves to be too much for you, I can do it alone."

Byron sat down beside her. "I'm never going to leave you alone," he promised, "not tonight, or any other time."

Arielle raised her hand to caress his cheek. "You may want to take that promise back in another couple of hours."

"Never."

"All right then, I already have the extra linens and towels we'll need stacked in the bottom of the wardrobe. There's string and scissors, too. Get those out, and then just talk to me for a while. It will help to pass the time until we have to work with the contractions. That's the only secret, you see, simply to flow with the pain, rather than fight it."

Byron moved the linens to the foot of the bed. His hands were shaking so badly, he dropped the scissors and string on the nightstand, but Arielle seemed not to notice. "First babies can take a long time, can't they?" he asked.

"Yes, but we should see our child before noon."

"It's a long time until noon."

"It won't seem that way tomorrow."

Byron returned to his place at her side and, after briefly searching his mind for a subject, realized he had never told her more about Elliott and Melissa than that they had died. "I want to tell you about my family," he began, "and the way things used to be."

When Arielle smiled encouragingly, he described his very first memories of his brother and sister, for he could not recall the time before they were born. One story led quite naturally into the next, and their adventures grew even more complicated after Alanna had come to live with them. Warmed by his recollections, at one point he felt so close to Elliott and Melissa, he turned, half expecting them to be there in his room. Embarrassed, he gave a halting explanation of what had happened.

"I know that sensation," Arielle revealed. "It's happened to me, too. There were many times after Bernard died that I could sense his presence. I never saw a ghost, but I could feel his love. It's been a long while, though. I think my memories of him stayed in Grand Pré."

"I'm glad." When Arielle looked startled, he rephrased his remark. "What I mean is, I'm glad he was a comfort to you there, but not here with me."

Arielle nodded, and encouraged him to keep talking until she could no longer hide her distress. She thought about Alanna then, reliving Johanna's birth in her mind so she could provide Byron with the specific instructions he would need before the strength of her contractions made it difficult to speak. "We haven't chosen a name," she then added.

Byron was doing his best to keep her calm, and welcomed that distraction. "If it's a boy, I'd thought about Elliott, or perhaps John Elliott, or Elliott Bernard, but now I think Alanna was right in giving her daughter a name all her own. I don't know what to choose now, and I've no suggestions for a girl."

"You're a wonderful help."

"Well, you didn't tell me I'd have to supply a name tonight, too."

Arielle's water broke before she could reply, and after that everything happened too quickly for the selection of names to continue. She had thought she understood how to ride rather than fight the pain, but it kept getting ahead of her, and had Byron not pulled her back to an oasis of calm between contractions, she would never have found the courage to face the next one. When at last their son was born, she was too weak to smile.

"Oh, damn it all," Byron cried. "I forgot to heat any water." Improvising, he used one of the small blankets Arielle had made to wipe off the squirming infant and then wrapped him in another. The first tentative light of dawn had just lit the sky when he handed him to his mother. He finished taking care of Arielle, removed the soiled linens, and stood back to admire his wife and child.

"Motherhood becomes you," he complimented sincerely. "I've seldom seen you looking so content."

Arielle peered into her son's bright blue eyes. "He has your eyes."

"I hope he has your hair." Exhausted, Byron stretched out on the bed beside her and snuggled close. "Do you suppose he's as tired as we are?"

Arielle studied the little boy's hands. They were perfect, as were his toes. "Probably. Babies like lots of sleep. Thank you for such a wonderful son, and for helping me bring him into the world."

Byron raised up to give her a kiss, then kissed his little boy on the head. Unlike little Johanna, he had only a few wispy strands of hair. "I can't even begin to thank you for all the love you've brought into my life. I'll do my best to make you happy forever."

"You've done more than enough for me already."

"No, I'll never stop finding ways to say thank you."

Arielle sighed softly and caressed her son's cheek. "Our son is thank you enough. He's a very handsome boy. Let's call him Beau. It means 'handsome' in French?"

"That's going to seem like bragging, isn't it? How about something a little more modest, like Michael, or Stephen?"

"I want to call him Beau."

"Fine, call him Beau, but that doesn't have to be his name."

Arielle started to laugh, which brought a cry from her babe she quickly hushed. "I had forgotten how we used to argue. Shall we compromise and call him Michael Beau and then you can call him Michael and I'll call him Beau?"

"Won't that confuse him terribly?"

"Oh, no, I'm sure he's very bright."

"All right then, his name is Michael Beau. Does that make you happy."

"Yes. Byron, I think this may very well be the most perfect moment of my life."

Byron raised himself up on his elbow to enjoy it more fully, then shook his head. "I don't know. The first time I kissed you was awfully good."

Arielle leaned over to kiss him again. "Yes, I've had a great many perfect moments with you."

In an hour or so, everyone would be up, and Byron would bring them in to see little Michael, but for now he wanted to keep the woman he loved and his first-born son all to himself. He didn't care where the English battled the French or what the citizens of Williamsburg thought of his choice of wife. The Barclays would survive, and, with them, every dream he had dared hope would come true.

"Byron?" Arielle spoke his name softly. "I loved hearing about your brother and sister, and I don't want Beau to grow up alone. Do you suppose we can give our children as happy childhoods as you had?"

Byron caught a faint trace of the loneliness Arielle had never admitted, and made a mental note to ask her to describe her own childhood soon. "Yes, we can give them lives filled with laughter and moments as perfect as this one, too."

Snuggled in her husband's arms, Arielle trusted him completely. "Did you hear that, Beau?" The dear little boy responded with a wide yawn, and she hugged him more tightly as he fell asleep. In the last year, her life had changed so enormously that at times it scarcely seemed to still be hers, but in that blissful hour, she felt dearly loved and the Barclay plantation truly became her home.

NOTE TO READERS

Despite earlier battles in the Ohio Valley, the French and Indian War officially began when England and France issued formal declarations of war in May 1756. William Pitt became England's Secretary of State in 1757, and his vigorous efforts to rebuild the British army and Royal navy enabled England to win the war with a series of decisive victories. British forces took Quebec in 1759, and Montreal in 1760. In an attack on France's ally, Spain, they seized the sugar producing islands of Guadeloupe and Martinique in the West Indies, and captured Havana, Cuba, and Manila, in the Philippines.

In the peace treaty signed in Paris in 1763, France lost her New World empire as she was forced to relinquish Canada and the land east of the Mississippi, except for New Orleans, to England, and all territories west of the Mississippi to Spain. England returned Guadeloupe and Martinique to France, Havana and Manila to Spain, but gained Florida.

In spite of optimistic predictions by Ben Franklin that the colonists would feel a renewed sense of loyalty to England, cries for independence would soon be heard in America, and France, which had recently been a bitter enemy, would become the Patriots' staunch ally against Great Britain. During the Revolutionary War, Nova Scotia became home to twenty-five thousand colonists who remained loyal to the British Crown, and was the site of Britain's main base of operations during the War of 1812.

Only one of the many ships carrying Acadians to new homes in the English colonies, the *Pembroke,* was overpowered and sailed to New Brunswick, but the incident served as inspiration for this book. Although widely dispersed, some Acadians were sent as far as Santo Domingo in the West Indies, vast numbers managed to reach New Orleans where their survivors are known today as Cajuns, who take justifiable pride in their French heritage.

I hope that you have enjoyed reading Byron and Arielle's love story. The Barclay family is becoming such an intriguing mixture of English, Iroquois, and French blood, they will surely inspire many more tales of romantic adventure during a fascinating time in America's history. I love hearing from readers. Please send your comments to me in care of Zebra Books, 850 Third Avenue, New York, NY 10022 and enclose a legal-size SASE for a bookmark.